LOVE AT FIRST BITE

Lucern unsnapped the buttons that ran down the front of Kate's dress and slid his hand inside, then under her bra to cup one breast in his cool palm. She moaned into his mouth. She shuddered as his thumb flicked the tip of her nipple.

Next he slid his leg between both of hers, forcing her dress upward until his upper thigh rubbed against the very center of her. Kate gasped, then kissed him almost frantically. When Lucern broke away, she moaned, her head dropping backward as she arched and shifted against his leg, wanting more. She felt his lips nibble along her neck, but everything felt so good she merely murmured her pleasure and tilted her head to give him better access. Then she was aware of his sucking at her neck. This time she didn't mistake it for a hickey.

Single White Vampire

LYNSAY SANDS

LOVE SPELL NEW YORK CITY

To Bobby, Shirley and Reg, Cathy and Bill, Mo,
Darryl, and David. For the friendship and the love.
Thanks for adopting me.

LOVE SPELL®

September 2003

Published by

Dorchester Publishing Co., Inc.
200 Madison Avenue
New York, NY 10016

ISBN 0-505-52552-6

Visit us on the web at www.dorchesterpub.com.

Prologue

January 30th
Dear Mr. Argeneau:

I hope this letter gets to you, finds you well, and that you had a happy holiday season. This is the second communication I've sent. The first was mailed just before Christmas. No doubt it was lost in the holiday confusion. I did attempt to contact you by telephone; unfortunately, the contact information we have doesn't include your phone number, and it is apparently unlisted.

As to the reason for writing; I am pleased to inform you that the vampire series you write under the name Luke Amirault is quite popular with readers—much more so than we ever expected. There has even been a great deal of interest in a possible book-signing tour. So many stores have contacted us regarding this possibility that I thought I should contact you and find out if and when you would be interested in undertaking such an endeavor.

Please contact this office with your phone number and your response.

I look forward to hearing from you.

Sincerely,
Kate C. Leever
Editor
Roundhouse Publishing Co., Inc.
New York, NY

April 1st
Dear Ms. Leever:
    No.
Sincerely,
Lucern Argeneau
Toronto, Ontario

April 11th
Dear Mr. Argeneau:

I received your letter this morning and, while I gather you are not interested in a book-signing tour, I feel I should stress just how strong is the public's interest in your books. Your popularity is growing rapidly. Several publications have written requesting an interview. I don't think I need explain how helpful such publicity would be to future sales.

As to a book-signing tour, not only have we had phone calls regarding one, but a highly successful bookstore chain with outlets in both Canada and the United States has announced that it would be willing to foot the bill to have you visit their larger stores. They would arrange and pay for your flights, put you up in hotels at each stop, and supply a car and driver to collect you from the airport, see you to the hotel, then to the signing and back. This is no small offer, and I urge you to consider it carefully.

As mail from here to Toronto appears to be quite slow—though your return letters seem to take the usual ten days—I am sending this by overnight express. I would appreciate your immediate response—and please remember to include your phone number this time.

Sincerely,
Kate C. Leever
Editor
Roundhouse Publishing Co., Inc.
New York, NY

June 15th
Dear Ms. Leever:
   No.
Sincerely,
Lucern Argeneau
Toronto, Ontario

June 26th
Dear Mr. Argeneau:

Once again you have forgotten to include your phone number. That being the case, I would first ask that you please call the office at once and speak to either myself, or, if I should happen to be unavailable when you call, my assistant Ashley. You may call collect if necessary, but I would really like to talk to you myself because I feel sure that you may not realize how popular you have become, or how important and necessary contact with your readers can be.

I do not know if you're aware of it, but fan sites are springing up all over the Internet and we receive tons of mail daily for you which will be boxed and forwarded to you separate from this letter. I have mentioned the requests for a book-signing tour in previous letters, but should tell you that those requests are now reaching unmanageable proportions. It seems almost every bookstore around the world would love to have you visit and are sure the signing would be a major success. While you could not possibly hit every store, we think that one store in every major city would be manageable.

I would also like to urge you to consider giving an interview or two, and am including the letters we have received from various publications regarding this. As you will notice, these requests come from more than just romance publications. Your popularity has gone mainstream, as is reflected by the fact that various newspapers and literary magazines are also requesting interviews. We have even had interest from a couple of the morning news shows. While the news shows would have to be in person, the newspaper and magazine interviews need not be; they could be managed either over the phone or even the Internet if you are on it. Are you on the Internet? If so, I would also like your e-mail address and would encourage you to get Windows Messenger or something similar so that I could speak to you in such a way. Several of my writers have Messenger, and we find it quite convenient and much quicker than normal mail.

There is much more I would like to discuss with you. Please remember to phone this office as soon as possible, collect if necessary. Again, I am sending this letter overnight express.

Sincerely,
Kate C. Leever
Editor
Roundhouse Publishing Co., Inc.
New York, NY

August 1st
Dear Ms Leever:
  No.
Sincerely,
Lucern Argeneau
Toronto, Ontario

Chapter One

"Rachel swears she never wants to see another coffin as long as she lives."

Lucern grunted at his mother's comment as he and his younger brother Bastien set the coffin down on the basement floor. He knew all about his soon-to-be sister-in-law's new aversion; Etienne had explained everything. That was why he was storing the thing. Etienne was willing to move it out of the mansion to keep his fiancée happy, but for sentimental reasons—he couldn't bring himself to permanently part with it. The man swore he came up with his best ideas lying inside its silent darkness. He was a bit eccentric. He was the only person Lucern could think of who would bring a coffin to his own wedding rehearsal. The minister had been horrified when he'd caught the three brothers transferring it from Etienne's pickup to Bastien's van.

"Thank you for driving it over here, Bastien," Lucern said as he straightened.

Bastien shrugged. "You could hardly fit it in your BMW. Besides," he added as they started back up the stairs, "I would rather transport it than store it. My housekeeper would have fits."

Lucern merely smiled. He no longer had a housekeeper to worry about, and the cleaning company he'd hired to drop in once a week only worked on the main floor. Their seeing the coffin wasn't a concern.

"Is everything in place for the wedding?" he asked as he followed his mother and Bastien into the kitchen. He turned out the basement lights and closed the door behind him, but didn't bother turning any other lights on. The weak illumination from the nightlight plugged into the stove was enough to navigate to the front door.

"Yes. Finally." Marguerite Argeneau sounded relieved. "And despite Mrs. Garrett's worries that the wedding was too rushed and that Rachel's family wouldn't have time to arrange to be there, they're all coming."

"How large is the family?" Lucern was sincerely hoping there weren't as many Garretts as there had been Hewitts at Lissianna's wedding. The wedding of his sister to Gregory Hewitt had been a nightmare. The man had a huge family, the majority of which seemed to be female—single females who eyed Lucern, Etienne and Bastien as if they were the main course of a one-course meal. Lucern disliked aggressive women. He'd been born and raised in a time when men were the aggressors and women smiled and simpered and knew their place. He hadn't quite adjusted with the times and wasn't looking forward to another debacle like Lissianna's wedding where he'd spent most of his time avoiding the female guests.

Fortunately, Marguerite soothed some of his fears by announcing, "Rather small compared to Greg's family— and mostly male, from the guest list I saw."

"Thank God," Bastien murmured, exchanging a look with his brother.

Lucern nodded in agreement. "Is Etienne nervous?"

"Surprisingly enough, no." Bastien smiled crookedly. "He's having a great time helping to arrange all this. He swears he can't wait for the wedding day. Rachel seems to make him happy." His expression changed to one of perplexity.

Lucern shared his brother's confusion. He couldn't imagine giving up his freedom to a wife, either. Pausing by the front door, he turned back to find his mother poking through the mail on his hall table.

"Luc, you have unopened mail here from weeks ago! Don't you read it?"

"Why so surprised, mother? He never answers the phone, either. Heck, we're lucky when he bothers to answer the door."

Bastien said the words in a laughing voice, but Lucern didn't miss the exchange of glances between his mother and brother. They were worried about him. He had always been a loner, but lately he had taken that to an extreme and everything seemed a bother. They knew he was growing dangerously bored with life.

"What is this box?"

"I don't know," Lucern admitted as his mother lifted a huge box off the table and shook it as if it were feather-light.

"Well, don't you think it might be a good idea to find out?" she asked impatiently.

Lucern rolled his eyes. No matter how old he got, his mother was likely to interfere and hen-peck. It was something he'd resigned himself to long ago. "I'll get around to it eventually," he muttered. "It's mostly nuisance mail or people wanting something from me."

"What about this letter from your publisher? It's probably important. They wouldn't send it express if it weren't."

Lucern's scowl deepened as his mother picked up the FedEx envelope and turned it curiously in her hands. "It is *not* important. My editor is just harassing me. The company wishes me to do a book-signing tour."

"Edwin wants you to do a book-signing tour?" Marguerite scowled. "I thought you made it clear to him from the start that you weren't interested in publicity."

"Not Edwin. No." Lucern wasn't surprised that his mother recalled his old editor's name; she had a perfect memory and he'd mentioned Edwin many times over the ten years he'd been writing for Roundhouse Publishing. His first works had been published as historical texts used mostly in universities and colleges. Those books were still in use and were celebrated for the fact that they'd been written as if the writer had actually lived through every period about which he wrote. Which, of course, Lucern had. That was hardly public knowledge, though.

Lucern's last three books, however, had been autobiographical in nature. The first told the story of how his mother and father had met and come together, the second how his sister Lissianna had met and fallen in love with her therapist husband, Gregory, and the latest, published just weeks ago, covered the story of his brother Etienne and Rachel Garrett. Lucern hadn't meant to write them, they'd just sort of spilled forth. But once he'd written them, he'd decided they should be published records for the future. Gaining his family's permission, he'd sent them in to Edwin, who'd thought them brilliant works of fiction and published them as such. Not just fiction, either, but "paranormal romance." Lucern had suddenly found himself a romance writer. The whole situation was somewhat distressing for him, so he generally did his best not to think about it.

"Edwin is no longer my editor," he explained. "He had a heart attack late last year and died. His assistant was given his title and position, and she's been harassing me ever since." He scowled again. "The woman is trying to use me to prove herself. She is determined that I should do some publicity events for the novels."

Bastien looked as if he were about to comment, but paused and turned at the sound of a car pulling into the driveway. Lucern opened the door, and the two men watched with varying degrees of surprise as a taxi pulled to a stop beside Bastien's van.

"Wrong address?" Bastien queried, knowing his brother wasn't big on company.

"It must be," Lucern commented. He narrowed his eyes when the driver got out and opened the back door for a young woman.

"Who is that?" Bastien asked. He sounded even more surprised than Lucern felt.

"I haven't a clue," Lucern answered. The taxi driver retrieved a small suitcase and overnight bag from the trunk of the car.

"I believe it's your editor," Marguerite announced.

Both Lucern and Bastien swiveled to peer at their mother. They found her reading the now-open FedExed letter.

"My editor? What the hell are you talking about?" Lucern marched over to snatch the letter out of her hand.

Ignoring his rude behavior, Lucern's mother moved to Bastien's side and peered curiously outside. "As the mail is so slow, and because the interest in your books is becoming so widespread, Ms. Kate C. Leever decided to come speak to you in person. Which," Marguerite added archly, "you would know should you bother to read your mail."

Lucern crumpled the letter in his hand. It basically said everything his mother had just verbalized. That, plus the fact that Kate C. Leever would be arriving on the 8 p.m. flight from New York. It was 8:30. The plane must have been on time.

"She's quite pretty, isn't she?" The comment, along with the speculation in his mother's voice when she made it, was enough to raise alarm in Lucern. Marguerite sounded like a mother considering taking the matchmaking trail—a path quite familiar to her. She'd taken it upon first seeing Etienne and Rachel together, too, and look how that had turned out: Etienne hip deep in wedding preparations!

"She's contemplating matchmaking, Bastien. Take her home. Now," Lucern ordered. His brother burst out laughing, moving him to add, "After she has finished with me, she shall focus on finding *you* a wife."

Bastien stopped laughing at once. He grabbed his mother's arm. "Come along, Mother. This is none of our business."

"Of course it is my business." Marguerite shrugged her elbow free. "You are my sons. Your happiness and future are very much my business."

Bastien tried to argue. "I don't understand why this is an issue now. We are both well over four hundred years old. Why, after all this time, have you taken it into your head to see us married off?"

Marguerite pondered for a moment. "Well, ever since your father died, I've been thinking—"

"Dear God," Lucern interrupted. He woefully shook his head.

"What did I say?" his mother asked.

"That is exactly how Lissianna ended up working at the shelter and getting involved with Greg. Dad died, and she started thinking."

Bastien nodded solemnly. "Women shouldn't think."

"Bastien!" Marguerite Argeneau exclaimed.

"Now, now. You know I'm teasing, Mother," he soothed, taking her arm again. This time he got her out the door.

"I, however, am not," Lucern called as he watched them walk down the porch steps to the sidewalk. His mother berated Bastien the whole way, and Lucern grinned at his brother's beleaguered expression. Bastien would catch hell all the way home, Lucern knew, and almost felt sorry for him. Almost.

His laughter died, however, as his gaze switched to the blonde who was apparently his editor. His mother paused in her berating to greet the woman. Lucern almost tried to hear what was said, then decided not to bother. He doubted he wanted to hear it, anyway.

He watched the woman nod and smile at his mother; then she took her luggage in hand and started up the sidewalk. Lucern's eyes narrowed. Dear God, she didn't expect to stay with him, did she? There was no mention in her letter of where she planned to stay. She must expect to stay in a hotel. She would hardly just assume that he would put her up. The woman probably just hadn't stopped at her hotel yet, he reassured himself, his gaze traveling over her person.

Kate C. Leever was about his mother's height, which made her relatively tall for a woman, perhaps 5'10". She was also slim and shapely, with long blond hair. She appeared pretty from the distance presently separating them. In a pale blue business suit, Kate C. Leever resembled a cool glass of ice water. The image was pleasing on this unseasonably warm September evening.

The image shattered when the woman dragged her luggage up the porch steps, paused before him, offered him a bright cheerful smile that lifted her lips and sparkled in her eyes, then blurted, "Hi. I'm Kate Leever. I hope you got my letter. The mail was so slow, and you kept forgetting to send me your phone number, so I thought I'd come visit personally and talk to you about all the publicity possibilities that are opening up for us. I know you're not really interested in partaking of any of them, but I feel sure once I explain the benefits you'll reconsider."

Lucern stared at her wide, smiling lips for one mesmerized moment; then he gave himself a shake. Reconsider? Was that what she wanted? Well, that was easy enough. He reconsidered. It was a quick task.

"No." He closed his door.

Kate stared at the solid wooden panel where Lucern Argeneau's face had been and fought not to shriek with fury. The man was the most difficult, annoying, rude, obnoxious—she pounded on his door—pigheaded, ignorant . . .

The door whipped open, and Kate quickly pasted a blatantly false but wide—she should get high marks for effort—smile on her mouth. The smile nearly slipped when she got a look at him. She hadn't really taken the opportunity earlier. A second before, she had been too busy trying to recall the speech she'd composed and memorized on the flight here; now she didn't have a prepared speech—didn't actually even have a clue what to say—and so she found herself really looking at Lucern Argeneau. The man was a lot younger than she'd expected. Kate knew he'd written for Edwin for a good ten years before she'd taken over working with him, yet he didn't look to be more than thirty-two or-three. That meant he'd been writing professionally since his early twenties.

He was also shockingly handsome. His hair was as dark as night, his eyes a silver blue that almost seemed to reflect the porchlight, his features sharp and strong. He was tall and surprisingly muscular for a man with such a sedentary career. His shoulders bespoke a laborer more than an intellectual. Kate couldn't help but be impressed. Even the scowl on his face didn't detract from his good looks.

Without any effort on her part, the smile on Kate's face gained some natural warmth and she said, "It's me again. I haven't eaten yet, and I thought perhaps you'd join me for a meal on the company and we could discuss—"

"No. Please remove yourself from my doorstep." Then Lucern Argeneau closed the door once more.

"Well, that was more than just a 'no'," Kate muttered to herself. "It was even a whole sentence, really." Ever the optimist, she decided to take it as progress.

Raising her hand, she pounded on the door again. Her smile was somewhat battered, but it was still in place when the door opened for the third time. Mr. Argeneau reappeared, looking less pleased than ever to find her still there. This time, he didn't speak but merely arched an eyebrow in question.

Kate supposed that if his speaking a whole sentence was progress, his reverting to complete silence had to be the opposite—but she determined not to think of that. Trying to make her smile a little sunnier, she cleared her throat and said, "If you don't like eating out, perhaps I could order something in and—"

"No." He started to close the door again, but Kate hadn't lived in New York for five years without learning a trick or two. She quickly stuck her foot forward, managing not to wince as the door banged into it and bounced back open.

Before Mr. Argeneau could comment on her guerilla tactics, she said, "If you don't care for takeout, perhaps I could pick up some groceries and cook you something you like." For good measure she added, "That way we could discuss your fears, and I might be able to alleviate them."

15

He stiffened in surprise at her implication. "I am not afraid," he said.

"I see." Kate allowed a healthy dose of doubt to creep into her voice, more than willing to stoop to manipulation if necessary. Then she waited, foot still in place, hoping that her desperation wasn't showing but knowing that her calm facade was beginning to slip.

The man pursed his lips and took his time considering. His expression made Kate suspect he was measuring her for a coffin, as if he were considering killing her and planting her in his garden to get her out of his hair. She tried not to think about that possibility too hard. Despite having worked with him for years as Edwin's assistant, and now for almost a year as his editor, Kate didn't know the man very well. In her less charitable moments, she *had* considered just what kind of man he might be. Most of her romance authors were female. In fact, *every* other author under her care was female. Lucern Argeneau, who wrote as Luke Amirault, was the only man. What kind of guy wrote romances? And vampire romances at that? She had decided it was probably someone gay . . . or someone weird. His expression at the moment was making her lean toward weird. Serial-killer-type weird.

"You have no intention of removing yourself, do you?" he asked at last.

Kate considered the question. A firm "no" would probably get her inside. But was that what she wanted? Would the man slaughter her? Would she be a headline in the next day's news if she did get in the door?

Cutting off such unproductive and even frightening thoughts, Kate straightened her shoulders and announced firmly; "Mr. Argeneau, I flew up here from New York. This is important to me. I'm determined to talk to you. I'm your *editor*." She emphasized the last word in case he had missed the relevance of that fact. It usually had a certain influence with writers, although Argeneau had shown no signs of being impressed so far.

She didn't know what else to say after that, so Kate simply stood waiting for a response that never came. Heaving a deep sigh, Argeneau merely turned away and started up his dark hall.

Kate stared uncertainly at his retreating back. He hadn't slammed the door in her face this time. That was a good sign, wasn't it? Was it an invitation to enter? Deciding she was going to take it as one, Kate hefted her small suitcase and overnight bag and stepped inside. It was a late-summer evening, cooler than it had been earlier in the day, but still hot. In comparison, stepping into the house was like stepping into a refrigerator. Kate automatically closed the door behind her to keep the cool air from escaping, then paused to allow her eyes to adjust.

The interior of the house was dark. Lucern Argeneau hadn't bothered to turn on any lights. Kate couldn't see much of anything except a square of dim light outlining what appeared to be a door at the end of the long hall in which she stood. She wasn't sure what the light was from; it was too gray and dim to be from an overhead fixture. Kate wasn't even sure that going to that light would bring her to Lucern Argeneau's side, but it was the only source of light she could see, and she was quite sure that it was in the direction he'd taken when walking away.

Setting her bags down by the door, Kate started carefully forward, heading for that square of light, which suddenly seemed so far away. She had no idea if the way was clear or not—she hadn't really looked around before closing the door—but she hoped there was nothing to trip over along the way. If there was, she would certainly find it.

Lucern paused in the center of his kitchen and peered around in the illumination of the nightlight. He wasn't quite sure what to do. He never had guests, or at least hadn't had them for hundreds of years. What did one do with them, exactly? After an inner debate, he moved to the stove, grabbed the teakettle that sat on the burner, and took it to the sink to fill with water. After setting it on the stove and cranking the dial to high, he found the teapot, some tea bags and a full sugar bowl. He set it all haphazardly on a tray.

He would offer Kate C. Leever a cup of tea. Once that was done, so was she.

Hunger drew him to the refrigerator. Light spilled out into the room as he opened the door, making him blink after the previous darkness. Once his eyes adjusted, he bent to pick up one of the two lonely bags of blood on the middle shelf. Other than those bags, there wasn't a single solitary item inside. The cavernous white box was empty. Lucern wasn't much for cooking. His refrigerator had pretty much been empty since his last housekeeper died.

He didn't bother with a glass. Instead, still bent into the fridge, Lucern lifted the blood bag to his mouth and stabbed his fangs into it. The cool elixir of life immediately began to pour into his system, taking the edge off his crankiness. Lucern was never so cranky as when his blood levels were low.

"Mr. Argeneau?"

He jerked in surprise at that query from the doorway. The action ripped the bag he held, sending the crimson fluid spraying out all over him. It squirted in a cold shower over his face and into his hair as he instinctively straightened and banged his head on the underside of the closed freezer compartment. Cursing, Lucern dropped the ruined bag onto the refrigerator shelf and grabbed for his head with one hand, slamming the refrigerator door closed with the other.

Kate Leever rushed to his side. "Oh, my goodness! Oh! I'm so sorry! *Oh!*" she screeched as she caught sight of the blood coating his face and hair. "Oh, God! You've cut your head. *Bad!*"

Lucern hadn't seen an expression of such horror on anyone's face since the good old days when lunch meant biting into a nice warm neck rather than a nasty cold bag.

Seeming to recover her senses somewhat, Kate Leever grabbed his arm and urged him toward the kitchen table. "Here, you'd better sit down. You're bleeding badly."

"I am fine," Lucern muttered as she settled him into a chair. He found her concern rather annoying. If she was too nice to him, he might feel guilted into being nice back.

"Where's your phone?" She was turning on one heel, scanning the kitchen for the item in question.

"Why do you wish a phone?" he asked hopefully.

Perhaps she would leave him alone now, he thought briefly, but her answer nixed that possibility.

"To call an ambulance. You really hurt yourself."

Her expression became more distressed as she looked at him again, and Lucern found himself glancing down at his front. There was quite a bit of blood on his shirt, and he could feel it streaming down his face. He could also smell it—sharp and rich with tinny overtones. Without thinking, he slid his tongue out to lick his lips. Then what she'd said slipped into his mind, and he straightened abruptly. While it was convenient that she thought the blood was from an injury, there was no way he was going to a hospital.

"I am fine. I do not need medical assistance," he announced firmly.

"What?" She peered at him with disbelief. "There's blood everywhere! You really hurt yourself."

"Head wounds bleed a lot." He gave a dismissive wave, then stood and moved to the sink to rinse off. If he didn't wash quickly, he was going to shock the woman by licking the blood off his hands all the way up to his elbows. The bit he'd managed to consume before she startled him had barely eased his hunger at all.

"Head wounds may bleed a lot, but this is—"

Lucern gave a start as Kate suddenly stepped to his side and grabbed his head. He was so surprised that he bent dutifully at her urging . . . until she said, "I can't see—"

He straightened the moment he realized what she was doing, then quickly bent over the sink to duck his head under the tap so she couldn't get at his head again and see that there was no wound.

"I am fine. I clot quickly," he said as cold water splashed on his head and ran over his face.

Kate Leever had no answer to that, but Lucern could feel her standing at his back watching. Then she moved to his side, and he felt her warm body press against him as she bent to try to examine his head again.

For a moment, Lucern was transfixed. He was terribly aware of her body so close, of the heat pouring off her, of her sweet scent. For that moment, his hunger became confused. It wasn't the smell of the blood pulsing in her veins that filled his nostrils, it was a whiff of spice and flowers and her own personal scent. It filled his head, clouding his thoughts. Then he became aware of her hands moving through his hair under the tap, searching for a wound she wouldn't find, and he jerked upward in an attempt to stand away from her. The attempt was neatly thwarted by the tap slamming into the back of his head. Pain shattered through him, and water squirted everywhere, sending Kate stepping back with a squeal.

Cursing, Lucern ducked out from under the tap and snatched at the first thing to come to hand; a tea towel. He wrapped it around his wet head, straightened, then pointed at the door. "Out of my kitchen. Out!"

Kate C. Leever blinked in surprise at his return of temper, then seemed to grow an inch in height as she marshaled her own. Her voice was firm as she said, "You need a doctor."

"No."

Her eyes narrowed. "Is that the only word you know?"

"No."

She threw her hands up in the air, then let them drop—as quick as that, seeming to relax. Lucern found himself wary.

Kate C. Leever smiled and moved to finish making the tea he had started. "That settles it, then," she said.

"Settles what?" Lucern asked, watching suspiciously as she threw the two teabags in the tea pot and poured hot water over them.

Kate shrugged mildly and set the kettle back. "I had intended on trying to talk to you, then checking into a hotel later tonight. However, now that you've hurt yourself and refuse to go the hospital . . ." She turned away from the steeping tea to raise one eyebrow. "You won't reconsider?"

"No."

She nodded and turned back to plop the lid again on the teapot. The clink it made had an oddly satisfied sound to it as she explained, "I can't leave you alone after such an injury. Head wounds are tricky. I suppose I shall have to stay here."

Lucern was opening his mouth to let her know that she most certainly was not staying there, when she moved toward the refrigerator and asked, "Do you take milk?"

Recalling the bag of blood ripped open in the fridge, he raced past her and threw himself wildly in front of her. "No!"

She stared at him, mouth agape, until he realized he stood before the refrigerator door with his arms widespread in a panicked pose. He immediately shifted to lean against it, arms and ankles crossed in a position he hoped appeared more natural. Then he glared at her for good measure. It had the effect of making her close her mouth; then she said uncertainly, "Oh. Well, I do. If you have any."

"No."

She nodded slowly, but concern filled her face and she actually lifted a hand to place it soft and warm against his forehead as if checking for fever. Lucern inhaled the scent of her and felt his stance relax somewhat.

"Are you sure you won't go to the hospital?" Kate asked. "You're acting a tad strange, and head wounds really aren't something to mess with."

"No."

Lucern was alarmed when he heard how low his voice had gone. He was even more concerned when Kate Leever smiled and asked teasingly, "Now, why aren't I surprised by that answer?"

Much to his dismay, he almost smiled back at her. Catching himself, he scowled harder instead and berated himself for his momentary weakness. Kate C. Leever, editor, might be being nice to him right now, but that was only because she wanted something from him. And he would do well to remember that.

"Well, come along, then."

Lucern stopped his woolgathering to note that his editor had collected the tea tray and was moving toward the kitchen door.

"We should move to the living room, where you can sit down for a bit. You took quite a blow," she added as she pushed through the swinging door with one hip.

Lucern took a step after her, then paused to glance

back at the refrigerator, his thoughts on the other full bag of blood inside. It was his last until the fresh delivery tomorrow night. He was terribly hungry, almost faint with it. Which was no doubt the reason behind his weakness in the face of Kate C. Leever's steamroller approach. Perhaps just a sip would strengthen him for the conversation ahead. He reached for the door.

"Lucern?"

He stiffened at that call. When had she stopped addressing him as Mr. Argeneau? And why did his name on her lips sound so sexy? He really needed to feed. He pulled the refrigerator door open and reached for the bag.

"Lucern?" There was concern in her voice this time, and she sounded closer. She must be coming back. No doubt she feared he had passed out from his injury.

He released a mutter of frustration and closed the refrigerator door. The last thing he needed was another debacle like spilling blood all over himself. That had already caused him unending problems, like the fact that the woman now planned to stay with him. He'd meant to nix the idea at once, but had been distracted by Ms. Leever approaching the refrigerator. *Damn!*

Well, he would straighten her out on that issue first thing. He'd be damned if he was letting her stay here and harangue him about all this publicity nonsense. That was that. He would be firm. Cruel, if necessary. She wasn't staying here.

Lucern tried to get rid of her, but Kate C. Leever was rather like a bulldog once she made up her mind about something. No, a bulldog was the wrong image. A terrier perhaps. Yes, he was happier with that comparison. A cute blond terrier hanging off of his arm, teeth sunk determinedly into the cuff of his shirt and refusing to let go. Short of smashing her against the wall a couple of times, he really had no idea how to get her jaws off him.

It was the situation of course. Despite having lived for several hundred years, Lucern had failed to come up against anything of the sort. In his experience, people were a bother and never failed to bring chaos with them. Women especially. He'd always been a sucker for a damsel in distress. He couldn't recount how many times he'd found himself stumbling across a woman with troubles and suddenly finding his whole life in turmoil while he fought a battle, a duel, or a war for her. Of course, he always won and saved the day. Still, somehow he never got the woman. In the end, all his efforts and the upheavals in his life left him watching the woman walk away with someone else.

That wasn't the situation here. Kate C. Leever, editor, was not a damsel in distress. In fact, she apparently saw *him* as the one in distress. She was staying "for his own good." She was saving him, in her mind, and intended to "wake him every hour on the hour should he fall asleep," to save him from his own foolishness in refusing to go to the doctor. She made that announcement the moment they were seated in his living room, then calmly set about removing the tea bags from the pot and pouring tea while he gaped at her.

Lucern didn't need her help. He hadn't really hit his head that hard, and even if he had, his body would have repaired itself quickly. But that wasn't something he could tell the woman. In the end, he simply said, with all the sternness and firmness he could muster, "I do not desire your help, Ms. Leever. I can take care of myself."

She nodded sedately, sipped her tea, then smiled pleasantly and said, "I would take that comment much more seriously were you not presently wearing a pretty but bloodstained flowered tea towel on your head . . . turban style."

Lucern reached up in alarm, only to feel the tea towel he'd forgotten was wrapped around his head. As he began to unravel it, Kate added, "Don't remove it on my account. It looks rather adorable on you and makes you far less intimidating."

Lucern growled. He ripped the flowered tea towel off.

"What was that?" his editor asked, eyes wide. "You growled."

"I did not."

"You did so." She was grinning widely, looking very pleased. "Oh, you men are so cute."

Lucern knew then that the battle was lost. There would be no argument that would make her leave.

Perhaps mind control . . .

It was a skill he tried to avoid using as a rule, and hadn't exercised in some time. It wasn't usually necessary, since the family had switched to utilizing a blood bank for feeding rather than hunting. But this occasion clearly called for it.

As he watched Kate sip her tea, he tried to get into her thoughts so that he might take control of them. He was beyond shocked to find only a blank wall. Kate C.

Leever's mind was as inaccessible to him as if a door had been closed and locked. Still, he continued to try for several moments, his lack of success more alarming than he would have expected.

He didn't give up until she broke the silence by bringing up her reason for being there: "Perhaps we could now discuss the book-signing tour."

Lucern reacted as if she'd poked him with a hot iron. Giving up on controlling her mind and making her leave, he leapt to his feet. "There are three guest rooms. They're upstairs, all three on the left. My room and office are on the right. Stay out of them. Take whichever of the guest rooms you want."

Then he retreated from the battlefield with all haste, rushing back to the kitchen.

He could put up with her for one night, he told himself. Once the night was over and she was reassured that he was fine, she would leave. He would see to that.

Trying not to recall that he'd been just as determined and certain about expelling her after she finished her tea, Lucern snatched a glass and his last bag of blood from the fridge. Then he moved to the sink to pour himself some dinner. He could probably get a quick cup while Ms. Kate C. Leever was occupied in choosing a room.

He'd thought wrong. Lucern had just started to pour the blood from its bag to the glass when the kitchen door opened behind him.

"Do you have any all-night grocery stores in town?"

Dropping the glass and bag, Lucern whirled to face her, wincing as the glass smashed in the sink.

"I'm sorry, I didn't mean to startle you, I . . ." She

paused when he held up a hand to halt her forward progress.

"Just . . ." he began, then finished wearily; "What did you ask?"

He couldn't really listen to her answer. The sweet, tinny scent of blood seemed rich in the air, though he doubted Kate could smell it from where she was across the room. It was distracting, and even more distracting was the rushing sound of it all running out of the bag and down the sink. His dinner. His last bag.

His mind was screaming NO! His body was cramping in protest. That being the case, Kate C. Leever's words sounded like "Blah blah blah" as she moved toward his empty refrigerator and peered inside. Lucern didn't bother to stop her this time. Apart from the blood from earlier, it was completely empty. However, he did try to concentrate on what she was saying, hoping that the sooner he dealt with her question, the sooner he could save his dinner. Try as he might, however, he was really only catching a word here and there.

"Blah blah blah . . . haven't eaten since breakfast. Blah blah blah . . . really don't have anything here. Blah blah blah . . . shopping?"

The last chorus of blahs ended on a high note, alerting Lucern to the fact that it had been a question. He wasn't sure what the question was, but he could sense that a no would probably provoke an argument.

"Yes," he blurted, hoping to be rid of the stubborn woman. Much to his relief, the answer pleased her and sent her back to the hall door.

"Blah blah blah . . . pick my room."

He could almost taste the blood, its scent was so heavy in the air.

"Blah blah . . . change into something more comfortable."

He was starving.

"Blah blah be right back and we can go."

The door closed behind her, and Lucern whirled back to the sink. He moaned. The bag was almost completely drained. It was flat. Nearly. Feeling somewhat desperate, he picked it up, tipped it over his mouth and squeezed, trying to wring out the last few drops. He got exactly three before giving up and tossing the bag into the garbage with disgust. If there had been any question before, there wasn't now. Without a doubt, Kate C. Leever was going to make his life a living hell until she left. He just knew it.

And what the heck had he agreed to anyway?

Chapter Two

"Shopping!"

Kate laughed at Lucern's disgusted mutter as they entered the 24-hour grocery store. He'd been repeating it every few minutes since leaving the house. At first he'd said the word as if he couldn't believe he'd agreed to go. Then, as they'd driven here in his BMW, that dismay had turned to disgust. You'd think the man had never gone food shopping before now! Of course, judging by how empty his cupboards were, Kate supposed he hadn't. And when she'd commented on the lack of food in his home on the way out of the house, he'd muttered something about not having replaced his housekeeper yet. Kate presumed that meant he ate out a lot in the meantime.

She hadn't bothered to inquire as to what had become of his previous housekeeper. His personality was answer enough. No doubt the poor woman had quit. Kate herself would have, she knew.

She led him to the rows of empty shopping carts. As she started to pull one out, Lucern grunted something that might have been "Allow me," but could just as easily have been "Get the hell out of the way." He then took over the chore,

In Kate's experience, men always preferred to do the driving—whether it was a car, a golf cart, or a shopping basket. She suspected it was a control issue, but either way it was handy; it meant she was free to fill the thing up.

She began to make a mental list of what she should get as she led the way toward the dairy section. She would have to be sure she got lots of fruits and vegetables for Lucern. The man was big and muscular, but far too pale. It seemed obvious to her that he was in dire need of some green leafy vegetables.

Maybe vegetables would improve his mood, too.

Lucern needed blood. That was the one thought pulsing through his mind as he followed Kate C. Leever through the dairy section, the frozen-food section, and now down the coffee aisle. The cart was filling up quickly. Kate had already tossed various yogurts, cheeses, eggs and a ton of frozen gourmet dinners in it. Now she paused in the coffee aisle and considered the various packages before turning to ask, "What brand do you prefer?"

He stared at her blankly. "Brand?"

"Of coffee? What do you normally drink?"

Lucern shrugged. "I do not drink coffee."

"Oh. Tea, then?"

"I do not drink tea."

31

"But you—," She narrowed her eyes. "Hot chocolate? Espresso? Capuccino?" When he shook his head at all her suggestions, she asked with exasperation: "Well, what *do* you drink then? Kool-Aid?"

A titter of amusement drew Lucern's attention to a plump young woman pushing a cart up the aisle toward them. She was the first shopper they'd come across since entering the store. Between the debacles with the blood bags, the tea in the living room, and the bit of time Kate had taken to settle in and change, it was now nearly midnight. The grocery store wasn't very busy at this hour.

Now that her giggle had caught his attention, the shopper batted her eyelashes at Lucern and he found himself smiling back, his gaze fixed on the pulse at the base of her throat. He imagined sinking his teeth there and drawing the warm, sweet blood out of her. She was his favorite sort to drink. Plump, pink women always had the best, richest blood. Thick and heady and—

"Mr. Argeneau? Earth calling Lucern!"

Luc's pleasant imaginings shattered. He turned reluctantly back to his editor. "Yes?"

"What do you like to drink?" she repeated.

He glanced back at the shopper. "Er . . . coffee's fine."

"You said you don't drink cof—Never mind. What brand?"

Lucern surveyed the choices. His eyes settled on a dark red can with the name Tim Hortons. He'd always thought that was a donut shop or something. Still, it was the only name he recognized, so he pointed at it.

"The most expensive one, of course," Kate muttered. She picked up a can of fine grind.

Lucern hadn't noticed the price. "Stop complaining. I am paying for the groceries."

"No. I said I'd pay and I will."

Had she said she'd pay when she'd mentioned it earlier? he wondered. He couldn't recall; he hadn't been paying much attention at the time. His thoughts had been on other things. Like the blood dripping down the sink and not into his parched mouth.

His gaze slid back to the plump, pulsing-veined shopper who continued past him. He imagined he looked like a starving man watching a buffet being wheeled past. He was hard-pressed not to throw himself onto it. Warm, fresh blood . . . much nicer than that cold bagged stuff he and his family had taken to ingesting. He hadn't realized how much he missed the old-fashioned way of feeding.

"Lucern?" There was a touch of irritation in Kate Leever's voice, and it made him scowl as he turned back. She wasn't where she'd last stood, but had moved on down the aisle and was waiting for him. She wore an annoyed expression, which in turn annoyed him. What did *she* have to be irritable about? She wasn't the one starving.

Then he had a vague recollection of her saying she hadn't eaten since breakfast, and he supposed she was hungry too and therefore had just as much right to be grouchy. It was a grudging admission.

"*I* am paying," he announced firmly as he pushed the cart forward. "You are a guest in my home. I will feed you." As opposed to feeding on you, he thought, which was what he most wanted to do. Well, not what he *most* wanted to do. He'd rather feed on the plump little brunette behind him. He had always found the blood of sleek, blond creatures like Kate C. Leever to be thin and bland. Plump-girl blood was better-tasting, more flavorful, fuller-bodied.

Of course, he couldn't feed on anyone. It was too dangerous nowadays, and even if he himself was willing to take the risk, he wouldn't risk the safety of his family just for a few moments of culinary pleasure.

It didn't mean he couldn't dream about it, though, so Lucern spent the next few moments trailing Kate around the canned food and dry goods aisles, absently agreeing with everything she said while he fondly recalled meals he'd enjoyed in the past.

"Do you like Mexican?" she asked.

"Oh, yes," he murmured, the question immediately bringing to mind a perky little Mexican girl he'd feasted on in Tampico. She'd been a tasty little bundle. Warm and sweet-smelling in his arms, little enjoyable moans issuing from her throat as he'd plunged both his body and teeth into her . . . Oh, yes. Feeding could be a full-body experience.

"What about Italian?"

"Italian is delicious too," he said agreeably, his memories immediately switching to a pleasing little peasant on the Amalfi coast. That had been his first feeding on his own. A man always remembered his first. And just the thought of his sweet little Maria made him warm all over. Such deep, dark eyes and long, wavy, midnight hair. He recalled tangling his hands in that hair and the deep groan of pleasure she'd breathed into his ear as he'd given her his virginity and taken her blood at the same time. Truly, it had been a sweet and memorable experience.

"Do you like steak?"

Lucern was once again drawn from his thoughts, this time by a package of raw meat suddenly shoved under his nose, interrupting his fond memories. It was steak, nice and bloody, and though he normally preferred human blood—even cold bagged human blood to bovine—the blood-soaked steak smelled good at the moment. He found himself inhaling deeply and letting his breath out on a slow sigh.

The package was jerked away. "Or do you prefer white meat?"

"Oh, no. No. Red meat is better." He moved closer to the meat counter she'd led him to and peered around with his first real interest since they'd entered the market. He had always been a meat-and-potatoes man. Rare meat, as a rule.

"A carnivore, I take it," Kate commented dryly as he reached for a particularly bloody package of steak. The blood was dripping, and he almost licked his lips. Then, afraid he might do something distressing in his present state, like lick the package, he stepped back and set the meat down. Taking hold of the cart, he began moving it along, hoping to get to a less tempting section.

"Hang on," Kate called, but Lucern kept walking, almost moaning when she rushed up with several packages of steak in her arms that she dumped in the cart.

Great! Now the temptation would follow him. He really needed to feed. He had to contact Bastien or Etienne and see about borrowing some blood. Perhaps he could make a quick stop at Bastien's on the way home. He could leave the unshakable Kate Leever in the car with the groceries, run in, gulp down a bit of nourishment and . . .

Dear God! He sounded like a junkie!

"Fruits and vegetables next, I think," Kate said beside him. "You're obviously in serious need of vitamins. Have you ever considered going to a tanning salon?"

"I can't. I have an . . . er, skin condition. And I'm allergic to the sun, too."

"That must make life difficult at times," she commented. Peering at him wide-eyed she asked, "Is that why you are so difficult about book signings and other promo stuff?"

He shrugged. As she began picking up all sorts of green things, he grimaced. In defense, he picked up a twenty-pound bag of potatoes to fill the cart, but it was soon covered in green: little round green things, big round green things, long green stalks. Dear God, the woman had a green fetish!

Lucern started moving the cart along a little more quickly, forcing Kate to hurry as she started on other colors. Orange, red and yellow vegetables flew into the cart and were followed by orange, red and purple fruit before Lucern managed to at last force her to the cash register.

The moment he stopped the cart, Kate began throwing things on the conveyor belt. He was watching her absently when the plump shopper pushed her cart by. She smiled and batted her eyelashes again, then gave him a little wave. Lucern smiled back, his gaze affixed to the pulse beating in her neck. He could practically hear the *thump-thump* of her heart, the rushing sound of blood, the—

"Lucern? Mr. Argeneau. Where are you going?"

Pausing, Lucern blinked his eyes, realizing only at Kate's question that he'd started to follow the plump shopper like a horse walking after a dangling carrot. His possible dinner looked back and smiled again before disappearing down the frozen-foods aisle. Lucern started after her. "We forgot ice cream."

"Ice cream?" He heard the confusion in Kate's voice, but he couldn't have stopped to answer had he wished. He hurried to the frozen-foods aisle only to find another shopper there in addition to his plump lovely. They hadn't crossed paths with any but the plump shopper all night, yet now there was another one present, hindering him from a quick bite! Sighing inwardly, he moved to the ice cream section and glanced distractedly, over the options. Chocolate, cherry, Rocky Road.

He glanced toward his plump lovely. She was watching him and giving coquettish smiles. She looked like a big, smiling steak on legs. Damned woman! It's not nice to tease, he thought unhappily and opened the cooler wider as he stared.

She approached, smiling widely as he pulled ice cream out of the cooler. She didn't say a word, just smiled naughtily as she walked past, her arm brushing against him.

Lucern inhaled deeply, nearly dizzy from the scent of her. Oh yes, her blood was sweet. Or was that the ice cream he held? He grabbed another carton and watched her disappear around the corner with a sigh. He wanted to follow. He could use his brain-control

37

trick to lure her into the back of the store for a little suck. But if he was caught . . .

Sighing, he gave up on the idea and grabbed some Rocky Road ice cream. He could hold out a little while longer. Just a little while more, and he would be free to escape to Bastien's or Etienne's. Surely Kate C. Leever was exhausted after her workday and flight, and would want to make a night of it.

"My, you do like ice cream," Kate commented as he returned.

Lucern glanced down at the four cartons he held and dumped them onto the conveyor belt with a shrug. He had no idea what flavors several of them were, and in his distraction hadn't even realized he'd grabbed so many, but it didn't matter. They'd get eaten eventually.

Kate protested his paying, but Lucern insisted. It was a man thing. His pride wouldn't allow a woman to pay for food intended for his home. Kate opened a bag of rice cakes to munch on the way back. She offered him some, but he merely sneered and shook his head. Rice cakes. Dear God.

Lucern managed to not stop at either of his brothers' houses. He was rather proud of his self-restraint. He and Kate carted the groceries inside his home; then he insisted she start cooking while he put them away. This made him look helpful and useful, when in truth he just wanted her to cook her damned meal, eat it, and go to bed so that he could go in search of what he needed. Not that he couldn't enjoy food, too. A little food wouldn't go amiss, but regular food wouldn't help his main hunger. His people could survive without food, but not without blood.

Fortunately, Kate C. Leever was apparently ravenous, because she made a quick meal, grilling a couple of steaks and then throwing together a bowl of a bunch of green stuff with some sort of sauce on it. Lucern had never seen the attraction of salads. Rabbits ate greens. Humans ate meat, and Lucern ate meat and blood. He was not a rabbit. However, he kept his opinions to himself and finished up with the unpacking at nearly the same time as Kate finished cooking; then they sat down to eat.

Lucern dug into his steak with fervor, ignoring the rabbit bowl. He'd asked for the meat rare, and he supposed it was rare to most people—but rare to him was *rare*. Still, it was tender and juicy, and he ate it quickly.

He watched Kate finish, but shook his head when she offered him salad. "You really should eat some," she lectured with a frown. "It's full of vitamins and nutrients, and you're still awfully pale."

He presumed she feared that his pallor was due to his supposed head injury. It was due to lack of blood, however, which reminded Lucern that he should see if Bastien was home. Excusing himself, he left the room and went to his office.

Much to his disappointment, when he called his brother, there was no answer. Bastien was either out on a date or had gone back to Argeneau Industries. Like Lucern, Bastien preferred working at night when everyone else was sleeping. The habits of a couple hundred years were hard to break.

Lucern returned to the kitchen, to find that Kate Leever had finished eating and had already rinsed off most of the dishes and set them in the dishwasher.

"I shall finish that," he said at once. "You must be exhausted and ready for bed."

Kate glanced at Lucern with surprise. It was hard to believe this was the same man who had written those short "nos" in response to her letters and been so rude when she'd first arrived. His helping her unload groceries and apparent consideration now made her suspicious. The hopeful look on his face didn't help much, either. However, she *was* tired. It had been a long day, so she reluctantly admitted, "I am tired, actually."

In the next moment, she found her arm grasped in a firm hand and herself being propelled out of the kitchen.

"It's to bed with you!" Argeneau sounded cheerful at the prospect, and he rushed her up the hall and then the stairs. "Sleep as late as you like. I shall probably work all night as usual and sleep most of the day. If you rise before me, eat whatever you wish, drink whatever you wish, but *do not poke around.*" The last was said in a hard tone that sounded more like the rude man she expected.

"I would hardly poke around," she said quickly, annoyed. "I brought a manuscript with me to edit. I'll just do that until you get up."

"Good, good. Good night." He pushed her into the yellow guest room she'd chosen earlier and pulled the door closed with a snap.

Kate turned slowly toward it, almost expecting to hear the door's lock click into place. She was relieved when that didn't happen. Shaking her head at her own suspicious mind, she moved to her suitcase to find her nightgown, then went into the en suite bathroom to

40

shower. She was just crawling into bed when she recalled the excuse she'd used to get to stay here. She paused to glance around.

Spotting the small digital clock on the bedside table, she picked it up and set it to ring in an hour. She had every intention of getting up to check to be sure that Lucern hadn't fallen asleep—and that if he had, he could still wake up.

Kate set the alarm back on the table and crawled under the covers, thinking of those few panicked moments in the kitchen. She drew a deep breath through her nose, recalling Lucern Argeneau standing before her, blood streaming down his head and face. Dear God, she'd never actually seen a head injury before. She'd heard they could be bloody, of course, and that they often looked worse than they truly were, but there had been so much blood.

She shuddered and swallowed a knot of anxiety. Kate hardly knew the man, and he'd been nothing but rude to her since her arrival, but despite the fact that it would serve him right after his behavior, she really didn't want to see him dead. How was she going to impress her boss that way? She could see it now. "No, Allison, I wasn't able to convince him to do the newspaper interviews. No, nor the television shows. Er . . . no, he won't be doing signings either. Actually, I might have been able to convince him, except I killed him instead. It was an accident, Allison. I know he is our latest cash cow, and I truly didn't mean to kill him despite the fact that he's a rude, pigheaded . . . No, really, it was an accident! Yes, I do realize I'm fired. No, I don't blame you at all for not giving me a reference. Yes, if you'll excuse me I'll just go apply at McDonald's now that my publishing career is ruined."

Sighing, she shook her head on the pillow and closed her eyes. Thank goodness Argeneau seemed healthy—except for the pallor. She sat up in bed, concern eating at her again. He really had been awfully pale.

"And why not?" she asked herself. It looked as if he'd lost a quart of blood. Or at least a pint. Maybe she should check on him now. Kate considered the matter briefly, partly wanting to check on him, partly reluctant to have him bark at her for interrupting him at whatever he was doing. He was surely going to bark enough when she checked on him every hour through the night. But he had been terribly pale after hitting his head.

On the other hand, she had noticed his pallor on the porch before he'd ever hit his head. Or had that been the lighting? It had been nighttime, and the light on the porch had been one of those neon jobbies. That might have simply made him appear pale.

She mulled over the matter briefly, started to slip her feet off the bed to go check on him before she went to sleep, but then she paused at the sound of a closing door. Stiffening, Kate listened to the soft pad of feet down the hall, then forced herself to relax and lie back down. The footsteps had been soft, but otherwise normal. Lucern didn't sound to be staggering or unduly slow. He was fine. She would stick to her plan to check him in an hour.

Relaxing, she lay back and closed her eyes. She wasn't going to get much sleep tonight and knew it. In truth, she'd really rather be in a hotel somewhere sleeping soundly. And she would be—head wound or no head wound—if she weren't so afraid that once he got her out of the house, Lucern Argeneau wasn't likely to let her back in. Kate couldn't risk that; she just *had* to convince him to do one of the publicity appearances. Any one of them would do. She very much feared that keeping her new position as editor depended on it.

"You're kidding? She really thought all that blood was from a little bump on the head?" Etienne gave a disbelieving laugh.

"Well, she would hardly imagine it came from a bag of blood in his fridge," Bastien pointed out, but he was chuckling too.

Lucern ignored his brothers' amusement and sank his teeth into the second bag of blood Rachel brought him. He'd already ingested the first. He had insisted on doing so before explaining why he'd shown up at Etienne's home pleading to be fed. The first bag had allowed him to get over his surprise that Bastien was there. It had also given his brothers time to explain that Bastien had come by to help sort out some last-minute problems with the wedding. Which explained nicely why Lucern hadn't been able to reach him.

"What I don't understand," Bastien said as Lucern finished off the second bag and retracted his teeth, "is why you didn't simply get into her head and suggest she leave."

"I tried," Lucern admitted wearily. He placed both empty bags in the hand Rachel held out, then watched her walk out of the room to dispose of them. "But I could not get into her mind."

43

The silence that followed was as effective as great gusty gasps would have been from anyone else. Etienne and Bastien stared at him, stunned.

"You're kidding," Bastien said at last.

When Lucern shook his head, Etienne dropped onto the chair across from him and said, "Well, don't tell Mother if you don't want her pushing you two together. The minute she heard that I couldn't read Rachel's mind was the minute she decided we'd make a good couple." He paused thoughtfully. "Of course, she *was* right."

Lucern grunted in disgust. "Well, Ms. Kate C. Leever is not perfect for me. The woman is as annoying as a gnat flying about your head. Stubborn as a mule, and pushy as hell. The damned woman has not given me a moment's peace since pushing her way over my doorstep."

"Not true," Bastien argued with amusement. "You managed to give her the slip long enough to come here."

"That is only because she was tired and went to bed. She . . ." He paused suddenly and sat up straight, recalling her promise to check on him every hour to be sure his head injury hadn't done more damage than he believed. Would she really do that? He glanced sharply at his brothers. "How long have I been here?"

Bastien's eyebrows rose curiously, but he glanced at his watch and said: "I'm not positive, but I'd guess you've been here about forty, forty-five minutes."

"Damn." Lucern was on his feet at once and heading for the door. "I have to go. My thanks for the drinks, Rachel," he called loudly at the other room.

"Wait. What . . . ?"

Bastien and Etienne got up to follow, questions slipping from their lips, but Lucern didn't stop to answer. He'd locked his office door before leaving the house, and Kate might assume that meant he was in there, but if she really did check on him hourly and got no answer when she knocked on the door, the damned woman might decide he'd died or something and call the police or an ambulance. She might even break down his office door herself. There was just no telling what that woman might do.

He came up with a couple of doozies as he hurried home.

Fortunately, she hadn't done any of them by the time he returned. She was up and trying to rouse him, though—that much was obvious the moment he opened the front door. He could hear her shouting and banging on his office door all the way downstairs. Rolling his eyes at the racket she was making and the panic in her voice as she called his name, Lucern pocketed his house keys and jogged upstairs. He came to an abrupt halt at the top of the steps.

Dear God, the woman didn't just eat rabbit food, she wore rabbit slippers.

Lucern gawked at the ears flopping over the furry pink bunny slippers she wore, then let his gaze slide up over her heavy, also pink and fuzzy, housecoat. If he didn't already know she had a nice figure, he wouldn't know now. Then he caught a glimpse of her hair and winced. She'd gone to bed with wet hair and had obviously tossed around a lot in her sleep; her hair was standing on end in every direction.

On the bright side, she obviously didn't intend on stooping to seducing him into doing any of those publicity things she was so fired up for him to do. Oddly enough, Lucern actually felt a touch of regret at that realization. He didn't understand why. He didn't even like the woman. Still, he might have been open to a little seduction.

"Good evening," he said when she paused in her yelling to take a breath. He found himself gaping again, as Kate C. Leever whirled around to face him.

"You! I thought . . ." She turned to the locked office door, then back to him. "This door is locked. I thought you were in there, and when you didn't answer, I . . ." Her voice trailed away as she took in his expression. Suddenly self-conscious, she pulled the edges of her ratty old robe together as if he might be trying to catch a better look at the flannel nightgown showing at the neckline. "Is something wrong?"

Lucern couldn't help it; he knew it was rude, but he couldn't stop the words from blurting through his lips. "Dear God! What is that goop on your face?"

Kate immediately let go of her robe and pressed both hands to her face, her mouth forming an alarmed "Oh" as she recalled and tried to hide the dry green mask.

It was obviously some sort of beauty treatment, Lucern deduced, but Kate didn't stick around to explain exactly what sort. Turning on her heel, she fled back to the guest room and closed the door. After a heartbeat, she called in a strained voice, "I'm glad you're all right. Mostly. I was worried when you didn't answer my knock. I'll check on you again in an hour."

Silence then filled the hall.

Lucern waited a moment, but when he didn't hear the sound of footsteps moving away from the door, he decided she was waiting for some sort of response. "*No*" was the first response that came to mind. He didn't want her checking on him. He didn't want her here at all. But he found he couldn't tell her that. She'd appeared terribly embarrassed to be caught looking as she had, and really he couldn't blame her; she'd looked awful in a cute, bunny type way.

He smiled to himself at the memory of her standing there in his hall looking like hell. Kate *had* looked bad—but in the sort of adorable way that made him want to hug her . . . until he'd seen the cracking green mask on her face.

Lucern decided not to further distress her with the "no" she no doubt expected and instead called out "Good-night" in an uncomfortably gruff voice. As he moved to his office door and unlocked it, he heard a little sigh from the other side of her door, then a very small "good-night" in return. Her soft footsteps padded away. She was going to bed, he thought.

There came a snap, and light fingered its way out from under the guest room door. Lucern paused. Why were the lights on? Was she resetting her alarm clock for an hour from now? The silly woman really did intend to check on him every hour!

Shaking his head, he stepped into his office and flicked on the lights. He'd give her fifteen minutes to fall asleep and then go in and turn off the alarm clock. The last thing he needed was for her to be pestering him all night. Although it did occur to him that if she didn't sleep much tonight, she would probably sleep longer in the morning to make up for it, which would give her less time to nose around on her own while he was sleeping.

No, he decided. She'd said she wouldn't poke around, and he believed her.

Mostly.

Chapter Three

Kate poked around.

She didn't mean to. In fact, she had made plans for the day which definitely did not include poking around—but, well, the best-laid plans and all that. They always went awry.

Kate woke up at ten a.m. Her first thought was to wonder where she was. Her second thought—once she recalled where she was and why—was "Oh, shit, the alarm didn't go off." Sitting up in bed, she reached for the alarm clock to look it over. It was set to the off position. Kate frowned at the thing, sure she had reset it after checking on Lucern the first time. She distinctly recalled resetting it and turning it on. But it was off. She set it back with a frown. Had she woken up the second time just to roll over and turn it off? That must be it, she realized and grimaced to herself.

"Way to go, Leever. The one excuse you had to stay here, the one opportunity to ingratiate yourself with the man, and you blew it." Her thinking had been that surely he couldn't oust her after she'd gone to the trouble of rousing herself every hour to be sure he was all right. But now that she'd failed at her task, he'd have her out of there by noon—if he hadn't written all night as he'd claimed he was going to do. If he had written all night, he might not wake up until two or three o'clock. Which meant she'd be out of there by three or four.

"Good show, Katie." She pushed the bedsheet aside and slipped out of bed. Now she'd have to come up with another good excuse to stay until she convinced Lucern Argeneau to cooperate.

Kate pondered the problem while she showered, while she dried off, while she dressed, while she brushed her teeth, while she fiddled with her hair and while she dabbed on a touch of face powder. At last she gave it up as a lost cause until after she'd eaten. She always thought better on a full stomach.

Leaving the guest room, she paused in the hallway and stared at the door opposite her own. Maybe she should check on her host. She hadn't done her checking through the night. The man might be lying comatose on his office floor.

She pursed her lips thoughtfully over the matter, then shook her head. Nope. Not a good idea, she decided. She'd neglected her duty to check on him last night; the last thing she wanted was to wake him up before she'd found some way to redeem herself.

Turning on her heel, she moved as quietly as she could to the stairs and down them. Her first stop was the kitchen. She put coffee on, then surveyed the contents of the fridge. Though she knew every single item in it, it was fun to look at all those goodies and pretend she might have something greasy and bad for her like bacon and eggs. Of course, she didn't. She settled for the less satisfying but healthy grapefruit and cereal. Then she poured herself a cup of coffee and sipped it as she peered out the window into Lucern's backyard. It was a large, neat, tidy lawn surrounded by trees, obviously professionally kept. Just as the house was.

Lucern's home bespoke wealth and class, both inside and out. It was large and filled with antiques, but outside was the true treat. The house was set on a good-sized property surrounded by trees and grass, all well kept and set up to disguise the fact that the home sat on the edge of a huge metropolis. It was gorgeous and restful, and Kate enjoyed it as she drank her coffee.

Pouring herself another cup, she wandered out of the kitchen and strolled up the hall, her mind searching for some plot to keep her in the house for at least another night. She really had to convince Lucern to do at least one of the interviews. Kate suspected he would never agree to do the book-signing tour and she had already let go of that idea, but surely he could be persuaded to do a couple of interviews. Possibly over the phone or via the Internet? A couple of her other authors had done it via e-mail. The interviewer sent an e-mail with the questions, the author answered by e-mail. Or there were the various messenger services; she'd heard of authors doing interviews that way as well. Geez, surely that wouldn't be such a big deal? Lucern wouldn't even have to leave his house.

She was about to turn into the living room with her

coffee when she spotted the box on the hall table. Kate recognized it at once. She'd packed the damned thing full of fan letters and sent it herself. Changing direction, she continued up the hall to the table and glared down at the box. She'd sent it three months ago! Three months! And he hadn't even bothered to open the damned thing, let alone answer any of the letters it held.

"Damned man," she muttered. "Ungrateful, stupid . . . *wonderful* man." The last was said with a dawning smile as she recognized her excuse for staying another night. "Oh," she breathed. "God bless your stupid hide and rude ways."

Salsa music. That was the first thing Lucern heard upon awaking. He recognized the tune; it was a hit at the moment. A brief image flashed in his head of a thin, handsome Latin man dancing around on a stage in dark clothes.

The music made it easy for him to find Kate. He merely followed the sound to his living room, where he paused in the doorway to gape at the shambles the room had become while he slept. The room that had been neat and tidy when he went to bed was now awash in paper. Every available surface had open letters and envelopes piled on it. Kate C. Leever boogied around a box in the center of the mess, pulling letters out, opening them, and gyrating to one pile or another to add the letter to it before boogying back for another.

"You poked!" he roared.

Kate, who had been doing some sort of bump and grind—a rather sexy bump and grind, to be honest—

with the half-empty box, gave a squeak of alarm. She whirled toward the door, upsetting the box and sending it to the floor.

"Now look what you made me do!" she cried, flushing with embarrassment. She bent to gather up the box and its contents.

"You poked," Lucern repeated. Moving forward, he towered over her as she scooped up the escaped envelopes.

"I . . ." She peered up at him guiltily, then irritation took over her expression. Standing, she glared back. "I hardly needed to poke. The box was right there on the hall table. I noticed it in passing."

"I am not sure, but I believe it is illegal to open someone else's mail. Is it not a federal offense?"

"I'm quite sure that doesn't apply when it's mail you sent yourself—and I *did* send this box. Three months ago!" she added grimly.

"But you did not write the letters inside it."

Kate scowled, then turned her attention to throwing the unopened envelopes back in the box. She explained, "I saw that you hadn't even opened it yet, and thought perhaps I could help. It was obvious you were overwhelmed by the number of letters."

"Ha! I had no idea of the number of letters. I hadn't opened it."

"No, you hadn't," she conceded after a moment. Then she asked, "What is it with you and mail? I've never met anyone who left mail lying about for months like this. It's no wonder you were so slow to answer my letters."

Before he could respond, she turned and added,

"And how could you ignore these letters like you did?" She waved at the mini-towers built around the room. "These are your readers, your fans! Without them, you're nothing. They pay good money for your books, and more good money to tell you they enjoyed them. Your books wouldn't be published without readers to read them. How can you just ignore them like this? They took the time and trouble to write you. They say wonderful things about you, your books, your writing! Didn't you ever admire someone's work or enjoy it so much you wanted to tell them of your appreciation? You should be grateful they've taken the trouble to do so!"

Lucern stared at her with surprise. She was quite impassioned, her face flushed, her chest heaving. And what a nice chest it was, he noted. She had a nice figure altogether, even in the comfortable jeans and T-shirt she'd chosen to wear today.

All of which was interesting to note, but not very useful at the moment. He reprimanded himself and took a moment to clear his throat before trying to speak. The problem was, he couldn't recall what she'd said or what he should say in response.

"Ha!" There was triumph on her face. "You have no answer to that one, do you? Because it's true. You have been terribly lax in tending to this matter, and I've decided—out of the goodness of my heart—to help you. You needn't thank me," she added in a rather self-righteous tone. Then she grabbed and opened another letter.

Lucern found a grin pulling at his lips as he watched her. He didn't have to be able to read her mind to know that this was not out of the goodness of her heart, but an attempt to remain in his home long enough to convince him to do some of her publicity stuff. He decided—out of the goodness of *his* heart—to let her stay long enough to help him with the letters. He hadn't intended to answer them. He didn't know any of these people and it was a burdensome task, but now . . . Well, her tirade had actually reached him. To some degree.

"Very well. You may help me with the letters," he announced.

Kate shook her head at Lucern Argeneau's magnanimity. "Well! How grand of you to allow me to . . ." She paused. Her sneering words were a wasted effort; Lucern had left the room. Damned man! He was the most frustrating, irritating . . . And what was with his proper speech all the time? The man had antique phrasing and a slight accent that she couldn't quite place. Both of which were beginning to annoy her.

She was just turning back to the box to continue sorting the letters into categories when a series of loud chimes rang through the house. Recognizing it to be the doorbell, she hesitated, then dropped the letters and went to answer. She opened the front door to find a uniformed man on the other side, a cooler stamped "A.B.B." in hand.

"Hi." He stopped chewing the gum in his mouth long enough to grin at her, showing off a nice set of white teeth. "You must be Luc's editor."

Kate lifted her eyebrows. "Er, yes. Kate. Kate C. Leever."

The man took the hand she held out and squeezed it warmly. "Aunt Maggie was right. You're a cutey."

"Aunt Maggie?" Kate asked in confusion.

"Luc's mom and my aunt. Marguerite," he added when she continued to look confused, but it didn't help Kate much. The only people she'd met since arriving were the pair who had been leaving when she got out of the taxi, and the woman certainly hadn't been old enough to be Luc's—er, Lucern's—mother. Kate shrugged that concern aside as the other connotations of what he'd said sank in. "You're Lucern's cousin?"

"Yes, ma'am. Our dads are brothers." He grinned, making it hard for her to see a resemblance. Oh, this man was tallish and had dark hair like Lucern, but Luc didn't smile, and this young man hadn't stopped smiling since she'd opened the door. It was hard to believe they were related. "I'm quite a bit younger though."

"You are?" she asked doubtfully. She would have placed both men around the same age.

"Oh, yes." He grinned. "I'm centuries younger than Lucern."

"Thomas."

Kate glanced over her shoulder. Lucern was coming up the hall, a scowl on his face as he glanced from her to his cousin. She sighed inwardly at his obvious displeasure. Apparently, he didn't like her answering his door. Geez, the guy was such a pain. Why couldn't Thomas here have written the vampire novels? He would have been much easier to deal with, she was sure.

"Here you are, Cousin." Thomas didn't seem surprised or disturbed by Lucern's expression. He held out the cooler. "Bastien said to get this here pronto. That you were seriously lacking and in need," he added with a grin and a wink.

"Thank you."

Lucern actually smiled at his cousin, Kate noted with surprise. And his face didn't crack and fall off.

"I'll return directly," Lucern added. As he turned toward the stairs he warned, "Try not to bite my guest. She can be . . . provoking."

Kate scowled at her host's retreating back, then smiled reluctantly at Thomas's chuckle. She turned with a wry smile and asked, "Has he always been this irritable, or is it just me?"

"Just you," Thomas said. At her crestfallen expression, he started to laugh. Then he took pity on her and told the truth. "Nah. It isn't you. Lucern is kind of surly. Has been for centuries. Although he seems to be in a good mood today. You must be having a good influence on him."

"This is a good mood?" Kate asked with disbelief. Thomas just laughed again.

"Here you are," Lucern called. He jogged down the steps and handed his cousin's cooler back to him. "Give Bastien my thanks."

"Will do." Then Thomas nodded, gave Kate another wink, and turned to walk off the porch.

Kate glanced at the driveway and the truck parked in it. "A.B.B. Deliveries" was stamped on the side, the same as the cooler, she noted. Lucern maneuvered her out of the way and closed the door.

"What . . . ?" she began curiously, but Lucern saved her from proving just how rude and nosy she could be. He turned away and started back up the hall before she could ask the questions trembling on her lips.

* * *

"I thought that, as there are so many letters—too many to answer individually, really—we could divide them into categories and come up with a sort of form letter for each. Then you could just add a line to each response to make it more personal."

Lucern grunted and took another sip of the coffee Kate had made while making lunch. Well, it had been her lunch, his breakfast. Although, if he counted the bag of blood he'd sucked down while stacking the rest Thomas had delivered in the small refrigerator in his office, he supposed the meal could count as his lunch, too. They had since moved to the living room, and he was seated on the couch while she explained her plans for his letters.

"I'll take that to mean you think my plan is brilliant and agree to cooperate," Kate said in response to his grunt. Because it seemed to annoy her, and because he liked the way she flushed when she was annoyed, Lucern grunted again.

As he expected, her cheeks pinkened with blood and her eyes sparked with anger, and Lucern decided that Kate C. Leever was a pretty little thing when angry. He enjoyed looking at her.

And despite her unhappiness with him, the irritation on her face suddenly eased and she commented, "You have more color today. I guess there was no lasting damage from that head wound after all."

"I told you I was fine," Luc said.

"Yes, you did," she agreed. Then she looked uncomfortable and said, "I'm sorry I didn't check on you after that first time. I intended to, but I didn't hear the alarm go off again. I must have turned it off in my sleep or something."

Lucern waved the apology away. He had turned the alarm off himself, so she had nothing to apologize for. And he didn't think she'd appreciate knowing that he'd crept into her room while she was sleeping. She most definitely wouldn't want to know that after finishing the task, he'd found himself standing at the side of the bed just watching her sleep for a while, staring with fascination at her innocent expression in sleep, watching the rise and fall of the bunnies on her flannel nightgown as she breathed. How he'd wanted to pull the top of that oh-so-proper nightgown away from her throat to see the pulse beating there. No, she definitely wouldn't want to know all that, so he kept it to himself and sipped his coffee again.

The drink was bitter, but an oddly tasty brew. Lucern couldn't think why he'd avoided it all these years. True, he'd been warned that the stimulant in coffee would hit his body twice as hard as a human's, but he really hadn't noticed any effects yet. Of course, he'd only had a couple sips so far. Perhaps he shouldn't risk any more. He set the cup down.

"So, what are we doing?" he asked abruptly, to get Kate off the topic of not waking up to check on him last night.

"Well, I've been dividing the letters into categories. A lot of them have similar themes or questions, such as requests as to whether you'll write Lucern's or Bastien's story next," she explained. "So I've been putting all those asking that question in one pile. That way, you can write a form letter for each pile, reducing the letters you write to twenty or so rather than hundreds and hundreds."

"Of course, it would be nice if you read each letter and wrote a line or two to personalize your response," she added, sounding tentative.

Lucern supposed she thought that the idea of all that work would annoy him. Which it did. He couldn't help but grumble, "I did not suffer these difficulties with my other books."

"Other books?" She blinked in confusion, then said, "Oh. You mean your historical texts. Well, that was different. Those were nonfiction. Most of them are used in universities and such. Students rarely write fan letters."

Lucern grimaced and gulped down another mouthful of coffee. It helped stop him from telling her that his novels were nonfiction as well, and that they were just peddled as vampire romance.

"Anyway, I think we have enough categories to make a start. I can tell you what each category is, and you can compose a sort of general response to each while I continue to sort the rest of the letters," she suggested.

Nodding his acquiescence, Lucern crossed his arms and waited.

"Wouldn't you like to get a pen and paper or something?" she asked after a moment. "So you don't forget any of them? There are at least twenty categories and—"

"I have an excellent memory," Lucern announced. "Proceed."

Kate turned in a slow circle, apparently trying to decide where to start. "Dear God, he sounds like that bald guy in *The King and I*," he heard her mutter.

Lucern knew he wasn't supposed to hear that, but he had spectacular hearing. He quite enjoyed her exasperation, so he added to it by commenting, "You mean Yul Brynner."

She jerked around to eye him with alarm, and he nodded. "He played the king of Siam, and did an excellent job of it."

Kate hesitated; then, apparently deciding that he wasn't angry, she relaxed a bit and even managed a smile. "It's one of my favorite movies."

"Oh, did they make a movie of it?" he asked with interest. "I saw it live on stage on opening night."

When she appeared rather doubtful, he realized that admitting to seeing the Rodgers and Hammerstein Broadway show—which had premiered in 1951, if he wasn't mistaken—was rather dating himself. As he looked to be in his mid-thirties, it was no wonder she appeared taken aback. Clearing his throat, he added, "The revival of course. It hit Broadway in 1977, I believe."

Her eyebrows rose. "You must have been all of . . . what? Seven? Eight?"

Unwilling to lie, Lucern merely grunted. He added, "I have an excellent memory."

"Yes. Of course you do." Kate sighed and picked up a letter. She read aloud, " 'Dear Mr. Argeneau. I read and adored Love Bites, volumes one and two. But the first was my favorite. You truly have a talent! The medieval feel to that novel was so gritty and realistic that I could almost believe you were there.' " Kate paused and glanced up. "All the letters in this stack are

61

along that line, praising you for the realism of your writing and the fact that it reads as if you were actually there."

When Lucern merely nodded, she frowned. "Well?"

"Well, what?" he asked with surprise. "That reader is right."

"That reader is right?" She gaped at him. "That's what you're going to write? 'Dear reader, You're right?' "

Lucern shrugged mildly, wondering why she was raising her voice. The reader *was right*. His books did read as if he'd been there in medieval times. Because he had been. Not during the precise time period when his parents met, but not long afterward—and in those days, change was slow enough that little had differed.

He watched his editor slam the letter back on the pile and move on to another. She muttered the whole time about him being an arrogant jerk, and added other uncomplimentary descriptions. "Insensitive" and "lacking in social skills" were just two. All of which Lucern knew he wasn't supposed to hear.

He wasn't offended. He was six hundred years old. A man gained some self-confidence in that time. Lucern supposed that to most people he *would* seem arrogant, possibly even a jerk. Insensitive certainly, and he knew his social skills were somewhat rusty. Etienne and Bastien had always been better at this social stuff. Yet, after years of living as a reclusive author, he was terribly lacking and knew it.

Still, he couldn't see any good reason to sharpen those social skills. He was at that stage in life where impressing someone seemed like a load of bother.

He'd taken a waitress for dinner once who'd explained the way he felt rather nicely. She'd said, "You can go along, working your shift and everything's fine. Most of the customers are pretty good, though there might be the occasional bad one. But sometimes you have that night where you get a real nasty customer, or even two or three in a row, and they bring you down, make you tired and miserable, feeling like the whole human race sucks. Then a baby might coo and smile at you, or another customer will say "Rough night?" with a sympathetic smile. Then your mood picks up and you'll realize maybe people aren't so bad."

Well, Lucern had suffered a couple of bad decades, and he was feeling tired and depressed and as if the whole human race rather sucked. He didn't have the energy or desire to put up with people. He just wanted to be left alone. That was why he'd started writing—a solitary pursuit that kept him busy and took him into much more pleasant worlds.

He knew that all it would take was someone to smile and say "rough decade?" to change that. Someone like Kate. As much as he'd resisted having to deal with her, he'd begun to enjoy her company. She'd even made him smile several times.

Realizing the path his thoughts were taking, and that they were rather warmer than he was comfortable feeling for his unwanted house guest, he drew himself up short and began to scowl. Dear God, what had he been thinking? Kate C. Leever was a stubborn, annoying woman who had done nothing but bring chaos to an orderly existence. He—

" 'Dear Mr Argeneau,' " she read grimly, drawing Lucern out of his thoughts. " 'I've read your vampire novels and enjoyed them immensely. I have always been fascinated with vampirism and read everything on the subject voraciously. I just know that there really is such a thing, and suspect you yourself really are one. I would love to be one. Would you please turn me into a vampire, too?' " Kate rolled her eyes and stopped reading, glancing at him. "What would you say to *her*?"

"No," he said firmly.

Kate threw the letter down with a snort. "Why does that answer not surprise me? Although I suppose it would be ridiculous to try to explain to someone of that ilk that you really aren't a vampire, that there truly is no such thing, so you couldn't possibly 'change' her." She laughed and moved on to the next pile. Looking at the first few letters there, she added, "It would be kinder just to tell her to go to her local psychologist to see if he couldn't help her with her reality problem."

Lucern felt his lips twitch, but he didn't say anything, merely waited as Kate settled on the next letter.

" 'Dear Mr. Argeneau,' " she began. " 'I haven't read Love Bites, One, but I will, I guarantee it. I just finished Love Bites, Two, and thought it was wonderful. Etienne was so sweet and funny and sexy that I fell in love with him even as Rachel did. He's my dream man.' " Kate paused and glanced up expectantly. "What would you say to those letters?"

That was easy enough. "Etienne is taken."

His editor threw her hands up in the air. "This isn't a joke, Lucern! You can't just—" She paused as the doorbell chimed, then turned away with a sigh as Lucern reluctantly stood to answer it. He already knew who it would be. Thomas had delivered the blood, which left the only other company he ever got: his family. And since Etienne and Rachel were busy with wedding preparations, and Bastien, Lissianna and Gregory would all be at work at this hour, the only person it could be was his . . .

"Mother." His greeting was less than enthusiastic as he opened the door to find Marguerite Argeneau standing there. He really had no desire to have his mother and Kate Leever in the same room; it would definitely give the older woman ideas. And since he already suspected she tended in those ideas' direction, he didn't think it was good to encourage her. But what could he do? She was his mother.

"Luc, darling." Marguerite kissed him on both cheeks, then pushed past him into the house. "Are you alone, dear? I thought I'd drop in for a spot of tea." She didn't wait for his answer, but followed her maternal instincts to the door of the living room and smiled brightly when she spotted Kate. "Well, it looks like I'm just in time. No doubt you two could use a break, too."

Lucern closed his front door with a resigned sigh, and his mother sailed fearlessly into his cluttered living room. The woman never simply stopped by for tea. She always had a purpose. And Luc very much feared he wasn't going to like her purpose in stopping by today. He just hoped to God she knew better than to try any of her matchmaking nonsense on him and Kate.

Chapter Four

"Why, you could be Luc's date!"

"Er . . ." Kate cast a frantic glance Lucern's way at his mother's suggestion, only to find him sitting with eyes closed, a pained expression on his face. She suspected he was begging for the floor to open up and swallow him whole, or even to swallow him in pieces, so long as it swallowed him. It almost made Kate feel better. It was nice to know that she wasn't the only one with parents who managed to humiliate her at every opportunity.

Still, Marguerite was really something else. Kate had spent the better part of the half hour since the woman's arrival merely gaping at her. This exotic and beautiful creature was Lucern's mother? Oh, certainly, the resemblance was there. And he was equal to her in looks, but Marguerite Argeneau didn't look a day over thirty herself. How could she possibly be Lucern's—or Luc, as everyone seemed to call him—mom?

"Good genes, dear," had been the woman's answer when Kate had commented.

Kate had sighed miserably, wondering why such genes couldn't run in her family, too. After that, she'd merely stared at the woman, nodding absently at everything said, while trying to spot signs of a face lift. She obviously should have been paying more attention to what Marguerite was burbling on about. Lucern's brother's wedding had been the topic of conversation. Kate wasn't quite sure how that had led to the last comment she had heard.

"Date?" she repeated blankly.

"Yes, dear. For the wedding."

"Mother." Lucern's voice was a warning growl, and Kate peered over to see that his eyes were open and sharply focused on his mother.

"Well, Luc darling. You can hardly leave the poor girl here alone tomorrow night while you attend." Marguerite laughed, apparently oblivious to her son's fury.

"Kate has to return to New York," Lucern said firmly. "She won't be here tomorrow ni—"

"That sounds like fun!" Kate blurted. Lucern fell silent and aimed his gimlet eye at her, but she ignored him. There was no way she was leaving without first gaining his agreement to at least an interview with one of the newspapers clamoring to speak to him. And falling in with Marguerite's suggestion meant that not only could he not force her on a plane back to New York, but by the time the wedding party was over, it would be too late for Kate to fly home the next night as well. Which gave her until Sunday to work on the man. That thought made her beam happily, and she silently thanked Lucern's mother.

The only thing that worried her was that Marguerite Argeneau was looking rather pleased in return. Kate had the sudden anxious feeling that she'd stepped neatly into a trap. She hoped to God that the woman didn't have any matchmaking ideas about her and Lucern. Surely Marguerite realized what a cantankerous lout her son was and that he wasn't Kate's type at all!

"Well, wonderful!" the woman said. Ignoring her son's scowl, Marguerite smiled like the cat who got the cream, then asked, "Do you have something to wear to the wedding, dear?"

"Oh." Kate's smile faltered. She'd packed something for every possible occasion except a wedding. There'd been no way to see *that* coming, and Kate didn't think the slinky black dress she'd brought to cover the possibility of an evening out would work.

"Ah-ha!" Lucern was now the one looking pleased. "She hasn't anything to wear, Mother. She can't—"

"A quick trip to my modiste, I think," Marguerite cut him off. Then she confided to Kate, "She always has something for just such an emergency. And a visit with my hairdresser will work magic on your hair, and we'll be set."

Kate felt herself relax, and could have hugged the woman. Marguerite was wonderful. Much too good to have a son like Lucern. The woman was clever, charming and a pleasure to be around. Unlike a certain surly man. Kate's gaze slid to Lucern, and she almost grinned at the misery on his face. She supposed she should feel guilty for forcing herself into his home and staying there, but she didn't. He was in serious need of assistance. He was terribly lacking in social skills and obviously spent way too much time alone. She was good for him—she was sure of it.

"Well, now that it's all settled, I'll be off." Marguerite was quickly on her feet and heading out of the kitchen—so quickly that Kate nearly got whiplash watching.

Getting up, she hurried after the woman. "Thank you so much, Mrs. Argeneau," she called as she jogged down the hall in pursuit.

Lucern's mother didn't just look young, she was as spry as could be for the mother of a man who had to be at least thirty-five. How old did that make her? Kate wondered. At least fifty-three. Impossible, she thought, but kept the thought to herself and merely added, "I really appreciate your generous offer to help me shop and—"

"Nonsense, dear. I'm grateful to you for being here to accompany Luc." Marguerite paused and allowed Kate to catch up. "Why, you should have seen the poor man at his *sister's* wedding. I've never seen Luc run so fast or hide so much. It's the ladies, you know. They tend to chase after him."

Kate's eyebrows flew up in patent disbelief at that.

A bubble of laughter burst from Marguerite. "Hard to believe when Luc is so curmudgeonly, isn't it? But I think it's the hunt that attracts them. He makes it obvious he isn't interested, and they react like hounds after a fox. With you there to act as his escort, he'll be able to relax and enjoy the celebration this time. And once he realizes that, he'll be grateful for your presence, too."

69

Kate didn't bother to hide her doubt that Lucern Argeneau could ever be grateful for anything. The man was more than curmudgeonly in her opinion.

"He may seem crusty on the outside, dear," Marguerite said solemnly, obviously reading her thoughts. "But he's rather like a toasted marshmallow, soft and mushy in the center. Very few people ever see that center, though." Leaving Kate to consider that, the older woman continued on to the door and opened it. "I shall pick you up after lunch. One o'clock. If that's all right with you?"

"Yes. But will that leave time to get everything done?" Kate asked with concern. In her experience, weddings were usually around two or three o'clock in the afternoon.

Marguerite Argeneau looked calm. "Oh, scads of time, dear. The wedding isn't until seven p.m."

"Isn't that rather late?" Kate asked with surprise.

"Late weddings are all the rage today. I hear Julia Roberts married her cameraman after midnight."

"Really? I hadn't heard that," Kate said faintly.

"Oh yes. She's started a trend. Till tomorrow then," Marguerite finished gaily. The woman then closed the door behind herself, leaving Kate standing in the hallway feeling rather as if she'd just survived a tornado.

Kate stood there for several minutes, just staring at the door, her mind whirring through everything she would need to do to be ready for this wedding, before the door to the kitchen opened and Lucern stalked out.

"I'll be in my office." His voice was short, his expression forbidding as he passed her on the way to the stairs.

Kate—always a smart girl when it came to matters of self-preservation—kept her mouth shut and merely watched him disappear up the stairs. He was angry, of course. Which was to be expected, but she hoped it would pass.

A door slammed upstairs. Hard.

Well, perhaps he wouldn't get over it tonight, but he would by tomorrow. She hoped. With a little help, maybe. She turned and peered at the mess in the living room. There was no way she was going to be able to get him to work on those letters tonight. Which she supposed was a good thing. She was beginning to fear that any letters he wrote were more likely to offend and scare readers than please them. She'd be doing him a big favor by composing the form letters herself and just having him sign them.

Kate grimaced at the idea. It meant a lot of work for her, and the readers were hardly likely to be all that happy. They'd certainly be happier with her meddling, however, than with receiving a letter that read:

Dear Reader.
No.
Sincerely,
Lucern Argeneau

Oddly enough, Kate found herself chuckling at the idea. He really was rather amusing in some ways, this author of hers. The problem was, he didn't mean to be.

Heaving a sigh, she turned into the living room to start to work.

*   *   *

Lucern grabbed a bag of blood from the small office refrigerator where he'd placed it earlier, then paced his office like a caged tiger. He did so for more than an hour before working off enough energy so that he could relax sufficiently to sit. He didn't know if it was his anger or the caffeine that had got him so wound up. And he didn't care.

Groaning, he leaned back in his desk chair and rubbed his face with his hands. His mother had just cursed him to two more nights of Kate Leever's presence. And Kate hadn't helped matters with her quick agreement. The woman was like lichen. Like muck you couldn't scrape off the bottom of your shoe. Like—well, none of the things popping to his mind were very attractive, and, as annoying as Kate Leever could be, she was also attractive, so Lucern gave up his analogies. He tried to be fair about such things whenever possible.

Letting his hands drop away from his face, he turned to consider the computer on his desk. He wanted to avoid Kate for a bit. He was still cranky enough that he was likely to hurt her feelings were he around her, and he didn't wish to hurt her—

"Well, hell! Now you're worried about her feelings?" he said to himself. This wouldn't do at all. He tried to be firm with his unruly sentiments and lectured, "The woman is your editor. She will use manipulation, clever ruses and any weapon necessary to get what she wants from you. Do not start getting all soft and sentimental about her. You don't want her here. You want to be left alone to work in peace."

The problem was, he didn't really have anything to work on. He hadn't started anything new since finishing

Etienne and Rachel's story—which had been in print for a month now. And Lucern didn't have a clue what to work on next. He knew that Kate and Roundhouse Publishing wanted another vampire romance, but Bastien wasn't showing signs of obliging his brother by falling in love any time soon.

Well, Lucern decided with a shrug, it wasn't as if he needed the money. His investments over the years had always done well. He could relax if he wanted. Roundhouse would just have to wait until he came up with something.

His gaze fell on the video game on the corner of his desk—*Blood Lust II*. The game was Etienne's newest creation. Part I had sold out several times and won countless awards. Its success wasn't a great surprise to Lucern; the game was fun and action-packed, with awesome graphics, lots of villains to slay, lots of puzzles to solve and a great story line. Lucern wasn't the only one in the family who could write a story. Blood Lust II was expected to do even better when it was released.

Grinning, he popped the seal on the package and pulled out the game CD. He had played the first couple of levels of the prototype before the game was even finished, and he and Bastien had got the first two full copies hot off the press. It paid to be brothers of the creator.

Lucern slipped the game into his computer and prepared to enjoy himself. He would work off some of his anger by slaughtering bad guys. And he'd also avoid Kate for a while. He'd found the perfect solution.

* * *

He had played for several hours and was deep into the game when he heard the knock at the door. At his distracted "What?" the door opened and Kate stepped into the room carrying a tray.

"I thought you might be hungry."

Her tentative words, along with the smell of food, drew Lucern's attention away from the game. He sniffed with interest, thinking he could manage some at that moment. He, like the rest of his family, ate food as well as ingested blood. If they didn't, they'd all be skinny wraiths.

"What is it?" he asked curiously.

"Well, I knew I was going to be busy—I've been working on the letters," she informed him. "So, after your mother left and you went upstairs, I threw the roast we picked up into the oven with some potatoes. That way it would cook while I worked. You said you like rare everything. I hope that includes roast, because this roast is pretty rare."

"Perfect." Lucern took the tray and set it on his desk, noting that there were two plates of food and two glasses of what looked to be wine and two glasses of water as well. She'd covered all the bases.

He was just relaxing when she began to drag a chair around the desk to join him and said, "I was hoping we could discuss—"

She was about to bring up the publicity issue again. Lucern immediately felt himself begin to tense; then Kate's gaze landed on the computer screen.

"That looks like Blood Lust."

"Blood Lust Two," he corrected.

"You're kidding. Really? It isn't supposed to be out until Monday. I have it on order."

"I know the creator," Lucern admitted reluctantly. "I got an early copy."

"No way. You lucky dog! Is it as good as the first?"

"Better." Lucern began to relax again as she continued staring avidly at the frozen screen. He recognized a fellow gamer when he saw one. Any talk of publicity had probably just bit the dust for the night.

He glanced at the screen and saw that his character had died while he'd been distracted. The game was waiting for him to decide what to do next. His options were to start over, or quit the game. He considered the matter briefly, then asked, "Do you want to play? You can play doubles on it."

"Really?" She looked terribly excited. "Yes, please. I love Blood Lust, and I've been waiting forever for Two to come out." She dragged her chair even closer. "This is great."

Lucern smiled to himself and started the game over. He'd say one thing for her: Kate C. Leever had good taste. She liked his books, and she liked Etienne's game.

She also proved to be one hell of a game player. The dinner she had made sat forgotten on the desk as they worked through the levels he'd already run through, then continued on to the next levels, working together to defeat the villains and save the damsel in distress. Every time they succeeded at accessing another level, Kate reacted with the excitement of a child and they did a high five or a little victory dance at the desk while they waited for the next level to load.

They played for hours, until the food was a shriveled

and congealed mess, until their necks and hands ached, and until Kate began nodding off in her seat. When Lucern reluctantly suggested it might be best if she went to bed, she agreed with equal reluctance that she should or she wouldn't be able to get up for the shopping trip with his mother.

Oddly enough, Lucern missed her once she was gone. He continued on through another level of the game, but it wasn't the same without her there to share the glee at succeeding. There were no high fives or little victory dances, and he was troubled to find he missed those, too. Even more troubling was the fact that for the first time in years, Lucern felt lonely.

Despite her late night, Kate was up and ready at one o'clock. She stood anxiously waiting by the front door watching for Mrs. Argeneau. When a limo pulled into the driveway, she hurried outside and started down the porch stairs, then paused and turned back uncertainly toward the door. She had unbolted it to leave and didn't have a clue what to do about bolting it again. Dare she leave it unlocked? Or should she wake up Lucern and have him bolt it?

"It's all right, Kate. Don't worry about the door," Marguerite unrolled the back window to call out. "Come along, we've lots to do."

Shrugging inwardly, Kate turned and walked over to the limo. The driver was out to open the door for her by the time she reached it, and Kate murmured a thank-you as she slipped inside; then she did a double take at the sight of Lucern's mother. The woman was bundled up as if they were in the midst of a winter storm.

76

She had on a long-sleeved blouse, gloves and slacks, then a scarf over her head and covering the bottom half of her face. Over-large sunglasses covered most of the rest. The only patch of skin showing was her nose, and that was slathered with a white cream Kate guessed to be sunblock.

"Don't tell me. You're allergic to the sun like Lucern?" Kate guessed.

Marguerite's mouth twisted in wry amusement. "Where do you think he got it?"

Kate gave a laugh and relaxed back in the limo, prepared for a day of both frantic shopping and pampering. And that was exactly what she got: a frantic rush to choose the perfect dress and see it tailored to fit her, then a couple of hours of delicious pampering at the spa where Marguerite Argeneau's hair stylist worked. She enjoyed herself immensely.

Luc didn't sleep well. He went to bed out of sheer boredom not long after Kate left, but he couldn't find rest. The woman hadn't just invaded his home, she'd made her way into his dreams, too. That fact was enough to make him terribly grumpy on awakening, and it was a surly Lucern who stumbled downstairs Saturday afternoon. He became even more surly when a quick search of the house showed that Kate hadn't yet returned from her shopping sojourn.

Grumbling under his breath, he made his way to the kitchen and—out of habit—opened the refrigerator door looking for blood. It wasn't until he had the door open that he recalled sticking his supply in the tiny fridge in his office, to keep it out of Kate's sight. He considered going back upstairs to fetch a bag, but didn't really feel like it. He didn't really feel like normal food either despite the fact that he and Kate had sacrificed supper the night before for Blood Lust II. And he knew he would be eating a lot of rich food at the wedding celebration, so it was better to put off eating now.

Deciding he'd grab a bag of blood later before leaving for the wedding, Lucern wandered aimlessly out of the kitchen and moved along the hall to the living room. He immediately grimaced. Kate had finished sorting the letters into categories, and there were several form letters awaiting his signature.

Curious, Lucern sat on the couch and began to read through them. They were all very nice, chatty letters that sounded gracious and charming and not at all like him. Kate was a good writer, too. She'd done a wonderful job, and Lucern supposed he'd have to thank her. He also supposed he should hire an assistant to manage such tasks in the future. Unfortunately, he knew he wouldn't. The idea of a stranger in his home, pawing through his things was not a happy one. That was the reason he still hadn't replaced his housekeeper, Mrs. Johnson. The woman had died in her sleep in 1995. Which was eight years ago, he realized with surprise.

Since, Lucern had hired a service to clean his home once a week, and he usually had his meals out or ordered them from a gourmet restaurant down the street. He'd intended to do that only until he found a replacement for the unfortunate Mrs. Johnson, which he'd never gotten around to. He'd think about it and all the trouble it meant, then would decide against it. Why go to all that time and effort only to have whomever he hired drop dead on him after ten or twenty years as both Mrs. Johnson and Edwin had done?

He muttered under his breath at the thought. Humans were so unreliable that way. They were forever dropping dead on you just when you had them trained.

He was pondering that annoying little habit of mankind when the front door of the house slammed. Kate was back from her shopping excursion. He ran his hands through his hair, brushed down his T-shirt and tried to look presentable. He sat up, peering expectantly toward the living room door . . . and was just in time to catch a glimpse of Kate flying upstairs. At least he thought it was Kate. All he'd really seen was a go-dawful bundle of shopping bags with various designer names on them, and feet.

Oh, yes. She'd been shopping. He slumped back on the couch with disgust. She hadn't even noticed him. Women!

A cacophony of sounds followed from upstairs—the slamming of the guest room door, then all sorts of unidentifiable banging and bumping. It sounded as if the woman was jumping around and throwing things willy-nilly.

It went on long enough that Lucern became concerned. Then there was a sudden and utter silence. Standing, he walked into the hallway and peered anxiously up the stairs. A door opened and closed; then he heard the clicking of high-heeled shoes on the hardwood hall floor, and Kate appeared at the top of the steps.

She was a sight. A vision. Her golden hair was piled

on top of her head with little ringlets dropping down to frame her pretty, flushed face. The gown she wore was a deep emerald green. It had a long skirt, a crepe neck, and was made of a soft-looking material that had a slight sheen as it draped gracefully over the contours and curves of her body. She was glorious. An angel. The most beautiful woman Lucern had seen in his life, and that was saying something. He was tongue-tied with amazement. He simply watched in awe as she descended the steps.

She was only halfway down when she spotted him. She immediately paused, blinked, then scowled. "You aren't ready!"

It was Lucern's turn to blink. His angel was bellowing. She was also frantic. The serene vision was gone.

"Lucern!" She glared at him with disbelief. "The wedding is at seven o'clock! It's six-fifteen now. We have to leave. You haven't even showered or anything! What have you been doing all this time?" She covered her lower face with horror. "We'll be late! I hate being late to weddings. Everyone will be seated in the pews, and they'll all stare and—"

"Okay!" Lucern held up his hands, trying to soothe her as he started up the stairs. "It's okay. I'm fast. I'll be ready. Just give me ten minutes. We won't be late," he assured her as he moved warily past her. "Really. I promise."

Kate watched with exasperation as Lucern disappeared up the stairs. Once he was out of sight, her shoulders drooped unhappily. After all her efforts, he hadn't even commented on how she looked.

Disappointed, she continued downstairs and went

into the living room to wait. She was all prepared to tap a hole in the floor with impatience. She didn't get the chance. Ten minutes after leaving her on the steps, Lucern came back downstairs all set to go. His hair was still damp from the shower and slicked back, and a tailored designer suit hung elegantly off his broad shoulders.

Ten minutes, Kate thought with disgust. Ten minutes, and he looked fabulous. It had taken her all day to put herself together, and it had taken him ten minutes! She glared at him as she joined him in the hall.

"See? I told you I'd be fast," Lucern said soothingly as he opened the front door. "We won't be late. We'll be right on time."

Still irritated that he'd been so quick, Kate merely made a face and led the way outside.

Lucern opened the passenger door of his BMW in a rather courtly manner she appreciated, then commented, "You look lovely." He closed the door before she could respond, but Kate smiled widely as she watched him walk around the car to the driver's side. Her mood was beginning to lift again. Kate generally disliked weddings, and she would definitely be uncomfortable at being called "Luc's date," but maybe tonight wouldn't be so bad.

Chapter Five

It was awful. Well, not entirely, Lucern admitted to himself. The wedding ceremony itself was beautiful. And much to his surprise, his stubborn, pesky editor got all teary-eyed as Etienne and Rachel exchanged their vows. She explained herself when he handed her the handkerchief he'd placed in his breast pocket with such care by saying, "They seem so happy. They're obviously deeply in love."

Lucern merely grunted and hoped the ceremony wouldn't be as long as Lissianna's had been last year. He only had the one hanky.

Fortunately, Rachel's minister wasn't as long-winded as the Hewitt family's minister had been. Still, Lucern practically ran Kate out of the church the moment it was done. Or tried to. Their escape was stalled by the bottleneck that formed at the exit as each and every single guest paused to wish Etienne and Rachel well. The couple had exited the church first, as per the custom, and were now standing atop the church steps, speaking to everyone as they left.

Of course, Kate would insist on congratulating them and wishing them well, too, which Lucern thought was ridiculous. She didn't even know them! But the woman ignored his attempts to urge her down the stairs, and stopped to wish the couple happiness.

Rachel and Etienne weren't surprised Kate was at the wedding, of course. The family grapevine was as healthy as ever. And much to Lucern's irritation, Rachel was one of those social people who liked everyone and liked to talk. Etienne was hampered with the same affliction, so they couldn't just say thank-you and let Kate go. No. They had to actually *speak* to Kate and ask if she was having a good time in Toronto.

Lucern felt himself tensing as he waited for her answer. He was vaguely surprised when she laughed and said, "Oh, yes."

Etienne seemed equally surprised. He asked, "You mean, my brother is actually entertaining you?" As if Lucern were some sort of heathen, incapable of being a good host.

"Yes." Kate nodded cheerfully. "He and your mother, too. Marguerite took me shopping and to the spa today. And last night, Lucern and I played Blood Lust Two until all hours of the morning."

"Oh!" Rachel exclaimed. "Isn't that a wonderful game? Etienne is so talented. Although I thought he'd drive me crazy with it when he was designing the end sequence. It gave him trouble."

"Etienne?" Kate glanced from Rachel to Etienne uncertainly.

"Yes. It's his game," Rachel explained. Then she glanced at her brother-in-law with surprise. "Didn't you tell her it was Etienne's game?"

"Yes, I'm sure I mentioned—"

"No, you didn't!" Kate exclaimed with a light slap at his arm. "Oh, my God! Why didn't you tell me?"

Lucern scowled. His editor didn't notice; she'd already turned back to his brother.

"I can't believe it! I love Blood Lust, both One and Two. They are amazing!"

She rambled on, gushing over Etienne in a way Lucern found annoying, then suddenly stopped with a small gasp, before saying, "Oh! I just realized, the primary characters in Luc's last book were named Rachel and Etienne. And Etienne was a game creator, too. Oh, wow." She gave a laugh and grinned at Rachel. "The next thing you'll tell me is that you're a coroner like the woman in the book."

Lucern, Etienne and Rachel all exchanged glances and shifted uncomfortably.

Kate's eyes widened at their silence. "You aren't, are you?"

"I like to base stories as much in reality as I can," Lucern said to break the silence.

"But you write vampire books." Kate sounded bewildered.

"Well, within reason," he amended, then took her arm firmly. "Come. We're holding up the line."

Lucern hurried Kate to his car, saw her inside, got in himself and immediately turned the radio on. He cranked the volume up high to prevent conversation and drove to the reception hall where the wedding dinner was to be held. In his rush to get there, where he hoped Kate would be distracted and forget the odd coincidence of the characters in his books matching his real-life family, Lucern somewhat exceeded the speed limit. As a result, they were one of the first to arrive.

Much to his relief, Kate didn't mention the matter again. She and Lucern were seated at a table, and his mother and his sister Lissianna with her husband Greg soon joined them. Bastien was seated at the head table with the rest of the wedding party, so it was just the five of them at the six-person table closest to the long head table.

Lucern spent the first several minutes simply fingering the glass of wine that was promptly set before him, his gaze darting nervously to Kate as she talked with Marguerite and Lissianna. The three women were making him terribly nervous. They had their heads together, and there seemed to be an awful lot of giggling and laughing mixed in with their quiet talking. He was dying to know what they were saying, but couldn't have heard had he tried, with all the talk and disruption as people arrived and greeted one another.

"Lissianna!"

Lucern stiffened at his editor's exclamation; then Kate turned on him. "Your sister's name is Lissianna! That's the name of the female vampire in your second book."

"Er . . . yes." He shot a glance at his mother and sister. Were they deliberately trying to complicate his life?

"Etienne and Rachel in the last book, Lissianna and Greg in the second. And Marguerite!" She turned on

Lucern's mother. "Your husband was named Claude, wasn't he?"

"It's pronounced with an 'o' sound dear, like load, not 'ah' like clod," Marguerite corrected gently. Then she nodded. "But, yes, my husband and my children's father was Claude."

"Oh." Kate was silent for a moment, but was obviously thinking, looking for other similarities. "And your family name is Argeneau, too. No, wait," she corrected herself. "In the novels it's Argentus, from the Latin 'argent' for silver, because the patriarch had silvery blue eyes. Like you!" She turned suddenly to peer into Lucern's eyes.

"Yes." Lucern shifted, feeling terribly uncomfortable, unsure how to explain. In the end, he didn't need to.

"I think it's terribly sweet of you to name your characters after your family like that," Kate said.

Lucern gaped at her in surprise. Sweet? He wasn't sweet. What the—

"It's obvious you care for them a great deal."

"Er . . ." Lucern was feeling oddly trapped when a tap on his shoulder drew his head around. He found himself staring at Bastien and Etienne. Relief at the distraction made him smile hugely, which surprised them.

"We need a hand from both of you." Bastien's look encompassed both Lucern and Greg.

"Oh. Oh, of course." Luc turned to Kate as Greg got to his feet. "They need us. We have to go," he explained.

Kate nodded solemnly. "It's a guy thing, huh?"

"Er . . . yes." Luc stood, tossed a warning glare at his mother and sister, lest they say something else to put weird ideas in Kate's head, then followed his brothers away from the table.

The foursome crossed the reception hall, left through a door half-hidden behind a decorated beam, walked up a long, narrow hall, then exited through another door that led into the parking lot behind the building. Bastien walked along the row of parked vehicles to his van. Lucern didn't know what was going on until his brother opened the back doors and dragged a medi-vac cooler closer.

"I don't know about you guys, but with everything that had to be done, I didn't get to feed before the wedding today. I thought I might not be the only one with that problem, so I packed a picnic for us." Bastien popped the cooler open.

Lucern grinned at the sight of the blood bags packed in ice. Good old Bastien. He was always prepared. He would have been a Boy Scout as a child had they had them in those days.

"Oh, thank God!" Etienne took the first bag Bastien held out. "I was so busy rushing around, I didn't get a chance to feed. Neither did Rachel, I'm sure."

"I brought enough for everyone," Bastien assured him. He handed bags to both Lucern and Greg. "I'll bring the ladies out after we go back. I just didn't think it would be good if we all left en masse. The Argeneau side would understand, but the Garretts would be confused."

"Too true, my friend," Greg said with a shake of his head. "I'm still not used to all this." He gestured to the bag in his hand, then lifted it and stabbed his elongating teeth into it.

Lucern smiled as he followed suit. For someone who claimed the opposite, his brother-in-law did a fair imitation of someone who was comfortable with his new situation. Mind you, that might be different if the therapist had to bite people to feed, as in the old days.

The four men all fell silent as they emptied their first bags of blood. Bastien then pulled plastic cups out of the van and split two more bags between those four cups, and the men stood talking as they drank. It wasn't long before the conversation came around to Lucern's unwanted guest. Etienne was the one to bring it up, commenting that she seemed quite nice.

Lucern snorted. "Don't let her fool you. That woman is as stubborn as a mule. She's like one of those damn ticks, burrowing under your skin and staying there. She's burrowed her way into my home and just won't leave!"

The others all laughed. Greg suggested, "Why don't you just do some of that mind-control stuff Lissianna's trying to teach me—just get into her head and plant the suggestion that she leave?"

"Luc can't get into her head," Etienne announced with a grin.

"You've tried?" Greg asked Lucern with surprise.

"Of course I did. The very first night." Luc scowled and shook his head. "But she seems resistant to suggestion. I can't even read her thoughts. The woman's mind is like a steel trap." He sighed. "It's damned frustrating."

"Yep. And don't tell Mother," Etienne reminded him.

"Why not?" Greg asked.

Bastien explained. "Mother says couples shouldn't be

able to read each other's thoughts, so when you come across someone strong-minded enough to block you out—which she says is rare—you should pay attention, they would make a good mate."

Etienne nodded. "So if she catches wind of this . . ."

"She'll be determined to put us together," Lucern finished for him. He immediately felt confused. The last thing he needed was his mother playing matchmaker and forcing him and his stubborn editor together. On the other hand, Kate was a hell of a game player. And she was attractive, and somehow she became less annoying the longer he knew her. He was even getting used to having her in his home. If he were going to be forced into marriage—

"So I wouldn't mention it to her if I were you," Bastien said.

"I'd have to agree with Bastien and Etienne on this," Gregory decided, looking at Lucern. "As much as I like your mother, she can be a tad persistent once she gets an idea into her head. If you don't want her interfering and trying to push you and Kate together, I wouldn't mention that you can't read Kate's mind."

"Too late."

All four men jumped guiltily at that sweetly sung comment. Whirling, they found themselves confronted by Marguerite. Lucern groaned at the predatory look on her face. She'd obviously heard everything. And judging by her expression, she was already plotting.

At least that was what he thought, so he was surprised when she took the bag of blood Bastien offered and turned to smile at her oldest son. "Luc, darling. If you want to get rid of the girl so badly, why not just agree to do one of the publicity things she's on about? The moment you agree, she'll leave."

" 'Cause I don't want to," he answered, almost wincing as he heard how childish he sounded.

"And I don't want to listen to you whine, but sometimes we have to do things we don't like in life." Her words made everyone fall silent; then Marguerite stabbed her teeth into her bag of blood and drained it. When she'd finished, she turned to Lucern and added, "Kate doesn't want to be here bothering you any more than you want her here. However, her job depends on being able to convince you to do one of those publicity events. She likes her new position. She wants to keep it. She won't leave until you agree to at least one."

Spotting his horrified reaction, Marguerite patted her son's cheek affectionately. "I suggest you tell her you'll do R.T. From what she told me at the spa today, it's probably the best option for both of you."

"What's R.T.?" Lucern asked suspiciously.

"*Romantic Times* magazine," his mother explained. "Just tell her you'll do it." Then Marguerite Argeneau turned and walked away, heading back along the row of cars.

"Hmm. I wonder how she found out Kate's job depends on convincing you to do one of those publicity events," Bastien murmured as they watched their mother walk away.

Greg shrugged. "She's very good at getting people to tell her things they never mean to say. She would have made a good therapist."

Lucern was silent, and they all handed their empty glasses back to Bastien. He didn't know how his mother had found out what she had, but he didn't doubt for a minute that it was true. Which made him about as miserable as he could be, for now he knew for certain that he would never be free of the woman. She was desperate, and desperate people were both as persistent as hell and unpredictable.

"Here you all are!"

The four men whirled away from the van again, this time to find Kate C. Leever facing them. There was a mischievous grin on her face as she took in their guilty expressions and the way they were all trying to hide something behind them.

"Rachel was looking for you. I said I thought I saw you come out here and said I'd check for her," she explained, still eyeing them with amusement. "She tried to stop me and said she'd go, but it's her wedding—I couldn't let her leave her guests to go chasing after you four reprobates."

Lucern exchanged a glance with the others. They all knew darned well that Rachel had probably hoped to slip outside for a quick nip as their mother had just done. Kate, in her kindness, had made that impossible.

"Why did you call us reprobates?" Gregory asked.

Kate gave an airy wave and laughed. "Because of what you're doing out here."

The four men exchanged glances and shifted into a tighter group, making sure that the open back of the van and the cooler of blood were hidden; then Lucern echoed, "What we're doing?"

"Oh, like it isn't obvious," she snorted. "Sneaking out here, crowding around the van." She shook her head and gave them a condescending look. "I may have been raised in Nebraska, but I've lived in New York long enough to be savvy about you artist types."

Now the looks the men exchanged were bewildered. Artist types? Lucern was a writer, Etienne a program developer, Bastien a businessman and Greg was a therapist. Artist types? And what did she think artist types did anyway? The only way to find out was to ask. Lucern did. "What is it exactly that you think we are doing out here?"

She gave a resigned sigh. "You're smoking pot-joints." She said it as one word.

The men all gaped at her; then Etienne released a disbelieving laugh. "What?"

Kate tsked with exasperation. "Pot. Marijuana. You guys snuck out here for a debbie."

"Er . . . I believe it's called a doobie," Greg interjected.

"Whatever. That's what you were doing, right?"

"Er . . ." Lucern began. Then he, Bastien, Etienne and Greg shared a grin.

"Yes. You caught us. We were smoking a debbie," Etienne agreed.

"Doobie," Greg corrected.

"Yes." Bastien nodded. "We'd offer you some, but we . . . er . . ."

"Smoked it all up," Etienne finished.

The two men sounded disgustingly apologetic to Lucern's mind. Good Lord.

"Oh, that's okay. I don't smoke anything." She smiled crookedly, then added, "Besides, dinner is about to be served. I think that's why Rachel was looking for you."

"Well then, we should go in." Stepping forward, Lu-

cern took Kate's arm firmly and turned her toward the
building. They'd barely taken two steps when he heard
the van doors closing and the other men fell into step
behind them. *Smoking debbies. Good Lord.*

Lucern was distracted through dinner, merely picking
at the food. It was apparently very good, if Kate's com-
ments were to be believed, but he didn't really have an
appetite. He found his mind stuck on his mother's claim
that Kate's job depended on her convincing him to cooperate. Lucern didn't know why, but that was really
bothering him. A lot.

". . . dance, Luc."

Lucern glanced around in confusion. He'd only
caught the end of his mother's words, he'd been so
deep in thought. He peered at her in question. "What?"

"I said, you should take Kate out on the floor and
dance. To support Etienne and Rachel. Someone has
to start everyone else dancing."

He glanced toward the dance floor, surprised to see
that the bride and groom were dancing. The meal was
over, and the first dance had begun. He, as the head of
his side of the family, would be expected to join next.
By all rights, he should be taking his mother, the matri-
arch, up there to encourage others to dance, but one
look at Marguerite told him that she had started her
matchmaking in earnest. She would not be dancing
with him.

Sighing, he pushed his seat back and held out a hand
to Kate. His editor looked terribly uncertain as she
placed her fingers in his and rose—a fact that annoyed
him no end, for reasons he couldn't possibly fathom

and had no intention of examining too deeply. Telling himself it was just a duty dance, and that his mother couldn't force him to dance with Kate again, Lucern led her onto the dance floor and took her into his arms.

It was a mistake. Kate C. Leever fit in his arms as if she'd been made for him. Her head came up just short of Lucern's chin, her hand was small and soft in his, and the scent of her perfume wafted tantalizing and vaguely exciting to his nose. Without even realizing it, he found himself urging her closer so that his body could meld with hers, his legs and chest brushing her with every step.

Lucern was used to hunger; he experienced it every morning upon awakening. While he slept, his body processed the blood he drank, repairing whatever damage the day had wrought and leaving him dehydrated and in serious need of more. Some days that hunger was worse than others. Some days it was mild enough that he could be distracted by other things as he had been this morning. Still, Lucern knew hunger. He understood thirst. He lived daily with a bone-deep yearning that could become so strong his body would cramp with it. And yet this . . .

He lowered his head, breathing in the scent of Kate's shampoo mingled with the spice and sweetness of her perfume. She smelled vaguely of vanilla, like a rich and luscious dessert or a bowl of ice cream, and he had the sudden mad urge to lick the nape of her neck and . . .

Lucern straightened abruptly as he caught hold of his thoughts. Lick her nape? More like bite it. Good Lord, he needed more blood. He'd been rather slack on the consumption end lately. What with Kate's presence and such, he hadn't been sticking to his usual four pints a day. He'd been running on mostly two—which explained his odd hunger now. He was confusing hunger for Kate's blood with hunger for her.

Relieved beyond measure, he smiled widely down at her when she murmured his name. She seemed slightly surprised at his smile, then asked uncertainly, "Is something wrong? You've stopped dancing."

Lucern peered around, surprised to realize that in his revelation he had stopped moving. He now merely stood in the middle of the dance floor holding her close. Very close. Her breasts, squashed against his chest, were being forced upward out of her gown. And they were very nice breasts. Round and a pale pink flesh tone that spoke of healthy blood. Lucern would have liked to lick his way over those orbs and . . .

"I have to talk to Bastien," he gasped. "Now."

Releasing her from his tight hold, he started to walk to where Bastien was dancing, then suddenly realized what he was doing. Whirling back to the bewildered Kate, who stood like an abandoned baby in the center of the dance floor, he took her arm and led her back to their table. He then walked around the dance floor, relieved that the music ended just as he reached his brother's side.

"Bastien, after you've seen your dance partner back to the table, I need to talk to you outside. At the van," he said meaningfully.

"Sure," his younger brother said. "Be with you in a moment."

Lucern nodded, and Bastien walked Rachel's sister, who was the maid of honor, back to the head table.

"Did I hear you say you were going out to the van?"

Lucern turned to find Lissianna behind him. She and Gregory had joined the dance floor just after Lucern and Kate. The couple had been standing nearby, waiting for the next song to start. He wasn't surprised she'd heard what he said.

He nodded in answer to her question, and felt it necessary to explain: "I haven't been feeding enough since Kate arrived."

Lissianna nodded in understanding. "Rachel and I will join the two of you. She was saying earlier that, what with preparing for the wedding and everything, she—"

"Fine, fine," Lucern interrupted. He didn't need the explanation. He was happy to have the women join them. "Go get her, then. Bastien will . . . Oh. He's brought her with him."

Bastien was leading their new sister-in-law across the floor.

"I'll keep an eye on Kate, so she doesn't come out and try to catch you with the debbies in hand," Greg said lightly as Bastien and the bride arrived. He moved off to invite the editor to dance.

"Good, good." Lucern didn't even smile. He just nodded his thanks and ushered the other three out of the reception hall.

Kate relaxed in Greg's arms the moment they started to move, something she hadn't been able to do in Lucern's embrace. She had seen the writer slip outside with his sister, Rachel and Bastien, and suspected they were out there smoking again. In her considered opinion, the man could use it. It would help him relax, surely. The man had been tense throughout the meal, and . . . Well, she supposed he had just seemed distracted through the meal—not that she'd let it bother her. She'd been busy talking to his mother and sister and listening to the amusing tales they told her about Lucern's youth.

If the mother and sister were to be believed, Lucern was really a very sensitive man with a crusty, grumpy shell. Having read his novels, Kate thought that was quite possible. There was a certain longing in the way he portrayed the couples in his book, a hunger that went beyond the bloodlust of vampires or even beyond sexual desire. His characters were lonely at heart, yearning for a soul mate to share their long lives. Kate wondered now if it wasn't a reflection of his feelings, if he didn't yearn for love.

Greg gave her a little twirl, and she smiled at him. Lissianna's husband was a much more relaxed dancer than Lucern. Luc had been almost vibrating with tension as he and she had moved across the dance floor, and it had transferred to Kate, filling her with a low-grade tension that was rather distressing. Despite that tension, however, she'd found herself melting into his embrace, resting her head on his shoulder and slipping her fingers closer to the nape of his neck to brush the hair there. She'd been relieved if a little stunned when he'd stopped dancing and walked away.

Well, all right, she'd been more stunned than relieved. She had stood there, gaping after him, unable to believe that he was reverting to his trademark rudeness right there in the middle of the dance floor for all to see. If he hadn't suddenly turned back and seen her to their table, she might have chased him down and given him a swift kick to the behind. Yes, it was definitely a good thing he was outside smoking. Surely it would relax him.

"I think you should just agree to do something for her," Bastien suggested. Of course, as ever, Kate had been the topic of conversation since they'd reached the van. And much to Lucern's irritation, everyone seemed to have advice.

"Why don't you tell her you'll do one of those interviews? Like that R.T. thing Mom suggested," Bastien continued. "Or tell her you'll do one of the publicity events, but only one and not the book-signing tour. Let her choose which is most likely to save her job. That way, she'll be happy and leave."

"Let *her* choose?" Lucern was horrified at the idea of giving her so much sway. "But what if she chooses one of the television interviews?"

Lissianna clucked impatiently. "It wouldn't kill you to spend half an hour in front of a camera, Luc."

"But—"

"Look at it this way," his sister added. "Half an hour in front of a camera during an interview, or Kate Leever camping out on your porch."

Bastien laughed. "If you even manage to get her out the front door."

Lucern glared at him, but his brother merely shrugged. "You've apparently gone soft on us, Luc," he continued. "A hundred years ago you wouldn't have had any trouble tossing her out on her heart-shaped little behind."

"You've been looking at her behind?" Lucern asked in outrage.

"Sure, why not? She's single. I'm single." He shrugged. "Is there a problem?"

Lucern scowled. There shouldn't be a problem, and he knew it. But for some reason, he didn't like Bastien checking out Kate at all.

"Poor Luc," Lissianna said. He peered at her in question, so she patted his arm as if he needed soothing. "Six hundred years old, and you just don't know how to deal with the feelings Kate raises in you. Surely with age some wisdom should come."

"It seems men remain emotionally dense no matter how long they live," Rachel commented dryly.

Lucern remained silent, his thoughts in an uproar. Lissianna was implying he was unaware he was falling for the girl. He wasn't. He was aware of it. But he didn't have to like it—or give in to it, either. As to the hunger he felt around her, Lucern admitted now it wasn't bloodlust he'd felt on the dance floor, but sexual lust. He wanted Kate C. Leever, editor. And that was a complication he could do without. If her mind wasn't closed to him, he might have been willing to indulge himself and enjoy her body as he wanted to. He certainly hadn't lived as a monk for six hundred years. But her mind *was* closed, making such an action dangerous.

Shaking his head, he left the others by the van and headed back into the reception hall. As far as he was concerned, he was just suffering a crush—a natural affection caused by being forced into close proximity with someone else. He'd get over it just as soon as Kate C. Leever was gone. He just had to get her gone.

Chapter Six

Marguerite was the only one at the table when Lucern returned and reclaimed his seat. A quick scan of the dance floor showed Kate and Greg were dancing. They looked awfully cozy. Kate was relaxed and smiling in Gregory Hewitt's arms—something she hadn't been in Lucern's—and they were moving in perfect sync, as if they'd been dancing together for years.

Gregory even looked pretty damned suave out there on the dance floor. Lucern had never thought of his brother-in-law as a ladies' man, but he certainly seemed to be doing a pretty good imitation right now. Logically, Lucern knew Greg loved Lissianna deeply and was no threat when it came to Kate. Besides which, Lucern reminded himself quickly, he himself wasn't even interested in a relationship with the woman. But his body didn't appear to be responding to his logic. Some primal part of him didn't give a hoot for logic. And as he watched Greg whirl Kate around the dance floor, Lucern could feel his muscles tensing and twitching. A low growl rumbled to life in his chest as he watched the pair dip and then recover.

"You should go cut in."

Lucern stiffened at his mother's words. He glanced her way and saw she was casting a pitying look upon him. He turned sharply, struggled briefly with himself, then jerked to his feet and strode onto the dance floor. If there was anything Lucern hated it was being pitied. Now he was mad.

Greg noticed his approach, took one look at his expression, nodded solemnly and quit the dance floor.

Kate turned in confusion when Greg suddenly released her and stepped away. She supposed she wasn't surprised to see Lucern there. However, she was surprised at his expression. His usually cold, grumpy exterior had been replaced by the intensity of a stalking animal. He looked hard and angry, but not cold. Anything but cold. His eyes were all silver with no blue. She now understood a description he had given of Claude in his first book: "Flinty eyes that spoke of the fires of hell and left his enemies quailing." She hadn't imagined that silver-blue eyes could look so ferocious, but there were vermilion fires burning there, almost seeming to snap out of his irises like the arc from a welder's flame.

Yet Kate wasn't afraid. For some reason a smile curved her lips, and she couldn't have stopped the words that popped out had she tried. "Smoking debbies didn't relax you, I take it?"

Lucern reacted as if he crashed into an invisible wall. His determined stride broke at once, and he stared at her with a blank expression that utterly erased the feral fever of moments before. Then he did the most amazing thing: Lucern Argeneau, that stubborn, stupid, ignorant man, actually let loose a gale of laughter. In truth, Kate hadn't thought such a thing possible. The man was such a . . .

Her thoughts died as he swept her into his arms and they began to dance. He was still chuckling softly, the action making his chest reverberate against hers. He urged her closer. When Kate lifted her head to peer shyly into his face, he smiled and said, "You're an evil woman, Kate C. Leever."

She found herself smiling in return. She had thought the man handsome from the first, but now, with laughter sparkling in his eyes and tilting the corners of his mouth, he was so much more than simply handsome. He was breathtaking. Literally. Kate honestly had some difficulty breathing as she met his gaze. Heat was radiating from every point their bodies met. She wanted to lay her head on his shoulder and melt into him. She wanted to feel his hands move over her flesh. She wanted . . .

To go home. Kate definitely wanted to go home. Or, really, she wanted to go anywhere that would take her far away from him. She didn't want to feel this way, she didn't want to want him. Hell, she didn't even like the man.

Well, all right, she admitted with painful honesty; she'd had fun playing Blood Lust Two with him, and he *could* be nice when he tried. She was sure. It wasn't as if he had tried yet. But surely everyone could be nice with a little effort? Yes, she assured herself. In fact, he was being nice to her right now. Sort of.

Kate sighed to herself. Dancing certainly felt nice. And when Lucern held her like this, she forgot how rude and pigheaded he could be. But—and it was a big but—she had absolutely no intention of getting involved with one of her writers. She was a businesswoman. A professional. And she would act professionally even if that's all it was, an act, and she really wanted to rip his designer suit off and plaster herself to his naked body.

Ohhhh. This wasn't good.

Lucern suddenly stopped dancing and announced, "I'm tired." When she didn't respond, he added, "Are you ready to leave?"

"Yes." She fired off the response like a bullet. She was more than happy to escape the possibility of suffering any more of this closeness.

Lucern apparently agreed. He immediately took her arm, led her off the floor and across the hall. He stopped only once, pausing briefly at the head table to tell his brother and new sister-in-law that they were leaving.

Kate spied Marguerite Argeneau frowning at them from her seat at the table they had shared, and she knew Lucern's mother wasn't pleased that they were leaving so early. She felt bad, but really it wasn't her problem. Marguerite was Lucern's problem. Kate's problem was maintaining a businesslike relationship while getting Lucern to do a publicity event. And she only had one more day to do it.

*   *   *

Lucern was silent on the way home, his thoughts a bit muddled. He wasn't certain what his intentions had been when he'd suggested leaving early, but . . .

Oh, who was he kidding? He'd been thinking about getting Kate home alone and possibly naked. The woman had gotten under his skin, and his family had made him admit it. Bastien had given him a nudge with the comment about her behind, and with the knowing smile on his face when he'd asked if his noticing was a problem; then Lissianna had made it worse with her "poor Luc." Just the sight of Kate in Greg's arms had roused the beast inside. But the look of pity on his mother's face had been the worst. Lucern realized that he could try to fool himself, but he was fooling no one else. And hell, he wasn't even fooling himself.

He liked her. Despite the fact that she was a modern woman, pushy and aggressive when necessary, who simply did not know her place, he liked her. Despite the fact that she seemed to have no dragons to slay, except perhaps him and his lack of cooperation, he liked her. And, dear God, he *wanted* her.

Lucern was a healthy male of 612 years. The number of women he'd been with in that time . . . Well, he couldn't even guess at the number. However, every single one had faded from his mind when he held Kate in his arms.

But she wasn't in his arms now; she was seated in the passenger seat, arms crossed defensively over her chest and staring blindly into the night as they drove. She was deliberately ignoring him, distancing herself. It helped to clear Luc's mind somewhat. Kate was his editor. He had to work with her. Sleeping with her would be a giant no-no. He felt inexpressibly weary as he pulled into his driveway.

Both he and Kate were silent as they got out of the car. She was the first to speak. She gazed up at the star-studded sky as they walked up the drive and murmured, "It's a beautiful night."

Lucern's steps faltered at her wistful tone. She sounded reluctant to see the night end, and he didn't want it to, either. Lucern knew he couldn't give in to his desire for her, but he was still loath to part from her.

"It *is* nice," he agreed. "Would you like to sit on the porch and have a glass of wine?"

He held his breath as she hesitated.

"Can we have coffee instead?" she asked. "I've had more than my usual quota of alcohol tonight."

Lucern let his breath out in a whoosh. "Certainly. Sit down and I'll—"

"I'll help." She smiled for the first time since they'd left the reception. "No offense, but I don't think you've made a lot of coffee."

Lucern wasn't offended. He was just happy that the evening wasn't going to end and that Kate C. Leever was smiling.

They worked in a companionable silence in the kitchen, Kate making coffee while he found bowls and scooped out some ice cream. Then they took their treasure out to the porch.

Kate stared up at the stars in the sky. It was such a peaceful night, so beautiful, and she was actually enjoying Lucern's company. Yes, she was actually enjoying it. His usual grumpy, terse persona was missing. She

106

didn't know if it was the alcohol or the debbies he had smoked at the wedding that had done it, but for the first time, he seemed very mellow in her presence. Oh, he had been pleasant the night before when they'd played the game together, but this was different. He'd been tense and ready to shoot the video-game bad guys then. Now he was incredibly relaxed and a pleasure to be with. They sat there for quite a while, drinking, eating their ice cream and chatting mildly about the wedding while avoiding looking at each other. At least Kate was avoiding looking at him. She had to—every time she gazed on the smile flirting on his lips, she wanted to kiss it.

You're a fool, Kate told herself. Her attraction to Lucern Argeneau was dangerous, and she shouldn't be encouraging it by suffering him being nice and even likeable. He was *one of her writers*. She was like a den mother to her authors. But her feelings for Lucern at the moment were far from maternal. And the longer this nice interlude went on, the harder it got for her to resist moving closer, touching him as she talked, leaning into him, kissing . . .

Cutting off her thoughts right there, she straightened and sought something to distract herself, something to end this interlude. The easiest solution was the reason for her being there. Kate took a deep breath, then blurted, "Luc, I know you don't want to talk about this, but I really wish you would consider a book-signing tour."

The writer tensed at once, the softness in his features disappearing. "No. I quite simply don't do book-signing tours."

"I know you don't, Luc. But . . . your books are so popular and—"

"Then I hardly need to do a tour, do I?"

"But the readers want to meet you, they—"

"No," he repeated firmly.

"Luc, please," Kate entreated, her voice husky.

Lucern stared at Kate silently, wishing with all his heart that what she was pleading for was something entirely different. *Luc, please kiss me. Luc, please take me to your bed. Luc, please* . . . But that wasn't what she was asking for. This was business. A desire for him to promote his books and make more money for her company. She wanted him to disrupt his life, risk the day with its damaging sunlight, and do a book-signing tour. Lucern wished he'd never written those damn popular books.

Standing, he abruptly tossed the rest of his coffee on the lawn and headed for the door. "I have work to do. Good night."

"No, wait. Lucern!" She was on her feet and after him at once. "We have to discuss this. I've been here three days and I haven't gotten a thing done."

Lucern ignored her. He merely stepped inside and started upstairs.

"Luc, please! None of the writers like book-signings, but they are so good for publicity, and readers want the contact. They want to meet the writer behind the stories they enjoy so much. Just a short tour would do," she wheedled when he made no response. "Half a dozen stops, maybe. I could go with you to be sure everything was just the way you wanted. If you would only—"

Lucern reached his office door. He stepped inside

and closed it behind him with a bang that was only slightly louder than the click of the lock.

Kate stared at the door. Slammed doors seemed to be a recurring theme in their relationship. She was beginning to hate doors.

Shoulders slumping, she leaned against the door and closed her eyes. She was a very positive person as a rule, and had always thought that a person could do anything they set their mind to if they worked at it hard enough, but that was before she'd met the immovable object: Lucern. The man was as stubborn as . . . well, as she was. Maybe more.

Kate considered giving up, packing her bags and heading back to New York with her tail between her legs, but it wasn't in her nature. She hated to be such a pest and wished she could just leave him to his peaceful existence, but in the company's opinion it wasn't unreasonable for them to expect Lucern Argeneau to do some promotion. They put out big bucks to advertise his books; the least he could do was put in a little effort himself. And she mostly agreed with that. She just had to convince him. Hell, at this point she'd consider it a grand victory just to get him to agree to a couple of interviews over the phone.

Kate straightened slowly. It might work. She'd been concentrating on the book-signing tour, but perhaps she would have more luck with interviews.

"Luc?" she called out. Silence was her answer, but Kate wasn't deterred. "Look, I know you don't want to do the book-signing tour, and that's fine. But, please, at least consider doing a couple of interviews?"

She waited in the silence, then added, "Just think about it. Okay?"

Deciding to leave it for the night, Kate turned to the guest room door. She had to think of an argument, some plan to persuade him. Then she'd tackle him again in the morning.

Lucern knew when Kate gave up and walked away. He felt her absence as well as heard the opening and closing of the guest room door. He sat for a long time at his desk listening to her moving around getting ready for bed, then to the sounds of the night when she stopped.

He considered playing Blood Lust II, but it wasn't the same without her. He considered writing but wasn't in the mood. So he sat there in the silent darkness, listening to the night. The cry of night birds, the song of crickets, the whisper of the wind, the sighs of. . . . Kate, he realized. That sleepy breathy sound had been Kate. Lucern could just hear it if he strained. He could smell her, too. The scent seemed to hang about him. Recalling her leaning against him as they danced, he ducked his head and sniffed his jacket. The scent was strong there. Disturbing.

Standing, Lucern shrugged off the jacket and slung it over the back of his chair, but the smell still seemed to cling to him. Or perhaps it was simply in the air, perhaps permeating his home just as she had. Giving up on trying to rid himself of her scent, he moved to unlock the door of his office and open it; then he stood there and closed his eyes. If he concentrated hard, the other night sounds faded and he was able to focus on the sound of her—the rustle of bedclothes as she shifted, soft little sighs as she dreamt, an occasional murmur, but mostly her breathing, soft and soothing, in, out, over and over again.

He could almost feel her breath against his skin, a warm, moist exhalation. Then he realized he *was* feeling it, soft and warm against his hand. He was standing next to the bed, his legs having carried him where his body longed to be—and all without his brain's awareness.

Lucern stared down at her through the moonlit gloom, smiling at the childlike way she slept. Kate was curled into a fetal position on her side, her hand tucked under her chin. Then his gaze drifted away from her face and down over her body. It was a warm night, and the air-conditioning didn't seem to reach the upstairs rooms as well as the lower ones. Kate had kicked off the sheets and lay in a thin white cotton nightie that had twisted up around her thighs. His gaze skimmed her slender limbs in their bent position. Kate had lovely legs, long and shapely. Luc managed to resist the temptation to run his fingers lightly over the pearly white skin revealed, but imagined what it must be like and knew it would be warm and soft to the touch.

A feathery sigh slipped from Kate's lips and she rolled onto her back in her sleep, one hand sliding slowly across her breasts before dropping to lie on the bed. Lucern followed the movement of the hand, then returned his eyes along the trail her hand had taken to settle at the neckline of her gown. The gown had buttons leading down to her waist. The top two were undone, and the third appeared ready to slip its hole, leaving a large expanse bare to view. Luc's gaze fastened on the milky tops of her breasts, and he watched them rise and fall with each breath. Rise and fall. He imagined freeing that third button to reveal more skin, then another and another, at last baring her breasts fully.

Lucern imagined how round and full they would appear in the moonlight. How luscious. He knew he wouldn't be able to resist touching them, caressing them, taking one hardening nipple into his mouth and suckling at its sweetness.

Kate arched in the bed and moaned low in her throat. Lucern almost moaned with her. Her perfume was stronger in here; it mixed with the smells of her shampoo and soap and essence. The combination was heady. He could taste it on his lips. Except for the lack of touch, he could imagine he really was: suckling, licking, nibbling a path across her skin from one breast to the other.

Lucern closed his eyes to imagine it better and could almost feel her warm skin beneath his lips. In his mind, he let his hands skim down her gown, slip beneath, then feather up the outsides of her thighs. He could feel her shudder under his touch, shift her legs restlessly as another moan sighed from her lips. Kate arched in invitation, wanting him, too—begging him to fill her and make her whole, to quench the fire he'd started.

Lucern was happy to oblige. He allowed his imaginary hands to drift over the tops of her legs, to push the flimsy cloth of her gown upward, then spread her soft thighs so that he could lick the vein there. He imagined touching her, caressing her, licking her glistening skin, then driving himself into her hot, welcoming body. He could almost feel her close around him, gasping and whimpering in his ear, her breath soft on his skin, her nails scoring his shoulders and back.

Kate would moan with pleasure as he drove into her over and over until she began to shake and shudder beneath him, her inner muscles clenching and unclenching.

"Lucern."

His name on her lips drew his eyes open, and he peered down to find Kate's sleeping face a portrait of ecstasy. She was panting, sweating and writhing on the sheets, her hands on either side of her head and tearing at the pillow as she convulsed with ecstasy. It was only then Lucern realized that while her mind was closed to him when she was awake, it was as wide open as anyone else's in rest. She'd just experienced everything he'd imagined, received it from his mind as if it were happening.

The knowledge was almost painful. He could have her if he wished. She would welcome him. Luc was breathing heavily with want, throbbing with desire, aching to drive himself into her. At the same moment, he yearned to fasten his teeth to her neck, consume her blood and body both at once. He knew it would be the most incredible experience of his life. But he couldn't. If he took her now, Kate would welcome it only because he wanted her to want him.

Shaking his head to erase the erotic images there, Lucern stumbled back from the bed, then out of her room. He didn't stop, but staggered drunkenly down the hall to the stairs. His head was full of her. He had to get away. The desire to take her was overwhelming.

He slammed out of the house and to his car. He had no plans when he started the engine, simply needed to get away from Kate and the temptation she presented. He ended up driving around for an hour or so before finally finding himself in Bastien's driveway. His brother's house was dark and silent, and he could sense that it was empty. He was about to back out of the driveway when Bastien's van pulled in beside him.

Lucern got out with relief, met his brother at the front of the vehicles and blurted out his troubles with Kate. It took a long while. He told his younger brother everything.

When he had finished, Bastien merely asked, "What will you do?"

Lucern was silent for a moment. Talking hadn't helped him clear his mind. He was still confused. He disliked confusion. He disliked any sort of disruption in his life. The answer seemed simple: Get rid of the confusion.

"I'm going to do whatever it takes to get her on a plane tomorrow," he decided.

There. Talking to his brother *had* helped.

Kate yawned and stretched in bed, a smile playing about her lips. She hadn't slept so well in ages. And she hadn't ever woken up feeling so great. She was so relaxed, so sated. Blinking in surprise, she realized it was true—she felt sated. Her body was a happy body, all warm and ready to do whatever she wanted.

Getting up, she got into the shower. It wasn't until she was humming and washing herself, running soap over her body, that she recalled the dream. Her hands slowed, her eyes dilating as the memories crowded in: Lucern caressing her, suckling her breasts, thrusting his body into hers.

A tingling drew her gaze down to her breasts, and she let her hands drop with embarrassment as she realized she'd unconsciously been caressing them. Her nipples were hard and erect. Even worse, she could feel the wetness building between her legs, and it had nothing to do with the shower at her back. Turning into the spray, she braced her hands on the shower wall beneath the nozzle head and allowed the water to pour across her body. But the dream didn't fade away—it was the most vivid she could ever recall having.

For one minute, Kate was afraid that it hadn't been a dream, that it had really happened and just seemed like a dream because she had been sleepy. But then she shook her head at the silly thought. If it had really happened, she would have wanted kisses, and he hadn't kissed her once. Kate would have grabbed him by a handful of hair and dragged his mouth to hers if necessary, but she would have had kisses. She liked kisses.

No, it hadn't happened, she thought, giggling as relief poured through her. It had just been an amazingly sexy dream. A *wet* dream.

Laughing at herself, Kate finished her shower and stepped out to dry herself. Dream or not, she felt great. She was also feeling rather benevolent toward her host for the pleasure of the dream. It didn't matter that he'd had nothing to do with it; he'd been the star of the dream, and in that dream he had given her great pleasure. Yep. He was a swell guy.

Smiling widely, Kate dressed, brushed her hair, then left her room and jogged downstairs to the kitchen. She was going to make Lucern some breakfast. A big breakfast. And she was going to sweetly tell him she'd given up on trying to get him to do the book-signing tour. Maybe then he'd be so relieved, he'd agree to do an interview or two.

She made the works: steak so rare it was still bleeding, eggs over easy, hash browns, toast and coffee. Then she was in a quandary. What to do? There was no sign of Lucern yet, but everything was ready. Should she go knock on his bedroom door and risk making him grumpy? That would hardly aid her cause. Should she carry the breakfast up on a tray and give it to him in bed? That didn't seem like a good idea. After the dream she'd had last night, she thought it might be best to stay far away from Lucern and beds—otherwise she might jump the poor man in the hope that the real thing would be as good.

Sighing, Kate considered the table she had set, then glanced at the oven where she'd placed everything to keep it warm. The things would be all right there for a little bit, but not long. She decided she would just clean the mess she'd made in his kitchen, and if he wasn't up by the time she finished, she'd risk his temper to wake him up.

Spying a radio on the kitchen counter, she turned it on and set to work, boogying around the kitchen to a classic rock station.

It was a screechy death shriek from an animal that woke Lucern. At least, that was what he thought. He sat up abruptly as the sound brought him awake, then paused to listen to the noises in his home.

Someone was banging around in the kitchen, and he could hear the tinny sound of music playing somewhere downstairs. But the shriek that had awakened him hadn't been either of these. Had it been Kate crying out in pain? he wondered, feeling himself tense. Was she being attacked by some madman who was even now destroying his kitchen?

"*Rahhhh-cksanne!*"

Lucern's eyes dilated in horror as the screechy voice sounded again, dragging along his nerves like nails on a chalkboard. Dear God, it was Kate attempting to sing.

He fell back with a grunt of disgust, exhaustion overwhelming him. He hadn't got to sleep until dawn. He was not ready to wake up yet.

"Roxanne!" the screech persisted.

It seemed *Kate* was ready for him to wake up, however.

Muttering under his breath, Lucern rose and stumbled into the shower. There he attempted to wake himself up and wash his bad mood away. He kept telling himself that he was getting rid of her today; he could sleep after that. It didn't help much. He was feeling incredibly grumpy as he staggered downstairs.

Kate heard Lucern on the steps and stopped singing. Whirling toward the stove, she grabbed pot holders, whipped the door open and quickly began retrieving breakfast. She was just setting the plate of hash browns on the table when he came into the kitchen.

"Good morning!" she sang cheerfully.

Lucern winced and groaned; then his gaze settled on

117

the table, and some of the grouchiness left his expression, replaced by surprise. "Did you make all this?"

"Yes," Kate breathed. She gave a sigh of relief. He wasn't going to be too terribly difficult about her waking him up. Just a *little* difficult. "Sit down and eat before it gets cold."

He sat and surveyed the offerings, then finally dug in. Kate poured coffee for them both, then joined him to eat. She allowed Lucern to eat in peace, deciding that she would broach the subject of doing an interview after he was full and happy.

Much to her surprise, however, she didn't end up having to.

When Lucern had finished his meal and pushed his plate away, Kate stood and grabbed the coffee pot to refill both their cups. She was working out what she would say as she set the pot back when Lucern suddenly said: "One event."

Kate turned back to the table in confusion. "One event?"

Lucern nodded. "If it's the only way to get rid of you, Kate C. Leever, I'll agree to one publicity thing."

"Really?" She tried to still the hope that leapt inside her. She waited for the catch.

"Yes. But this is the deal. I do the one event. One only. After that you have to let me alone."

"Okay," she agreed.

Lucern eyed her suspiciously. "You won't call and harass me anymore? No express letters? No camping on my doorstep?"

"No. I promise," Kate said solemnly.

"Very well." He sighed. "One event—preferably the R.T. thing my mother mentioned."

Kate's eyes nearly popped out of her head. "The R.T. thing?"

"Yes. Would my doing that keep your bosses happy?"

"Oh, yes," Kate breathed, hardly able to believe her luck. She'd mentioned the conference to Marguerite at the wedding, and admitted that she wished she could convince Lucern to attend, but she'd never guessed he would agree. It seemed the woman had taken up the cause. Kate decided she loved Marguerite Argeneau. Marguerite was a wonderful woman.

"Good. Then arrange it. I'll do the R.T. interview. Now, when are you going to leave me in peace?"

Kate glanced at the kitchen clock. It was almost noon. She had called earlier and found out there was a one-o'clock flight, a three-o'clock and a five-o'clock. She had thought she would have to take one of the later flights, and she still could if she wanted to spend more time with him. But then his words clicked. *"Good. Then I'll do the R.T. interview."* R.T. hadn't asked to do an interview yet. The only R.T. event was the conference. Had Lucern's mother led him astray? Deliberately?

"Er . . . Luc, what exactly did your mother say about the R.T. thing?"

Her author shrugged. "She said, 'I suggest you tell her you'll do R.T.' She thought it was probably the best option for both of us."

"And that's all she said?" Kate asked carefully.

Lucern nodded, then added, "Oh, and she said it was a magazine."

Kate had to consider this. Marguerite had led her son

astray all right, and the only reason she could imagine the other woman would do that was to try to help her. Kate felt a twinge of guilt.

A moment later, she let it go. Marguerite wouldn't do anything to harm her son. She must think he would go, too. And that it would be good for him. Kate wasn't going to get into the middle of it. He'd said he would do the R.T. "thing"; she would leave it at that.

She would also get the heck out of there before he realized it was a conference, not an interview, and tried to back out.

"Oh! I didn't realize it was so late," she gasped, peering at her wristwatch with feigned surprised. Then she smiled at Lucern sweetly. "You asked when I was going to leave you in peace. Well, there's a one-o'clock flight that I can just make if I hurry!"

And with that, she whirled and rushed out of the kitchen.

Lucern gaped at the swinging kitchen door. He'd wanted her gone, but her eagerness to comply was a bit disconcerting. He tilted his head and scowled at the ceiling as banging and bumping erupted upstairs. She was obviously rushing about like a crazywoman up there. It seemed she couldn't get out of his home fast enough. It also seemed she was mostly packed, because it wasn't long before he heard her rush along the hall overhead.

He stepped into the hall in time to see her rush down the stairs. A car honked out front at the same moment her foot landed on the ground floor.

"Oh!" Kate turned toward the kitchen, then paused. She smiled in relief when she saw him. "There you are!

Good! My taxi's here and I didn't want to leave without saying goodbye."

"Taxi?" Lucern echoed with disbelief.

"Yes. I called from my room while packing. Boy, they're fast here, huh?"

When Lucern simply stared at her blankly, Kate hesitated. Finally, hefting her suitcase she said, "Well. Thanks for everything. I know I was an unwanted guest, but you were pretty good about it, all things considered. And I appreciate—oh, damn!" she muttered as the cab honked again.

"Wait!" Lucern called as his editor turned and opened the front door. She hesitated, waving at the cab to let the driver know she was coming, then turned back. Lucern didn't really have anything to say; he was just reluctant to see her go. After searching his mind for something—anything—about which to speak, he finally came up with, "What about the interview? When will you arrange it? And you should have my phone number so that you can call and let me know when it is. And my e-mail address, too," he added as the thoughts struck him.

"Um . . ." She winced, then admitted, "Your mother gave me both your number and e-mail address."

"She did?" He was startled, though he knew he shouldn't be. Not with his busybody mother.

"Yes." Kate sidled a little further out the door, a fascinating expression on her face. She looked torn, as if she knew she had to tell him something but didn't really want to. Lucern's fascination deepened when she took another crablike step sideways before blurting, "R.T. doesn't want an interview."

"It doesn't?"

"No, they don't. The R.T. thing your mother was talk-ing about is a *conference*." A look of pain crossed her face; then, while Lucern was trying to absorb that, she added, "But don't worry. You won't regret this. I'll be there with you and will look out for you the whole time." She was still sidling and had almost made it out the door as she added on a babble, "I'll send you all the information and the tickets and pick you up from the airport and everything. So don't worry!"

The taxi chose that moment to give another impa-tient honk.

"Gotta go!" Kate cried, and pulled the door closed with a slam. The sound echoed through the house, fol-lowed by the *tap-tap* of her rush down the porch steps. Then silence fell.

Lucern was transfixed. It was as if he had been pole-axed. Conference? His mother hadn't said anything about a conference. She'd said *Romantic Times* was a magazine. A book club. Someone who would want an interview. Kate must be confused. Dear God, she'd *bet-ter* be confused.

He hurried to the door and stared through the shaded glass just as the taxi pulled away. Lucern watched it.

He stood for a moment, Kate's words playing through his head; then he turned and started up the stairs. *R.T.* She must be confused. He would look up Romantic Times magazine on the Internet just to make sure she was confused.

Barely three minutes later, Lucern's roar echoed through the house.

Chapter Seven

"I am not doing it," Lucern announced, fury underlying his calm proclamation.

"Yes, you are." Marguerite Argeneau filled in another word in her daily crossword puzzle. She'd been working on the damned thing since he'd arrived.

Marguerite disliked the smell and noise of the city. Lucern's father, Claude, hadn't liked it any better. Besides which, living in the city meant moving every ten years to avoid drawing unwanted attention from the fact that they didn't age. Lucern's parents had avoided it all by purchasing several lots of land an hour outside of Toronto, and building their home in the midst of them. They thus had no neighbors near enough to be a concern, and needed not move at all if they did not wish. At least, they hadn't had to move in the thirty years since they'd built it.

Lucern now sat in the family mansion and watched his mother fill in another word. He had no idea why she bothered with the bloody crossword; centuries of living combined with a perfect memory made it less than challenging. Shrugging, he glared at her and repeated, "I am not doing it."

"You are."

"Am not."

"Are."

"Not."

"Are."

"All right, you two. Stop it," Bastien interrupted. He had ridden out to the Argeneau family home after Lucern had called him, ranting unintelligibly about being tricked and shouting that he was going to wring their precious mother's neck. Bastien hadn't really believed his brother would do it, but curiosity had made him rush out to see what would happen. He'd arrived just behind Lucern, entered the house on his brother's heels, and still didn't know what the man was upset about.

He really wanted to know. It was rare to see Lucern with the fire presently burning in his eyes. Grumpy, surly, impatient? Yes, Luc was often all of those. Impassioned with rage? No. Kate C. Leever had lit a fire under him the likes of which Bastien hadn't seen in his five hundred years. And Bastien *was* sure this had something to do with that inestimable editor. Luc had shouted her name like a curse several times while ranting on the phone. It was one of the few words Bastien had actually caught.

Turning to his brother, Bastien asked, "So what exactly is the problem, Luc? I thought you were willing to trade an interview with this *Romantic Weekly* magazine to get rid of Kate. What's happened to change that?"

"*Romantic Times*," Lucern corrected shortly. "And it isn't a bloody interview—that's what changed it. It's a damned conference."

"A conference?" Bastien glanced at his mother suspiciously. "Did you know this?"

Marguerite Argeneau shrugged mildly, which was as close as she would come to a confession. "I don't see the problem. It's just a couple days in a hotel with some readers."

"Five days, mother," Lucern snapped. "Five days in a hotel with some five thousand fans. And then there are balls, book-signings and—"

"One book-signing," his mother interrupted. "One book-signing with a couple hundred other writers there. You won't be the focus. You'll be lucky to get any attention at all."

Lucern was not calmed. "And what about the balls and awards dinners and—"

"All the functions are held in the hotel. You won't need to risk the sun. And—"

"I won't need to risk the sun because I'm not doing it!" Lucern roared. "I can't go."

"You *are* going," Marguerite began firmly, but Bastien interrupted her. "Why can't you go?" he asked Lucern.

"It's in the states, Bastien," his brother said grimly. "I can't possibly get blood through Customs at the airport. And I can't go without blood for five days." He could, actually, but not very comfortably. Cramps would cripple him, and his body would begin to consume itself.

Bastien frowned. "I could ship blood to you once you're there. We do such things all the time."

"There. You see!" Their mother crowed with triumph. "You are going."

"Thanks, Brother." Lucern sneered at the younger man, then glared ferociously at his mother. "I am *not* going!" he said again.

"You gave your word."

"I was tricked into giving my word. You led me to believe it was an interview."

"I never said it was an interview," Marguerite argued. Then she stressed, "You gave your word you would go and you are going."

"I may have given my word, but I didn't sign a contract or anything. I am not going."

Marguerite jerked upright as if he had slapped her. Her words were slow and cold. "A man's word used to be his bond."

Lucern flinched, but he growled, "It used to be. Times have changed. In this world, a man doesn't have to do anything unless it is in writing."

"In this day and age, that's true," she allowed, eyes narrowing on him. "But that isn't how you were raised, Lucern Argeneau. Are you no longer a man of your word?"

Luc gritted his teeth, his fury and helplessness combining. His mother was pulling out the big guns, questioning his honor and using his full name to show her shame that he would even suggest going back on his word. Could he really disappoint her?

Kate chewed on her thumbnail and paced the carpet by the arrivals gate. Her plane had arrived early and Lucern Argeneau's plane was late, which meant she'd been waiting for nearly two hours. And she wasn't even sure if Lucern was on the plane.

She had sent the tickets and all the information on the Romantic Times Conference the day after leaving Toronto. She hadn't received a letter back stating that Lucern would *not* be coming, but then neither had she received word that he would. For all Kate knew, he hadn't even read her damned letter. As usual. She could have called—she had the number—but Kate suddenly found she had a yellow streak. She hadn't called for fear that he would tell her where she could stick her tickets.

Groaning, she turned and paced back the way she'd come. It had been four weeks and three days since she'd left Toronto. She had been petted and congratulated that entire time in the offices of Roundhouse Publishing. Allison had been amazed that she had succeeded where Edwin had failed—a nice little tidbit they had neglected to mention. It seemed her job hadn't been in jeopardy after all; but her convincing Lucern to attend the conference had raised her in their esteem. Allison was now positive that Kate "could get the job done." Her position was secure.

Barring any big screw-up on her part, she added to herself. Which would include Lucern's simply not showing up after all the money they had put into registering him, purchasing his first-class plane tickets, and securing the three-room suite she'd insisted on getting at the hotel. Kate had told Allison she'd promised Lucern these arrangements. And in a way she had; she'd promised him on the way out the door that she would be sure he didn't regret coming, and that she'd be with him at all times to ensure everything went well.

She'd considered how best to make him happy on the flight back to New York, and she'd continued to plan at home that night, thinking that if she got to the office on Monday to find a message from Lucern refusing to attend, she could pull all these special arrangements out to try to persuade him. It turned out she hadn't needed to persuade him, but she would still follow through on all the things she'd planned.

She would be glued to Lucern's side almost twenty-four hours a day, and when she couldn't be there—for instance, when he had to use the men's washroom, or when she had to slip away to the women's—someone else would be there. She had enlisted Chris Keyes, one of the two male editors at Roundhouse Publishing, to aid her in the endeavor.

She'd been prepared to beg, bribe and even resort to blackmail to get the senior editor to assist her, but in the end, she hadn't had to do any of that. Despite the fact that Chris had a slew of his own writers to look after at the conference, he had immediately agreed to help her.

Kate supposed the promise of his own room in a three-room suite, rather than sharing a normal two-bed room with Tom, the V.P. of Promotion, had helped. But C.K., as she sometimes called him, was also a big fan of Lucern's vampire series. Chris had asked a ton of questions about the man after Kate's return from Toronto, but she had just kept answering with, "You'll be meeting him soon. Wait and see." She'd been terrified that if she told him the truth, he'd refuse to help.

An increase in the noise level around her drew Kate's

attention to a mass of people moving up the hall. The plane had arrived, and she was about to find out if Lucern had come. Kate prayed his mother had badgered him into it, but she wasn't at all sure even that formidable woman could manage to do so.

Hands fisted at her sides, Kate searched the crowd of approaching faces. The conference officially began on Wednesday; but she had booked Lucern on a Tuesday-evening flight to prevent his using his allergy to sunlight as an excuse not to come. She and Chris had flown in early to meet him. Their arrivals had been an hour apart, precluding Kate from risking going to the hotel and checking in and then returning to collect Lucern, so Chris had good-naturedly taken control of their baggage and headed to the hotel while Kate waited for Lucern's flight.

Mind you, had she realized that Lucern's flight was going to be delayed so long, she might have gone with Chris and stopped for a drink or two or three before returning. She was so nervous about this conference that she was developing a sour stomach. Or perhaps it was an ulcer—she had heard that was a common editors' complaint.

Kate's thoughts died abruptly as her gaze settled on a man who had been somewhere near the back of the pack. She'd recognize anywhere that muscular frame and the majestic way he held his head. *Lucern*. He was bearing down on her, his long-legged stride quickly bringing him to the front of the disembarking passengers.

"Thank you, Marguerite," she whispered, not even caring that the man looked as surly as ever. She would

129

expect nothing less. He was here, and that was all that mattered. A smile of relief stretching her lips, Kate moved forward to greet him.

"You came." She hadn't intended to speak those words, or for her relief to show, but so it was.

Lucern scowled. "I said I would. I'm a man of my word."

Kate's smile widened even further; then she glanced down at the suitcase, overnight bag, briefcase and portable computer he held. "Here, let me take those for you."

She relieved him of the briefcase and portable computer before he could stop her. He didn't appear pleased by her help.

"I can carry my own things, thank you," he said. His words were stiff, and he tried to retrieve the articles. Kate ignored the attempt and merely turned to lead the way out, babbling with determined cheer. "Chris went ahead to the hotel to check us in, so all we have to do is ride there and settle in. I arranged for your flight to be tonight because I recalled you were allergic to the sun. The best I could do was to have you leave late in the afternoon and arrive in the early evening, which I figured was better than leaving and arriving in the daytime. This works out nicely, though, because now we have the whole night to relax before the others show up tomorrow."

Lucern had been scowling at Kate's back—her heart-shaped butt, actually, if he was honest—but at those words he jerked his eyes up to the back of her head and grimaced. He had wondered why his flight was booked for the night before the conference began, but he had just supposed it was what everyone did. Now he knew she'd done it out of concern for him. Or, more likely, concern that he would refuse to fly during daylight due to his "allergy." What a pain; now he had to be grateful.

"Here we are."

Lucern had been debating commenting on her kindness in having him fly at night, but gave up the idea as he saw the car she'd stopped beside. It was a black sedan, mini limo. She handed his portable and briefcase to the driver with a smile, then turned and tried to take Lucern's overnight bag while waiting for the driver to stow the items in the trunk. Lucern frowned and evaded her reaching hands. He moved to the trunk and put them in himself. The silly woman was trying to be helpful, but Lucern was used to things being the other way around. In the era in which he'd been raised and his attitudes formed, *he* was supposed to carry things for *her*—not allow her to carry his burden.

The driver closed the trunk and led the way to the back passenger door where Kate stood. Apparently, she didn't appreciate Lucern's gallantry in refusing her help. That fact was just as exasperating to Lucern. Someone should teach the silly woman that men were given the physical strength to bear the burdens in life. Women were given beauty to please the men. Deciding to ignore her, he followed her into the back seat when the driver opened the door, then fixed a dignified you-don't-exist-for-me look on his face and stared straight ahead.

The moment the door closed, he was enveloped in a cloud of her tantalizing perfume. He didn't know what it was she wore, but it should come with a warning: "Heady, and likely to cause confusion in those who smell it." He himself was certainly suffering confusion from it.

Annoyance overtook him. He'd been feeling betrayed for four weeks, ever since she'd rushed out of his house, and he'd been nursing that anger. Yet now, as the smell of Kate's perfume surrounded him, his anger was overwhelmed by an entirely different but equally passionate reaction.

Men suffered a terrible handicap, he decided with disgust as he found his anger edged out by lust. The amazing thing was that it had taken him six hundred years to recognize that fact.

"I tried to do everything I could to make sure this was as comfortable for you as possible," Kate said, drawing his attention. "What I'd like to do is outline what I've arranged. Then, if you have any suggestions, perhaps I could take care of them tonight so we'll be all ready before everyone else arrives. Okay?"

Lucern grunted assent, then wished he hadn't when she dug out a file from her capacious purse and shifted closer so that he could watch her open it. He really didn't want her closer. The scent of her was upsetting enough to his equilibrium; the feel of her was going to be . . .

Lucern inhaled deeply and sighed as she opened the file and unintentionally brushed his arm with hers. Then his gaze landed on the top page of the agenda. He frowned. "According to this, the conference started on Sunday."

"No," Kate said. Then she corrected herself, "Well,

yes. They had some events for anyone who wanted to join ahead of time, but the official start isn't until tomorrow."

"Hmm." Lucern decided to keep his mouth shut. He should be grateful that she hadn't forced him to go through the pre-conference crap, too.

"So," his editor said with a return of her determined cheer. "Tomorrow starts with the morning walk with cover models. Then the brunch—"

"What the deuce is a morning walk with cover models?" Lucern interrupted. He'd already seen the agenda, of course—both on the internet and in the paperwork she'd sent him. But nothing had described any of the listed events.

"Er . . . well, actually, I'm not sure," she admitted. She cleared her throat, her smile a tad strained. "But it doesn't matter—you don't have to attend."

"I don't?" He peered at her suspiciously. Something she didn't want him to attend? That seemed strange. He had been sure that she was going to drag him to every single function.

"No. Your first official event will be the Welcome Brunch and R.T. Awards."

Lucern nodded. Those didn't sound so bad. He could eat. Although the awards part would probably be boring.

"Then there's the Reader Hospitality Suite and discussion," she went on. "Allison and Chuck want you there."

"Who are Allison and Chuck?"

"Allison is the head editor, my boss," Kate explained. "And Chuck is the company president. They'll definitely expect you to attend the Hospitality Suite."

Lucern grimaced. "What is it?"

"It's . . ." She appeared to be at a loss for a moment. "Well, each publisher—most of them, anyway—rents out a reception room at the hotel, and writers and editors talk to the readers who come in."

"You want me to talk to people?" he asked in horror. Dear God, he should have done the signing! That would have been less bother, just scribbling his name.

"Of course I want you to talk to people," Kate said with exasperation. "You can do it. I've seen you speak." She fell silent and stared at him, alarm growing on her face. She bit her lip. "Or maybe we can skip that. No, Allison and Chuck would have a fit. You have to go." She sighed heavily. "Oh, damn. This isn't good."

"No, it isn't," Lucern agreed with a nod. Then he jerked around with surprise as the door opened beside him. They had apparently arrived. Without his realizing it, the car had stopped, and the driver was now waiting for him to alight. Nodding his thanks, Lucern slid out then turned and took Kate's hand when she followed.

"We'll need to work on you tonight," she decided as she straightened next to him.

Lucern stiffened and dropped her hand. "Work on me?"

"Yes. Work on you," Kate repeated. They followed Lucern's luggage into the hotel. It was on a trolley, being pulled by a uniformed bellhop. Apparently the driver had seen to the luggage before opening the door for them.

"I don't need 'work,'" Lucern said irritably as they stopped at the elevator.

"Yes, Lucern, you do." Kate smiled sweetly at the bellhop as the doors opened, and he gestured for them to enter.

"I do not," Lucern insisted, following, squeezing himself up against Kate to leave room for the luggage trolley.

"Can we talk about this later?"

Kate gave an impatient nod at the bellhop and pushed the button for their floor. At least Lucern presumed it was their floor. He hadn't a clue, though she had said someone named Chris had already checked them in. He supposed this Chris was another editor. He wondered if she would be as annoying as Kate.

He glanced at the bellhop, confused at Kate's desire to put this off. The man was a servant, hardly worth worrying about. Although he didn't want to argue either. "No. There is nothing to discuss. I do not need to be worked on."

"You do," Kate insisted. "And I'm not going to talk about this now."

"There is nothing to talk about."

"There *is*," she snapped.

The bellhop gave a soft chuckle, and Lucern glared at him. There had been a time when servants knew their place and would have been deaf and dumb to such discussions. That time wasn't now. He constantly forgot how rude the world had become.

The doors opened and the bellhop moved the trolley out; then he led them down a long hall past countless doors. At the end he stopped, pulled out a card key, opened the door, then pushed the trolley in.

"Which room do these go in, ma'am?" he asked,

pausing in the center of a large chamber set up as a living room.

His question drew another scowl from Lucern. He was the man; the fellow should have addressed the question to him.

"I'm not sure. Just set them here. We can manage, thanks." Kate accepted the card key from the fellow and handed him a tip, making Lucern scowl again, this time at himself. He was the man; he should have tipped the bellhop. He should be more on the ball. His only excuse was that it had been a long day. His flight had been at three p.m., but he'd had to leave for the airport at one to get through security. He had worn a business suit, hat and sunglasses, and slathered on sunscreen, but of course, some of the sunlight had got through. His body had sustained damage that his blood was already working to correct. He was feeling depleted and needed to feed—a state he was beginning to associate with Kate Leever.

The click of the door closing drew his gaze back to her, and Lucern picked up their argument immediately. "I do not need to be worked on."

"Lucern," his editor began wearily. Suddenly losing her temper, she said grimly, "Look. You're named after a dairy product, you look like an Angel wannabe, and you talk like a bad Bela Lugosi. You need work!"

"Wow, Kate."

Lucern turned to see a tall, slender blond man entering the room. He was clapping his hands slowly, an irrepressible grin on his face. "You'll have to give me pointers on handling writers. I've never seen it done quite like that."

"Oh. Chris." Kate sighed unhappily.

"This is Chris?" Lucern asked with dismay.

His editor stiffened again but said simply, "Yes."

"You never said he was a man. Make him leave."

Kate's eyes narrowed on him, fury burning out of them. "Look, Lucern—"

"Nope," Chris interjected. He put his hands up in a conciliatory gesture. "Kate, he doesn't sound like Bela Lugosi. The smarmy accent is missing."

Kate's ire turned on her coworker. "I meant he uses old-fashioned terminology."

Chris merely arched an eyebrow. A moment later he added, "And his hair's too dark for him to be an Angel wannabe."

"Shut up! Stay out of this."

The editor laughed, apparently unoffended. "And Allison and Chuck were worried you couldn't handle this guy."

"Who *is* this gentleman?" Lucern asked Kate stiffly. If she said it was her husband, boyfriend or lover, he feared he might have to perform some violence.

"Chris Keyes," Kate announced. "He's an editor at Roundhouse, too. Chris Keyes, meet Lucern Argeneau, aka Luke Amirault, the vampire writer."

"A pleasure, Mr. Argeneau." The lanky editor stepped forward and offered his hand in welcome.

Lucern automatically shook, but he asked, "You're an editor?"

Keyes nodded.

"What do you edit?"

"Romance, like Kate."

137

Lucern nodded slowly, then asked hopefully, "Are you a homosexual?"

Chris Keyes's eyes rounded in shock.

"Lucern!"

Lucern glanced at Kate with annoyance. She sounded just like his mother when she barked like that. Taking in the way his editor was flushing and then paling by turns, he decided not to mention it.

A sudden burst of laughter drew his gaze back to Chris. The young man's stunned expression had given way to a deep belly laugh. Lucern waited patiently for him to recover himself.

When Chris's mirth had died down to a chuckle, he asked, "What made you ask such a question?"

"You are a romance editor. That is a woman's job."

"Ah." Chris grinned. "But you write them. Are you gay?"

Lucern stared for a moment, then grinned, caught. "Touché."

Kate was not amused. Moving between the two, she glared up at Lucern. "Chris has kindly agreed to help look after you this weekend. You will not be rude to him." She scowled and added, "At least, no ruder than you usually are."

Lucern scowled back. "I do not need to be looked after."

"You—"

"Kate," Chris interrupted. "It's getting late. If you still want to go to Bobbi's kick-off party, you should probably—"

"Oh, damn!" Kate glanced at her watch. She seemed to forget all about Lucern and asked her coworker,

"Where did you put my stuff? It's a Western theme. I have to change."

"I put it in that room." Chris pointed to a door on their right. "I figured if you didn't like it, we could shuffle later."

Kate merely nodded. Rushing into the room, she slammed the door behind her. Chris just shook his head.

Lucern scowled after Kate. If she expected him to go to this party, she had another think coming. He had no intention of going to a Western themed party after just flying in.

"So, I guess it's you and me tonight, Luc," Chris said cheerfully. Lucern suddenly rethought the party. Kate would be there. Not this guy.

"Why are you here?" he asked the male editor.

Chris grinned. "I'm supposed to keep you safe. When Kate can't be around. Like tonight."

"Keep me safe?" Lucern echoed. "From what?"

Chris pursed his lips and considered. Then he grinned. "You've never been to a Romantic Times conference, have you, Luc?"

Lucern shook his head. He gave a start of surprise when Chris clapped a hand on his shoulder and steered him toward the bar in the corner. "Let's have a drink while I tell you. You're going to need it."

Lucern fretted as he watched Chris pour the glass of Scotch he requested. He was beginning to believe this conference would be even more of a pain than he'd feared.

"There you are." Chris handed him his drink. The editor then gestured for them to move to the couch, which was set against the walled window.

Lucern moved toward it, suddenly thinking how hungry he was. "Was there a package delivered here for me?"

"Not that I know of. I'm sure they would have mentioned it when I signed in," Chris answered. He settled in the room's one chair, leaving the couch to Lucern. "But then, I don't know that your name is registered for this room."

Lucern stiffened. Was he not to be the man in any of these situations?

The bedroom door Kate had disappeared through suddenly opened, and she rushed out. Lucern automatically got to his feet at her entrance, forgetting about his hoped for blood delivery. He gaped at the woman. She was wearing the tightest pair of hip-hugging jeans he had seen in all his born days. They were complemented by knee-high cowboy boots, a checkered shirt, a fringed suede jacket, and a cowboy hat that looked like it had seen rough use. She looked sexy as hell.

"Katie," Chris called. "Did you put Lucern's name on the room?"

Kate glanced over with surprise. "Of course not. I was afraid someone might connect the names Lucern Argeneau and Lucern Argentus and figure out this was his room. The whole idea of this suite was so that none of his fans could find him. Why?"

"Luc was expecting a delivery. I guess they would have turned it away if they didn't think he was here."

Kate turned an apologetic gaze on Lucern. "Sorry. Just call and have them deliver it to my name. Okay?"

Lucern nodded slowly, his eyes feasting on her. She

blushed under his perusal, then said, "I'll try not to be out late. Chris will look after you until I get back. Anything you want, he's the man to go to, okay?"

Lucern nodded again, his tongue stuck on the roof of his mouth.

"Chris." She turned her attention to her coworker. "Make him watch some TV. Maybe he can update the way he speaks by watching it."

The other editor laughed. "Katie, dear, if watching television hasn't changed his speech before now, one night is hardly going to do it."

"He doesn't have a TV," she explained dryly. "At least, I didn't see one." She turned a curious gaze to Lucern. "*Do* you have one?"

He shook his head. Television, in his opinion, rotted the brain.

"I didn't think so," she said with satisfaction. She instructed her friend "Make him watch it. I'll see you guys later."

Both men were silent until the door closed behind Kate. Lucern sank back onto the couch.

"Why did you stand?" Chris asked curiously.

"A lady had entered the room," Lucern answered absently. His vision was still full of Kate the cowgirl. He usually preferred women in more feminine dress, but there had been nothing masculine about Kate in that outfit.

"You're kidding about the TV, right?" Chris asked. "Do you really not have one?"

"No. Never have."

"Man!" Chris picked up the remote control off the table. Lucern recognized it; he had one for his stereo system at home. This was to the television. The editor clicked it and grinned. "You're in for a treat, Luc. You're gonna love television."

Lucern grimaced. He very much doubted that he would love television. He was more a theater type of guy. Old habits died hard.

Chapter Eight

Lucern loved television. He didn't know why he had allowed prejudice to prevent him from at least trying it before now. TV was a marvelous invention. It was like a mini-stage with little players. And what players! In the last three hours he had watched a movie by some guy named Monty Python . . . or had that been the character?

Anyway, they'd watched that first. When it ended, Chris had looked through a television guide and cried, "Yeah! A Black Adder marathon!" And they'd been watching that ever since. It was a grand show! Marvelous and amusing. Lucern hadn't laughed so hard in years.

"They have history all mixed up, but it is quite amusing," he announced, reaching for a fresh beer from the six-pack on the coffee table.

Chris burst out laughing, then stopped abruptly, his eyes going wide. "Oh, shoot! Kate's going to kill me!"

Lucern arched his eyebrows. "Why?"

"Because I was supposed to make you watch modern American television, to help with your speech." He pondered for a minute before shrugging. "What the hell. It's kind of late in the game to change your speech, anyway."

Lucern nodded absently. The mention of Kate made him remember her accusations of earlier. She had said he spoke in old-fashioned ways. Lucern supposed he did; it was hard to change speech patterns. He'd been born in Switzerland in 1390. His parents had moved around a lot in those days, but that was where he'd been conceived and born. They had subsequently moved back to England, and he had learned to speak using the King's English. Despite all the countries he had lived in since, and all the languages he had learned and spoken, he still did and probably always would bear a slight accent and lean toward speaking the way he'd been taught.

What else had she said? He recalled something about an angel. That he looked like an angel wannabe? What did that mean exactly? Her voice had been too snarly for it to be a compliment. His gaze shifted from the TV screen to Chris. "Who, or what, is an angel wannabe?"

Chris turned a blank expression on him. "Huh?"

"Kate said I looked like an angel wannabe," Lucern reminded him. Understanding immediately lit the young editor's face. "Oh, yeah. Well, you know. Angel. Buffy and Angel? Vampire slayer and vamp? Oh, that's right. You don't watch TV, so you wouldn't know," he said finally. "Well, Angel is this vampire, see. And he is,

144

or was, Buffy the Vampire Slayer's boyfriend. But he has his own show now."

"Vampire slayer?" Lucern asked with dismay. Did they still have those? Dear God, he had thought that craze had died out a century or so ago. Life had been pretty tense for a bit. He and his family had had to be terribly cautious—or more so than usual. They had always had to be cautious. Their natural proclivities had made them a target many times over the centuries. Many had been burned at stakes as witches during the Inquisition, and when Stoker had come out with his damned book, vampire slayers had popped up everywhere. It had been a damned nuisance. And scary, too. His family had only really begun to relax since the advent of blood banks, which had lessened both vampires hunting and being hunted. Now it seemed to be a false security. There were still slayers out there.

Well, there was nothing he could do about it at the moment, though he meant to warn his family. He would mention it to Bastien when his brother called back.

Lucern moved on to the other accusation Kate had made. "What did Kate mean by my being named after a dairy product?"

"Oh." Chris made a face. "Lucern is a dairy company here in the States."

"A dairy company?"

"Yeah, you know—milk, cottage cheese, ice cream," Chris explained in exasperation.

"I know what dairy products are," Lucern said testily. "But I am not named after dairy products."

"So what are you named for?"

"The lake in Switzerland where I was conceived."

Chris nodded. "I think I've heard of it. But doesn't Lake Lucerne have an e on the end?"

"Yes, well . . . I think my mother thought the e made the name feminine. She took it off."

"Ah." Chris nodded again. "It's a cool name. Don't let what Kate said bother you. She's just a little testy lately. Working too hard or something." He gestured to the pizza box on the table. "Is there any left?"

Lucern leaned over and saw that there were still two slices of the meat-eater's special they'd ordered. He took one, then handed the box to Chris.

Besides television, pizza was something else he'd never tried. It wasn't something served in the gourmet restaurants he frequented. Lucern was beginning to think that his snobby ways had been making him miss out on many pleasures he might truly enjoy. He had never been a great fan of beer, but it had a nice bite to it with pizza. It went even better with the peanuts Chris had run out to buy. It had been kind of fun, too, cracking the peanut shells and strewing them all over the place.

Lucern peered at the coffee table with interest. It was awash in empty beer cans, peanut shells, used paper plates and napkins. He had at first tried to clean up as they ate, his fastidious nature kicking in, but Chris had told him to just stop, he was blocking the TV. Now Lucern found himself rather comfortable amid the mess.

His gaze slid curiously to his companion. Kate's editor friend was an interesting fellow, mostly good-tempered but with a caustic wit at odds with his youth. Lucern had learned the man was in his late twenties—a babe to his own advanced years, though the editor would probably resent him thinking so. Despite that, Lucern was enjoying his company.

He had, though, found himself looking at the man's neck a lot the last hour or so. Now that he had eaten regular food, and satisfied his more natural hunger, the missing blood delivery was beginning to gnaw at Lucern. He had called Bastien twice from his bedroom but got no answer either time. His brother was never home! But that was Bastien's nature.

His younger brother worked hard, played hard, and ran on staggered hours, sometimes braving the day to work, sometimes working nights at the family company. Bastien was the son who had taken up the reins of Argent, Inc. after their father's death. Lucern had never been interested. He'd always preferred the arts, alternating between painting and writing the last couple hundred years.

In contrast, Bastien had always enjoyed the wheeling and dealing of business. The boy had worked in the family company most of his adult life, and he was good at it. Bastien was the one who had convinced their father to diversify from farming and shipping to production in the eighteenth century. He was also the one who had decided they should move into feeding from blood banks. Bastien was an innovative thinker.

He was also damned hard to keep track of. The family business often took him on unexpected trips to foreign countries for indefinite periods. Lucern often couldn't be sure of where his younger brother was or when he would be back. Bastien might simply have been out to dinner when he called, or he might be on his way to Europe to handle a problem at the head offices. Whatever the case, he would get Lucern's message and return the call sooner or later. But Lucern was hungry now.

His gaze slid to Chris's throat again. The editor had a good healthy pulse. Lucern could probably get a pint out of him without harming the fellow. Of course, it would be alcohol-soaked blood, he realized unhappily. And his own blood had a goodly portion of alcohol in it already. He frowned, but his gaze stayed fixed on the other man's neck. Chris laughed at something that had happened on the latest Black Adder skit. Lucern didn't look toward the television; he hungered.

The craving for blood was nothing like that for food. It was somewhat similar to thirst, but wasn't just a dry mouth. It affected his whole body. His skin seemed to be shriveling and aching with want of nourishment.

He knew it wouldn't be as bad right now if he hadn't been out in the sun. The walk from the car into the airport had been a short one, but the airport was all glass and he'd had an aisle seat on the plane. So he'd been unable to close the window shade. He had been stuck with the sun shooting in the window and striking him. The sun was dangerous to his sort. It caused damage in everyone, of course, people of his own race and humans, too. But his body, his blood, was constantly repairing that and other daily damages, and the sun's rays could do a lot, using up his reserves at an accelerated pace and leaving him dangerously dehydrated, bringing a thirst that no amount of water would cure. Only blood.

"What are you doing?"

Chris's question made Lucern realize that he had stood and moved around behind the other man. The editor twisted in his seat, peering back at him curiously.

Nothing. I am sitting on the couch. Watch the show, Lucern commanded, slipping inside the man's mind with little effort and taking control.

"Watch the show," the editor echoed, and turned back in his seat.

Lucern smiled. He hadn't lost the ability to slip inside another's mind and take control. His inability to do so with Kate had made him worry that he had forgotten how. He hadn't, of course. Which meant that Kate was one of those strong-minded and strong-willed individuals his mother swore were the . . .

Lucern pushed the thought away. Thinking of Kate at this moment stirred guilt in him. He was contemplating dining on her coworker, after all, and knew she would not be pleased.

His gaze narrowed on the man sitting before him, and he quickly sifted through the editor's thoughts, looking for anything regarding Kate. He was relieved to find little but friendship and affection. Chris and Kate were not now nor never had been in any sort of relationship. This was good. Lucern liked the young man. He wouldn't have liked him nearly so well had he been romantically involved with Kate.

Lucern proceeded to blank out Chris's thoughts, forcing him to concentrate only on the Black Adder show. He would be unaware of Lucern, who touched the top of his head and tilted it to the side to allow him better access to the carotid.

Lucern bent forward. He would only have a little nibble, take just enough blood to quench the worst of his thirst. Just a little.

Kate stepped off the elevator and started down the hall with relief. She had spent the last several hours involved in shop talk, encouraging, assuring and praising her various writers at the party. All of them were wonderful women, but they had little personal contact with her, so when they got the chance to see her in person they were all rather needy. Though enjoyable, the encounters were mentally and emotionally exhausting, and Kate couldn't wait to get back to the suite and relax.

She thought of Lucern. Taking off her hat, she ran her hands unhappily through her hair. She had been unnecessarily mean to him earlier. Her only excuse was frustration and weariness. She was frustrated because she'd managed to get the man here to the conference and was now worried it would do more damage than good. And she had worked late hours the last month trying to get ahead so her absence this week at the conference would not be a problem. Added to that, she had been nervous the entire time, worrying over whether Lucern would show up or not.

Kate sighed to herself and dug around in her pocket for her room key. She would be extra nice to him to make up for her earlier irritability. After all, it wasn't his fault he was named after dairy products, was as pale as death half the time or spoke in such an old-fashioned way. He had been tricked into giving his word to come, then had kept it. He wasn't all bad. He was . . .

A pervert! That was Kate's first thought upon opening the door to the three-bedroom suite. She couldn't believe her eyes. She wasn't even sure at first as to what she was witnessing. Chris was sitting in the chair, and Kate would almost have believed he was watching television, except Lucern was bent over him, an arm around his shoulder and trailing down his chest as he buried his face in the editor's neck.

Kate gaped in horror. Lucern Argeneau *was* gay: And he was making a pass at her coworker!

"What the hell are you doing?"

Lucern straightened abruptly and whirled to face the door where Kate stood gaping. His first thought was, uh-oh. His second was that it was a damned shame she was resistant to mind control, because he would have used it on her. Then the phone rang.

Lucern took a moment to reinforce his control over Chris so that the editor wouldn't hear or see what was going on; it was better not to free his mind until Lucern knew how he was going to explain this. Then, since Kate seemed incapable of moving at the moment, he left her standing by the door and walked into his bedroom to answer the phone. He was hoping it was Bastien.

As he'd hoped, it was his brother's voice on the line. Though the timing sucked. If his brother had called half an hour earlier, Lucern might have been able to control his bloodlust and avoided the scene in the other room. How the hell was he going to explain this to Kate?

"Lucern? *Lucern!*"

He gave up and turned his attention to Bastien. "Where are you?" he asked.

151

"I'm in Europe. I got your message, but you didn't say what the problem was. What—?"

"Hang up the phone." Kate was suddenly at his side. He should have locked the door. It appeared she had recovered from her shock, and judging from her expression, she was not a happy camper.

"Just a minute, Kate," Lucern scowled at her. "Go wait in the other room."

"No. I want to talk to you. Now." She grabbed for the receiver, but Lucern turned away, moving it out of her reach.

"Look, Bastien. I . . ." He paused and stared at the receiver in his hand after a click sounded in his ear.

"What were you doing to Chris?"

Lucern turned. "You hung up the phone!" He gaped at Kate.

"You're damned right I did," she hissed. She glanced toward the door to the other room. The Black Adder laugh track could be heard beyond. She turned back and accused in a harsh whisper, "I leave you alone for a few hours and come back to find you hitting on my friend? For your information, he isn't gay, so you're wasting your time. I can't believe you'd act like this, but you're going to explain yourself right now."

Lucern recoiled as if she'd hit him. "I wasn't hitting on your friend. What kind of man do you take me for?"

"Well, what kind of man am I supposed to take you for? You've never shown the least bit of interest in me, and I come back to find you all over Chris!"

Lucern stared at her for a moment, then slammed the dead phone down in its cradle. Snatching her by the wrist, he tugged her into his arms. She got out one gasp of surprise before his mouth closed over hers.

It was no soft, tentative kiss. Lucern had something to prove. Besides, he'd wanted her for so long that he couldn't have been soft had he wanted to. The kiss was a taking—he ravaged her mouth, forcing her lips open and thrusting his tongue inside, his body clenching at the taste of her. She was as hot and sweet as he had imagined.

And she was as willing. Oh, not at first. For the first moment or two Kate was stiff and still in his arms, but then she gave a groan of surrender and melted into him, her body forming itself against his like a soft sweater. Her breasts nudged his chest as she slid her free arm around his neck and tilted her head slightly to make it less awkward as she kissed him back.

It only served to fan the flame of Lucern's desire. Forgetting his original intent to prove he wasn't gay, he released her wrist and slid his arms around her. Letting his hands slide down over her back to her heart-shaped bottom, he cupped those round curves and lifted her against him until they were groin to groin; then he gyrated his hips to press into her. Kate was warm sunlight in his hands, arching and writhing against him as she moaned. Her mouth went wider, then sucked at his almost frantically.

"Lucern." She gasped his name in protest when he paused to glance around. But Lucern wasn't stopping. He had no intention of stopping; he merely wanted to know where the hell the bed was. He wanted to touch more of her. He wanted to take her. He couldn't touch and take her while they were standing.

Seeing the bed directly behind Kate, he urged her

back onto it. Following her down, he pressed his body insistently into hers and lowered his mouth to kiss her again. Kate relaxed at once, her hands roving over his back, side and arms. Lucern felt her tugging at his shirt, trying consciously or unconsciously to pull it free of his pants, and he was suddenly grateful that he'd removed his jacket and tie earlier. There was less to take off that way.

Kate, of course, was wearing far too much. He decided to help her with that problem; but when he started to break their kiss, she protested with a loud groan and dug her claws into his lower back, trying to hold him in place.

Lucern chuckled breathlessly into her mouth, pleased with her passion. He gave her another deep kiss, filling her mouth with his tongue, then withdrawing it in imitation of what was to come. He broke the kiss and nibbled his way down her chin, along her throat as he started to work on the buttons of her shirt. He hesitated as his lips found and paused on the pulsing vein in her throat. He could feel the excitement in her blood, could almost taste it. He wanted to bite her. Wanted to feed. But he would wait. He would take her blood as he took her body. They would both find the heights of ecstasy that way. It would be better for the wait.

Lucern let his mouth move on, kissing Kate's tender flesh until he reached where the round tops of her breasts pushed out of her bra. His hands had been busy. Her shirt was undone down to where it was tucked into her jeans. Lucern rose up, his knees settling on either side of her hips, and he tugged the shirt free, opening it fully so that it dropped to lie on either side of her. She lay, naked except for a white cotton bra.

Lucern had seen many women in various states of undress. He'd seen women in corsets that had curled his toes, in slinky French negligees that had left him breathless, in little bits of nothing that couldn't even really be called clothing—but he didn't think he'd ever seen anything as sexy as Kate in her cotton bra. Her cowboy hat had tumbled off and lay next to her, her hair was a tangled mess around her flushed cheeks, and her eyes were sleepy with desire. He wanted to eat her up. Wanted to take her into his body and keep her there for eternity. He wanted *Kate*.

She shifted restlessly beneath him, her hands reaching to feather over his belly through his shirt, and Lucern reluctantly gave up looking at her. Leaning forward, he caught her by the arms and pulled her into a seated position; then he kissed her as he slipped his hands around her to undo the bra. He would have just ripped it off, but it would be a shame to never see her in it again.

Kate wasn't inactive as he worked. She finished tugging his shirt free of his dress slacks and ran her hands underneath, over his hard back then around to explore his chest.

Lucern smiled against her mouth. He undid the last clasp and felt the cloth slip loose. Quickly pushing her shirt off her shoulders, he pushed her back on the bed and tugged the frustrating scrap of cotton off so that he could see her properly.

"Perfect." The word slipped from his lips as he reached to cup her breasts. Kate moaned and arched her back, pressing upward into his touch. It was all the urging Lucern needed; he shifted lower on her body so that he could bend forward and take one perfect, hardened nipple into his mouth. His eyes closed with pleasure as he suckled the nub and felt it stiffen even further with excitement. Kate allowed him to attend her breasts for a bit, then caught his hair and tugged his head demandingly upward.

Lucern gave in to the demand. Shifting to kiss her, he slid his leg to nestle between hers. He pressed upward, nudging his thigh against her sex as he kissed her. Kate responded heatedly, rubbing back in return and tugging viciously at his shirt. Several buttons snapped. Lucern suddenly found his shirt open, and he pushed closer so that their flesh met. Kate's nipples grazed the hair of his chest, then his skin, sending tingles through him. He felt her hand slide down over his stomach to his groin.

Lucern went a little wild. He thrust against her, grinding closer, her hand caught between them. The phone began to ring. Lucern heard it, but it was a far-off sound, a distant concern he couldn't be bothered with. Kate filled his mind. She was all he saw or heard—her gasps and soft sighs, her scent, her touch. She swamped him. The world could go to hell for all he cared. Kate was with him, and he wanted her there forever. For longer than forever.

Lifting his mouth from hers, Lucern moved to her neck, found her pulse and sank his teeth into her flesh. She cried out, her neck arching, and Lucern closed his eyes, grinding his lower body against her. Her lifeblood filled his mouth. It tasted sweet despite her slender body. Lucern had always preferred larger women, finding their blood thick and rich and fulfilling. But while Kate's blood was different, it was still heady. He felt a rush as it filled him.

"Hey, Lucern! Some guy named Bastien . . . Oh! Uh, sorry."

Lucern straightened abruptly, rising to his knees on the bed. Whirling he caught sight of Chris moving quickly away from the open door. He stared in amazement, unable to believe that he had got so carried away that he'd forgotten to close the door, and was even more amazed that he'd lost control to such an extent that he had released his power over the editor's mind. Worst of all, he had allowed Chris to catch him and Kate together. He had no fear that the man would know he'd been feeding, but Chris's other assumptions would be just as bad. Kate certainly wouldn't be pleased about it. And Lucern had no desire to cause her discomfort with her coworkers.

Then what the other man had said sank in, and Lucern recalled the ringing phone. Bastien was on the line, calling back! Hurtling himself off the bed, Lucern rushed to the door just in time to see Chris hang up.

"Oh," the editor said, spying him in the doorway. "I told him you were busy."

Lucern cursed under his breath. Opening his mouth to snap at the younger man, he paused when he realized the editor was avoiding looking at him. Keyes was also blushing furiously. Lucern peered down at himself, grimacing when he saw that Kate hadn't only got his shirt open; she'd managed to start on his pants. The belt was undone, the button open, and his slacks were half-way down his thighs.

He doubted that was what had got Chris upset, however. No doubt the man was discomfitted by finding Kate in flagrante delecto with one of her writers.

Lucern was trying to decide what to do when he was suddenly pushed from behind. Shifting to the side, he half-turned to see Kate rush out of the room past him. Her shirt was done up and her hat was back on her head, and the glimpse he got of her face showed it cherry red with embarrassment.

Lucern tried to grab her hand, but she was already out of reach. Kate called something unintelligible but for the word "bed," then disappeared into her room. The door closed with a snap, followed by the *snick* of the lock. She definitely wanted to be alone.

Lucern sighed unhappily and pushed a hand through his hair. He'd made a mess of everything.

"Well, I guess I'll . . . er . . . go to bed, too," Chris announced. He then disappeared.

Shaking his head, Lucern walked to the bar. He poured himself a stiff drink, then carried it back to his room, closing the door behind him.

"Now that it doesn't matter," he muttered to himself as he walked to the bed. He'd muddled everything and knew it.

What could he do now? He hadn't a clue what Kate was thinking. Was she aware that he'd bitten her? Usually people weren't, but he usually controlled their mind while doing it, pouring the pleasure it gave him back into them while he fed. It was usually a very erotic experience for them. For the women, anyway. He didn't bother to do that with the men, but merely blanked their mind so that they wouldn't recall what had happened. They were simply left with two tiny holes in their neck and no idea where they'd come from. Lucern had opened his mind to Kate as he'd bitten her, but he was not sure she'd felt his pleasure as her own. Had she felt his bite? Had it been painful? Or had she felt the pleasure and jubilation?

If she had felt the pain of the bite, Kate would probably think he was some insane freak. She'd think he wrote about vampires because he mistakenly thought himself one. She'd be wondering just what she had on her hands. Or, worse, she'd know the truth. But Lucern suspected it would be the freak thing. A sensible modern woman like Kate would never believe in vampires.

Chapter Nine

Kate woke up feeling awful. She didn't understand why at first, but then the memories hit her like a sledgehammer: Coming back to find Lucern hanging over Chris. His going into the bedroom to answer the phone. Her following him, rage consuming her. *How dare he be gay?* she had been thinking. *How dare he?* The very idea had stunned her. She was attracted to him. Had had erotic dreams about him. He couldn't be gay!

And it appeared he wasn't. She could still feel his lips on hers.

Her first reaction to his sensual assault had been shock; then her anger had turned to relief, and, just as quickly, to desire.

The man could kiss. She recalled his kiss as she pushed the covers aside and slid out of her bed. The man could kiss like no one she'd ever met. His kisses had reached down inside her soul and pulled out every want, every desire, every drop of lust residing inside her body, and had brought it to the surface. She'd wanted him. She still did. Her nipples were erect just at the memories. And he had definitely been excited, too. It had felt as if he had a big steel rod in his pants when she'd put her hand there.

Which was all great. Except that she was his editor and had no business knowing how big his steel rod was. And her coworker had caught them going at it!

Groaning, she walked into the bathroom, turned the cold water on in the shower and stepped inside. She had no idea how she was going to face either man again. But somehow she had to. Should she act as if nothing had happened? Should she talk to Chris about it? Should she talk to both of them? And if she talked to either of them, what could she say? She knew what she *should* say to Lucern. She should say it was an aberration and could never happen again. But she didn't want to say that. And with Chris, she didn't have a clue. There really was nothing to say.

Sighing, Kate turned off the water and grabbed a towel off the rack. She wrapped it turban-style around her wet hair, then grabbed a second towel to dry off. Next, she grabbed the terrycloth robe the hotel had provided and, bundled in that, she walked to the mirror and made a face at herself. She had to dry her hair, do her face, dress and then go out and see Chris and Lucern. Ugh.

Kate reached for the towel around her hair, meaning to get the worst of the water out before blow-drying it, when she noticed marks on her neck. Pausing, she stared for a moment. Then, leaning into the mirror and turning her head to the side, she peered out of the corners of her eyes at her neck.

For the longest time she just stared at the two small puncture marks, all sorts of thoughts running through her mind: Lucern's books, with characters all bearing the same names as his family. The evening wedding. Lucern and his mother being allergic to the sun. The head wound that had appeared to bleed so copiously, but that she couldn't find and that didn't appear to bother Lucern at all after he washed the blood away. The way he'd been leaning over Chris when she'd returned, his mouth against her friend's neck. The fact that Chris hadn't even seemed to be aware of his presence, and hadn't reacted at all to Kate's return.

Yet she didn't recall Lucern biting her last night. Did she?

Oh. Suddenly she saw an image of being half-naked in Lucern's arms, her breasts brushing his hard chest as he thrust himself against her hand and nibbled on her neck. She had assumed he was giving her a hickey, maybe; hadn't cared, it had felt so good. "Dear God," she'd moaned. And "Don't stop." She'd even turned her head to allow him better access.

Her hands dropped to her sides. He'd bitten her. Not only was Lucern Argeneau a vampire, he'd had the balls to bite *her*!

Turning on her heel, she charged out of the bathroom.

"You bit me!"

Lucern's eyes popped open, and he sprang upright on the bed to stare at the woman in the doorway. His eyes were bleary with exhaustion. He hadn't slept at all well or long. A body couldn't take six hundred years of sleeping during the day and switch to sleeping at night just like that. He had lain in bed awake for most of the night, wondering if Kate was very pissed at him and when he would be able to get her into his arms again. Judging by her expression now, he wasn't guessing anytime soon.

Sighing, he flopped back on the bed with a groan. He didn't have the energy to deal with Kate at the moment. He had barely got a couple of sips out of Chris before she had returned, then had barely got a couple more out of Kate. He was *hungry*, dammit.

"Don't you ignore me, Lucern Argeneau!" Kate snapped, storming forward. "You *bit* me."

Her words made their way through his sleep-fogged mind and his eyes blinked open again. Damn. She'd noticed. He watched her approach, then noticed Chris hovering worriedly outside the door.

"Close the damned door," he snapped.

Kate turned in surprise to the door. Spotting Chris there, she looked at his neck. There were marks there, too.

Chris's eyebrows flew up at her angry expression. He grabbed the door handle and started to pull it closed. "I'll just close this."

"Just a minute. Let me see your neck," Kate demanded. She was at the door in an instant and jerking his head to the side. She stared at his throat for a minute, then whirled furiously on Lucern. "You son of a bitch."

"Geez, Kate. Take a pill. It isn't Lucern's fault. I cut my neck shaving."

She whirled back to Chris in shock. He was already closing the door behind him as he left.

The room was enclosed in darkness for a moment; then Lucern flicked the switch on the bedside lamp. Kate started toward him. "What did you do to him? How could you possibly make him think that is a shaving cut?"

Her incaution was foolish. She got too close and, just like that, Lucern rose up in bed, caught her by the arms and dragged her over him until she slammed down on the mattress. In the next moment, he moved to cover her.

"Get off of me." She had meant to sound commanding. Instead her voice came out weak and breathless. Kate scowled to try to reinforce her words. She wasn't scared exactly, but there was a quaver in her voice. Lucern's eyes had turned that silver color, though not in anger. He looked like a predator, and Kate was pretty sure she was the prey. The problem was, she wasn't sure she didn't want to be. Her body was already responding to the feel of him pressing down on her.

Lucern hesitated, then let his eyelids droop over his eyes. He looked like a sleepy lion. It really wasn't much better.

"I am sorry," he said in that proper English of his. Another clue to his vampirism, Kate thought unhappily. He was probably real old.

"What for?" she asked after several moments of silence.

"For biting you," he answered promptly, then added, "without your permission."

Kate scowled. "What about Chris?"

"It was just a nibble," he said with a shrug. "And you did say I should go to him if I needed anything."

"I didn't mean you should bite him!" Kate yelled.

Lucern had the nerve to grin. "And what should I have done?"

"You could have . . ."

When she fell into a confused silence, he asked, "What? Said, 'Oh. Say, Chris, would you mind picking up a pint of blood while you're out getting peanuts? I'm a tad thirsty at the moment.'" He made a face. "You didn't put my name on the room, so the blood that was supposed to be delivered here was turned away. I was hungry," he explained simply.

Kate stared at him, her mouth gone dry. He really was a vampire. She suddenly realized that she hadn't really believed it yet. Now she did. Mostly. Shifting under him, she demanded, "Show me your teeth."

He bared them. They looked perfectly normal to her. His canines were a little pointy but not overly long, and she muttered, "No sharp, pointy, canine teeth. . . ."

"Oh, *those* teeth." Lucern opened his mouth again. To her horror, the canines extended out of his gums like a cat's claws.

"Oh, God," Kate whimpered.

He retracted the teeth at once. "It's okay, Kate. I would never hurt you."

"You bit me!" she cried. Which was followed by another chorus of "Oh God, oh God, oh God." She couldn't seem to stop saying that.

165

"But it didn't hurt," he argued. "Did it?"

"Oh God! Get off me, get off me, get off me!" She began to struggle beneath him, but it was a useless attempt. He was much bigger than her. And stronger. She stopped struggling, tried to calm herself, then said, "Please."

Lucern peered at her for a moment, suspicious, then shook his head. "I can't. Not until you promise that you won't tell anyone about this."

She opened her mouth, but he forestalled her by adding, "It's for your own good, Kate. People would just think you are nuts."

He was probably right about that, she realized. They would all think she'd been working too hard and gone off her rocker. A shifting from below drew her attention to the fact that something was moving down there, and it wasn't Lucern. At least not most of him. Dear God, he was getting aroused. She could feel him growing and pressing against her. Kate cleared her throat. "Umm, Lucern?"

"Call me Luc," he suggested. He gave a wicked grin. "Lucern sounds so formal, and we're a bit beyond that."

Kate didn't smile. She cleared her throat again. "Luc. If you're dead, how can you get . . ." She shifted her eyes downward. He got the drift without her having to explain further, thank goodness, and he shifted away so he wasn't pressed quite so intimately against her.

"I apologize, but I fear I find you quite attractive," he said with great dignity.

"You do?" she asked.

"Yes."

"Oh." She wasn't sure whether she should be happy

about that or not, so she returned to her question. "But, if you're dead—"

"I am not dead," Lucern informed her, rolling his eyes.

"You aren't?" she asked. He shook his head solemnly, so she continued, "Then, you aren't soulless?"

"No." A smile quirked his lips.

"And the rest of your family . . . ?"

He shook his head solemnly.

Kate digested this news, her mind processing that he had written factual history books before his vampire romances. She processed that the first vampire romance had characters named after his parents, the second was about Lissianna and Gregory—a social worker and a therapist, just like the real Lissianna and Gregory—and the third was about Rachel and Etienne, a coroner and a game designer. It seemed pretty obvious that he was still writing historical fact. "How old are you?"

"Six hundred and twelve," he answered calmly. As if it were a normal enough age. Dear Lord, Kate realized with dismay. She *had* lost her mind. She whimpered again.

"It's okay, Kate." Luc brushed the hair back from her face. "I know this is a lot to accept, but it's okay."

"How can it be okay? You're a vampire. And you bit me." She still couldn't believe he'd done that. And why had it felt so good?

"It was just a little nibble," he said. When she glared at him, he tried again. "I'm sorry I bit you, but I was hungry . . . and you smell so delicious." His eyes dropped to her neck as he spoke, and longing crossed his face. Alarm coursed through her, and Kate covered her neck with both hands.

Much to her irritation, he began to chuckle. His chest shook against hers.

"This isn't funny," she snapped. "How would you like to feel like a slab of veal?"

"My dear Kate. You are hardly a slab of veal," he said. Forcing a solemn expression, he added, "You're at least a steak."

Her mouth dropped open in horror. Lucern took advantage of the moment and closed his mouth over hers. Much to Kate's chagrin, the passion he had ignited in her the night before immediately flamed to life again. Apparently, her body didn't care that he was a blood-sucking demon. It liked him just fine. More than fine. And now Kate was having to fight both him and herself. It was a losing battle. A bare moment passed before she gave in with a wrenching moan and slid her arms around his neck.

It was all Lucern was waiting for, apparently, for a heartbeat later she found the sheet that had been caught between them gone and her robe wide open. Which not only left her naked beneath him, but alerted her to the fact that Lucern Argeneau slept in the nude.

Her eyes widened. He slept in the nude and in a bed. When he broke their kiss to nibble at her ear, Kate gasped, "What about your coffin?"

"I left it at home." His voice was a velvet growl laced with laughter.

Kate wasn't sure if he was joking or not, but she stopped worrying about it when his hand closed gently around one breast and squeezed. Moaning, she arched into the hot caress; then her eyes popped open. "Why aren't you cold? I thought vampires were cold."

"I told you, I'm not dead," Lucern reminded her.

"Oh, yeah," Kate muttered. Then Luc claimed her lips again. Shifting down her body, he enclosed one breast in his warm, wet mouth. He suckled on it like a hungry baby, his tongue flicking her nipple as he did. Kate suddenly didn't mind being dinner. Which made her think. "What about garlic?"

"Love it," he said, and shifted his mouth to her other breast. "Someday I'll rub it all over your body and lick it off as proof."

Kate squirmed at the erotic image, then realized it was not unsimilar to the one they were already playing out. She was naked; he was licking her. *Dear God!* She lost track of her thoughts as his hand slid between her thighs.

"Luc," she breathed. Much to her amazement, he stopped, heaved a sigh and shifted to sit beside her.

"Okay. Let's get this out of the way. We're obviously not going to get anywhere until we do," he said with exasperation.

Realizing he'd thought she was going to ask another question, Kate opened her mouth to correct him, then decided against it. She really did want to understand.

"My great-great-grandfather was from what you people call Atlantis."

Kate recoiled. This was the very last thing she'd expected him to say. He sounded like a nut.

Lucern ignored her reaction. "As some have speculated, Atlantis was far advanced scientifically. My great-great-grandfather was a scientist. Just before the city's fall, he developed what people today call nanos—tiny little computerized gizmos. I won't bother explaining the whole of it, but suffice it to say that he combined the science of nanos with microbiology to create microscopic little nanos—a virus of sorts—that when shot into the bloodstream, live there and replicate. They're a parasite of sorts," he explained. "They live off the host, but in return repair and regenerate the host. Which keeps the host, and in turn themselves, young and vital for an indeterminate length of time."

"A virus?" Kate asked with disgust.

"It cannot be caught by touching, and it cannot be caught by kissing."

"What about biting?" she asked, her hand going unconsciously to her neck.

"No. Not by biting. The nanos have to be either shot directly into the bloodstream or consumed."

"Like when Dracula cuts himself and presses his wrist to Mina's mouth?"

"Dracula!" Lucern heaved out a sigh. "Bram's character was based on a cruel, boastful, barbarous bastard. And if he could have kept his mouth shut whilst drinking, Bram Stoker would have never written that damned book—which was mostly wrong due to the fact that his informant was dragged off before he could say too much."

Kate stared, wide-eyed, unsure whether she believed Luc or not. Perhaps they'd both lost their minds.

"I am alive, not dead. I have a soul. I can smell, eat and touch garlic. Crosses have no effect, and I can go into churches as you very well know since you attended my brother's wedding."

"But you can't go out in the sun," Kate said.

"I can," he corrected. "It is just that the sun does a great deal of damage to flesh, which means more blood is needed for the nanos to repair it. Tanning isn't really good for people. It ages the skin. Our bodies won't tan, and the nanos try to replace the skin as it ages. That consumes quite a bit of blood. The more skin exposed and the longer the exposure, the more blood is needed. In the old days there were no blood banks, which meant we had to take the blood from humans and increased the risk of our drawing attention. It was easier to avoid the sunlight and limit our blood-intake requirements. It was also easier to hunt at night."

"And you hunted 'humans.' "

He nodded.

"So you're not a human?"

"Yes. Well." He frowned. "I'm an Atlantian. Same species, different race."

"Oh." She breathed out a sigh, then just sat there digesting it all until her eyes drifted to Lucern's leg. His very pale leg. She supposed a tanning salon was out, and recalled how sometimes he was terribly pale and other times flushed with color. "So when you're really pale it's because—"

"Because I am in need of feeding," he finished. "I'm dehydrated, and the blood has all moved closer to my organs to keep them functioning. When I am flushed, I have fed."

"Dehydrated." She nodded. "Why can't you just drink lots of water? Why do you have to have blood?"

"The nanos use blood to repair and reproduce themselves. The body can't make blood at a fast enough rate.

171

The nanos cause the hunger for blood when they need more by creating some sort of chemical reaction in the body."

"And the teeth?"

"They create those first. It's some sort of genetic encoding." He sighed wearily. "Kate, I've entrusted you with my life and the lives of my family by telling you this. Were you to tell anyone . . . well, most people would think you mad. But it's possible someone might believe, and just one person is enough to endanger all my people."

"How many of you are there?"

"Under five hundred."

She let her surprise show. "So few?"

"Yes. It would be dangerous to have too many. Each of us is only allowed to have one child per century to keep the population down."

"But there should still be more of you. If there are five hundred now, and all of them have children—"

"The five hundred include men, women and children. Out of those, there are perhaps one hundred couples. And then we have a certain number of deaths in each century, too."

Kate was surprised. "I thought you couldn't die."

"We don't age. Everything dies," he explained patiently. "Diseases and viruses have no effect on us—the nanos see to that—and we don't age. But there are other ways to die. For instance, many of us were burned at the stake during the Inquisition."

"What about a stake to the heart?"

Lucern nodded.

"A bullet to the heart?" she asked.

He shook his head. "The nanos would repair the damage quickly."

"Then why does a stake kill?"

"Well, it will kill if you leave it in long enough. The nanos will try to repair the heart around it, but can't force the stake out. The heart won't beat, there will be no fresh blood or nanos brought to help, and they and the body will die."

"Oh. I see." Kate dropped her gaze and found herself staring at his flaccid penis. All this explaining had ruined the mood somewhat—which was a damned shame. Clearing her throat, she lifted her gaze to his face again. "So . . . Bastien sent you blood, but because I left your name off the registration it was returned, and now you're . . ." She hesitated. He was as pale as death. She would have looked like hell had she been as pale as him. He still managed to look strong and sexy, though. It really didn't seem fair. "What happens if you don't get blood?"

"The nanos will start to eat tissue to get the nutrients they need," he admitted reluctantly.

Kate's eyes widened in horror. "That sounds painful."

"It is," he said simply.

"Would it kill you?"

"Eventually, but there would be a lot of pain first."

"And I hung up on Bastien last night," she realized with horror. "Were you able to tell him to send more before—"

"No." Lucern suddenly sounded a little testy.

"Did you call him back?"

"I don't know where he is. All he said was that he was in Europe before you hung up."

"Oh, dear," she said faintly. "How long until it starts to hurt?"

"Four o'clock this morning."

Kate closed her eyes. *Great!* That meant the nanos were eating him already. She had a hungry vampire on her hands. One who was so hungry he was in pain. And she had him in a hotel with over two thousand romance fans waiting to throw themselves at him. It would be like bringing a lion to a hog farm. Kate heaved a sigh. This was all her fault, of course. She supposed she had better fix it.

"All right. How much blood do you need until we can think of a way to get you more?"

He looked surprised. "A full pint would be enough to get me through the day, maybe. But I need—"

"A pint!" Kate shrieked. *Dear Lord.* "A pint? That's like a milk-bag full."

"Roughly, yes."

Kate considered the matter seriously, it hadn't hurt when he bit her last night. Actually, it had felt damned good. But a pint?

"That's how much they take when you give blood," he told her helpfully.

"Is it?" She had never given blood. But she had seen footage of people giving blood on the news whenever they had those big drives. She supposed he was telling the truth.

"Yes, it is," he assured her. "I really need a lot more, but that's all that it's safe to take without side effects. And it would get me by for a bit."

Heaving a sigh, Kate held her arm out, wrist up toward his mouth. "Go ahead."

Lucern blinked, his nose quivering slightly. She wondered if he could smell her blood. The idea that she smelled like dinner to him was rather distressing.

"Go ahead?" he echoed uncertainly.

"Go ahead and bite me," she said impatiently. Turning her head away, she squinted her eyes in case it hurt this time. It was her wrist, after all, not her neck. Maybe she should have given him her neck.

She stiffened as he took her fingers in his. Kate held her breath, waiting for the bite. Her heart stalled, and she nearly snatched her hand away when she felt his lips touch the sensitive skin of her wrist. But there was no great sharp pain; it just felt like he was nibbling the skin.

Well, she thought as the nibbling sensation moved slowly along her wrist, this wasn't so bad. Much nicer than giving blood at the blood bank, she was sure. Much nicer. Exciting even. She squirmed a bit when the nibbling reached the sensitive inner curve of her elbow. Obviously, he hadn't bitten yet. Or had he? Blinking one eye open, she peered at him. All she could see was his head bent over her arm. He had nice hair. Thick and dark and—

"Oh," she breathed as he took a little nip at her skin. It didn't hurt, just startled her in a sexy kind of way. But Kate didn't think he'd drawn blood or anything. He was already moving further up her arm. The vein must not have been good there, she thought vaguely, watching his head rise farther and farther. When he got to the inside of her upper arm, even with her breast, he suddenly shifted to the side and latched onto her nipple. She started in surprise. She almost protested, but as he drew on her sensitive skin, she decided it might be better if he bit her there anyway. It wouldn't show. He laved and suckled her, then drew her deep into his mouth, and Kate decided that if he was biting her, he could do it anytime.

One of his hands slid up along her stomach to find her other breast. Kate slowly drifted back on the bed, telling herself that it was to prevent feeling faint after he took the pint, but the truth was her body was shaking horribly, her muscles quivering with excitement. She didn't think she could have stayed upright under his sensual onslaught had she wanted to.

Lucern followed her down and braced himself with one elbow as he continued to pleasure her. Kate closed her eyes and let her hands drift into his hair. They knotted and tugged there of their own accord. She didn't mean to interrupt his meal, but she had a sudden hunger of her own—she desperately wanted him to kiss her. When he raised his mouth from her nipple, Kate saw that her flesh was still intact. No biting yet. It appeared that feeding was a rather involved ordeal. She should have known. Lucern wasn't the eat-and-run type.

His mouth came down on hers as she'd wanted, and Kate sighed into the kiss. She also allowed her hands to drift down over his back to find his behind, and she pushed him tight against her even while arching up to meet him. He ground against her without entering, but it seemed to excite him as much as her, because his kiss grew hard, his mouth demanding.

Kate moaned when he tore his lips away and shifted to her neck. Somehow, she knew the time for biting had come and felt herself tensing in preparation. Then she was distracted by the way he moved over her, urging her legs apart. He settled in the cradle of her thighs, his hardness pressing against her.

"I want you," he whispered in her ear, then nibbled at the tender lobe, a sharp tooth running lightly over the skin.

Kate suddenly had the mad idea that, were her ears not pierced, he could have done it for her.

"Kate?"

She forced herself to concentrate. He was asking permission. She wasn't sure for what exactly. To bite her, or to sink his body into hers? Probably both. Kate opened her mouth to vaguely tell him to go ahead when there was a knock at the door.

"Hello? Hey! You two!" Chris called through the door. "Look. I hate to bother you, but the welcome brunch and RT awards start in about fifteen minutes. Are you guys ready?"

Chapter Ten

"Is Lucern okay? He looks awfully pale."

At Allison's comment, Kate glanced worriedly at her author. Luc *was* awfully pale. She'd thought so in his room, but he seemed even more so under the lights here in the large reception area of the welcome brunch. She should have insisted that he bite her.

She had tried, of course. She'd told him to just do it, but Chris had been knocking insistently on the door, and Lucern had refused. He'd feared she might be faint afterward, and he didn't want her trying to get ready, suffering a dizzy spell and perhaps falling. Besides, there wasn't time, he'd said. He'd do it later.

Now, as she took in the pallor of his skin, she could have kicked herself for not being more insistent.

"Kate?"

She turned and forced a smile for her boss. "He's a little jet-lagged. He'll be okay."

Allison accepted the lie and turned her attention

back to her meal, leaving Kate to fret over Lucern. She was going to make him bite her first thing upon leaving the brunch; they could run upstairs for a quickie before going to the reader hospitality suite. And then she'd have to find a way to get him a real supply of blood. She'd considered the matter, and even if they were able to get hold of Bastien today, she was sure it would be tomorrow before he could arrange another shipment to be delivered.

Kate frowned as she realized that Bastien could be calling right this minute, and there was no one in their room to answer the call. And there wouldn't be all day. Or tonight either if they attended the cover model reunion. Perhaps they could skip that. Lucern wasn't really needed there. The fans would all be interested in the male cover models and might not notice his absence. Allison and Chuck would, however. Kate frowned down at her plate. Allison wouldn't mind, but Chuck would. As far as he was concerned, the company had paid for Lucern to be there and he would want his money's worth.

"Does he speak?"

Kate glanced sharply up at Chuck's acidic question. She had made sure that Chris was on one side of Lucern and she on the other. Allison was directly on her right, and Chuck was next to Allison, but the publisher was leaning in front of the editorial director, his chin practically resting on her chest as he spoke. Allison was seething, and Kate couldn't blame her. Chuck was something of a pig, hitting on all the women in the office and trying to look down their tops. He wasn't well liked by the staff, and they could hardly wait for him to be replaced. As a rule, presidents at Roundhouse were changed almost yearly. Kate just hoped Chuck Morgan wasn't the exception. No one at Roundhouse had been happy when he had arrived to replace George Sassoon. Their last president had been an exceptional man who had moved to publishing from radio and television, bringing all of that savvy with him. He had done wonderful things for Roundhouse. No one had been surprised when he had been snapped up by a bigger company. Chuck Morgan was a poor replacement.

Her gaze drifted past his sneering face to Jodi Hampton, the writer who sat beside him. Jodi was throwing curious glances at Lucern. Kate wasn't surprised. Aside from him being an attractive man, Lucern was receiving an unusual amount of VIP treatment. The editors and personnel of Roundhouse were supposed to be spread out among a couple of tables so that all their writers felt included. But Chris and Kate weren't going to leave Lucern's side all week, and Allison and Chuck had wanted to meet the mysterious Mr. Argeneau, so they were all grouped around him. Which left only Deeana Stancyk and Tom Duchamp, the VP of Promotion, to circulate among the thirty other Roundhouse writers in attendance.

"I said, does he speak?"

Kate's gaze shifted back to Chuck. He was one of the few men whose features reflected his unpleasant nature. He had a pockmarked, florid face, a drooping gray mustache and a bespeckled, balding head.

Kate considered the question. Unfortunately, Lucern was rather taciturn at the best of times. At the moment, he was silent as stone. She opened her mouth to offer an excuse for his silence, then just as promptly changed her mind. They had wanted him here; she had got him. Perhaps if they weren't happy with his performance, they wouldn't make her pester him in the future. She merely shrugged and said, "Not much."

Chuck didn't seem pleased. Kate didn't care. It was the truth, and she couldn't be held responsible for Lucern's nature. Her gaze slid to the writer again. Chris was talking, and Lucern was nodding dully. There were lines of tension around his eyes that worried her. It made her wonder if he was in a lot of pain. She immediately began trying to think of a way to get him blood—and more blood than the pint he'd said it would be safe for her to give him. She briefly considered finding him a lineup of victims to bite, but as much as she enjoyed the idea of putting Chuck at the front of the line, there was no one else she wanted to feed to him.

Kate was still pondering the problem when the plates were cleared from the tables and the awards ceremony began. She listened halfheartedly as the nominees were named for each category, followed by the winner. Kate clapped when the others did, but she was mostly lost in thought.

"And the final nominee is Luke Amirault's *Love Bites.*"

Kate jerked upright in her seat as Luc's pseudonym was called out. She wasn't at all surprised that Lucern was doing much the same thing next to her. She'd forgotten to tell him that his book was nominated in three different categories. She winced when he turned an accusing glare on her.

181

"You're nominated. That doesn't mean you'll win," Kate said soothingly.

"And the winner is . . . Luke Amirault for *Love Bites*!"

"*Merde*," Lucern muttered.

"Shit," Kate echoed in English. She hesitated for a moment, but when Lucern showed no sign of getting up, she leaned toward him to explain, "You have to go up and get your award."

"I don't want to."

Kate felt her heart squeeze at the childlike complaint. Six hundred years old and he still sounded like a baby. Men were the same no matter the species . . . or was it race? Whatever. Catching his elbow in her hand, she stood abruptly, forcing him up with her. "Neither do I. So we'll do it together."

Much to her relief, he allowed her to force him to his feet and then toward the stage at the far end of the room. People were clapping and calling out congratulations, some yelling they really enjoyed his books. Lucern seemed oblivious to it all. The skin on his face was tight, his expression almost pained as he walked doggedly forward. Kate couldn't decide if it was due to hunger or a reaction to being the center of attention. She knew he must hate this sort of thing. She'd learned of his reclusive ways while in Toronto. And if she hadn't caught on after three days in his company, his mother and sister had revealed a lot about him at the wedding.

Kathryn Falk, Lady Barrow—the woman behind Romantic Times Book Club Magazine, the conference, and various other concerns—was waiting on stage to present the award herself. She smiled widely as Kate and Lucern mounted the steps to the podium; then con-

cern flickered on her face as she noted their odd behavior. Kate tried for a brighter smile to reassure the
woman, but she could have used a little reassurance
herself. Lucern wasn't the speech-making sort, and
some sort of speech would be expected.

"Congratulations, Mr. Amirault," Lady Barrow said as
she handed over the award. "I've very much enjoyed
your vampire series."

Lucern grunted, took the award and started to walk
offstage. Kate gaped after him, then muttered under her
breath and hurried after him to catch him by the arm.

"You have to say thank-you," she hissed, urging him
back toward Lady Barrow and the podium.

"I don't want to."

Kate frowned at the weakness in his voice. She almost preferred his "No's" and had to wonder just how
much the lack of blood could affect his mind. If she
didn't find him some blood soon, might he lose it entirely and just go nuts? She cringed at the idea.

"Just say thank-you," she ordered grimly, steering him
to the podium.

"Is he all right?" Lady Barrow asked in a whisper as
Lucern paused in front of the microphone. He stared
blankly out at the sea of faces. Kate wondered if the
crowd looked like a feast of steaks to him, then nodded.

"Jet lag," she lied.

"Are you sure that's all?" Kathryn looked doubtful, so
Kate added, "And a bit of a tummy flu, I think." Then
she gave in, admitting, "He isn't at all well."

"Oh, dear," Lady Barrow murmured.

"But we're hoping it passes quickly," she assured the

woman. "We might miss the cover model reunion to go to the doctor."

"Doctor? At night?"

"It was the earliest appointment we could get," Kate lied.

"Oh." Lady Barrow shook her head, then seemed to realize that Lucern had been standing silently at the microphone for several moments. The room had fallen into an expectant hush.

Kate moved to his side and gave him a nudge. "Say thank-you."

"Thank you," he said dutifully. It was a rather ungrateful growl. And he immediately stepped back after saying it. Kate cringed, but Lady Barrow saved the day by stepping up between them and catching his arm. She urged him forward again, then took control of the microphone and said, "Ladies . . . and gentlemen." She added the last with a grin toward the table of male models, the only males present other than the handful of male publishing personnel and the occasional writer's husband. "As you can see from his pallor, Mr. Amirault isn't feeling well, but he insisted on attending today's ceremony to thank you all for your support." She allowed a moment to pass for that to sink in, then continued, "I for one am grateful he showed up. Let's all give him a round of applause and thank him for his wonderful stories. Thank you, Luke."

Kathryn Falk turned to give him a hug, and the crowd broke into applause.

Relief coursed through Kate. Lady Barrow had saved the day! Then she noticed how Lucern's nostrils were flaring, and that he lowered his face to the woman's neck. Even more disconcerting was the silver glow that had come into his eyes. His lips moved along Lady Barrow's skin in search of a pulsing vein.

Kate's eyes widened in horror. He was about to bite Lady Barrow right there on the damned stage!

"No!" The shriek left Kate's lips as she saw Lucern's teeth extend. It was a loud shriek. The entire room fell into stunned silence. But Kate didn't care, because Lady Barrow jerked out of Lucern's arms and whirled around in amazement. Lucern scowled at her for the interruption of his meal.

"Er . . ." Kate said into the deafening silence. Moving to the microphone, she added, "No. There's . . . er . . . no need to thank him. Lucern is . . . he's just grateful he . . . er . . . had this opportunity to thank you all. Er . . . thank you."

The crowd began to clap again, but Kate hardly noticed. Lucern was moving closer to the unsuspecting Lady Barrow, that hungry look still in his eyes. Forcing a smile, Kate snatched his arm and marched him away.

"You were going to bite her," she accused.

"I just wanted a bit." He sounded sullen.

"Just a bit?" she exclaimed. "Right there on the stage for all to see?"

"They would have thought it a publicity stunt," he defended himself. Then he sighed and admitted miserably, "I couldn't help myself. She has strong, sweet blood."

Kate stared at him. "You didn't—"

"No, you stopped me in time. But I can tell by the smell."

Kate grimaced, then noted that the lines around his

185

eyes had deepened and were around his mouth as well. "How bad is the hunger right now?" It was a stupid question. The man had nearly bitten Lady Barrow on-stage. The hunger was bad. What she really wanted to know was, "I mean, are you in pain?"

He nodded grimly.

"That little bit of sunlight yesterday caused this much trouble?" she asked. If so, it seemed to her that vampires were weaker than humans in some ways. Rather fragile, in this respect at least.

"That little bit of sunlight yesterday, the guy seated next to me on the plane with a cold who kept coughing at me, the—"

"Being around sick people uses up more blood?" Kate asked with alarm. They were in a hotel with a couple thousand people—germs were probably rampant here. No wonder he was such a shut-in.

"Yes." Lucern nodded. "The nanos apparently surround disease and kill it off, but it takes up more—"

"Blood," Kate finished unhappily.

"Yes. And then there is the sunlight in here today."

Kate peered around the bright room with surprise. The walls were solid without windows, but there were skylights overhead. They were frosted skylights, and it hadn't occurred to her that they might be a problem. She should have thought of it. Her gaze moved to the table they sat at, and Kate almost groaned as she realized that she had chosen a table positioned directly under a skylight.

"The alcohol last night didn't help either," Lucern continued. "It dehydrates the body, too."

Kate frowned. She'd noted the crushed beer cans, empty pizza box and piles of peanut shells around the coffee table in front of the television this morning. It looked as if Chris and Lucern had enjoyed a boys' night. Now Luc was paying for it in spades. It seemed his state was a result of a lot of things. The latest reason was her fault, however.

They had nearly reached the table. Kate steered Lucern away from it and toward one of the exits. "Come on."

"Where are we going?" He sounded confused.

"To find you food." She stepped out of the reception hall and peered around. There really wasn't time to go to their suite. Somewhere closer was needed. She dragged him toward the men's room.

"Go inside and see if it's empty," she suggested. "If it isn't, make whoever's in there leave. You can do that, can't you? You know, control their mind and—"

"Yes. But—"

"Just do it," Kate insisted.

Lucern shook his head, but pushed through the door. A couple minutes later, the door opened and a man walked out. Kate recognized him as one of the male models. She smiled nervously at him, but he didn't smile back—he didn't even seem to notice her standing there. His eyes were glazed, his expression blank.

She watched him walk away, then slid into the bathroom, relieved to find Lucern alone.

"Okay." She walked determinedly to him. "Let's do it."

Lucern shook his head as she held out her wrist. "I can't."

"What do you mean, you can't?" she snapped in exasperation. "You've already bitten Chris and me once, so of course you can. Just get your teeth out."

"Kate, I can't. It would hurt."

"It didn't hurt last night," she pointed out.

"That was because you were overwhelmed with sexual desire."

Kate flushed, but didn't bother denying it. She *had* been rather hot and bothered. "What's that got to do with it?" Her eyes narrowed. "Chris wasn't—"

"Of course not." He was starting to sound impatient. "But I can control *his* mind."

"So control mine."

"I can't, Kate. Your mind is too strong."

"It is?" She felt pleasure fill her. Her mind was too strong. Wasn't that nice? She had a strong mind. Oh, she realized suddenly, she even had a stronger mind than Chris, because, from what she'd seen upon returning to the room last night, Lucern had no difficulty in controlling him. She would have liked to gloat about that, but Lucern was still speaking.

"The only time I can get into your head is when you're sleeping, or when you're wrapped up in passion. At least, I assume I can then. You didn't feel any pain when I bit you last night, did you?"

Kate shook her head. "No. No pain at all."

He nodded. "Then your mind must have opened enough for me to infuse it with pleasure."

"Hmm." Kate digested that. "How do you know you can get into my head when I'm sleeping?"

Guilt crossed Lucern's face, and Kate suddenly recalled the erotic dream she'd had in his home. "You didn't . . ." she said.

He flinched at the accusation, then raised his hands placatingly. "I was just . . . checking on you. And you looked so sweet and sexy, I started thinking about what I'd like to do to you and I didn't realize you were receiving my thoughts until you . . . er . . ." He shrugged uncomfortably. "I stopped right away."

Kate glared at him, feeling vulnerable and exposed. The dream she'd had in his home hadn't been a dream at all. Or had it? His fantasy? Was it a dream? A waking dream? It hadn't been hers.

The bathroom door opened, and both she and Lucern glanced sharply toward it as a middle-aged man started into the room. Lucern scowled at him, his eyes flashing silver fire. *Leave.*

The man stopped abruptly, his eyes glazing over; then he turned and obediently left the room.

The minute they were alone again, Kate grabbed Lucern's hand and pulled him into one of the stalls—she could hardly let him keep putting the whammy on people who entered the bathroom. The stall was a close fit, but she supposed it was good enough for biting. "Just do it, Luc. You need the blood. You're starting to look like the walking dead."

"I don't want to hurt you."

She heaved a sigh of exasperation, but was secretly pleased that he was so reluctant to cause her pain. Especially when he was obviously suffering so horribly himself from something she could ease. The pain would be the equivalent of a shot. At least, she hoped that was the extent of it.

"Look. What if I open my mind to you?" she suggested, though she hadn't a clue how to do it. She supposed she would just think open thoughts. "Let's try that, shall we? I'll open my mind and—"

"Kate," Lucern began, and she knew he was going to refuse. She was standing in a damned men's john—in a stall, no less—offering the stupid man her blood like she was some freak female Renfield, and he just stood there being all chivalrous and Old World. He must be really old. In her experience, men these days took what was offered regardless of whether it was good for the woman or not. Hell, sometimes they took what wasn't offered.

"Dammit, Luc," she interrupted impatiently. Grabbing the collar of her scoop-necked dress, she twisted it over to reveal the pin she'd used to attach her bra strap to the material.

"What are you doing?" He was scowling again.

Good, she thought irritably. She was feeling rather crabby, herself. She'd thought only babies needed spoon-feeding. Undoing the pin, she slid it free of her bra, quickly jabbed herself on the tip of a finger, then squeezed it viciously until a nice fat drop of blood came to the surface. She shoved it under his nose determinedly.

"Are you hungry?" she asked. She followed when he backed up against the stall wall trying to avoid her finger, then waved it under his nose. Triumph rose within her when she saw his nostrils flare. "Come on. You're hungry. Have a taste. Just a lick. If you don't like it, we'll find you someone else. If you do, a little nibble at my neck will make you feel better. Come on, Lucern, try a little Kate for breakfast and . . ." Her words died on a startled gasp as he licked the blood off the tip of her finger. It was such a quick scrape of his tongue across her finger she hardly felt it, but much to her satisfaction, his eyes glowed silver. She had him.

Kate tipped her head to the side and squinted in preparation for what was to come, then remembered about the opening-her-mind thing. She thought, *My mind is open. Lucern can come in. My mind is open. Lucern can come in.*

Apparently, opening one's mind wasn't so easy. She felt Lucern's hands on her arms, then the brush of his lips against her neck, then agonizing pain as he began to insert his teeth.

"Ow, ow, ow." Despite herself, Kate began to struggle. Lucern pulled away at once. He still held her, though, his hands digging into her arms, his breath coming heavy, the silver fire in his eyes an inferno as he fought to control his thirst.

Kate bit her lip unhappily, ashamed to learn that she was a wuss. But it had hurt so much. No shot had ever been that bad. But, then, shots weren't nearly as large as Lucern's teeth. She pressed a hand to her throat. "I guess I don't know how to open my mind."

Lucern pulled his hands away. "You'd better leave. I don't think I can control myself much longer."

Kate hesitated, then moved forward, sliding her arms around his neck.

"What are you doing?" he asked harshly.

"Well, if I have to be sexually excited to let you in so it doesn't hurt, you'd better get busy and excite me," she said.

"Kate, we're in a water closet. This is hardly the place to—"

"Not very adventurous, are you?" she asked. "Forget where we are and get to it, buddy. This is a public washroom—someone could come in at any moment," she pointed out. Leaning up, she pressed her lips to his. It was all she had to do. Lucern promptly began to kiss her back, his arms closing around her like steel bands.

Kate supposed what followed was the vampire version of a quickie. It was not at all like the passionate moments they had shared in their suite. She couldn't explain it, but there was intent behind his every action, as if he weren't fully involved, but performing certain acts to excite her as necessary steps toward biting her. He seemed distant somehow. Uninvolved. His kisses were practiced and still exciting, but even as she moaned in response and opened to him, she was aware that he wasn't completely there. At least, she was aware of it at first. As his tongue thrust into her mouth, she became a little too preoccupied to care.

Lucern unsnapped the buttons that ran down the front of her dress and slid his hand inside, then under her bra to cup one breast in his cool palm. Kate moaned into his mouth. She shuddered as his thumb flicked the tip of her nipple.

Next he slid his leg between both of hers, forcing her dress upward until his upper thigh rubbed against the very center of her. Kate gasped, then kissed him almost frantically. When Lucern broke away, she moaned, her head dropping backward as she arched and shifted against his leg, wanting more. She felt his lips nibble along her neck, but everything felt so good she merely murmured her pleasure and tilted her head to give him better access. Then she was aware of his sucking at her neck. This time she didn't mistake it for a hickey, but there was no pain . . . until her foggy brain told her what he was doing and that there should be pain. The excitement started to fade away.

Just as Kate felt the first faint stirring of pain, Lucern seemed to realize what was happening and distracted her. He slid his hand under her skirt, his fingers feathered lightly up her inner thigh, urging her legs a little further apart. Then he pushed the wispy cloth of her panties aside and stroked her. Kate forgot all about what was happening at her neck She gasped and murmured in pleasure, squirming in his caress, then cried out as he slid a finger into her.

"Oh, Luc." She gasped, sliding her fingers through his hair and clutching his head to her as if it were her only anchor to sanity. She moaned as she rode his hand, her body humming with an excitement so fierce her legs grew weak. Kate opened her eyes and tried to warn him that her legs were giving out, but she was distracted by the fact that everything seemed blurry. She wanted to tell Lucern that, too, but it seemed too much effort. An odd lassitude was stealing over her.

The stall wall at her back vibrated as the door of the next cubicle banged open. Kate supposed that someone was in the washroom with them. It didn't bother her too much, but then Lucern lifted his head and frowned. He glanced back at Kate, and concern covered his expression.

Cursing softly, he adjusted his hold and turned Kate, lowering her to sit on the toilet. He didn't say anything, but his expression was grim as he straightened her clothes and did up the buttons of her dress. Once he'd put her back together, he unlocked the stall door, peered out, then lifted her back to her feet, pulled her arm over his shoulder and half-walked, half-carried her out of the bathroom. Kate didn't see anyone, but the stall door next to the one they'd been in was closed and she could see feet under it. Someone *had* come in, she realized with vague interest.

"There you are! I've been looking for you two everywhere."

Kate peered around and spotted Chris coming toward them. His expression was tense, his voice urgent. "Chuck is livid. Lucern won both of the other categories he was nominated for and wasn't around to accept the . . . Jesus, Kate, are you all right? You look like hell."

"She isn't feeling well," Lucern explained, mentally kicking himself. It was his fault. He'd taken too much blood—he hadn't been able to help himself. Once the sweet, warm fluid had burst over his parched tongue and into his mouth, he'd been lost. If someone hadn't distracted him, he didn't know what would have happened. His anxious gaze slid to Kate's wan face, and he berated himself again. Fortunately, he hadn't taken enough to cause serious damage, but Kate was going to feel weak and—

"I thought you were the one not feeling well," Chris said with confusion. The editor moved to take Kate's other arm and some of her weight.

"It's catching," Lucern muttered. He steered them toward the elevators.

"Great," Chris said. "Then I'm sure to catch it next." He brightened. "But you seem to be getting over it. You've got some color in your cheeks again. At least it passes quickly."

Lucern flinched guiltily. The color in his cheeks was thanks to Kate's blood. It was also the reason she was now so weak. He was feeling a bit better. A bit. He'd guess that if he could get another couple of quarts of blood, he'd be back to his old self.

"Where are we going?" Chris asked as they waited for the elevator to arrive.

"I'm taking her upstairs to lie down."

"No." Kate suddenly forced herself to straighten. She managed the attempt, but swayed weakly. "We should go to the hospitality suite."

"You're in no shape to go to some stupid hospitality suite," Lucern argued. "You need something sweet and rest. To rebuild . . ." He paused, not wishing to say more in front of Chris.

"I just have to sit there. They'll have refreshments," Kate insisted. She turned to Chris. "Are they almost done with the awards?"

"Yes. Another half-hour, I would think." The editor glanced at Lucern as the elevator doors opened and they helped Kate aboard. "She should be okay in the hospitality suite. We can keep an eye on her. Chuck will have a fit if she doesn't show."

Lucern remained silent as Chris pressed an elevator button. He wasn't happy with the decision, but he didn't want to jeopardize Kate's job. And he would keep an eye on her.

Chapter Eleven

Kate tipped the bags over and watched everything she'd purchased tumble out onto the bed; then, she began to sort through the pile. Snatching the black sweater and black wool hat, she hurried to the closet and grabbed her black dress pants. She pulled them on quickly, donning the sweater, too, but stuffing the hat into a pocket. Then she hurried back to the bed to start tossing the things into her new black backpack. Once she was done, she checked her watch.

Kate had spent the better part of the afternoon sitting in a chair next to Lucern in the Roundhouse hospitality suite, eating all the food he kept shoving at her and dutifully drinking the orange juice he'd made Chris go out and find. It had been interminable. Kate had started to feel better rather quickly after drinking the orange juice and eating, at least physically better, but Lucern had hovered anxiously over her. The man had acted like a mother bird.

Lucern had also reeked of guilt, for which Kate could have kicked him. He had nothing to feel guilty for—she had practically forced him to take her blood. And, yes, it had briefly weakened her, but it hadn't harmed her in the end. Still, she did not have aspirations to be on a dinner menu. Even if being there had been mostly pleasurable, she would avoid offering herself up as another meal. So she'd fretted with the problem of how to feed him all afternoon.

Kate had been to several conferences and had never seen the Roundhouse hospitality suite so busy. The fans had arrived en masse, filling the room to bursting, the overflow spilling out into the hall. Chuck had been clearly pleased. Allison, Tom and Deeana had had their hands full answering questions, and giving out little key chains with miniature book covers on them to the readers. Chris had been forced to leave Lucern and Kate several times to confer with some of his own writers, but that had been all right, they'd done fine. With Lucern, the fans had been blessedly gentle. Perhaps that was because of Lady Barrow's announcement that he wasn't feeling well, or perhaps it was because, while he no longer looked like a walking corpse, Lucern was still pale and apparently fragile. Whatever the case, the fans Kate had feared might overwhelm him had all been gracious and sweet. They had also done most of the talking, telling Lucern how much they enjoyed his work and not seeming to notice that he said little in response.

It was at the hospitality suite that Kate had come up with her plan. It was risky and dangerous and utter madness, but it was the only thing she could think of. Knowing that Lucern would balk at it, she'd kept the plan to herself, asked Chris to accompany him to the cover model reunion dinner, and had slipped out to collect what they would need. Now she checked to be sure that she had everything and peered at her wristwatch again.

She had instructed Chris to bring Lucern back to the room directly after the dinner and skip the rest of the evening. That should be soon. Her gaze went to the hotel window. The sun had set while she'd been about her task; it was dark night outside. That was good. They would need darkness.

Laughter coming from the other room told Kate the men had returned. Curious as to their levity, she slipped into the living area. Her eyebrows rose as she took in Lucern's chagrined expression and Chris's amusement.

"Had a good time?" she asked lightly. Her curiosity grew as Chris laughed again.

"You wouldn't believe it, Kate," her friend exclaimed. "I've never seen anything like it. I mean, you know how the women can be, gathering around the few men in attendance like bees around a flower, but this was madness. I swear, one woman actually plopped herself in Luc's lap and propositioned him for everyone to hear. I thought he was going to bolt." He laughed again. "Luc looked terrified."

Lucern grimaced as Chris went on to describing several other advances he'd had to parry. It *had* been madness down there. Lucern detested modern women with their aggressive behavior—except for Kate, of course, who was only aggressive in the nicest possible way. But the women he and Chris had just escaped . . . dear God! Lucern hadn't been so worried since that time when he was a boy and the villagers had attacked the castle, torches and pitchforks in hand.

He gave a shudder as Chris recounted the tale of the woman who had leapt into the elevator after them. She'd actually begged Lucern to father her child, claiming she desperately wanted a son as talented as he. Despite the woman's plump flesh and prodigious breasts, Lucern hadn't had trouble refusing the generous offer. He had, however, had trouble resisting the urge for a little taste of her blood. If Chris hadn't been there, he very well might have tried despite the risk. The relief Kate's donation had given him earlier had not lasted long. His body was in too much need. He was again quite literally desperate to feed. It was so bad that he had decided to retire to his room, slip through the door leading directly out into the hall, and go find himself a snack. Several snacks. Although he had to remember not to drink too deeply, as he had done with Kate. His mother and father had taught him long ago that one did not slaughter the cows that produced one's milk.

"I'm heading back now."

Lucern turned his attention to what was going on around him. Chris moved toward the door.

"Willing to brave those women again?" Kate teased.

Her friend grinned. "I have to talk to a couple of my authors. Besides, they weren't bothering me. Not with Lucern there. Maybe they will without him," he added with a wink. But as he opened the door, he was nearly run down.

Lucern gaped in horror as he suddenly found himself surrounded by a pack of excited, yammering women.

Every one of them was pushing and grabbing at him. Lucern backed away until he found himself up against a wall, but still they crowded forward, pressing against him, the sweet smell of their blood the only thing he could really concentrate on. He caught words and bits of phrases here and there, but none of it made sense.

". . . just love your books . . ."

". . . couldn't afford to attend the conference, but live here . . ."

". . . waited around the lobby . . ."

". . . recognized you from your picture at the back of the book . . ."

". . . followed you to your room . . ."

". . . just love you!"

". . . please bite me. Turn me into a vampire . . ."

". . . autograph my breasts?"

"Out!"

Lucern definitely heard and even understood Kate's shout. He also heard her next strident words: "A little of your *special help* wouldn't hurt here, Luc!"

Lucern smiled. He loved it when she called him Luc. Then understanding struck him. She wanted him to use his mind control to convince the women to leave. He only hoped he could focus enough to do so. Doing his best to ignore his hunger, Lucern tried to focus. He sent the message out to the women that they wanted to leave.

Kate and Chris both helped, each grabbing two women by an arm and urging them toward the door. Lucern dealt with the others by mind control, releasing their minds the moment the door was closed behind them.

"Geez," Chris muttered as he turned the lock. " 'Bite me?' 'Turn me into a vampire?' These women have to learn the difference between reality and fiction."

Lucern and Kate exchanged glances, but they said nothing as Chris moved to the door of his bedroom.

"I guess I'll slip out the door from my room. Hopefully, the women aren't watching that one. I'll stop at the front desk and have security men sent up to remove the women from the hall."

"Okay. Thanks." Kate waved him off. Both Lucern and she were silent as they waited for the sound of his door opening and closing.

Kate sighed when it came. She turned to Lucern with a determination that, even in his depleted state, he knew couldn't be good. Her first words didn't reassure him.

"I have a plan."

"What do you have in the bag?" Lucern asked with bewilderment as they left the hotel.

"Stuff," Kate answered a tad shortly. She wasn't pleased with him at the moment, because he hadn't immediately fallen in with her plan. He'd heard her out, a disbelieving expression on his face, then had tried to talk her out of it. He had done his best to convince her to let him simply go bite a couple of conference guests, thinking it a much more sensible plan, but she seemed offended he'd even consider it.

He'd briefly wondered whether her upset might be because she didn't like the idea of his indulging with another woman the delights he did with her, but then he'd tossed that thought aside. She already knew,

201

thanks to walking in while he was trying to feed on Chris, that he needn't bother with such methods. He supposed she was just generally offended on behalf of mankind itself. Humans didn't mind slaughtering baby cows for veal, but seemed testy at the idea of being food themselves.

"If it's too heavy, I'd be happy to carry it—as I told you upstairs," Kate added through gritted teeth.

Lucern felt a smile threatening at her irritation. He forced it back at once. He rarely smiled. Chalking up his desire to do so now as just a symptom of his blood-less state, he shifted her bag to his other hand. The woman hadn't given it up easily. After more than an hour of arguing, Lucern had finally given in to her plan. Mostly because he was starved, she was stubborn, and it was the only way to get out of their room. He knew darn well she would hound him until he agreed.

Having relented and agreed to try her plan to garner him a one-stop meal, however, didn't mean Lucern had given up courtesy. When she'd produced her "bag of tricks," as she referred to it, he'd immediately insisted on carrying it. Kate seemed to see the move as some slight to her strength. She could carry her own bags, thank you very much. But he wouldn't let her.

Sheesh, Lucern thought. Modern women sure were a pain.

"Here we are," Kate announced, leading him to a taxi. She gave the driver an address as Lucern followed her in. Apparently, she had done her research. She obviously believed in being prepared—just like Bastien.

Despite the pain he was suffering, Lucern felt his lips

twitch with amusement. He couldn't help it; Kate was just so delightfully cute.

It wasn't a long ride. When the taxi stopped and Lucern got out, it was to find they had been dropped in front of a restaurant, of all places. Luc stood staring at the building in bemusement as Kate followed him out.

"Kate, I think we're in the wrong place," he said as the taxi pulled away. "I don't see—"

"This way." She took his arm and steered him up the street. "I didn't want the cab to drop us off in front, in case our little adventure made the papers tomorrow. The cabbie might have remembered picking us up and dropping us off there, and they would be able to trace us back to the hotel. Now, that isn't a worry." Her voice was brittle. Despite this being her idea, she seemed extremely tense.

"Ah. Good thinking," Lucern murmured. He didn't want to point out that the way they were dressed—not to mention the metallic clinking of the backpack he carried—would make them memorable anywhere. And being dropped off a couple of buildings down would be of little help. Still, it wouldn't be a concern. Lucern would see to that. He had no intention of endangering Kate.

He spotted the building they sought, but Kate grabbed his arm and led him past it. He was about to ask why, when suddenly she turned down an alley that ran along the opposite side of the building.

"I cased the place before I went shopping," she whispered as she skulked down the alley, dragging him behind her with one clawlike hand entrapping his wrist. She was walking in the most peculiar fashion; crouched

203

over as if she thought that would reduce the chance of being seen.

Lucern eyed her behavior with some bewilderment, and wondered if her usually sensible mind had snapped. Surely she understood that walking in such a manner made her no less visible, and also made her look as if she was up to no good. Apparently not.

He sighed as the toe of his shoe hit a stone and sent it skittering, which in turn sent Kate skittering, too. She burst into a run, dragging him along with her until they reached a dumpster a little more than halfway down the alley. She pulled him behind it, then crouched there and peered out fearfully.

"Did you hear that?" she asked in an anxious whisper. "I thought I heard something. I don't see anyone, though. Maybe it was just a cat or something."

"Or a rat," Lucern bent to whisper in her ear. He knew it was a mean thing to do, especially when he knew what she'd heard. But he simply couldn't help himself. She was so easy to tease. He hadn't had this much fun in . . . well, centuries, he realized with surprise.

"A rat!" Kate straightened abruptly, her head slamming into the bottom of his chin.

Lucern jerked back. Wincing, he rubbed the spot even as Kate grabbed her head and issued a howl of pain. She cut the noise off almost at once, of course, but still, Lucern couldn't help but think that perhaps stealth was no longer possible in this endeavor. Kate wasn't very good at this crime business.

"Shh," she said sternly, as if Luc had been the one who'd just let out the caterwaul. Lucern let her get away with it, instead watching with interest as she pulled two woollen hats from her pocket. She donned one, tugging it onto her head and pulling it down over her face. It was a ski mask. When she had the holes adjusted so that only her eyes and lips showed, Kate handed him the other.

"Put it on," she ordered. Taking the backpack he held, she set it on the ground with a clank.

"I am *not* putting this on," he said with disdain.

Kate heaved an impatient sigh. "Put it on, Lucern. I don't want to open the papers tomorrow and find your wan face glaring back at me."

"How could—"

"Security cameras," she interrupted grimly.

Lucern snorted. "They would hardly have security cameras in a—"

"They have security cameras everywhere nowadays," she interrupted again. "It lowers the insurance or something."

Muttering under his breath, Lucern gave in. Donning the stupid thing, he felt like an idiot, and was grateful none of his family members were there to witness it. Etienne in particular would have enjoyed taunting him for decades. Knowing Kate could not see his scowl did not prevent his aiming a particularly ferocious one at her. Not that she noticed; she was quite busy sifting through whatever was in her bag. There was an awful lot of banging and clanking going on.

What the hell had she brought? he wondered irritably.

"In your years of living," she began in a strained tone, "I don't suppose you learned anything about burglary, did you?"

"A thing or two," Lucern admitted.

"Good." She sounded relieved. "Because all I know about it is what I've seen on TV."

Lucern raised an eyebrow, but since again he knew she couldn't see it, he said in a solemn tone, "One would never credit it."

"It's true," she told him earnestly. "I like cop shows, and I just went by those. I hope I got what we need. I wasn't sure—I just went through the hardware store and grabbed anything that looked useful."

Ah. This explained why she hadn't attended the cover model reunion. Lucern knelt at her side and peered curiously into her bag. The first thing he saw were several long, pointed tools. They looked like screwdrivers but with sharpened ends. There were several of them, in a variety of sizes. "Scratch awls? What are those for?"

"They always use sharp, pointy things to break into places on TV," Kate explained. "To pick locks." She paused, her expression thoughtful. "Or credit cards." She frowned briefly, then cursed. "I knew I should have brought my purse."

Lucern wasn't really paying attention; he was sorting through the bag. "A pipe wrench?" he asked, lifting the large, heavy plumber's tool.

Kate bit her lip and shifted uncomfortably. "I thought maybe if you couldn't pick the locks, you could break a window."

Lucern arched an eyebrow, then pulled out a coil of . . . "Rope? Rope, Kate? What the heck did you bring rope for?"

"In case you had to climb into or out of a second-story window," she explained defensively.

"It's a one-story building," he pointed out.

"Oh, yes." She peered at the building with displeasure, as if suspecting it may have shrunk a floor while she wasn't looking.

"I thought you cased the place."

"I did. I just . . ." She waved her hands wildly. "Okay, so you won't need to climb out a window. You might have to tie someone up, though."

"Hmm." Lucern reached for the next item. "Duct tape?" He drew out a roll of the silver tape. Even through the darkness, he could see her blush.

"Dad always said there wasn't a job where duct tape didn't come in handy," she said lamely. Then she straightened her shoulders and added, "You can tape the glass before you break it, if you have to break it. That would reduce the noise and mess. Or if we have to tie someone up, duct tape is impossible to tear."

"I thought the rope was for tying them up."

"Fine," she said irritably. "Use the rope to tie them up. You can duct tape their mouths shut to gag them."

Lucern nearly laughed aloud but managed to hold it back. She had obviously considered every eventuality. Except one. He didn't need any of this nonsense. Packing all the tools back into her bag, Lucern closed it, and stood up.

"Wait here," he ordered. Then he walked up the alley to the side door.

As usual, the woman didn't listen, but chased after him. Her voice was panicky as she asked, "What are you going to do?"

"What we came here to do," he answered. "Rob the blood bank."

He knocked at the door. Kate could hardly believe it. She *didn't* believe it. Lucern's idea of breaking into the blood bank was knocking at the bloody door? He really needed to get a TV so that he could get a grip on reality. One didn't pull a break and enter by knocking.

Maybe he'd lost his mind, she thought unhappily. That thought took hold, and Kate considered it seriously. It was definitely possible. The hunger and pain caused by his lack of blood could have pushed him over the edge. He might now be a raving lunatic, she thought. So she told him so.

"You're insane," she muttered in the silence that followed his knock. "The bloodlust has driven you over the edge. You—"

She snapped her mouth closed as the side door opened. Kate was so surprised she merely stood and gaped as a man appeared. Sandy-haired and about her age, he wore a lab coat and a questioning expression as if it were only slightly out of the ordinary for people to be knocking at the side door after hours.

Kate hadn't really expected anyone to answer but, if she had, the last person she would've expected was one of the blood-bank workers. They should all be at home, shouldn't they? She'd expected a security guard, or maybe a member of a cleaning crew.

Her thoughts were distracted when the fellow seemed to notice their ski masks. She was pretty sure that was the cause of the sudden panic on the man's face. When he started to close the door, Kate glanced at Lucern and gave him a nudge. Apparently, she needn't have bothered. In the next moment, the man halted. Lucern was already working to control his mind.

There was silence as Lucern merely stared at the man, whose face slowly became blank. Lucern asked pleasantly, "Are you alone?"

"Yes." The blood-bank worker's voice was dull, almost sounded drugged.

"Are their security cameras here?" Lucern asked.

Kate felt justified in having insisted on the ski masks when the man said yes. Lucern, though, looked less than pleased. She supposed he'd hoped to take his mask off.

"Would you be so good as to show us to your supply of blood?" Lucern asked next. Kate rolled her eyes at his Old-World courtesy. It seemed the man did everything that way. Even break-and-enter.

When the blood-bank worker turned and started up the hall, Lucern glanced at Kate. "Wait here. I'll return directly."

"Yeah, right," was her answer. She hefted her bag over her shoulder and followed him inside. This had been her idea; she'd be damned if she was going to wait out in an alley, wringing her hands like some wimpy heroine in a novel.

Lucern glared at her. She glared back. Moving to follow the man in the lab coat, she left Luc to fall into step behind her.

She glanced around nervously as they walked up the hall. The blood bank was as silent as a tomb. Not a happy thought, she decided, but it brought to mind coffins and she wondered about them. Obviously, Lucern didn't need to sleep in one. While he had reinforced the darkness in his hotel room by hanging a blanket over the curtains, he wasn't sleeping in a coffin. She supposed that was something else Stoker had got wrong. But, then, according to Lucern, he didn't need a coffin because he wasn't dead. He was just old.

Kate was scowling as she, Luc and their guide entered a room with metal and glass refrigerators around it. Luc was *very* old. She usually preferred to date men her own age. Lucern did not fit in that category. She could safely say he was the oldest man she'd ever dated. Maybe he was the oldest man anyone had ever dated.

She paused just inside the door and merely watched as Lucern walked past her to one of the refrigerators. He opened its door, revealing neat rows of the red liquid he so needed.

Kate peered curiously at the man in the lab coat. He looked completely out of it, a zombie at Lucern's mercy, and she felt a moment's gratitude that she had a strong mind. If not, Luc could have put the whammy on her and gotten her to do anything he wanted. Which was a scary thought.

She turned her attention back to Lucern, then watched with interest as he selected a bag and poked his teeth into it. The procedure was pretty clean. He was apparently able to suck the blood directly up through his teeth like through straws, because he just stood there, teeth inserted as the blood drained away. It was relatively quick. Still, Kate found herself glancing nervously up the hall as she waited for him to finish.

Lucern went through eight bags that way, one right

after the other. When he had finished with the last, he started to close the refrigerator door. Kate rushed forward and stopped him.

"What are you doing?" he asked as she opened her backpack. She began shoving bags in.

"Getting some to go. You'll need more tomorrow," she pointed out. "And I don't want to go through this again."

Lucern nodded. "Take the empty bags, too," he instructed. Then he moved to the blood-bank worker, murmuring something she couldn't hear.

"What did you say?" Kate asked as they hurried back up the hall through which they'd entered.

"I instructed him to change the records to reflect the difference, so that the blood isn't missed."

"Oh." Kate fell silent as she stepped outside. The cool air on her face as she removed the mask was a relief, and she felt some of her tension drain away. But she didn't relax completely, not even once they were in a cab and headed back to the hotel. She was as wound up as a clock, and had been all day. She could hardly believe it had been so easy. Knock on the door? Sheesh.

Lucern's hand closed over hers, and Kate glanced at him in surprise. The man was actually smiling. Sort of. At least, his usual scowl was missing. That was the equivalent of a smile with this man, she thought, noting his cheeks were now flushed with color and the lines of pain were gone from his face. She couldn't believe how much blood he'd drunk, but it appeared to have done him good. He looked healthier than she'd ever seen him.

Her gaze dropped to his hand covering hers, and she

turned hers over to clasp it. She knew he had sensed the tension still gripping her, and he was trying to tell her without words that it was all right. But she felt like a teenager holding hands with her boyfriend for the first time. She was sorry when they arrived at the hotel and he released her to pay the driver.

They were both silent as they walked inside and took the elevator to their floor, Kate wondering if he would kiss her and thank her for her help once they got there. She hoped he would. She hoped he'd do more than that. But she knew it wasn't likely when they entered the room and heard the television playing. Chris was back, relaxing on the couch.

"Oh, hey! I was wondering where you two had got to. A delivery came while you were gone." He gestured to a large box on the table by the window. "It's addressed to Lucern Argeneau c/o Kate C. Leever. I guess your brother must have re-sent it. He must have figured everything out on his own." He frowned at his words, then shook his head. "Though, I guess the first box couldn't have got back to him yet—it's only been a day." He shrugged. "He must just have sent you something else."

Kate wasn't listening. She was gaping at the box on the table with disbelief. It had "A.B.B." stamped on its side. Argeneau Blood Bank? Dear God. All that stress and anxiety had been for nothing.

Chapter Twelve

Lucern glanced across the hospitality suite to where Kate was talking to Deanna Stancyk. Kate was easy to find in her sunny yellow skirt and matching jacket, aglow with life and vitality, smiling, her face animated, her hands moving as she talked and laughed. She was beautiful. Just looking at her caused an ache in Luc's chest. Although it could be indigestion, he thought, recalling the greasy breakfast he'd eaten that morning.

Kate had been terribly quiet with him since they'd returned to the suite last night to find the box from Bastien. She hadn't even followed him into his room to see for sure what the box held, but had merely handed him the backpack with the six bags of stolen blood, murmured good night and slipped into her room. Which had turned the night flat for Lucern.

He'd unpacked the box in his room and stored all the blood—from their adventure as well as from Bastien—in the mini fridge. He'd had to remove everything

213

from the fridge to do so. He'd stacked the cans of pop, the little bottles of alcohol and the snacks on the dresser, and then had wandered to the living room and dropped onto the couch to watch TV with Chris for a while, hoping Kate would reappear. She hadn't.

The temptation to go to her had been strong. With his need for blood satisfied, Lucern had found other cravings bothering him—top among them to just be in Kate's presence. Her company somehow made him feel lighter, younger. As if he hadn't existed six hundred years and become weary of living. The woman was playing havoc on his psyche.

After watching a bad vampire movie—dear God, why was the vampire always the villain?—Lucern had left Chris and gone to bed. He'd awoken early, consumed a couple more bags of blood, put the Do Not Disturb signs on both his door to the hall and the one leading into the living area of the suite—so that the cleaning lady wouldn't find his blood in the fridge and pitch a fit—then had joined Kate and Chris to head out for breakfast.

The three of them had eaten in the main dining room, joined by a handful of other Roundhouse authors. Lucern hadn't said much at the meal, just listened with interest as Kate and Chris talked to the others. It was then that he'd realized how much of their time he was monopolizing. They were babysitting him as if he were a child. He'd almost felt shame.

His pride had made itself known, then, and when they'd all moved on to the hospitality suite, Lucern had insisted that Kate circulate and talk to her other writers, telling her he could take care of himself. She'd appeared torn, but at last had given in to the need to spend time with as many authors as she could. She glanced his way often, stopping by occasionally to make sure he was all right, but she had spent the better part of the morning circulating the room, talking and laughing, reassuring and praising.

Chris, too, had gone about his business, tending to his own authors, leaving Lucern to sit with the writers with whom they'd breakfasted. Luc had spent the morning mostly listening, only commenting once in a while. These were nice women, interesting and creative, and they had included him in their circle without question. But they also tended to act a touch protective toward him, helping him handle his never-ending droves of fans.

He appreciated their assistance, but Lucern was starting to get something of a complex. Why did everyone think he needed protecting? They acted like he was fragile and—he shuddered—sensitive. Lucern was the least sensitive man he knew. Why, in his youth he'd been a warrior, thinking nothing of hacking men down with his sword. When pistols had been invented, he'd fought countless duels, shooting men dead, then riding to his club for breakfast. He could take care of himself. But Kate and the others didn't seem to realize that. Though she had left his side, Kate still watched him as protectively as a mother bird watching her chick make its first shaky flight. He had no doubt that, should she deem him in need, she'd be at his side at once.

Kate happened to glance his way just as he had that thought, so Lucern glared at her for thinking so little of him.

"Kate's a beautiful woman," Jodi Hampton said softly by Luc's ear. "She's also very sweet and giving. Many of her writers would be quite upset if someone were to hurt her. And that includes me."

Lucern turned to the writer in surprise. Jodi had been at his side through breakfast, and she had remained there once they'd reached the hospitality suite. Fifty years old, but with the vitality of a much younger woman, Jodi Hampton was one of Roundhouse Publishing's top authors. She'd built her career the hard way, increasing her readership book by book rather than making a sudden splash, and she'd built it to the point where her last five books had hit the *New York Times* bestseller list. Perhaps it wasn't surprising then that, as well as being attractive, she was also confident and interesting. Less obvious, but something Lucern had quickly discerned, was that she was also terribly kind—though right now she sounded like a mama bear warning a predator off her baby. Lucern liked that. At last, here was someone who did not see him as helpless, but as a possible danger. If only emotionally.

"I would never hurt Kate," he assured the woman feeling fond of her. He liked intelligent women.

Jodi nodded slowly. "I hope not, Luke Amirault, because I like you."

"My name's really Argeneau. Lucern Argeneau," he told her. "I only write as Luke Amirault."

Jodi nodded again and held out her hand. "And my real name is Teresa Jordan. A pleasure to meet you, Lucern."

"Call me Luc." He shook her hand and felt his lips

twitch into something simulating a grin. "I gather you write historical romances, Teresa?"

"Yes. And I have all of your historical texts to help me with the research. You're much younger than I expected. I should have realized, though. Your books aren't like most dusty old histories. You bring other eras to life. Your books make research a pleasure."

Lucern felt his mouth twist again in a pleased grin. It felt odd. He wasn't used to smiling so much. He had only started to do so since the advent of Kate in his life. But he thought he could get used to it.

Aware that the flood of fans in the hospitality suite had died down, Lucern relaxed a little and began to discuss history with his new friend. Soon the whole group of Roundhouse writers had joined in.

"It's grown a bit quiet."

Kate nodded as Chris appeared at her side. It had been a long but productive morning. Kate was pretty sure she had managed to have a word with every single one of her writers in attendance at the conference. She was ready for a break.

"It's lunchtime," she pointed out. "Everyone is probably eating. It will pick up again in a little while."

"Maybe we should collect Luc and go grab some lunch, too," Chris suggested.

"Good idea." Kate turned to find Lucern, and saw him deep in conversation with Jodi.

"He sure is loosening up now that's he's feeling better," Chris whispered as they walked across the room. "He isn't as difficult as Edwin always said. Either that, or you've had a good influence on him."

Kate gave a dry laugh. "More likely that 'little boys' night out' you two enjoyed that first night loosened him up."

Chris laughed. "I couldn't believe he had never watched television. He took to it like a duck to water, though. He has a good sense of humor under all that stuffy proper English personality. I like him."

"So do I," Kate responded automatically, suddenly realizing it was true. She *did* like Lucern. She wasn't sure why, but she did. And it wasn't just his kisses or his importance to her career. She pondered why she liked him as they reached the group of debating writers, and waited for the appropriate moment to let their presence be known.

Lucern had been rude and surly when she'd first arrived on his doorstep, but not rude enough to push her out of his home and send her on her way. Which he'd had every right to do. He'd allowed her to drag him out shopping, followed her uncomplainingly around the grocery store, and eaten her cooking. He had been difficult about those letters, but Kate now understood it hadn't been deliberate.

She recalled reading the letter from the reader asking if Lucern would turn her into a vampire, and Luc's abrupt "no." Then she recalled the letter from the reader who had fallen in love with Etienne, and Lucern's response: "He's taken." At the time, she had thought he was being deliberately difficult, but now it all seemed clear. She almost laughed aloud, though she'd been ready to shriek at him then.

Luc was an honest man, a man of his word. He'd promised to do R.T. and, despite being tricked into thinking it was just an interview, had stuck to his word. He was now attending a conference she knew nothing on earth would have dragged him to if he hadn't given his word. He was a man of honor. He was also very caring and chivalrous. Just look at how he had refused to bite her and cause her pain when he'd been in such need.

Of course, she was beginning to suspect he had a wicked sense of humor beneath his proper facade and all that surliness. Sometimes she caught a glint in his eye—usually when he was being most obtuse—that made her think he was deliberately working her up.

"Oh, hello."

Kate pulled herself from her thoughts and smiled as Jodi greeted her.

"We were thinking of slipping out for lunch while it's slow," Chris said. "Any takers?"

The writers were all on their feet at once, grabbing their stuff. It seemed everyone was ready for a break. Kate smiled at Lucern, who moved to her side and took her arm. The action felt proprietary, almost possessive, but Kate suspected it was just his upbringing. His natural chivalry.

Someone suggested leaving the hotel and getting away from the conference atmosphere for a bit, but Kate felt concern about the sun's effect on Lucern. Seeming to sense her worry, Luc glowered at her. He muttered that he'd be fine; he had his "medicine."

"What medicine?" Jodi asked.

"Lucern has something of an allergy to the sun," Kate explained reluctantly. Then she rushed on to add, "But he has some . . . er . . . medicine upstairs, so I'm sure he'll be fine. We can find a restaurant nearby if you guys want."

"No. There's no sense dragging him around while we find someplace. Wouldn't want to make him sick. We haven't eaten in the hotel pub yet. We can try that," Jodi suggested. The other women agreed.

As they made their way down, the other authors began teasing Lucern, commenting that he wrote vampire romances and was allergic to the sun. "Hmm. Perhaps we should watch our necks," Jodi joked.

Kate was horrified. What had she started? She grew quite tense and anxious at the teasing, but Lucern seemed to take it in stride. Eventually, the conversation moved on to other subjects. They reached the pub and were seated.

Lunch was delicious, the company adding to the experience. When they finished, everyone seemed reluctant to leave, so Kate decided a little fun wouldn't go amiss before she herded them all back to the hospitality suite. "Maybe we should check out the other events taking place, here," she suggested.

Jodi pulled out her conference agenda and read the options. There were educational programs for writers, a cooking demonstration called "Cooking with Love," psychic and astrological readings, and dance lessons.

Two of the authors wanted to check out the writers' programs, but they promised they'd drop back into the hospitality suite later. Two more left for the cooking demonstration with the same promise. One wanted to take dance lessons and dragged a groaning Chris off to that. Which left Jodi, Kate and Lucern.

"Well, that leaves the psychic reading and astrology,"

Jodi announced, folding her agenda and slipping it back in her purse.

"Sounds fun." Kate pushed back her chair to rise. She happened to glance at Lucern, and was surprised to see him looking uncertain. Jodi noticed as well.

"What's the matter, Luc? Scared the psychic will see something bad in your future," the writer teased.

Lucern grimaced. "Or in my past."

He had spoken in his usual surly tone, but there was a teasing glint in his eyes Kate found she was beginning to recognize. Jodi apparently recognized it, too, because she laughed. Still, Kate wondered. Lucern had a long past. Six hundred years. That was a lot of time. She found herself wondering about all the years he'd lived. Had he ever loved someone? Been married? Had children? He was single now—at least he seemed to be. Dear God, she wasn't even sure about that. He might have a wife. He might have kids. He might . . .

"So, how have you managed to avoid marriage so long, Lucern? Or are you married?" Jodi asked, as if she'd been reading Kate's thoughts. The woman had always had a way of doing that, which made Kate a tad nervous. Perhaps the writer had a touch of psychic ability. Heck, she might even be a mind reader, and know that Lucern was opening Kate's mind to all sorts of possibilities she would have laughed at before. Kate decided she would guard her thoughts around the woman from now on . . . just to be sure.

"And how old are you, anyway?" the author continued. "Thirty-five or so?"

Kate watched Lucern's mouth quirk in a rare crooked smile.

"Or so," he answered. "And no, I've never been married."

"Why not?" Jodi apparently had no problem in being nosy. Much to Kate's amazement, Lucern seemed more amused by the question than annoyed. It seemed Chris was right. Luc was loosening up.

"Who would have me?" he asked lightly. There was a wicked glint in his eye.

Jodi glanced at Kate then, and Kate felt herself flush. Had the woman picked up on her attraction to Lucern? Dear God, she really had to be more careful.

"Here we are," she announced with determined cheer. Ahead was the sign to the room with the psychic and astrological readings.

A number of small tables were distributed around the room. Each table was assigned to a psychic or astrologer, their signs and paraphernalia set up around them. There was only one chair at each table besides that of the reader. One client at a time, thank you. There were also tables where one could buy crystals and such. It was rather like a psychic fair.

"I'm going to have my astrological chart done," Jodi announced. "Then I'm going to have an astrology reading, too. And a psychic one." The writer's green eyes were shining. She was obviously excited.

Kate had never been to a psychic in her life, and she didn't have a clue where to start. One glance at Lucern showed him looking bored, so Kate nodded at Jodi and smiled. "Lead on, MacDuff."

"You're a very young soul, light and bursting with love and enthusiasm to experience all the world has to offer."

Lucern remained silent as the supposed psychic batted her eyelashes at him, but Kate snorted with derision behind him. The psychic stopped fluttering over his hand long enough to glare at her, then went on, "You have lived many, many lives."

Kate snorted again. "When has he had time?"

"I beg your pardon?" The psychic sneered up at her.

"I thought he was a young soul," Kate pointed out. "How can he be a young soul who has lived many lives?" She touched Lucern's arm. "Come on. This is a waste of money."

Lucern was on his feet at once, ushering her and Jodi away under the psychic's baleful gaze. He was steering them toward the exit when Jodi stopped, forcing Kate and Luc to stop as well.

"No, wait. I want a reading from her." The author pointed toward a table where a white-haired lady sat alone, without a line like at the other tables. Kate supposed it was the lack of a flashy display that had made her less popular. The rest of the psychics wore bright clothes and had dramatic signs and flashy tablecloths; this woman hadn't bothered with a tablecloth, and wore a beige outfit guaranteed to fade in a crowd, and a plain sign.

"Her?" Kate asked doubtfully. The woman didn't look very successful, if she did look serene.

"Real talent doesn't bother with flash," Jodi said. They all walked over.

Kate and Lucern watched solemnly as the woman took Jodi's hand. She said Jodi was a writer—which Kate didn't think was hard to work out, since this was a writing conference. It was a fifty-fifty chance that Jodi was either a writer or a reader. The woman next said she was quite successful at it, which wasn't that big of a revelation either. She might have recognized Jodi's picture from the back of her books.

The next statement surprised Kate. The reader said Jodi was still suffering from a painful loss she had endured some time ago, the loss of her soul mate. Kate felt the hair on the back of her neck prickle. It wasn't common knowledge, but Jodi's husband had died four years earlier, a year before she'd been published. Kate also knew Jodi still wept for him. She claimed he had been her one true love.

The psychic rubbed Jodi's hand soothingly and told her that her love was there with them now, and that he was always nearby. But she also said he wanted Jodi to continue living. Someone would come into her life soon, and while he wouldn't be a soul mate as her first love had been, he would be Jodi's dear friend, lover and companion for the rest of her days—and the psychic said Jodi's first love wished for it to be so.

Jodi's eyes glazed with tears. She stood and turned to Kate and Lucern. Kate was trying to think of something to say to lift the mood, when Lucern suddenly commented, "So, looks like you'll get laid before you die after all."

Kate turned a horrified gaze on him. She had never heard the man speak so crudely. She'd never even heard him use such modern terms. She turned to Jodi in shock, but the author just burst out in peals of tinkling laughter.

"Yes, it does. Isn't that nice?" Jodi sighed and touched Luc's arm. Then she explained to Kate, "The women were talking about sex, of course, when it got slow back in the hospitality suite. Beth was bemoaning the fact that her characters had better sex than she did, and I snorted and said that at least she was getting some, I doubted I ever would again before I died. But now it sounds as though I shall!"

She smiled at Lucern, then urged him toward the chair. "Your turn, my friend. I want to hear what she has to say about *you*."

Kate watched the older woman badger Luc into sitting. For a moment, she felt a touch of discomfort. It was obvious that the pair had developed something of a friendship this morning, and Kate was ashamed to realize that what she felt was jealousy. Shrugging off the petty feelings, she turned her attention to the psychic, who had claimed Lucern's hand and was now running her fingers lightly over it. Her eyes were closed in concentration.

"You're very old," the woman said in hushed tones. She blinked her eyes open to look at his handsome young face, frowned in confusion, then closed them again. "It's your soul that must be old," she corrected. "Very old. You have had many loves."

Kate felt something tighten in her chest before the woman corrected herself again: "No, not loves. Lovers. You have had many. Many, many," she added, sounding surprised again. Then she blinked her eyes open to ask with some vexation, "When have you had time to sleep?"

Kate's lips twitched. She supposed Lucern *had* been with many women. He was a healthy male of over six hundred years. Even if he'd only had one lover per year, it meant six hundred. If he'd had more than three a year . . . The mind boggled. In dismay, she decided she would have to ask him if vampires could get and pass on STD's. She hoped not, but really, it was something she needed to know.

"You had begun to weary of life," the psychic went on, grabbing Kate's attention. "It all seemed so hard, and the cruelties of man had begun to wear you down. But something—no, not something, but someone— someone has reinvigorated you. Made you feel it might be worth living again. That there is still joy to be had."

Kate's tongue seemed stuck to the roof of her mouth. Someone? Who? Some secret part of her hoped it was she. At the same time, the idea terrified her. She was attracted to Lucern. She had even come to like and respect him, but—

"Hold on to her." The woman was staring deeply into Luc's eyes. "You will have to fight for her, but not in the way you are used to. Weapons and physical strength will do you no good in this battle. It is your own pride and fear you will have to fight. If you fail, your heart will shrivel in your chest, and you will die a lonely, bitter old man, regretting what you didn't do."

Lucern jerked his hand free, then stood and walked away. Kate turned to follow, but the psychic suddenly latched onto her hand. "Wait. Your man will be all right for a minute."

Kate stiffened. "He isn't my man."

The psychic's expression suggested that Kate wasn't fooling anyone. The woman said, "He is special, your man. But to be with him you will have to make a choice. You will have to give up all. If you have the courage, everything you ever wanted will be yours. If not . . ." She shrugged and released Kate's hand. "Now go to your man. Only you can calm him."

Kate hurried after Lucern, aware that Jodi was on her heels. The skin of her wrist still tingled where the psychic had touched her, prickled as if she had been shocked. Kate rubbed it absently, her thoughts scattered. She would have to give up all, but would gain everything she ever wanted? How was that even possible? She shrugged the concern away as she rushed out of the room and spotted Lucern disappearing around a corner.

By the time the two women had caught up with him in the Roundhouse Publishing hospitality suite, Luc was seated at a table, surrounded by fans.

Allison was gesturing for Kate to join them across the room. Kate glanced uncertainly from her boss to Lucern.

"I'll see if Luc's okay. You go see what your boss wants," Jodi suggested, giving her a push toward the head editor. "We haven't much longer here, anyway. They're closing up early to allow everyone time to prepare for the Renaissance costume ball and banquet."

Oh, yes, Kate thought as she moved toward her boss. Tonight was the costume ball.

Lucern nodded solemnly as the reader he had been speaking to stood and went to speak with Jodi. He was becoming used to talking to readers. He had tried his best not to at first, but Kate's lecture in his home kept popping into his mind—how, without them, he wouldn't be published. That he touched their lives, and that they only wished to tell him so. He'd learned to respond in somewhat of a pleasant manner to the embarrassing compliments they gave, but had found that with this little effort the readers opened further to him. They told him things, gave him parts of themselves he didn't know how to handle.

One woman had told him she'd just lost her young son, that life seemed bleak and endlessly cruel to her but that she'd found escape and hope in his books. Perhaps life would be good again someday. Then she had forced a laugh and told him she only wished that vampirism were true, that if she had believed in it, she would have searched the earth for a vampire to save her child.

Lucern had ached for the woman. He'd felt her pain reaching out to him and seeping into his body. He knew it was wrong, but he hadn't been able to let her just walk away. He'd slipped inside her mind and . . . not removed her pain, but veiled it somewhat, easing it for her so that the good memories were stronger than the bad. She'd walked away smiling.

He had met many wounded people today. Once he'd opened to them, he couldn't seem to close them out. But he had met many people who were just fine, too. He had found the whole experience interesting, to say the least. He had written his books for purely selfish reasons, to record the truth. But now he saw that the books were touching the lives of many others. It made him want to try his hand at genuine fiction, something he had never considered. He had started his life as a warrior. After a hundred years of that, he'd been something of a rakehell. When he had tired of that, he had donned a scholarly persona and buried himself in history. Perhaps it was time to turn to more creative pursuits. But would he be good at it?

"Okay. Time to go." Kate suddenly appeared at his side. "Allison is closing the hospitality suite early so everyone has plenty of time to prepare for the Renaissance ball."

Luc breathed a sigh of relief. The other writers seemed to echo it. While it was rewarding to speak to readers, it was also wearying. Lucern was surprised at how exhausted he felt.

As he walked with Kate to the elevator, he reminded himself to definitely remember to feed before the ball. It was imperative. Which brought his thoughts around to the matter of the ball. A Renaissance ball.

Well, he had very fond memories of that period. For that reason, Lucern was sure the night's ball would be fun.

Chapter Thirteen

The Renaissance ball was awful. When thinking about the era, Lucern had forgotten one thing: the dresses the women wore. He remembered unhappily just as Kate stepped out of her bedroom and into the shared living room.

She wore a full-length Elizabethan gown of burgundy brocade and white lace. It had a velvet bodice with the traditional pointed stomacher. Her long skirts and sleeve caps were pleated. She looked lovely. Truly. But the bodice was what really made the gown; it forced her breasts together and up so that they appeared ready to tumble out at any moment. Lucern's mouth began to water the moment she appeared. Then it struck him that he wouldn't be the only one looking at those luscious round orbs on such display. Kate was going to wear this damn thing in public. He didn't like that thought at all.

Lucern had opened his mouth to tell her so when she

froze and blinked at him. "What the hell are you wearing?" she asked.

He stiffened in surprise. Glancing down at the dark blue costume he wore, he said, "This is traditional sixteenth-century wear," he said. "Did you not order it?"

"Yes, of course. But I just told them the sizes and didn't specify . . ." Kate's voice trailed off, and she frowned at him.

"You don't like it?"

"Like it? Well, it's just . . . you look kind of . . . er . . . froufrou," she said at last. "I mean . . . the black leotards show off your legs nicely, but . . . ?"

"They are called trunk hose," Lucern informed her. He was still trying to figure out what froufrou meant. It didn't sound complimentary, the way she said it. Unhappily, he did not keep up with modern euphemisms. He really should get out more. "I thought you edited historical romance, too," he said, perhaps a touch peevishly.

"Mostly medieval," she explained. "Renaissance hasn't been that popular." Her lips pursed, then twisted somewhat to the side. "So, what is that . . . er . . ."—she waved in the general direction of his groin—"that duck thing?"

Lucern sighed. "It is a codpiece."

"Oh." She nodded slowly, considering the rather exaggerated item.

Lucern peered down and considered it as well. It was huge, a puffed and slashed bag ornamented with several jeweled pins. It was also a tad misshapen from storage and did vaguely resemble a duck. This was obviously an early Renaissance costume. The codpiece had fallen out of favor during Queen Elizabeth's reign.

"I have read about those, but I thought they were supposed to be . . . er . . . rounder or something. You're going to hurt yourself. Someone will walk past you, bang into it and—"

"Hey! You two look great!" Chris came out of his room wearing a red and burgundy outfit not unlike Lucern's. His codpiece was a tad more normal, however.

Lucern smiled at the younger man, feeling the tension seep out of him. He hadn't cared for having Kate pick on his costume, and even worse was having her attention focused on his codpiece. Knowing she was staring had made the bit of anatomy it covered stir with interest.

"So"—Chris glanced from one of them to the other— "are we ready to go?"

Kate was positive her breasts were going to pop out of her gown. She was doing her best not to breathe, in order to prevent it from happening, but every time she had to curtsy she also said a little prayer that they stay in place. Fortunately, they did—but each time she straightened it was to find Lucern glaring at every man within looking distance. Kate found it rather amusing.

What she didn't find amusing was the way women were staring at Luc's codpiece. The damned thing sparkled and glittered, to jeweled pins catching every passing light. Kate's own eyes had been drawn repeatedly as well. It was damned embarrassing how distracting the thing was. Not that Lucern seemed to notice. If he was aware of the way two thousand women in the room were gawking at his groin, he pretended not to be and walked with pride. She didn't know where he got the courage. Had she walked in wearing sparkling cones on her breasts, she would have been cringing and trying to hide them.

"Wow, what a bash, huh?" Chris commented.

Kate peered around at the entertainment. There were musicians, jesters, dancers and minstrels. It really did resemble how she imagined a ball of old would appear. Her hand tightened on Lucern's arm, and she leaned up to his ear to whisper, "Is this how it really was?"

He hesitated. "Somewhat. Of course, the lighting would have been dimmer. We had only candlelight then, no electricity. The floor would have been covered with rushes. Dogs and rats would have been scavenging for spare bits of food. The smell would have been far less pleasant and—"

"That's okay," Kate interrupted. "I like our ball better."

"Hmm." He nodded.

They found a table and were barely seated when Jodi and several other writers joined them. The conversation was at first dominated by amazement at Lady Barrow's accomplishment. The jesters were amusing, the minstrels played ancient instruments. The dinner, when it was served, was delicious if not quite true Renaissance fare.

Once the plates were cleared away, the dancing began. Lucern murmured that he would be back in a moment, and Kate, presuming he had to go to the men's room, nodded absently, her attention on the dancers swirling around the room. She turned to say something to Jodi, who had taken the seat on Lucern's other side, but paused when she saw Lucern was still there. "I thought you were . . ."

Her voice trailed away as she noted that his hands were under the table. He appeared to be . . . doing something. "What . . . ?" she began in amazement.

"I am caught on something," he said shortly.

Kate blinked, confusion filling her mind. "What do you mean, you're caught on something?" She was imagining . . . well, it was best she didn't think too long on what she was imagining. She soon learned it was worse than that.

"The tablecloth," he said, ducking slightly to the side in an attempt to see the problem. "One of the pins."

It was all he had to say; Kate got the picture at once. One of the jeweled pins on his codpiece had somehow gotten caught on the tablecloth. Much to her horror, a burst of laughter slipped from her lips.

Lucern wasn't amused. "This isn't funny," he told her grimly. "I have to relieve myself rather urgently. And I can't get up."

"So . . . you people have to go to the bathroom, too?" Kate asked with interest.

Lucern glared at her as if she'd lost her mind. "Where do you get your thoughts?"

"Well," she explained in self-defense, "Bram in his books, never had Dracula relieve himself. I just never thought—"

"I doubt if he had Mina relieve herself, either," Lucern growled. He jerked at the tablecloth, making it and everything on it slide an inch or so toward him.

The conversation around the table stopped. Kate glanced up to see that everyone was staring at Lucern with varying levels of horrified fascination. Knowing that Lucern would never ask for help, Kate decided to save him from his pride. She drew attention to herself by clearing her throat, then smiled at Chris. "C.K., can you help Lucern? He's in some difficulty."

"Sure, what's the problem?" Her friend started to rise.

"One of the pins on his codpiece has attached itself to the tablecloth. Maybe you could crawl under the table and set him loose," she suggested.

Chris laughed and paused. "You're kidding, right?"

When she shook her head, he dropped abruptly back into his seat. "Sorry. Codpiece removal is not my department."

"Chris!" Kate said grimly.

"Kate," he responded dryly. "He's *your* writer. *You* crawl under the table and undo him."

"I thought you liked him," she said accusingly.

"Not that much," Chris shot back. Then he glanced apologetically to Lucern. "Sorry, Luc."

"I quite understand. I'll manage." He responded with dignity, but he was blushing fiercely, Kate noted with interest. She hadn't known that vampires could blush.

He jerked the tablecloth again in his efforts, and Kate frowned. He was going to upset the table or wreck the costume she'd rented. Neither option was a good one. She had no desire to find the remnants of the dinner on her rented costume; she didn't want to have to pay to clean it. Nor did she want to replace the ridiculous codpiece Lucern wore because he'd ruined it. Swallowing the last of her wine, she set her glass down and turned to Lucern.

"Okay. Get your hands out of the way and let me have a look."

Lucern hesitated, then brought his hands out and onto the table. Kate promptly bent down to try to see what was going on. She was at the wrong angle. "Can't you back any further out?" she asked.

"Not without taking the tablecloth with me," he snapped.

She straightened and peered around self-consciously, not surprised to see the tableful of writers all watching avidly. Her gaze found Jodi's on the opposite side of Lucern. "I can't see anything from this angle. I'm going to have to get under the table."

Jodi's eyes rounded; then she got to her feet. "Come on, girls. There's no need for everyone to know what's going on. We can act as a barricade."

The other authors all promptly got to their feet and moved around the table. Kate watched with relief as they formed a semicircle around her seat and Lucern's, their wide skirts making a nice curtain. Chris was the only one left seated. He watched the operation with wide eyes, apparently unsure whether he should be horrified or laugh.

"Go ahead," Jodi said once everyone was in place. The other writers nodded.

Kate felt ridiculously like a soldier being sent on a solo secret mission. Wishing she'd had more wine, she took a deep breath then slid off her seat and under the table. It was terribly dark. And hot. She knelt to the side of Lucern's hosed legs, her head twisted, attempting to see the pin and what it was caught on, but she wasn't quite at the right angle and wasn't close enough.

Muttering under her breath, Kate eased closer, around his leg until she knelt between his knees; then she reached tentatively for the bunched-up tablecloth. She was absolutely not going to touch his codpiece, at least not if she could help it. She lifted the cloth a bit, but it really was attached.

"Do you need a candle or something under there?" Jodi asked helpfully. Her head suddenly appeared under the table, then it disappeared and Kate heard her ask, "Does anyone have one of those pen light things in their purse? I usually carry one, but . . ."

The rest of what she said was lost to Kate as the other woman straightened.

"You sure get yourself into some interesting situations, Katie my girl," Kate muttered, trying to unbunch the cloth so that she could find where it was attached to Lucern. It was her job to be sure that things ran smoothly for her writers at these things, and to help them out of sticky situations. But it was her considered opinion that this situation was beyond the call of an editor's duties. If it hadn't been Lucern in this bind, she wouldn't even have thought of fixing it herself. Which was an interesting point, one she would contemplate later. She gave a start when something bumped the underside of her hand. It was the codpiece, Kate realized with amazement. It was growing and had bumped into her. Well, what was under it was growing. It seemed Lucern was finding the ordeal something more than just embarrassing.

Lucern wished the ground would open up and devour him. It could even take every one of the writers surrounding him, and Kate too if it liked, so long as it ended this misery, the most embarrassing moment of his life. It wasn't bad enough that his codpiece was attached to a tablecloth, but now Kate was kneeling between his legs trying to untangle him, and that was giving rise to thoughts that had nothing to do with getting free so he could visit the men's room. He was imagining what it would be like if, instead of untangling the tablecloth, she would simply shift the codpiece aside, pull him out and wrap her lips around him. Then he realized he had gone hard, and he hoped to God she didn't notice.

How had he ended up in this position? He was a man who liked order and routine. He did not attend conferences, or Renaissance balls. How had his life got so out of control? Something nudged against his codpiece, and he jerked upright in his seat, drawing the attention of the women around him.

"Sorry." Kate's voice came muffled from under the table. It sounded like she was speaking through gritted teeth. Lucern closed his eyes in humiliation and wished himself staked through the heart.

"Did she stick you with the pin?" Beth, one of the writers, asked in concern.

Lucern grunted in answer, but it came out more like a whimper. Taking that for a yes, Beth patted his shoulder sympathetically.

"Here you are!"

Lucern turned his head to see Lady Barrow making her way to him through the gathering of authors, Jodi pressed herself against the table next to his leg, blocking the view of Kate underneath. Lady Barrow appeared a little curious as to why the women were all clustered there, but she didn't ask. Instead, she smiled at Lucern.

"Allison told me you were feeling better, but I wanted to see for myself."

Lucern stared at her, knowing his eyes had gone as round as pumpkins. Normally, he would have stood when a lady approached; but that was impossible. That wasn't the reason his eyes had gone round, though. The fact was, unaware of Lady Barrow's presence, Kate had just grabbed his codpiece and shifted it. She had also—unintentionally?—grabbed hold of the part of his anatomy that was expanding in size, filling to capacity the overlarge codpiece.

"Sorry." Kate's voice came from under the table again. "I'm having trouble seeing this pin."

Lady Barrow's smile froze. Her eyes shot down to where Jodi's skirts hid the table, then traveled up to the writer's alarmed face, then slid to Lucern's mortified expression. Before she could say a word, Kate's voice sounded again. It was irritated and short. "Dammit, Lucern! The moment I get you unhooked, I insist you take these damn pins out. They're a bloody nuisance."

"Luc's codpiece is stuck to the tablecloth," Jodi blurted as Lady Barrow opened her mouth. "Kate's trying to free him."

"His codpiece, she means," Beth put in helpfully. "Kate is trying to free his codpiece from the tablecloth. Not him from his codpiece."

"I see," Lady Barrow murmured, looking not at all sure how to handle the situation. Her dismay lasted only a moment, however; then she gestured for Jodi to move aside, lifted the tablecloth out of the way, and knelt to peer under the table. "Can you see in there,

Kate? Or shall I have someone bring a light?"

Lucern felt Kate's hand tighten on him in alarm, and he closed his eyes with a moan.

"Lady Barrow?" Kate's voice sounded incredibly small.

"Yes, it's me. Do you need some light under there?"

The muffled curse that came from under the table was almost drowned out by a sudden guffaw from above. Lucern opened his eyes to see Chris covering his mouth. The man was losing it. Lucern supposed he couldn't blame him. Were he not at the center of this debacle, he might find it horribly amusing as well. As it was, he just found it horrible.

Lucern couldn't hear Kate's muttered answer to Lady Barrow, but it must have been in the affirmative, for the woman straightened, peered around, then summoned one of her workers to find a flashlight. The man was off like a shot; then Lady Barrow turned to survey Lucern's pained expression. She patted his shoulder soothingly. "Never mind. This sort of thing has happened to all of us at one time or another." Her mouth quirked. "Well, not precisely this sort of thing, but you know what I mean."

Lucern groaned and closed his eyes again. Then a bluff voice said, "Well, what's going on here? Why are all my writers just standing about?"

Kate recognized Chuck Morgan's voice and could have wept. Instead, she leaned her head weakly against Lucern's knee and wondered if the situation could possibly get any worse. First Lady Barrow was witness to this humiliating event, and now the president of her company had arrived. Oh, she was really impressing

240

her superiors with this conference! It had all been much easier when Edwin had been in charge and she had only been an assistant.

"*What?*" Chuck's horrified roar was probably heard from one end of the reception hall to the other, Kate thought—and judging by the way the general talking and laughter suddenly quieted, she knew she was right. Dear God, soon everyone was going to know she was under here.

Kate heard Lady Barrow's voice, sharp and firm, and she smiled to herself. Kathryn could be as kind as anyone, but she wasn't a woman to take guff and she wasn't afraid of anyone, as far as Kate knew. She had probably just put Chuck in his place for drawing attention to what they had all been trying to hide, and Kate could have hugged the woman.

"There you are!" she heard Lady Barrow exclaim. "Thank you."

The tablecloth lifted, and the woman appeared. Much to Kate's amazement, rather than hand over the flashlight, Kathryn Falk, Lady Barrow, knelt and slid under the table next to her. "It's hot under here, isn't it?" she commented conversationally, as if she did this sort of thing every day. Lady Barrow situated herself, turned on the light, shined it where the tablecloth and codpiece were tangled, then nodded solemnly at Kate. "Get to it, girl. The sooner you get it untangled, the sooner we can get out of here."

It was easier said than done. Lucern was well and truly caught. At least three of the half-dozen pins on his codpiece were stuck at various places in the tablecloth. One pin had probably just snagged at first, then

Lucern's tugging had entrapped the others. It took a bit of work to free him.

Lady Barrow remained patient throughout, keeping the light steady, holding the cloth out of the way when Kate needed an extra hand, giving advice and cracking the occasional joke to relieve the stress of the moment. However, even with her help it seemed an excruciatingly long ordeal. And embarrassing, too. As much as she wanted to avoid touching Lucern's codpiece, it was impossible—and more often than not she was holding it in her hand. She was terribly aware of the hard flesh beneath as she twisted the material this way or that, trying to unhook all the pins without getting others caught. She didn't even want to guess at how Lucern felt. It had to be some horrible torture.

If Kate didn't soon stop, Lucern was positive he was going to shame himself right there at the table for all to see. She wasn't touching him in any sexual way, but the very fact she was between his knees and shifting him had him reacting like a teenage boy. He had lived a long, long time, but Lucern had never found himself in quite this situation before. And he hoped to God he never did again.

"There's another one free."

Kate's voice came from beneath the table, and everyone standing around made noises Lucern supposed were congratulatory and encouraging. He tried not to wiggle in his seat as her grip on him again shifted. Generally, his erections didn't point that way—but he supposed she was trying to get at the last pin. By looking down, he could actually see her fingers wrapped around him where they poked out from under the cloth. He glanced up at Jodi and saw her wide-eyed gaze fixed on his lap. He managed a lame smile.

"Oh, dear."

That exclamation from one of the other writers drew both his and Jodi's attention. It was Beth, and she looked absolutely horrified. Lucern felt his heart sink. He had thought that the arrival of the president of Kate's company was the worst thing that could happen, but the writer's expression suggested otherwise.

"What is it?" he asked, deciding it was best to find out.

"You know those documentary people? The ones who have been filming everything?" she asked.

"No." Lucern hadn't heard of any documentaries being filmed.

"They're always shooting documentaries at the R.T. conference," Jodi put in. "They love filming all the women and the finery and such."

"Yes. And don't look now, but they're coming this way. And so is that photographer from the local paper."

"Oh, dear," Jodi murmured. "He's probably looking for Lady Barrow. He's been trailing her all night."

"Damn," Lucern breathed. It had all definitely just got worse.

"Last one," Kate told Lady Barrow with a relief that was echoed by the founder of Romantic Times.

"Good," the woman said.

Kate couldn't blame her; they were both bent, heads tilted to the side and backs pressed against the bottom of the table. Kate had to really respect the woman for coming under here with her. There had been no need, but Lady Barrow had that kind of if-there's-something-to-do, let's-get-it-done personality. Energy and enthusiasm seemed to shimmer off her.

Sighing, Kate forced herself to concentrate on the task at hand. One last pin to free and they would be out of there. Then she was going to insist Lucern head straight to the men's room and remove the jeweled pins. She couldn't imagine he had put them on his damned codpiece in the first place, and was grateful she hadn't danced with him before this had happened—she might have found her dress caught. Wouldn't that have been fun, to untangle right there in the middle of the dance floor for everyone to see? As it was, enough people knew she was under a table working on Lucern's codpiece; she didn't need every last attendee of the conference seeing her author's predicament.

"Got it! You're free," Kate called out in relief as the last pin came loose. She started to pull away, only to find her sleeve pulling up short. Somehow, while she had been untangling the tablecloth from the last pin, her sleeve had gotten caught on another. She was now attached to Lucern, wrist to codpiece.

"Damn," she said.

"What is it?" Lady Barrow asked, frowning. Something of an uproar started on the other side of the tablecloth. Everyone seemed to be talking at once.

"I'm caught on one of the pins of his . . ." Kate gasped, rushing forward on her knees to keep her sleeve from ripping as Lucern suddenly scooted backward. The squeal of his chair legs on the floor drowned out her cry of alarm, and she was forced to hurry out from under the table as he started to rise. Kate blinked against a sudden flash, heard Lucern cursing, but was briefly blinded. It had been dark under the table.

"Watch out, Mr. Amirault," Lady Barrow warned, crawling out from under the table. "She's got her sleeve caught on your . . ."

Lady Barrow went silent upon seeing the newest additions to their audience. Kate became aware of them, too, her eyes adjusting and slowly noting the film camera pointed in her direction. There was a photographer, too, with a very professional-looking camera. The flash had been him taking a picture, she realized.

Lucern, doing his best to ignore her hand hanging in front of his groin, said in a pained, polite tone; "Call me Luc, please, Lady Barrow."

"My, my, my," the man with the professional-looking camera said. "You didn't mention *this* event to me, Lady Barrow."

"Who . . . ?" Kate began, just knowing she didn't want to hear the answer.

"The local paper," Lady Barrow said grimly. She got to her feet. "And now that this emergency is over, I guess I'd better take care of the next."

Jodi and the other writers helped the woman brush down her skirts; then Kathryn Falk took the reporter's arm, turned him away and started to walk him toward her own table.

"I'll lay money she has that man eating out of her hand in ten minutes," Jodi said with admiration. Turning to Lucern and Kate, she smiled encouragingly. "That picture won't make the papers. I guarantee it."

Chapter Fourteen

They made the front page of the *Daily News*.

"That weasel of a reporter swears he didn't give it to his editor, but I don't know who else could have," Kathryn Falk said in a disgruntled tone. She had called Kate and Luc first thing in the morning and requested they meet her in the main restaurant for breakfast. Kate had immediately suspected the worst. And she'd been right.

She stared miserably at the newspaper photo. There was Lucern, half-standing and looking all handsome in his froufrou costume, and there was she, looking like some cheap wench crawling out from under the table to grab him by the . . . She sighed miserably and read the headline again. "Medieval Moments?" it screamed in big letters.

Roundhouse Publishing Editor Kate C. Leever grabs all the gusto she can from vampire romance author Luke Amirault, as Kathryn Falk, Lady Barrow, CEO and founder of the Romantic Times Magazine, looks on at the Renaissance Ball last night.

Kate groaned and started to slam the paper down, but paused to reread the byline. She looked more carefully at the picture.

"When I get my hands on that man, I'm going to—" Lady Barrow began.

"I think he's telling the truth," Kate interrupted wearily. "It seems to me that newspaper man's flash went off just as I came out from under the table. You were still under there. But you're in this picture."

Lady Barrow took the paper and peered at it, a frown forming on her face. "I think you're right. But who else could have taken it? Cameras weren't allowed. We had hired a photographer to take photos of people. The only guests with cameras were reporters and . . ." Her voice trailed off, her eyes narrowing. "Why, that . . ." She cut herself off, clearly displeased. "If you'll excuse me, I have something to take care of."

She stood, then paused and forced a smile. "Don't worry about this. It's all a tempest in a teapot. It'll pass quickly if you don't give interviews about it."

Kate and Lucern nodded, then watched Lady Barrow leave the restaurant—no doubt to skin a certain photographer.

Kate sighed. Lucern did too. They avoided looking at each other. They had been avoiding looking at each other ever since last night. Jodi had helped untangle Kate's sleeve from his codpiece, after which he had promptly excused himself. Kate had then settled at the table where Jodi and the other writers had tried to cheer her, while Chris had tried valiantly not to laugh. Chuck had come by twice to talk to the writers and toss glares her way. Allison had come by at least three times to reassure her that everything would be fine. Chris had again tried not to laugh.

When Lucern hadn't returned after half an hour, Kate had excused herself and gone back to their suite. Lucern had just been coming out of his room. His gaze had touched hers, then shifted quickly away as he asked if the ball was over. Kate had told him it wasn't, but she had a headache and wanted to lie down. He'd made a sympathetic comment, told her that he'd just come upstairs for a drink—from which she gathered that he'd had some blood—then had said perhaps he'd just relax in the suite, too.

Kate had merely shrugged. She felt depressed and miserable, a gigantic failure at life and wondered how everything had gone so wrong.

And that had been before her folly was plastered all over the newspaper.

She sighed again.

"I guess we should head to the hospitality suite," Lucern finally suggested.

Kate grimaced. She'd had to drag him to the blasted thing that first day; now he was all eager to go. And she wasn't. The last thing in the world Kate wanted was to go anywhere she might have to face Chuck Morgan. If the publisher hadn't been pleased with her last night, today, after seeing the headlines, he would be livid. If she still had her job by noon, she'd be a lucky woman.

But, she told herself, there was no sense in dragging it out. She might as well go learn the awful truth.

*   *   *

It wasn't as bad as she'd feared. In some ways, it was worse. Kate still had a job. In fact, Chuck was terribly pleased with the publicity. Lucern had made the front page, after all. As had Roundhouse Publishing. The man kept congratulating her as if her public humiliation was some sort of grand promotional scheme. Kate would have liked to choke him. By the end of the day, she decided that if he patted her in that congratulatory manner one more time, she was going to.

It was more than a relief to Kate when they closed up the hospitality suite and everyone was freed to prepare for the night's Rock 'n' Roll party.

Her gaze went to Lucern. The man had come out of his shell with a vengeance. Every time she'd looked his way today, he'd been talking to a fan or another writer. Kate couldn't be sure, but she suspected he'd done more talking since arriving at this conference than he had in the past several decades. He'd become more loquacious with each passing day, and today had been no exception.

Of course, there wasn't a single solitary conference attendee who hadn't seen the headlines. The news of the situation had also made the rounds, and while most people were terribly sympathetic with both her and Lucern, there were a few who still snickered. They offered their "You poor dears" or their "How embarrassing it must be for yous," while they chuckled nonetheless. Of course, Lucern wasn't suffering those little snickers. Everyone seemed to feel great sympathy for him, saving all their amusement for her.

Which was usually the way of it, Kate thought wearily

as she walked toward the table with Lucern and the other writers; the woman always suffered the scorn and humiliation, while the man walked away with the glory or sympathy. Unfortunately, try as she might, Kate couldn't be angry at Lucern for the way other people acted. He had apologized repeatedly while Kate and Jodi had worked to untangle her sleeve from his codpiece, and she knew he really felt bad about the whole thing. But it hadn't been his fault. It had just been one of life's unfortunate incidents.

Lucern glanced at her as she approached, and Kate managed to pull a smile from the depths of herself.

"Time to go?" he asked.

"Yes." She smiled at him, then the table in general. "Time to get ready for the Rock 'n' Roll party."

Lucern stood and took her hand, his gaze moving over her face with a tinge of what she thought might be concern. "You look weary."

"It was a long day," Kate agreed with a small shrug. They left the hospitality suite. They didn't speak again until they reached their own. Chris hadn't returned yet, and the suite was empty and silent.

"What does one wear to a rock and roll party?" Lucern asked as he closed the door behind them.

"Well, I gather it's an oldies type party. Fifties. Jeans and T-shirts will do. I brought a leather jacket and boots for you to wear," Kate explained. She had said she would take care of everything, and she had to the best of her abilities.

"A leather jacket?" Lucern asked, one eyebrow raised.

"Yes. You know, the Fonzie look."

"The who?"

She frowned at his bewildered expression, then recalled he didn't watch television. He'd missed loads, she realized with amazement. "He's a cool fifties character from a series. Leather jacket, jeans, leather boots and greased back hair. Very cool."

"Ah. Yes, I recall a couple characters like that from those days." Lucern nodded. "But how did you know what boot size to get?"

Kate flushed and shrugged, then turned toward her door. She was slipping through it when she admitted, "I called your mother and asked."

She didn't wait for his response, simply closed the door on his startled expression. Then she went to pull out the bagged clothing from the costumers. She set the bag holding the leather jacket and boots on the bed, then held the see-through bag with her own costume up for inspection. This was certainly going to be an adventure. The costume didn't look at all appealing. She'd bet anything that those crinolines were going to itch like crazy.

Actually, she'd been wrong, Kate admitted sometime later as she surveyed herself in the mirror. She wore saddle shoes, bobby socks, the pink poodle skirt and a cream sweater set. She'd pulled her hair back into a ponytail and gone light on the makeup, and she looked about sixteen. She shook her head at her reflection, then decided she was ready and walked out to collect the bag with Luc's costume.

Chris and Luc were both watching television when Kate joined them in the living room, and her gaze slid from one's oil-slicked head to the other. She gaped. "What have you two done to your hair?"

Chris turned and grinned. "Isn't it great? Luc helped me with it. I didn't bring a leather jacket, but he said if I stuck a pack of cigarettes under my T-shirt sleeve I'd look just as cool."

Kate looked at Lucern. Great. Now she had two grease-slicked Fonzies on her hands. Still, other than the hairstyle, they were very different. Chris's hair was light, while Lucern's was as dark as midnight. Chris was tall and wiry, his body lanky rather than having the muscular breadth of Luc's. Chris's T-shirt was plain white; Lucern's was black and pulled tight across his chest, showing every ripple of his muscles. God, he looked hot. Even with enough grease in his hair to fry donuts.

"Is that for me?" Lucern stood and walked over, his gaze sliding across her in a slow caress.

"Yes." Kate handed him the bagged clothing, aware her face was flushing. She not only looked sixteen, she felt sixteen at the moment.

"You look lovely," he said in a whisper-soft voice. "Sweet and cute. The picture of youth."

Sweet and cute. Kate chewed over those words as Luc unwrapped his boots and jacket, then donned them. Puppies were cute. And who wanted to look like "the picture of youth"?

"A perfect fit."

Kate glanced at Lucern where he stretched, testing the fit in the shoulders of his jacket. Her gaze didn't settle on his shoulders, though, but on his chest where the muscles bunched. *Cute and youthful*. She sighed.

252

"Looks great." Chris got to his feet and joined them at the center of the room. "Let's get going. I have to stop and pick up a pack of cigarettes to stick under my sleeve."

Kate managed to tear her gaze from Lucern's chest. She nodded, then turned to lead the way out.

The Rock 'n' Roll party was in full swing when they arrived. Kate took one look at the dancers—mostly women—and winced. Some of them were very good. Some obviously didn't have a clue what they were doing. Kate very much feared she would fall into the latter category.

"I suppose *you* know the dances?" she asked Lucern. At her pained expression, he grinned one of his rare grins and nodded.

"Very well, actually." Then he added, "I'll teach you."

To Kate, who was of the considered opinion that she had two left feet, that sounded very much like a threat. But Lucern was a very good teacher and, being one of so few men, he was much in demand. He took everything with a good grace that nearly sent Kate into coma from the shock. She watched him dance with twenty or so women at a time. He lined them up in rows, patiently teaching them steps amidst much giggling, then twirled the women about in the air with the strength and stamina of a bull. The women thought he was marvelous. Kate did, too. She couldn't believe this was the same surly man who'd once slammed a door in her face. This man smiled. This man had the patience of Job. This man was every woman's dream. She even let him teach her how to dance.

The party was great fun, but Kate had suffered a stressful day and she found herself growing tired early. Lucern apparently noticed the yawns she was trying to hide. "You have to leave," he said, coming over and collecting her. He then lectured her all the way back to their suite—mostly about not eating enough. He had apparently noticed she'd been too busy talking to her writers to eat more than a few bites from the buffet.

"I don't like it. You have to take better care of yourself," he insisted firmly. "You expend far too much time and energy on behalf of your writers, myself included," he complained.

Kate tried to defend herself, pointing out that this was only one week a year.

Luc wasn't fool enough to fall for it. "Jodi mentioned many other conventions that are held throughout the year," he said. "And I hear you frequently work nights and even weekends, editing and reading books from your 'slush pile.' "

Kate made a mental note to block Jodi from her Windows instant messenger after hours, if the author was going to go and tattle on her. She always kept her instant messenger signed on while she was in the office, in case one of her writers had a question. Jodi often berated her for working so much, but the last thing Kate needed was Lucern knowing she had absolutely no social life.

Of course, he had apparently lost interest in pursuing the passion they had briefly shared. He hadn't tried anything since that first night and the morning after. That had been Tuesday and Wednesday. It was now Friday night, and other than holding her hand in a calming

manner, Lucern hadn't done anything to initiate another such occurrence.

Of course, neither had she, Kate admitted to herself.
She eyed him consideringly. Perhaps . . .

"You're going to bed the moment we get back in the
room. And I don't want to see you again until at least
seven a.m. That means ten hours of sleep. You need it,"
Lucern said firmly, interrupting her thoughts as they
stepped out of the elevator.

Kate sighed inwardly. There was no "perhaps" about
it; the man wasn't interested in bedding her any longer,
and he had just made sure she wouldn't get the idea
herself. Had those first two passionate encounters been
caused purely by his need for blood? Perhaps he had
deliberately seduced her only in an effort to "have a
nibble." Perhaps she hadn't noticed his lack of true interest the first two times because she had been so overwhelmed, hadn't been aware of the fact that he might
deliberately excite her only to bite her. She had certainly been aware of it the third time and noticed it
then, but only until his practiced, deliberate assault on
her senses had overwhelmed her. Perhaps he wasn't at
all interested in her as anything but dinner.

Why had she thought otherwise? And when had it
started to mean so much?

Kate sighed unhappily as they entered their suite. It
was rather disheartening to be nothing but a snack.

"Sleep well." Lucern gave her a gentle push toward
her bedroom door, and Kate went without comment.
She managed to murmur good night before slipping
inside, but that was just for pride's sake. Her shoulders
slumped, her heart sore as she began to undress.

255

*   *   *

Lucern watched the door close behind Kate and frowned to himself. The woman worked too hard, ate too little, and was killing herself to keep everyone happy—including himself. She needed rest. She needed to eat more. And, above all, she needed to relax. He could think of many ways to help her do that. Unfortunately, most involved both of them naked, and he wasn't at all sure she would welcome that now that she knew the truth about him. It had been his experience that most women were repulsed by his being a vampire. Kate certainly wasn't the first woman who had learned his secret over the years, and he had found, more often than not, they became afraid of him upon learning the truth. To keep himself and his family safe, he had often had to exert himself to veil their memories, or persuade them the revelation was just a dream.

Kate hadn't appeared frightened, though. She'd seemed to look at his vampirism as just a problem. Luc was a vampire, but he was also one of her most successful writers, and he needed blood. She had had to find him some. She had even been willing to indulge in intimacies in the men's washroom to accommodate him. Other than that, however, she had shown no sign of interest.

He recalled, his first night here and the first morning, when they had found themselves in passionate circumstances. But that had been before Kate knew he was a vampire. She might very well find him repulsive now.

Suddenly aware of tension in his neck and shoulders, Lucern removed his leather jacket and tossed it over a chair. He rotated first one shoulder then the other, then his head as well, trying to ease the muscles there. It was Kate's doing. He wished he knew what she was thinking and where she stood on the matter. He wanted her to want him. He wanted her. He grimaced. It was a foolish want. Kate was a modern woman with career aspirations and a life and home in New York. She had left life in sleepy Nebraska to pursue a job in the publishing industry. She would hardly give that up to move to Canada to carry out an affair—and Lucern didn't know her well enough to be sure he wanted a life with her. For the average human, a bad marriage was only a forty- or fifty-year sentence; it could be much much longer for him.

His gaze slid to the small bar in the corner, and he considered a Scotch before bed. He decided against it. He wasn't much of a drinker and didn't want to start relying on it. Alchohol had done serious damage to his father, Claude, even killing him in the end.

Shrugging, he decided he might as well go to sleep.

The first thing that struck him when he entered his room was the sweet smell of blood heavy in the air. Then he realized that the bedside lamp was on, and he stiffened. He had turned the light out before leaving for the ball. It was now on. His body began to pump adrenaline even as his gaze swept the room.

The partially open fridge door, and the slashed bags of blood lying before it, explained the scent in the air. Other than that, nothing seemed disturbed. There didn't appear to be anyone around. Of course, the scent of blood was so thick, his usual ability to sense anyone nearby was hampered.

He took a step toward his looted blood supply, intending to see if anything was salvageable. But even as he did, he heard the whisper of the bedroom door swinging closed behind him. He whirled just in time to feel the stake slamming into his chest.

Kate had removed her clothes and was debating whether to shower or simply go to bed when she heard a crash. She paused, her head tilting as she listened. When something slammed hard into the wall separating her room from Luc's, she snatched for her robe, dragged it on, and tied the sash as she ran into the living room.

The door to Lucern's room was closed. Kate didn't bother to knock, but thrust it open and rushed inside. She nearly crashed into two men locked in combat. At first, all she saw were the two men grappling with each other; then she noticed the stake, its tip buried in Lucern's chest and blood seeping out. She shrieked in horror, though she didn't know it. She heard the yell as a distant sound.

At last, breaking out of her shock-induced paralysis, she glanced wildly around. The only weapon she could see were the bedside lamps. She ran to grab one, cursing when the damned thing didn't move. It was fastened to the bedside table. Her gaze shot back to Lucern and his assailant. There was more blood, and it seemed to her the stake had gone deeper. Lucern appeared to be weakening. Yet there wasn't a single damned thing around to use as a weapon. Desperate, she grabbed a pillow and ran over, batting at the stranger, then slamming the pillow into his head and shoulders. Her attack had little effect on the man. He didn't even glance around.

Letting loose a howl of rage as her gaze shifted to Lucern's pale face, Kate caught the pillow at each end and swung it over the attacker's head and slammed it into his face. Pulling it tight, she proceeded to try to climb the fellow's back. Much to her relief, he released Lucern and stumbled backward, trying to grab wildly at her. She managed to avoid his flailing hands, and held on to the pillow with all her might. He couldn't possibly breathe like this, and she was praying he would pass out before he managed to get her.

She released an "oomph," but managed to stay on his back as he staggered back into the wall next to the closet. Kate held on, knowing both she and Luc were lost if she didn't.

Kate glanced desperately at Lucern. He was on his knees by the bed, his hands weakly gripping the stake in his chest. She recalled him saying that a stake would kill him if left in too long, and she knew she had to get to him fast. Her thoughts were scattered as the man she was riding slammed backward again, this time propelling them into the closet. Kate grunted as her head slammed into the clothing rod.

The pain was like an explosion inside her head, blinding her with searing white flashes behind her eyes. She wanted to grab her head and hold it in her hands until the agony passed, but she couldn't let go of the pillow and so hung there blind and in agony, clinging to consciousness by a thread.

When the pain finally began to wane, Kate wasn't sure how much time had passed. It took a moment before she realized her view had changed. She was lower to the ground. She turned her attention to the man she clung to, and she saw that he had sunk to his knees, taking her with him. She let her feet drop to the floor, her gaze returning to Lucern. Alarm again coursed through her. He was slumped forward, his head down. Realizing that she couldn't wait any longer for her assailant to pass out from lack of oxygen, she released one end of the pillow to search around the floor of the closet.

She tried to keep the pillow in place over the man's face with her one hand, but she was aware she was failing. She heard him taking great gasps of air, and she knew it wouldn't take long for him to recoup enough to become a serious threat again. That thought had barely managed to panic her when Kate's searching hand bumped something. She snatched it up, recognizing it for a shoe, and without a thought slammed it down on her attacker's head. He didn't immediately fall forward under the blow, and she realized she was holding the shoe by the heel. She gave up on holding the pillow in place, turned the shoe around and this time slammed the heel down on the back of her enemy's skull with all the strength she could muster.

Much to her satisfaction, the blow worked—the man fell soundlessly forward on his face. Leaving him where he lay, Kate struggled to her feet and stumbled over to Lucern.

The first thing she did was grab him by the shoulders and urge him up. He fell onto his back without a sound. His head slammed against the floor, hard, and his knees bent, his lower legs caught under him. Kate peered at him unhappily. He was gray. She had never seen him this color. But there wasn't much blood lost that she could tell. The stake still protruded from his chest, allowing only a bit of seepage. But she recalled his saying the heart couldn't pump with a stake there, and she knew that if she didn't remove it, he would die.

The stake was made of the light wood usually found at do-it-yourself places, and it looked like a dowel or something. Lucern's attacker had bought and sharpened a dowel to a point so that he could stake Lucern. Now she would have to unstake him or he would die.

She didn't waste time thinking about what she was doing; she knew that every second counted. Reaching out, she grabbed the dowel firmly and pulled it free— which wasn't as easy as she'd expected. She hadn't really thought about it, but if she had, Kate supposed she would have expected it to pull free like a knife from butter. Lucern's body wasn't butter. There was some resistance to the removal, and she had to exert some strength. The sloppy squelching sound as she removed it made what little food she'd managed to down at supper threaten to make an encore appearance.

Kate swallowed determinedly. Tossing the stake aside, she quickly covered the wound in Lucern's chest as blood began to pour out in great gushes. She applied pressure in an effort to keep him from bleeding to death, praying all the while that his blood would repair the damage. As she sat there, she wondered if she was really helping to save him or killing him.

She sat like that for several minutes, just pressing

down on his chest, until a moan from Lucern's attacker warned that he was coming around. She felt torn between staying to hold in Lucern's blood, or somehow incapacitating the man again. It seemed to her that if the man came around, she and Luc would probably both be dead. Surely he would finish Lucern off, then kill her as a witness. On the other hand, she would risk Lucern's bleeding to death if she left him.

Her gaze slid back to Lucern's face and she hesitated, then cautiously removed her hands from his chest. Much to her relief, blood didn't come gushing out as before. His body was repairing itself. She hoped so, or he was dead.

Banishing that thought, Kate got to her feet and peered around the room for something to tie up their enemy. She spotted the black backpack with all the burglary paraphernalia, and relief soaked through her. She had handed it to Lucern to take the blood with him and never bothered to ask for it back. Hurrying to it, she found the rope, but tossed that aside and snatched up the duct tape and the knife instead. She wasn't very good with knots. Besides, she suspected the tape would be harder for the man to get free.

Another groan from her attacker made Kate rush to his side. She pulled his hands behind his back and quickly began wrapping tape around his wrists, running the roll between his lower arms and hands for good measure. Once satisfied that he couldn't free himself, she moved to his feet and bound his ankles the same way. Then she rolled him onto his back so that he lay on his bound hands, and began to wrap tape over his mouth and around his head. It would be a bitch to get the tape off his hair, but she didn't care. He deserved that and more.

Kate was just finishing when the attacker's eyes suddenly blinked open. She gave a start as he jerked, trying to break free. Hatred blazed from his eyes. She met his gaze for a moment, then finished with the tape, ignoring his useless struggles.

Had Lucern been a normal man, she would have called the police. But Lucern wasn't a normal man. How could she explain the situation? Kate's gaze swept the room, falling on the partially open fridge door and the slashed bags of blood. She couldn't explain any of this to the police. No, she was on her own.

Pushing herself to her feet, Kate moved almost reluctantly back to Lucern's side. Then she hesitated, unsure what to do. There still didn't appear to be a great deal of blood loss. On the other hand, she suspected it would probably take a lot of blood to repair the damage done to Lucern. He would need blood.

Her eyes went to his mouth. He didn't seem to be breathing, let alone in any shape to drink from her. On the other hand, she saw that the wound in his chest was not gushing. It wasn't bleeding at all. If anything, she was sure the hole was smaller and there was less blood present.

Kate recalled that Lucern had said that something in his blood used blood to repair injuries. Was it using that blood even now? Could it repair him and keep him alive . . . if he was still alive.

Kate leaned forward and grabbed the ragged edges

of Luc's T-shirt where the stake had torn it. She rent it open, pulling one long strip of cloth free. Setting it on the floor next to her, she shifted her head over Luc's chest for a closer look at his wound. Yes, there was definitely less blood. Surely, that was a sign he still lived?

Biting her lip, she glanced down at the knife in her hand. He couldn't feed off her. But could she feed him?

Acting before she could think about it and change her mind, Kate slashed her wrist, then she held it over his wound, allowing her blood to drip freely into it. She stayed like that, stopping only when she started to feel a little lightheaded. Then she quickly grabbed the slip of T-shirt she had ripped free. Using that, she tightly bandaged her wrist. It was an awkward procedure, but she managed.

At last, Kate sat back and cast a glance at the man who had attacked Lucern. He was where she had left him, still tightly trussed. If he had fought the binding, it was holding fast. Noting that with relief, she turned her attention back to Lucern. His eyes were still closed, his face pale and still. He didn't open his eyes or smile at her as she had hoped. The wound wasn't closing miraculously. It wasn't anything like the movies. She wished it were.

Kate resolved herself to a long vigil. She wasn't at all sure he would open those silver eyes again, but she wasn't going to give up either.

Weariness overtaking her, Kate shifted to lie beside him and rested her aching head on his uninjured shoulder. She lay there in silence for a moment, listening, but no heartbeat met her ears. The stake had stopped his heart. She just wasn't sure if it had stopped it for good.

"Come back to me, Lucern," she whispered, closing her eyes to shut out the light. "Please."

Chapter Fifteen

Lucern woke with a gasp, his body sucking oxygen deep into his lungs and just as quickly forcing it out again. The sound of his heart was like a drum in his ringing ears, and his eyes saw only darkness. That darkness slowly gave way to blurred color. Lucern lay still for several moments as his body struggled to recover, knowing he had come close to death.

He slowly became aware of pressure on his shoulder, and he glanced down, relieved to find that his eyesight had returned. He was able to see the top of a head. He couldn't see the face, but he recognized Kate's honey-blond tresses and felt an odd warmth flow through him to know she was with him.

Letting his eyes drift closed, he took stock. There was no brain damage from what he could tell; his memory was intact. Kate had saved him. The idea was a bit mind-boggling. He was used to being the warrior, the savior, the hero. But Kate had been the hero today, fending off his attacker with—of all things—a pillow.

He would have chuckled if he had the energy to do so. The woman had felled their attacker with a pillow, an attacker who had got the best of him. It really did boggle the mind. Her courage and cleverness were a formidable combination. He tried to lift his hand to caress the soft strands of her hair, wanting that further connection with her, but didn't yet have the strength.

Frustrated by his weakness and lack of control, Lucern forced himself to be patient. His body would be working like mad to send blood to repair his brain and vital organs first. Once they were in working order, the blood would concentrate on the rest of him. Then some of his strength would return.

As he lay there, he wondered about his attacker. Who was the man? It was a question he would like answered, but Lucern also wondered what had become of him. He could only assume that Kate had tended to the matter, or she surely wouldn't have fallen asleep on him. If she was asleep.

His eyes popped open again.

From prior experience with injuries, Lucern guessed that he had been unconscious for perhaps half an hour. It seemed a relatively short period of time for Kate to have handled their attacker, removed the stake from his chest and fallen asleep. This time, when he tried to move Lucern was able to raise his hand and rest it weakly against the side of her head.

Much to his relief, Kate murmured sleepily. She cuddled kittenlike against him, snuggling into his body. The action managed to relax Lucern. She was alive. Everything else could wait. He closed his eyes and fell into a light rest as his body finished its repairs.

When next he opened his eyes, it was hunger urging him back. His strength hadn't fully returned—Lucern was still weak, comparatively speaking—but his weakness was equivalent to an average man's strength. Moving carefully, he shifted out from under Kate, easing her head to the floor before sitting up and peering around. He immediately spotted his attacker lying on the floor by the closet. The man was trussed like a turkey.

Luc's eyes went to the refrigerator and he noted the four slashed bags. He twitched with realization. *Four* bags. There had been eight left after his last feeding. Standing up, he moved to the refrigerator, pulled the door the rest of the way open and peered inside. A breath of relief slipped from his lips at the sight of four intact blood bags. He must have interrupted the fellow's work before the man got the chance to destroy the whole supply.

Lucern grabbed one of the pints and stabbed his teeth into it as he turned to survey the room. There would be a bit of work setting it to rights. He had to clean up the blood on the carpet and take care of the gentleman now imitating a bear rug on his floor.

He contemplated what to do with his assailant as he went through two more bags of blood. At last, he decided he would have to find out more before making a decision. He needed to know if this had been an attack on Luke Amirault the vampire author, or Lucern Argeneau the vampire. The difference could affect the safety of his family.

Lucern felt pretty good once he'd finished his third bag of blood. He decided to leave the fourth and final bag for later, and he closed the refrigerator door and set to work. He took care of everything as best he could—including handling his assailant—then turned his attention to Kate, who still lay sleeping in the middle of his floor. He debated whether to take her back to her room, but the last he had seen she had hit her head on the closet rod. He didn't like the idea of leaving her alone all night. What if the injury caused her some difficulty later? She should sleep here in his room, though not on the floor.

Moving to her side, Lucern knelt and slipped his hands under Kate, then lifted her into his arms. She barely stirred as he carried her over and laid her on the bed. He noticed the strip of cloth around her wrist as he started to straighten. Picking up her hand, he unwrapped the makeshift bandage. Concern filled him. The gash in her flesh had clotted and was no longer bleeding, but he couldn't tell how deep it was. He didn't think she needed stitches, since it was already closed, but . . .

He grabbed the phone and called down to the front desk, requesting bandages and antiseptic, then pondered how she might have received the injury. The only thing he could think of was that she had gotten it somehow during the battle. He now regretted letting the man go so lightly. He should have—

His thoughts were interrupted by a knock at the outer door. The first-aid items had arrived. He went and got them without letting the bellhop in, then went back to attend to Kate. He cleaned her injury and carefully wrapped it, then set her hand gently on her chest and pulled the covers up over her.

He left her sleeping while he stripped off his ruined clothes and showered the blood away. Then he slid into bed, too, being sure to stay as far away from her as he could. He didn't want to risk bumping Kate's arm or have her getting upset when she awoke. He would sleep on his side of the bed.

Of course, he hadn't considered that Kate might not stay on her side. He had just started to doze off when Kate rolled over, throwing her hand across his chest and snuggling up like she belonged there. Oddly enough, it felt like she did.

Kate was slow to wake, almost reluctant to face the world. It took a moment for her foggy brain to remember what had happened; then Lucern's image slipped into her mind. She stiffened and opened her eyes. The first thing her gaze fell on was Lucern's chin. She stared at it for a moment, then reluctantly lowered her eyes to his chest, afraid to find the gaping hole there. When she saw bedding, she sat up abruptly, startled to find herself in bed with him. Her gaze swept the room in confusion—only to find it all in order. Had it all been a dream? she wondered vaguely.

Her eyes fell on the floor in front of the mini-refrigerator, and her tongue stuck to the roof of her mouth. Obviously, someone had tried to wash away blood, and had managed to remove the worst of it, but there was still a large, faint stain. Turning back to Lucern, Kate tugged the blankets down.

A sob surprised her by breaking from her throat at the sight of his unmarred chest. Both relieved and amazed, she ran the tips of her fingers lightly over the perfect skin there, then she closed her eyes and tried to calm her wildly beating heart. He was alive!

A warm hand closed over hers, and Kate opened her eyes again. Lucern was awake, and he peered at her and clasped her hand.

"You saved my life," he said solemnly. "Thank you."

Kate glanced away, her gaze finding the closet and the empty floor in front of it. "The man who attacked you—"

"I cleared his mind and sent him home."

She stared at him in horror. "Sent him home? He attacked you."

"I could hardly call the police and try to explain the situation," Lucern pointed out. He shrugged, then added, "Besides, he wasn't well. His mind is . . . wrong."

"Why did he attack you? Was he at the conference? Does he—"

"No, he wasn't a conference attendee. He lives here in the city. Apparently, his wife was a big romance fan. When she left him, he wanted someone to blame it on. He decided it was all those books she was reading." He shrugged. "He started reading them for himself, and when he got to mine, he got the idea that I was a vampire. He saw our picture in the paper and knew that I was in town, and he decided that I had taken control of his wife's mind and lured her away from him. He began to believe that if he could just destroy me, her mind would be set free. He believed she would come back to him."

Kate stared at Lucern, her thoughts racing. He sounded so understanding.

She had felt helpless and useless last night, and had

suffered a great sense of loss at the possibility that he might be dead—more loss than was appropriate for one of her writers. There was really no use fighting it anymore. Kate knew her feelings for this man ran deep. She had thought him brilliant and talented before ever meeting him, had found him surly and rude on arriving at his home, then had seen other sides of him slowly show themselves, like the legs, arms and head of a turtle. She had come to see that the hard shell he showed the world was just that, a shell, a shield meant to protect himself. He was smart and strong, but he was also compassionate and kind. A man had nearly killed him, and yet Lucern found it in his heart to feel sorry for him. She heard the compassion in his voice. It was as soft and open as his expression. His shield seemed to be missing entirely this morning, and she had no idea why. She almost wished it weren't so. Perhaps then she would be able to battle the wealth of feelings welling up within her.

"Kate?"

Her eyes refocused on his face.

"How is your head?" he asked. "I saw you hit it on the clothing rod before I lost consciousness last night."

"My head is in bad shape," she told him solemnly.

Concern entered his gaze. "It is?" He sat up and reached for her, his fingers running gently over the back of her head. "I took a look last night, but there wasn't much of a bump. I thought . . ." He fell silent when she placed her hand against his chest where the stake had been. The bedding pooled around his waist, leaving endless flesh bare to her view.

He looked fine. Still, Kate knew he would need to

replenish the blood used to repair his body. She would also have to replace the bags of blood the attacker had destroyed. Luc needed enough to see him through the rest of the conference. It was Saturday morning, six a.m, she saw with a glance at the bedside clock. There was only that day and the next to get through—but Lucern had been injured and would need a large infusion. She was willing to offer him her own. Unlike last night, this time it would be a pleasure to give it. He would make sure of that, she knew. Her fingers moved across his chest of their own accord.

His skin was slightly cool to the touch—not the cold flesh of a corpse, but a degree or two cooler than her own. It felt nice. Kate almost felt as if she were suffering a temperature, but knew her overheated flesh had nothing to do with ill health and everything to do with the naked man in bed next to her. She was pretty sure he was naked. She had learned that first morning that he slept in the nude, and she vaguely recalled her legs scraping bare skin as she had shifted this morning. Of course, he might be wearing jockey shorts or something.

Lucern caught her wayward hand in his, ending her mental debate as to whether he was naked. Kate dragged her gaze from his lap where it had drifted. He caught her eyes with his own, held them as he raised her hand to his mouth and pressed a kiss to her palm.

Kate's breath caught. His caress caused a tingling in her palm that ran up her arm, eliciting from her a small shiver.

"Does your head hurt very badly?" he asked.

Kate slowly shook her head. "That's not what I meant by its being in bad shape, Luc."

"Then, what . . . ?"

Kate ignored his question and raised her hand to caress his cheek. The clean bandage on her wrist surprised her. "Did you—?"

"Yes." He caught her hand and drew it to his mouth. Again he pressed a kiss on her palm just above the edge of the bandage. There was a flicker of anger in his eyes. "Did *he* do this?"

"No. I did," she admitted. "To help you."

His gaze followed hers to his chest, and realization dawned on his face. It softened the anger of a moment before.

"Kate," he began, his voice husky. But she didn't want his gratitude. She hadn't done it wholly for him. Her reasons were much more complex and partially selfish. She had done it for herself. Because she couldn't imagine a world without him in it. She didn't want to, and she didn't want a thank you. She wanted to give him the chance to take the blood he no doubt needed, and she wanted him.

"I want you," she admitted. "You're one of my writers, a vampire in serious need of blood, you nearly died last night, we both could have died, and yet now, this morning, I don't care about any of that. I want to push you back on the bed, crawl on top of you and take you inside me."

Lucern stared at Kate, his mind blanked by her words, filled with the image she painted. He could see her pushing him back, dragging the sheets and blankets aside, shrugging out of the bulky terrycloth robe she wore, then shifting over him and reaching down to guide him into her.

A moment before, what she suggested would have been impossible. His body would not have cooperated. Now, however, he was awake and peering expectantly up from under the blankets. *Damn,* he thought with mild amazement, there was definitely something to be said for modern, aggressive women.

Clearing his throat, Lucern managed a smile. "I think that idea shows merit," he said.

Oddly, his gruff formal words had the effect of making Kate burst out laughing. Lucern was trying to decide if he should join her or be affronted when she suddenly sobered, straightened beside him on the bed, and untied her robe. She slipped it off her shoulders. As it pooled around her waist, she said solemnly, "I hope you have a condom."

Lucern stared at the pale creamy flesh of her body. He had gotten her almost naked just days before in this very room, but he hadn't had the view he had now. Kate was slender and shapely, her curves generous but not overly so. She had rosy nipples, which topped breasts pointing at him like a pair of binoculars. He wanted to reach out and grasp them as he would binoculars, but rather than look through them, he wanted desperately to lick and suck and . . .

"A condom?" he asked, as if he'd never heard the word before. Fortunately, his mind cleared enough for him to grasp the meaning: she was concerned about the sexual diseases of the day. "Oh. Not to worry; diseases can't survive in my body."

He smiled one of his rare smiles, pleased to be able

to pass along the information. Not having a condom wouldn't be a problem. Besides, at that moment, he was positive that *a* condom wouldn't be sufficient. Many would be needed. Many, many, he thought as he reached out to run his finger over one of her erect nipples.

He glanced up with a start when Kate slapped his hand away. Much to his dismay, she didn't appear impressed with his announcement. She was frowning.

"But don't vampires have sperm?"

Lucern had to think about that question for a moment before his poor besotted mind understood. *Sperm? Sex. Babies. Oh!*

"Oh!" He glanced wildly around the room, his mind working frantically. He didn't have a condom. He didn't use condoms. STD's weren't a fear to him, and pregnancy had never been much of a concern. It was rare for a human and his sort to manage a baby. His cousin, the mad scientist of the clan, had explained why to him, but he couldn't remember at the moment. Still, he didn't think Kate would take that rare chance. He needed a condom.

"Uh, just a minute. Just . . . uh . . ." Sweeping the blankets aside, he leapt from the bed and grabbed the bloodstained pants he'd removed last night. He began searching through the pockets. When he found his wallet, he took it out and smiled at her—an admittedly pained smile. "I just have to . . . er . . . just one minute."

He ran out of the room and into the living room. He paused halfway to the door to the hall when she shouted, "You don't plan on going to buy some, do you? You're naked, Luc!"

That stopped him.

"Luc?"

"No. No, I'm not—Just a minute," he finished at last, his mind feverish. He considered dressing, but then an image of Kate rose in his mind. No, there wasn't time to dress. What if she changed her mind? Had second thoughts? He couldn't risk that. It would be faster if . . .

Hurrying to the phone, he snatched it up and dialed the front desk.

"Good morning," a cheerful female voice sang. "Front desk. Can I help you?"

"Condoms," Lucern blurted.

"Excuse me, sir?"

"Condoms. I need condoms," he barked.

"I see, sir." The cheerfulness went out of the voice. "What size?"

"Size?" They had sizes? Lucern peered down at himself. "Big."

"Of course, sir. They're always big," the voice said dryly. "Your choices are fitted, regular, large or extra large."

Lucern stared down at himself again. He seemed smaller than he had been moments ago. His erection was dwindling. He decided to forgo the extra large. "Large."

"Luc? What are you doing?"

Lucern turned to find Kate standing naked in the bedroom doorway, her gaze moving nervously between him and the door to Chris's room. His gaze swept her from top to toe, and he was grateful that his eyesight hadn't been damaged last night. Neither had his sense of smell. Her sweet, spicy scent was wafting to him, surrounding him with its succulence. She smelled good enough to eat. That thought brought other thoughts to mind: licking every inch of her flesh and—

"Luc?" Kate was starting to look concerned. "Are you all right? You look . . . odd."

"Sir?"

Lucern's gaze dropped to his erection. He said into the phone, "Make that extra large."

"Extra large what? Lucern, what are you doing?" Kate asked. She was starting to sound irritated.

"Just a minute," Lucern barked into the phone. Setting it on the table, he hurried to Kate's side to catch her by the arms. "I'll be right there. Go back to bed. You have goosebumps." She had them everywhere— on the arms his hands were absently caressing, on her breasts which his eyes were caressing, on— Perhaps extra large wouldn't be big enough.

Shaking his head, Lucern turned Kate around and pointed her toward the bed. "I'll be right there. I promise."

"But—"

Lucern closed the door on her protest and hurried back to the phone. "Hello?"

"Yes, sir." The woman was definitely annoyed at waiting. "Now, what size package do you want? We have six-packs, twelve-packs, twenty-four and thirty-six."

"Six, twelve, twenty-four and thirty-six?" Lucern repeated. This was like some sort of test. Dear God, he couldn't think. The scent of Kate still enveloped him, and his brain had gone all fuzzy. He wondered briefly if he shouldn't have consumed more blood. Perhaps he had lost more than he'd thought, and his blood supply was so low that his body was now having to take blood from elsewhere to support his erection. If so, it had definitely chosen to remove it from his brain. His thoughts were as muddy as a pigsty after a rainfall.

"Sir?"

"All of them," he said at last. The more the merrier.

"Lubricated or nonlubricated?"

"Urgh," Lucern choked into the phone.

"Very good. Lubricated," the woman said. "Now . . . do you want For Her Pleasure, Ribbed, Ultra-fit, Extra Strength, Ultra Pleasure, Shared Sensation, Textured, Sensitive, Ultra-thin, Magnum, Supra, Pleasure Mesh, Extended Pleasure or Magnum XL?" The woman sounded like she was really enjoying herself.

Lucern wasn't. He peered down to see that his erection was definitely suffering from this barrage of questions. It was a sad sight, and he whimpered into the phone.

"I'll just send a variety, shall I?"

Lucern was sagging against the table in relief when she added, "That should be no more than half an hour. Have a good day, sir."

Lucern was erect at once. Well, his body was. His penis was still flagging as he roared, "Half an hour?" into the phone.

His answer was the dial tone.

"Luc?"

He slammed down the phone and turned to find his bedroom door open again. Kate was once again standing in it. But, she had re-donned her robe. He noted this with horror, his sinking heart telling him that the moment was passing. If he didn't do something soon, she was going to change her mind. Uncertainty was already creeping into her expression. "Maybe we should just give this a pass. You're one of my writers, and it probably isn't very professional to—"

Lucern almost groaned aloud. This was exactly what he'd feared might happen. Faced with it now, he did the only thing he could think of. Crossing the room, he caught her in his arms and kissed her. It was no "Good morning, nice to see you" kiss. It was "I want your body hot, sweaty and plastered against mine." Kate hesitated the barest moment, then—much to Lucern's relief—gave in with a moan. She melted against him.

Lucern's erection gave him a thumbs-up. It poked at Kate's robe. That was enough to urge him to take her in his arms and carry her to the bed. Setting her on her feet beside it, he quickly removed her robe and tossed it aside, then set to work convincing her she hadn't made a mistake on admitting she wanted him.

His plan—he began to worship her body—was to drag out the foreplay until the condoms arrived. Half an hour shouldn't be any problem at all. It would take that long to make his way across every inch of her skin. He started with her breasts, sweeping his hands up beneath them and catching their bottoms with his thumbs as the rest of his fingers closed around the sides. Then he bent his head and took one perfect nipple into his mouth. He would coax it back to its former glorious state of erection.

Kate moaned and shuddered as her nipple pebbled in Lucern's mouth. She had begun to think this wasn't a very good idea when Lucern left her side, but now, as he suckled on her breast, drawing its peak into his mouth and pulling her desire back from where it had briefly hidden, she let her doubts drift away. She wanted him. Oh, yes, how she wanted him.

Her hands roamed over his shoulders and down his back, clawed his flesh as he nipped playfully at hers.

Lucern chuckled against her breast and urged her onto the bed. He lay atop her at once, his mouth finding hers and devouring it. Kate kissed him back with every ounce of her being, her hands sliding into his hair and holding him there as she did. Then she let her hands drift down over his body.

Lucern stiffened against Kate, his eyes closing with pleasure as her fingers wrapped around his erection. She squeezed gently before sliding her hand along its length.

Ah, the aggressive modern woman, he thought vaguely. Renaissance and Regency women had been much more timid. Not all of them, of course, but the majority had allowed the man to set the pace and do most of the work. Not his Kate, however. She grabbed for the gusto, urging him on, and once again Lucern saw that there was something to be said for modern women after all. They were smart, business savvy, sexy as hell and not afraid to go after what they wanted. They were . . .

Horrible, he thought suddenly as he thrust into her caress. He had half an hour to kill before the condoms arrived. He hadn't been with a woman for a while. Several hundred years of sex had rather stolen the novelty of it, and he had grown tired of the bother more than fifty years ago. He'd led a rather asexual life since. However, Kate had reinvigorated that side of him—with a vengeance. And if she continued to touch and caress him the way she was, he was going to lose control like a teenager. Oh, this wasn't good.

Reaching down, Lucern caught her by the wrist and pulled her hand away. He broke their kiss and moved down her body, shifting his erection out of reach. He was determined to keep her busy and excited until the condoms arrived.

Kate moaned with mingled desire and displeasure when Lucern's mouth slid from hers and he began licking and nibbling his way down her body. She had the brief thought that it was a shame he didn't have two mouths so she could continue to kiss him as he ravaged her flesh.

Catching the hand that had stopped hers from exploring, she drew it to her mouth. Grabbing one thick finger, Kate sucked it into her mouth and nipped. Lucern paused to pay special attention to her breasts.

Her body tingled everywhere, and Kate shifted restlessly beneath Luc, clutching his hand and gasping as his mouth dropped to her belly. The muscles in her stomach contracted and rippled under his onslaught; then they clenched as he moved lower still and urged her legs apart. Oh, this was . . . She hoped he wouldn't *bite* her there.

The thought, silly as it was, forced a gasping laugh from her lips, but it died as quickly as it was born. What he was doing to her didn't leave breath or thought for such concerns, and moments later she didn't care if he did bite her so long as he didn't stop everything else.

Dear God, he would kill her with pleasure and she would be happy in the dying, she thought dazedly.

Then, losing the capacity to think as her body imploded, she cried out, arching her hips upward and tearing at the bedsheets. She shuddered out of control, grabbing Lucern's shoulders as he shifted. The only thing that would make this better was to have him inside her. She was sure of it. "Please, Lucern," she gasped.

"What is it, sweet?" he asked as he lay between her legs.

"I want you inside me. Put on the condom," she begged. When he stiffened and paused, she frowned. "Luc?"

"Er . . ." Much to her dismay, he pulled away from her. "I, er . . ."

"Didn't you get a condom?" she asked. "I thought—"

"Yes, yes. I, er, I just forgot it in the other room," he assured her quickly. Pushing himself from the bed, he added, "I'll . . . er . . . just be a moment. Stay here."

Then he hurried out of the room, pulling the door closed behind him.

Chapter Sixteen

Lucern yanked the door open and peered out into the hall, hoping to see a bellhop sauntering up with condoms in hand. Of course, there was no such thing. The hall was completely empty. He slammed the door with frustration, then turned to peer around the suite. There should have been condoms in each room. Hotels should stock them like they did candy bars and booze. Really, Luc didn't know why no one had thought of it.

A small sigh and the rustle of sheets drew his gaze to the door to his room. His hearing was working exceptionally well at the moment. All his senses were buzzing. His entire body was jumping with excitement, and all of it, every aching inch of him, wanted to be with Kate. This was like some sort of hell. Some sort of . . .

Lucern scowled toward his room and the soft, willing woman in his bed. He had known that this conference would be a hellish excursion. Little had he realized it would be full-body torture, though.

A snore from the other direction drew his attention. Chris Keyes's room. Sure, the guy was sleeping peacefully. He wasn't suffering the tortures of the damned and—

Chris is a guy.

The thought interrupted Lucern's internal rant, and he gazed hard at the door. Kate's coworker might have a condom. His gaze shot to his own room. He didn't think that Kate would want Chris to know what they were getting up to, though; he was pretty sure she would be extremely displeased if he asked her friend for a condom.

Another sigh issued from his bedroom, followed by another rustle. He could just imagine Kate shifting restlessly on his bed, her nipples still erect, her face softened by desire and—

He just wouldn't tell her where he got the condom, Lucern decided. Hurrying to Chris's door, he didn't knock or make any other sound that Kate might hear, simply opened it and slipped inside. He rushed to the bed where Chris lay sleeping. Grabbing the sleeping editor by the shoulders, he gave him a violent shake.

"Wake up," he hissed.

Chris came awake at once, his eyes blinking open with alarm. "What? What's happened?" he asked anxiously. "Is the hotel on fire?"

"No. I need a condom. Do you have one?"

Chris blinked stupidly at him. "What? A condom?" He started to lift his head; then his gaze hit Lucern's naked body. He froze, his mouth dropping open with horror. "Oh, geez, don't point that thing at me. Oh, my God." He pulled free of Lucern's hands and rolled away

285

with disgust. "I'm sleeping here. Go away."

Lucern scowled at Chris's back, straightened, and crossed his arms. "I need a condom."

"And I need sleep! Go away," the editor repeated.

"Don't you have any?" Lucern persisted.

Apparently realizing Lucern wasn't going to go away, Chris rolled back over. He glared. "Yes, I do. But do I look like a pharmacy to you?" he asked. He sat up. "Look, Lucern, I like you. But Kate is my friend and . . ." He paused to scowl. "Will you stop pointing that damn thing at me? You're giving me a complex here. Thank God all of my writers are female. Not one of them would stand there naked, waving themselves in front of me. I shouldn't know this much about Kate's personal life. We're friends and coworkers and . . . Have you two slept together yet? The other day—"

"No." Lucern interrupted to shut him up. "Not *yet!* All I want is a damned condom, not a lecture!"

"Yeah? Well, all I want is to sleep and to not see Kate hurt, and you . . ." He paused as a knock sounded on the door to the suite.

When Lucern started to leave, Chris caught his arm. "You aren't answering the door like that! What if it's a fan who managed to track you down?" The editor thrust his blankets aside and got out of bed in one move. He was topless but wearing boxers. He stalked out of the room without bothering with a robe. Lucern followed at a discreet distance, just in case it *was* fans at the door and not the condoms he had ordered.

"Good morning, sir!" A uniformed bellhop stood in the doorway, smiling widely and holding out several boxes. "I believe these are for you."

Chris goggled. Lucern didn't know if it was the quantity or the variety that had so horrified him. When the editor continued to stand there, Lucern lost his patience and strode forward.

"Give them to me." He took the boxes from the now also gaping bellhop, then hesitated. "I don't have a tip. Chris, do you have a tip?"

"What?" The editor stared at him blankly.

"A tip for the man," Lucern repeated irritably. He gestured to his nakedness. "I don't have anything. I'll pay you back later."

"Oh." Chris patted his boxers where pockets would have been on slacks. He scowled. "No, of course I don't—"

"That's okay. You can just catch me later," the bellhop said quickly. Looking uneasy, he held out a pen and a clipboard with a slip of paper. "Just sign this so they can be charged to your room, and I'll be off."

Chris quickly signed the slip and handed the pen and clipboard back. "Er, thanks."

"You're welcome, sir. You two have fun now." The bellhop winked, then pulled the door closed.

Chris whipped around to face Lucern, horror dawning on his face. "He thinks we—that you and I—he . . ." He was almost incoherent with horror.

Lucern was too impatient to get back to Kate to calm him down. He took the vampire shortcut and slipped into the editor's mind. *Go to bed, Chris. This was all a dream. You're sleeping.*

The man calmed at once. He started to walk toward his door, muttering, "Oh, yes. I'm sleeping."

Lucern watched Chris's bedroom door close, then

hurried back to his own room. He nearly ran Kate down. She had re-donned her robe and was apparently coming to find him.

"Oh," she gasped and took a step back at his sudden appearance. "I thought I heard a knock at the door and voices."

"Yes. Hotel delivery," Lucern said. Noting the way her eyes widened as Kate took in the boxes he held, and afraid she would be put off by the number of condoms, he added, "I wasn't sure what kind to get, so I ordered all of them."

"I see." Her face turned pink, but she managed a smile. "Well, that's . . . er, that shows forethought . . . or something."

Lucern sighed inwardly. This condom business could really put a crimp in the act of lovemaking.

Displeased with the discomfort now between himself and Kate, he set the boxes on the dresser, pushed the door closed and pulled her into his arms. He wanted her warm and wet and aching for him again. He hadn't gone to all this trouble to have the moment ruined. He kissed her with a deliberate passion meant to stoke the embers of the fire he'd built earlier, but when Kate didn't immediately melt against him, it occurred to him once more that it was a shame her mind was locked to him. It would have been so much easier to simply communicate his desire to her and infuse her with it. Instead, he had to do this the hard way.

Urging her around to lean against the dresser, he broke their kiss to lean back and untie the sash of her terrycloth robe. He froze as the cloth gaped open.

Damn, she took his breath away. He raised his hands to capture her breasts.

Kate released a shuddering sigh as he caressed her, and Lucern realized there might be something to be said for the hard way. He wanted to hear more of those sighs. He wanted moans and groans, and for her to say his name in that sexy pleading voice. He wanted to sink inside her and drive her wild with pleasure. And he didn't want to waste time moving to the bed.

Releasing her breasts, Lucern pushed the boxes of condoms out of the way, caught Kate under the arms and lifted her to sit on the dresser. Pushing the robe off her shoulders, he let it fall to the hard wooden surface, then stepped between her legs. He wanted her on fire again. He wanted her mindless, all his. Catching her by the back of the neck, he drew her forward for another kiss. His other hand played over her body. Using fingers and mouth, he planned to trace every line of her body, neglecting not an inch. He wanted to fondle, nibble, caress and devour.

Kate had a few demands of her own, however. He felt her hand encircle and slide along his length, and he nearly came undone. He managed to contain himself, but his kiss became almost savage. His hand immediately slid between them to find the heart of her.

Kate gasped and nearly leapt off the dresser. Lucern's touch was a shock to her still sensitive skin. She moaned and scooted closer, her legs closing around his hips, her hands moving over his body. He was hard and strong and a pleasure to touch, and he was driving her mad. He had already pushed her over the edge once earlier and she was aching for the experience again. But this time she wanted him inside her.

Lucern moaned and shuddered when she found his hardness and caught it in hand. Kate smiled against his mouth, pleased at this proof that she could affect him, too; then she felt blindly about until she caught one of the boxes on the dresser. Somehow she got it open one-handed and retrieved a condom. She had no idea what kind it was and couldn't have cared less. She just wanted him inside her. Now.

Lucern heard a vague crinkling sound, then tearing. He was about to break the kiss to glance around when he felt something press against the tip of him and begin to slide over his length. Now he did break the kiss to look. Much to his amazement, Kate was sliding a condom onto him.

"Kate," he got out through gritted teeth. "I—"

"I *want* you," she breathed, finishing her work. Catching him by the behind, she drew him closer to her. *"Now."*

That was all she had to say. Lucern had thought it would take a bit more work to get her back to this point, but her cheeks were flushed with color and her body was straining. She wanted him. Without further ado, he caught her under the knees, slid her forward on the dresser and pressed his mouth to hers. He plunged into her. Then he had to stop at once. The feel of her closing warm and wet around him was like nothing he had ever experienced. He was enveloped in her scent and feel, was almost one with her in body and soul. Almost.

Acting instinctively, he slid his mouth from hers and down to her neck, and he partially withdrew. Kate murmured with pleasure, her lower body wiggling against him. Her head tipped back to allow his caress. Lucern felt his teeth protract and plunged them into her neck as he thrust back into her body. It was a purely animal action, like a dominant male cat catching a female by the neck, as he drove into her. Kate C. Leever was his, and he was marking her as such.

Kate cried out and strained against Lucern as her mind was suffused with pleasure. It was a sudden rush, an overwhelming wave as his mind merged with hers, gifting her with what he was experiencing. Her pleasure—almost unbearable before—was suddenly doubled, and for a moment she was sure her heart couldn't take it. Then her body shuddered and contracted, her legs clenching around his, her nails unintentionally raking the length of his back, and lights exploded behind her tightly closed eyes.

She felt Lucern's hands slip under her bottom and pull her tighter to him, and she moaned. The movement made another wave of pleasure course through her. The waves were battering her, riding one atop the other as she experienced both his pleasure and her own. She clutched her hands in his hair, held on for dear life as the overdose of excitement made her woozy. She was afraid to open her eyes, afraid the room would be spinning as wildly as her mind.

Mere mortal lovers would seem tame after this experience, she realized sadly. Lucern had ruined her for all others, and she very much feared it was like a drug. All Kate could think was that she wanted more. Her heart was hammering, her body writhing, and she wanted more. She wanted to drown in it. She *was* drowning in it, she realized as she began to lose consciousness. Yet still she wanted more.

Lucern felt Kate sag against him as his pleasure overcame him. He cradled her against his chest as his body shuddered, then waited another moment for his strength to return. Pulling her back enough to peer into her face, he saw that she had fainted.

He wasn't terribly surprised. It had nothing to do with his bite. While he had sunk his teeth into her, his body was presently sated and he had not drunk. This faint was purely a result of what they had just experienced. It had happened in the past on those few occasions when he had poured all of his pleasure into the mind of his lover, and none of those times in the past had been as explosive as this one. He would have been more surprised had she not fainted.

Smiling, he pressed a kiss to her forehead, then again rested her against his chest. He had to regain his strength; the experience had hit him pretty hard, too. Lucern had never felt quite so weak yet satisfied in his life, and this woman in his arms was the reason. He rubbed her back with one hand, sifting the fingers of his other through her hair.

Finally, once he felt able again, he caught her under her bottom and lifted her from the dresser. He carried her like that to the bed, her legs and arms sagging but their bodies still joined. Yet by the time they reached the bed, he had once more grown hard within her. He was relieved when she murmured and opened her eyes. He knelt on the bed with her, then laid them both down.

"Luc?"

"Yes." He brushed the hair off her forehead and pressed a kiss to the tip of her nose.

"That was . . ."

"Yes," he agreed solemnly. Shifting, he moved to one elbow to take some of his weight off of her. Kate's eyes went wide as she felt him move inside her; then she appeared disappointed.

Lucern didn't understand why until she said, "You didn't—"

"Yes, I did," he interrupted, unwilling to let her think for even a moment that she hadn't pleased him. "But you're intoxicating, and I want you again." He withdrew a little and slid back in as he spoke.

Kate's eyelids drooped to half-mast, leaving her looking sleepy and sexy and with a mischievous twinkle in her eyes. "Oh, well, I do try to keep my writers happy, Luc," she said.

Then, before he could comment on her comment, she caught his head and drew him down for a kiss. She arched against him, pulling him into her body.

"Luc's out of books," Chris said.

"What? Already?" Kate turned away from the male cover model she had been talking to. The man was one of the most popular models around, his name and face selling books as much as any author's name. He was considering getting into the writing end as well, to make more money on his name and face. Unfortunately, from the sample chapters he had sent her several weeks ago, it was obvious he couldn't write worth a damn. Kate had been trying to convince him to use a ghost writer for the last two hours. Now she gave up on him and frowned at Chris.

They were at the Book Fair. There was no hospitality suite today; the book-signing was scheduled for ten a.m. to two p.m., and every single author in attendance was there signing books and talking to readers.

Kate and Lucern had arrived at 10:01. They had been a minute late, but would have been even later if Chris hadn't harassed them into hurrying by pounding on both their doors at 9:30 and shrieking, "Get up, get up! We have to go." Of course, Kate hadn't been in her room. She was grateful her coworker didn't know that. She and Lucern had made great inroads into using those condoms. It seemed vampires had much more stamina than the average human male. They were also terribly inventive, although Kate didn't know if that was a racial trait or just Lucern. She supposed that after six hundred years a man learned quite a few tricks. She had enjoyed every one.

"Yes. He's been very busy and the crowd just descended on him, grabbing his books up like crazy," Chris explained.

Kate glanced at her wristwatch. It was only noon. There were two hours left of the signing. "We brought extra boxes of his books. They're—"

"Gone," Chris announced. "He's been through all of those, too."

"We should have brought more." Kate sighed. "What's he doing now?"

"Just sitting there, talking to readers. Which is fine, but he complained he was kind of tired. He sent me to ask if he could catch a nap. Do you want me to walk him up?"

"No, I'll . . ." Kate paused.

She had been about to say that she would see him upstairs, but now had second thoughts. She had no doubt Lucern was tired. It had been a very wearing night, what with the attack and their lovemaking marathon. It had been early when they had first woken up, and they had fooled around for hours before Chris had interrupted to remind them of the signing. The poor vampire must be exhausted. If she went upstairs with him, though, he might be inclined to start up where they had left off—and Kate wasn't at all sure she had the willpower to be firm and refuse.

"What's wrong with your neck?" Chris asked suddenly. She had been rubbing it absently.

Kate removed her fingers. She had bite marks on her neck and on several other spots on her body.

She had expected Luc to bite her, of course. She had intended to help replenish him. She simply hadn't expected him to bite her quite so many times or in all the places he had. The man was an animal, and she couldn't get enough of him. Especially since she felt just great. She hadn't suffered any weakness or dizziness after his feeding off her. Well, she had fainted a couple of times at first, but that seemed a small price to pay for the pleasure she had enjoyed. He really had ruined her for all other men.

"Kate. What's wrong with your neck?" Chris repeated.

She waved his question away. "Nothing. And yes, please. I'd appreciate it if you walked him up to the suite. Just in case there are lurking fans who might bother him."

Actually, Lucern seemed to be handling the fans fine. And they in turn were being incredibly nice to him. Kate was really more concerned about another wacko attacking him like the one last night. But Chris didn't know about that. No one did.

"Okay," Chris agreed easily. "I'll be back in a minute, if any of my writers need anything."

"Thanks. I'll look out for them till you return," Kate assured him.

"Oh, *that's* a nice costume."

Lucern grunted at Jodi's comment, tearing his gaze away from Kate to peer at the couple promenading on the stage. This was the Mr. Romance cover model competition and Historical Fashion Spectacle. Which translated into watching men in tight black pants and loose white pirate-style shirts promenade with women in old-fashioned gowns.

In truth, Lucern did find the costumes the women wore rather impressive reproductions of gowns worn when he was younger. And he probably would have enjoyed the spectacle more if Kate were seated with him. He was instead at a round table with Chris and several other writers. Kate was seated in the first of four rows set up directly in front of the stage.

She was a judge for this competition. Which Luc understood. He had no problem being on his own while she went about her work. What he didn't like was the fact that she was sitting right next to the long-haired model she had been so busy talking to at the book-signing earlier. Lucern hadn't really been tired at the book-signing; he had hoped to lure Kate back to their room for more lovemaking. But Kate had been too busy with this model—a long-haired muscle-head who stood a little too close and tended to look down her top a little too often.

Lucern might not have minded so much if the guy were a writer and she had business with him, but the guy was a model. What could they possibly be discussing? He scowled as the man leaned close to Kate and murmured something in her ear. Lucern had never thought of himself as the jealous sort. He was learning different. And he didn't like it.

"Oh, that one is lovely, too."

Lucern tore his gaze away from the couple in the judges' area again. Glancing to the stage, he nodded grimly in agreement with Jodi as he saw the burgundy costume worn by the woman there. The gown was lovely, a perfect example of late Renaissance wear. Kate would have looked lovely in it. Luc's gaze slid back to her, and he scowled when he saw that she wasn't even looking at the stage but was talking intensely to the model.

Damned man. Didn't he know she was taken? Apparently not. And whose fault was that? Kate. She should have let him know she wasn't available.

And why hadn't she wanted to sleep with him this afternoon? Hadn't he pleasured her over and over that morning? He had certainly enjoyed their lovemaking. And he was just as sure that she had enjoyed it. Hadn't she?

"Katie's having a little trouble with Robert," Jodi observed.

Lucern glanced at her. "Robert?"

Jodi nodded. "He's the most popular male model around. His name is as recognized as most authors'. He wants to trade on his name by writing romances himself *and* by modeling for the covers. Unfortunately, he can't write. His books are all throbbing and heaving." She gave a laugh, then explained: "That's the stereotypical view of Romances—that all they are is throbbing and heaving."

Lucern grunted. He didn't have a single throb or heave in his books, yet they were considered romances.

"Kate has been trying to convince Robert to use a ghost writer," Jodi went on. "But he's fighting it. He thinks he's a wonderful writer."

Lucern nodded solemnly and turned fresh eyes on Kate. So the model was a writer. His head was close to Kate's again. As Luc watched, Kate burst into laughter. Then she touched the man's shoulder. Luc had seen her do that with the women writers—Kate was a toucher, he had noticed that about her. She often patted his hand or his shoulder or arm while talking to him. He had seen her do it to others as well. It had never bothered him when he saw her doing it with women. But he didn't care for her touching this Robert person that way. He didn't care for it at all.

Irritated by the jealous tendencies he hadn't realized he had, Lucern picked up his drink and downed the rest of it, then glanced around when everyone burst into applause. On stage, the judges had chosen the winning romance model. The show was over.

"Okay," Chris suggested to the rest of the table as he got to his feet. "You guys have a little time before the Roundhouse party. Why don't you go grab something to eat and drink. I have to go help Kate and the others set up. Jodi, will you keep an eye on Luc, make sure he doesn't have any problems?"

"Sure," the writer agreed. When she took in Lucern's scowl, she slipped her arm through his and said, "Chris means well, Luc. You're new to conferences, and everyone's just worried you might be overwhelmed by it all."

Lucern merely grunted. He hadn't been scowling at Chris's assumption that he needed looking after—though that was rather annoying, too—he had been scowling at the fact that Kate was going to be busy setting up the party. He wouldn't get a chance to talk to her. He hadn't talked to her since they had arrived at the Book Fair that morning. He was starting to feel a little abandoned—a new sensation, and one he didn't enjoy at all. He was becoming dependent on the woman, his mood affected by her presence. He didn't like it. His life was becoming a series of highs when she was near, and lows when she wasn't. It seemed to Lucern that the boredom and sameness of his life before Kate was far preferable. Safer. Perhaps he should create some distance between them. After all, the conference would be over the next day; he would fly home to Toronto, and she would return to New York.

And all this passion and laughter would become a memory, he thought sadly. Kate had brought him back to life for a bit. He had enjoyed it, but it was going to be painful to go back to that old empty existence. He had not bothered with friends for a long time, as they always died or had to be left behind when he moved. It had just become easier to not bother with them. He almost wished—

"Come along, Luc." Jodi stood and waited beside his chair. "We're going to the pub here in the hotel for a quick dinner. Then we'll all separate to get ready for the Roundhouse party."

Lucern shook off his melancholy and got to his feet. "And what is the theme for this party?"

"Don't you know?" She seemed surprised.

"Should I?" he asked. Wariness nipped at him.

"Well, it's a vampire ball. You'll be the star attraction!"

Lucern managed not to flinch, but he wasn't a happy vampire. He had enjoyed the rock 'n' roll party the night before, but he really wasn't in the partying mood tonight. And being the star attraction sounded rather alarming.

Chapter Seventeen

"I think we're ready here."

Kate nodded at Allison's comment as she peered around at their handiwork. Black tablecloths, blood-red roses on each table and dim lighting. It was ready.

"You'd better go change. The guests will start arriving in half an hour, and you and Luc are supposed to be in the receiving line," the head editor warned. Kate grimaced, but nodded and gestured to Chris that it was time to go. She started out of the ballroom.

Allison, Chuck, Tom and Deeana had all already changed; they had been exiting one at a time to get into their costumes, leaving the others to continue decorating. Kate and Chris were the only ones left. Kate had deliberately put it off until now. She wasn't looking forward to telling Lucern that he was the star attraction at this ball. She knew he was not going to be pleased, and after the laughter and passion they had shared, she was fearful the annoyed and surly Lucern would return.

"Buck up," Chris said as they stepped out of the elevator. "Luc has loosened up quite a bit. He may take this in stride."

Kate forced a smile for her coworker. She only hoped he was right. She felt guilty for not having told Lucern about this from the start, but she was a coward.

The vampire ball hadn't been her idea. Chuck had come up with it. He'd considered it a brilliant bit of promotion, and when Kate had tried to talk him out of it, telling him that Lucern wasn't a very social person and that it might overwhelm him, Chuck had steamrolled over her protests. He had even ignored the fact that the conference attendees would have little time to prepare for the switch from the spy party that had originally been planned. Kate was worried sick that half the attendees would arrive in trench coats, the other half in capes. It might all turn farcical!

These worries faded from her mind as she paused at the entrance to the suite. C.K. pulled out his key card and unlocked the door. Kate spotted Lucern immediately. He was seated on the couch, watching television. His hair was wet and he was in a robe, obviously waiting to finish getting ready. He didn't notice their entrance at first, seemed instead quite involved with whatever he was watching. There was a look of abject horror on his face. What was he watching?

Kate glanced at the TV, recognizing a rerun of *Buffy the Vampire Slayer*.

Lucern suddenly sat forward, a sound of disgust slipping from his lips. It sounded very much like "bitch," though Kate couldn't be sure.

Aware that they had very little time to get ready for

the party, she cleared her throat. "Er . . . Luc?"

He glanced at her sharply, a scowl on his face. "Did you see that? Buffy just staked that poor vampire. He had yet to even *do* anything untoward, he just crawled out of his grave and she staked him. That is just not right. She is taking out her problems with that Angel fellow on vampires, that is what she's doing." Luc muttered a curse as he turned back to the screen.

A little burst of laughter slipped from Chris's lips, as he headed for his room. "Um, I'm going to get ready."

Kate bit her lip as she watched him go.

"Look!" Luc snapped, sitting forward again. "She's just done it again. Stake-happy is what she is. She's just staking them left and right, sometimes for no reason at all. This Buffy person is—"

"Luc?" Kate interrupted.

"Hmm?" he asked. His gaze was still fixed on the screen.

"We have to get ready to go."

"Yes. I showered and shaved, I just have to dress. I was waiting for you to return to see what I am supposed to wear. I didn't know if you had another costume or— she did it again!" He launched to his feet, glaring furiously at the screen. "Who writes this nonsense? We don't turn into slavering beasts when we bite, and did I turn into a puff of smoke when I was staked? No. No, I say. This is shameful nonsense. Just ridiculous. I ought to write and . . ."

Kate didn't catch the rest. She left Lucern waving his fist at the television and retreated to her room to collect the costume she had rented for him. So, Lucern had discovered television. It was a shame, really. It was even her fault. She had insisted that he watch TV that first night.

He was still ranting about writing to whomever was in charge of the Buffy show and straightening them out, when Kate returned. She paused beside him and shook her head mournfully.

"I suppose I should be grateful that you haven't discovered sports yet. Men can be impossible when they're sports freaks," she commented.

Lucern tore his gaze away from the TV and snorted. "Sports. I saw what you people call sports. Sheesh. If you want sports, you should watch a joust. Now, *that* was a sport. Matches won, lives lost, blood shed." His gaze dropped to the bag she held. "Is that for me?"

"Yes." Kate handed it over. She started to turn away, but gasped in surprise when he caught her hand and tugged her off balance. She landed in his lap with an ungraceful plop. Before she had quite recovered, his mouth covered hers and he subjected her to a thorough kiss.

"Oh," she sighed when it was over. Her mind was awhirl. Somehow her arms had crept around Luc's neck, and she was plastered to his chest like a wet cloth.

"Hello," the vampire growled. His hand slid up the inside of her leg, pausing to run over a bite mark he had left on her upper thigh.

Kate stiffened and wiggled as a thick ache started between her legs.

"Does it hurt?" he asked quietly, rubbing his fingers over the mark.

"No." She reached down to try to stop him, but the

straight skirt of her business suit was pulled tight over her legs. She couldn't hamper him.

He began to nibble at her ear, and his fingers slid further up her leg.

"Luc," Kate protested, dismayed at how breathy she sounded. She tried for a firmer tone. "I have to get ready."

Lucern grunted and slipped a finger under the elastic of her panties. "You feel ready to me."

"Oh." She arched slightly into his caress. Her body was eager to recreate a little of the magic from that morning. Her mind, however, was lecturing her. The ball. Lucern was the star attraction. And Chris was just on the other side of the door. This last thought, more than any other, made her scramble out of Luc's lap and away from his touch.

"I have to dress," she blurted. Rushing into her room, Kate slammed the door on any comment he might have made, then leaned back against it, her hand to her chest. She was panting as if she had run a race, her legs trembling, her flesh tingling. And she was fighting her own instincts. She would have much rather taken him by the hand and dragged him to bed. In fact, she was hard-pressed not to do so right that moment. But duty called.

Duty. She sighed. She still had not told Lucern that he was the focal point of tonight's ball. He was feeling lusty now, but he wouldn't be once he learned what she'd gotten him into.

Forcing herself not to think of that, she pushed herself away from the door. She had to get ready. She had brought a long black gown of her own from home. She donned the slim sheath of black silk, then used makeup to give her skin the fine white sheen of bone china before adding a blood-red lipstick. That done, she released her hair from its bun and brushed it out until it fell around her shoulders in soft waves.

Deciding she was as done as she was going to get, Kate grabbed the two pairs of vampire teeth she had brought from New York and hurried out of her room.

Lucern was standing in the living room, dressed and ready to go. Kate felt a gusty sigh slip from her lips at the sight. The man looked absolutely fabulous in the tuxedo and cape she had brought. He was every woman's fantasy. She really wished she wasn't about to anger him with the news she had to impart.

"You look ravishing," Lucern said solemnly.

Kate forced a smile and walked forward, holding out one set of teeth.

Lucern glanced down with distaste at the cheap plastic vampire teeth, then stiffened. His gaze shot back to her face. "Please say you jest."

Kate bit her lip to stifle the laugh that was suddenly eager to burst from her; Luc looked so horrified at the very thought of wearing the tacky teeth.

"Everyone will be wearing them," she informed him. "It's a vampire ball."

"I have my own teeth," he said with great dignity.

"Yes, I know. But no one will expect that. Please, just put them on. Please, Lucern?" She touched his arm.

His gaze settled on her lips in a way she found most distracting; then he sighed heavily with exasperation. "Oh, very well."

He snatched one of the pairs of teeth from her palm

and popped them into his mouth. Then he proceeded to move them about, making faces and shifting his jaw in an effort to make them more comfortable. "Vees ore asrocious."

Kate blinked at his slurred words. Deciding it would be best not to encourage his whining, she shrugged and popped the second set of teeth into her own mouth, then understood exactly what he meant. They *were* atrocious. They were damned uncomfortable. They were so bad, she almost considered leaving both pairs behind.

Chris sauntered into the room in his own tuxedo and cape. "You two look great," he said.

He smiled at them both, revealing a pair of realistic-looking vampire teeth.

Lucern immediately scowled. "Ou ee? 'Is eeth ook eal. An a amn ight ore omorta-ul."

Kate was trying to translate his attempted words when Chris winced. "Man, Kate," he said. "Where did you get your teeth? Sheesh. Those are so out-of-date it isn't funny."

Kate glared at her friend's betrayal. Deciding to ignore both men, she headed for the door, saying, "Let's go, I don't want to be late." At least, she tried to say that. It came out more like " 'et's o ah own an oo ee ate." Sighing as Chris burst out laughing, she dragged the door open and led the way out.

Lucern tried to remove his teeth in the elevator, but Kate managed to convince him to put them back in. She then removed her own, cleared her throat and said, "Luc, I really should have mentioned this before, but—"

"I a uh oco oin uh uh awe."

"What?" Chris gaped at him, then glanced at Kate. "What did he say?"

"He said, 'I am the focal point of the ball,'" she answered distractedly. Then she asked Lucern. "How did you know?"

Lucern spat his teeth out before answering, "Jodi told me."

"Oh." Kate bit her lip and surveyed his face, trying to figure out why he wasn't angry. "It wasn't my idea," she informed him quietly.

"It really wasn't," Chris said. "This was Chuck's brainchild. Kate tried to talk him out of it."

When Lucern merely nodded and didn't say anything else, Kate frowned. "You aren't angry?"

He shrugged. "I was a tad annoyed at first. But it's only a couple of hours out of my life. I have a lot of hours to fill, Kate. This whole conference is barely a heartbeat of time for me."

Chris looked perplexed. Kate wasn't perplexed as to Luc's meaning—he had lived hundreds of years, and would no doubt live hundreds more; these few days were barely a grain of sand on the beach of his life—but what she did wonder about was whether his words held a secret meaning for her. She was one of hundreds, perhaps thousands, of women who had passed through his life in those hundreds of years. Was the relationship they were enjoying just as unimportant to him as this conference? Was *she* just another grain of sand?

The idea bothered her, yet it made perfect sense. What else could she be? In another twenty-four hours she would be back at home in New York, and he would be back in Toronto. Life would go on as it always had. Eventually, she would meet some nice man, settle down and have a couple of kids, grow old. And Lucern would be still young, sexy, and taking some other woman to the heights of ecstasy. The idea really bothered her.

Taking a deep breath to try to dispel the ache in her heart, Kate put her teeth back in her mouth and followed Chris out of the elevator.

"There you are!" Allison greeted as they arrived. She stood just inside the ballroom doors with Lady Barrow and Chuck. "You're just in time. One or two people have arrived, but that's all."

"Good. It would be shameful to be late for my own party," Lucern said dryly. He gave the publisher a glance that made the man shift uncomfortably.

"Yes, well," Chuck muttered, but Lucern had already turned to greet Lady Barrow.

Luc smiled at the woman in her lovely crimson gown, took her hand and bowed low over it. "Lady Barrow," he said, pressing a kiss to the back of her hand. "You look and smell good enough to eat."

Lady Barrow gave a good-natured laugh at this, but Kate tensed. She distinctly recalled him almost biting the woman. She also recalled that she had yet to replace Luc's emergency blood supply. As far as she knew, he needed more than the blood he'd gotten from her this morning while they made love. She'd meant to make a quick trip to the blood bank at some point today, but it had slipped her mind. And now Luc must be starving. And no doubt in pain from lack of blood.

Still, he didn't look to be in bad shape. She peered

at Luc as he laughed and talked to Allison and Lady Barrow. He was a touch pale, but not gray as he had been. And there were no pained lines on his face.

Kate considered the matter as she reminded Lucern to put his teeth back in, and they took their positions at the door to greet the ball attendees. She concluded that they would have to leave the ball early and rob the blood bank again. She hated to do it. Blood banks were always short of blood. But Lucern was as needy as any patient, and she could hardly let him suffer.

They were at the door for an hour before Allison announced it was time to circulate. Kate stayed close to Lucern, afraid that he might—out of desperation—bite one of the guests. She might not have worried so much if women didn't keep coming up, asking to have their picture taken with him doing just that. She could only imagine the torture he must be suffering, pretending to bite their necks. It was rather like asking a dieting woman to hold a forkful of cheesecake in her mouth all night and not chew.

Aside from that, though, everything went fine. Well . . . except for the damned teeth she had supplied. It was terribly difficult to speak coherently with them in and Lucern's dropped into his wineglass at least three times as he tried to drink. The fourth time he dropped them, Kate caught Lucern's arm and dragged him to a stage across the ballroom. Slipping backstage, she led him through the first door she came to, flicked on the lights and closed the door behind them.

Lucern peered around. The room was a dressing room, and he raised his eyebrows. "What—"

310

"Give me your teeth," Kate interrupted, holding out her hand.

Lucern didn't bother to hide his relief as he popped them out. When he handed them over, Kate walked back to the dressing table and tossed both his fake fangs and hers into a garbage can. "You can use your real teeth. We'll just tell everyone that a nice fan saw the trouble you were having and offered you a spare pair."

She turned, giving a start when she found him directly behind her. She hadn't heard him follow. Managing a smile despite her suddenly tripping heart, she said, "We should probably wait a few minutes before going back. I'm not sure how long it usually takes to put in teeth like Chris has, but I imagine the glue needs a few moments to dry."

"Hmm." Lucern ran a hand up her arm, smiling when she shivered.

Kate tried not to look ready to leap on him. The man had just to touch her and she wanted him. Dear God, her legs were shaking. Clearing her throat, she shifted away and sank onto the upholstered bench in front of the dressing table. Turning to face the mirror, she set her purse down, took out her lipstick and quickly applied a fresh coat. Her eyes darted to the man standing behind her when he placed his hands on her shoulders.

Luc didn't say anything, just caught her gaze in the mirror. Kate's mouth went dry. She swallowed at the sight of the silver fire sparking out of his eyes. She recognized that look. He had nearly burned her alive with it this morning. Luc wanted her.

His hands slid off her shoulders, and Kate's gaze

shifted to follow his hands as they dropped down to cover her breasts. The dress had no back, which meant she'd had to forgo a bra. There was nothing between his hands and her breasts except for black silk.

"Lucern—"

"Shhh." He placed one knee on the bench by her hip, then nudged her head to the side. Urging back her hair, he placed a kiss on her neck.

Kate leaned back into him and watched in the mirror. A sigh slipped from her lips as he ran his thumbs over her erect nipples. Then he removed one hand and raised it to catch her chin and turn her head. He kissed her. Kate moaned, opening to him, arching into his caress, her hands sliding up his arms toward his shoulders.

She was taken by surprise when he suddenly lifted her to her feet. "What?"

"Come," was all he said. Then he was leaving the room and pulling her behind him. Kate thought he was taking her back to the party, but he led her onto the curtained stage. He quickly crossed it. Kate tried to follow quietly, knowing all that stood between them and the ballroom full of people was the stage's closed curtain, but her high-heeled shoes went *click-click-click* as she walked. Luc led her down the stairs on the opposite side and out a door.

"Where are we going?" Kate hissed, glancing nervously back down the hall at the doors to the ballroom.

Luc stopped at the elevators and pushed the button. "You look tired," he said. "You worked too hard today. You need rest."

Kate spoke sharply. "Luc, we have to—Ohh," she

cried as the elevator doors opened and he tugged her inside.

"Luc," she repeated. He pushed the button for their floor, but Kate slipped between him and the panel and hit the open button. "We have to—" She nearly swallowed her tongue when he pressed close against her back and slid his hands up to cup her breasts. She let go of the elevator button to grab his hands. "Lucern!"

He ground his lower body against her buttocks, and she closed her eyes as she felt his hardness. The elevator's doors closed, and the car started to rise. "A nap does sound good," she breathed. Then she shook her head. "No, we have to . . ."

She swallowed her words again as he bent to catch her legs just above the knees. His hands skimmed up over her skin, sliding under her skirt as he straightened.

Kate groaned and widened her stance. He cupped her between the legs with both hands and pressed her back against him.

"You want me."

"I want you," Kate echoed. Then she blinked her eyes. "Hey!"

Struggling out of his hold, she whirled to scowl at him. "Don't pull that mind-control crap on me."

"Don't you want me?"

Kate merely scowled harder. He knew she wanted him. He couldn't have slipped inside her mind if she didn't. Still, that didn't matter. She was finding it difficult enough to fight her desires and do what was expected of her—having him take control of her mind was not helping. And he had slipped in so easily!

The elevator stopped, the doors opened, and Lucern grabbed her hand and pulled her out.

Kate tried to dig her feet in as he dragged her up the hall. "Lucern. One more hour at the ball. One hour. Then we can go visit the blood bank and take care of your little problem. We can't—Okay, half an hour," she argued desperately as he stopped at their door and used his key card. "Half an hour more at the ball!"

He tugged her inside, pushed the door closed, then walked to the couch.

"Or maybe we could make a quick trip to the blood bank now, then go back to the ball," Kate pleaded. Luc dropped to sit on the couch, still holding her hand. "We can take care of your need for blood, *then* go back—"

"Kate," Lucern interrupted.

"What?" she asked warily.

"I do not need blood." He tugged her off balance and into his lap. "All I need is you."

Kate didn't get a chance to respond; Lucern prevented it by sealing her lips with his. She kept her mouth closed at first, ignoring the temptation to kiss him back as she struggled to retain control. But his lips weren't the only thing moving on her—one of his arms was around her back, the fingers having slipped through the side of her dress to caress the ticklish skin under her arm and along side her breast. The other was working busily at the ties of her gown at her shoulder.

Kate moaned deep in her throat, but managed to keep her lips shut as first one shoulder tie was pulled free, then the other. The material pooled around her waist, and Lucern gave up trying to kiss her and bent his head to her breasts.

"Damn," Kate breathed as he suckled one nipple, then the other. "Screw the ball."

Grabbing him by the hair, she dragged his head back up and kissed him voraciously. This was their last night together. Chuck and her job could go to hell. She was going to make the most of this.

Kate heard Lucern growl in response to her surrender; then he set to work with a passion. His hands were everywhere, skimming her breasts, her waist, her hips, sliding up her thighs.

Kate wasn't satisfied simply being the recipient of his touch, and with his help, she shifted to straddle him on the couch, forcing the narrow skirt of her dress up her legs to her hips. She wanted to touch and taste him everywhere. Breaking their kiss, she leaned back and set to work removing his clothes. She undid his cape and pushed it off his shoulders, then pushed the tuxedo jacket off too.

Leaving both garments bunched up behind him on the couch, Kate set to work on his shirt. She breathed a sigh of relief once she had him bare to the waist. Sliding off his lap, she knelt on the floor between his knees and turned her attention to his pants. When she got the button undone and slid the zipper down, Lucern made as if to stand, but Kate shifted forward, blocking his ability to rise. She pushed his slacks and boxers down and caught hold of his erection. Lucern jerked and gasped as she took him into her mouth, groaned as she ran her lips down him and back again.

"Kate," he growled and caught his hands in her hair. He couldn't seem to make up his mind what to do. She suspected he wanted to pull her head away but couldn't quite manage it and so simply held on as she pleasured him. He allowed her to do so for a moment or two; then he did exert pressure and pulled her head away.

He was growling again, his face strained, and Kate knew she had woken the beast. Catching her by one arm, Luc stood, pulling her up with him; then he kissed her roughly, his hands shoving her gown down her hips. It barely hit the floor before he caught the fragile cloth of her panties. He gave a tug that ripped them clean off.

Kate gasped and trembled. Then his hand was there, his fingers delving between her legs. Kate squeezed her eyes closed and pressed into his touch, aware that her legs wouldn't hold her upright for long. Lucern seemed to realize it, too, because he broke the kiss and turned her toward the couch. Pushing her onto her knees on it with his body, he followed her, bending her over its back and pressing close.

Kate cried out and clutched the back of the couch as he slid into and filled her. She cried out again as he reached his arms around, one hand catching under her breasts for support, the other slipping between her legs as he slid in and out.

It was fast and furious this passion, overwhelming them both quickly. Kate never felt Lucern bite her, but she definitely noticed when he suffused her mind with his passion. Already teetering on the edge of fulfillment,

Kate plunged into it, screaming out with ecstasy. Luc's pleasure joined hers in her mind. But the sound seemed faint to her ringing ears, and Kate feared she was about to . . .

Chapter Eighteen

She hadn't fainted. She'd come awfully close, though, Kate admitted to herself as she showered the next morning. It was a good thing that she was young and healthy; otherwise these passionate encounters quite possibly might have killed her.

Smiling, she turned into the water and let it wash the lathered soap away. Lucern was better than chocolate. As a child, Kate had once asked her mother how she would know she was in love. Her mother had said she would know she was in love when she would be willing to give up chocolate forever to be with that person for even an hour. Kate, a dedicated and hopeless chocoholic, had decided right then that she would never fall in love. She had been sure that no male was worth such privation.

Lucern was worth giving up chocolate. Dark chocolate, white chocolate, milk chocolate—she would happily give it all up for him. But her grin quickly faded.

She doubted she would ever be given a choice.

Sighing, she turned off the shower and stepped out onto the small towel she had laid on the floor. She snatched one of the large bath towels from the rack to dry off, then paused as she caught sight of herself in the mirror. Letting her towel drop away, she stared at her reflection.

Her body was a mass of bites. There were very few places that Lucern hadn't marked her. And every bite had been bliss. Anywhere there was a vein, and some places there weren't, her body was marked. These marks should hurt now that she wasn't caught up in passion and Lucern wasn't infusing her mind with his pleasure, but they didn't.

Kate ran her fingers over a set on her shoulder and shuddered as she recalled Lucern biting her there as he drove into her. Her body immediately flared to life, yearning for Lucern again.

"Dear God, I'm a junkie," she breathed, letting her hand drop. Worse, she was a junkie who was about to lose her fix. This was Sunday, the last day of the conference. There was a tea in the afternoon and a farewell party that night, but those were the only functions scheduled. There was to be no hospitality suite. Most of the attendees were leaving in the afternoon or evening. Some would even be flying home that morning.

Due to his "allergy to the sun" Kate had booked Lucern on a 4:30 flight back to Toronto, and herself and Chris on a 5:30 flight back to New York. That way, they could see him off and still get back to their respective homes early enough to unpack and relax tonight before going back to work in the office tomorrow.

How long did that leave her with him? she wondered. She had woken up at six a.m. and considered crawling onto Lucern, waking him up with a smile, but had come in here to take a shower first. By her guess it was maybe 6:15 or 6:30. That meant she had about ten hours left. Her mouth went dry. Ten hours. Ten hours and then . . .

Her eyes were suddenly blurry, her heart aching.

Kate brushed away her tears with a disgusted swipe of her fingers. Jesus, what was the matter with her? So they had great sex. She hadn't done anything stupid like fall in love or anything, she told herself.

But she was lying. It wasn't just great sex. She'd fallen for the big lug. Cripes. She wasn't the sort to break the law and rob a blood bank for just any writer. She thought the world of Jodi, but she wouldn't have done it for her. And she wouldn't have offered Jodi her wrist for a little breakfast nibble either. Yep, she'd fallen for Lucern. Hard.

How had this happened? *When* had it happened? Obviously before breakfast on Wednesday. Maybe when Luc had proven he was a man of his word by actually showing up at the conference. No, more likely before she'd ever left Toronto. She was honest enough to admit—at least, to herself—that she hadn't been able to get the man out of her head during the month between meeting Lucern and seeing him again. She'd taken great joy in reserving his room, registering him at the conference, and choosing and ordering all of his costumes. She'd even dreamt about him—hot, sweaty dreams like the one she'd enjoyed in his home.

Dear God, she was an idiot. She should have realized. She should have recognized her feelings and stayed away from him. She might have gotten over him in time if she had. No. Now that she had seen his soft side, watched him handle his fans with infinite patience and kindness, smiled and laughed with him and enjoyed the ecstasy only he could give her . . .

Kate began to cry. Big fat tears rolled down her cheeks. Their reflection in the mirror terrified her. She was afraid she would react the same way at the airport, crying like a baby when she had to say goodbye. Her heart would be on her sleeve, bleeding for him. Lucern would be embarrassed and disgusted. Modern women were supposed to be able to handle such things. They were supposed to embark on affairs with insouciance, then shrug and move on when they ended.

Kate's heart, ever hopeful, suggested that perhaps this was more than an affair to Lucern, too. She viciously squelched that hope. Luc had never spoken of feelings for her, not even liking. And, as painful as it was to admit, she feared she was just a pleasant meal to the man. He couldn't control her mind to bite her; he had to impassion her. And he *had* impassioned her. Yet the reason for it was plain to see. He was using her. They had shared passionate moments the night he arrived and the morning after, when he had needed blood. Then they'd avoided it again until after the attack by a fan's husband, when Lucern had again found himself in need.

She was just supper to Lucern. Which was humiliating. But even more shameful was the fact that, if that was her only value to him, Kate wasn't sure she wouldn't offer herself on the menu for the rest of her life just to be near him.

She closed her eyes and hugged herself. She couldn't face Lucern again. She couldn't risk shaming herself that way. And if he rejected her . . .

No. She couldn't risk seeing him again.

Lucern rolled onto his side and felt around for Kate, but his hand encountered an empty bed. Scowling, he opened an eye and glared through the darkness. She wasn't there. Forcing himself to sit up, he peered around the room. The damned woman had gotten up and left him alone in bed. He wasn't finished with her yet. He intended to keep her busy in bed all day. He didn't give a damn about her schedule. This was their last day together, and he planned on making the most of it.

Shoving the blankets aside, he slid out of bed and marched to the bathroom. Kate wasn't there. His gaze went to the bedside clock. It was a little after 7:30. The only reason the room was dark was because of the blanket he had hung over the blinds on the windows. Turning away from the bed, he jerked his door open and stalked out of his room.

Chris was sitting on the couch watching cartoons. He glanced over his shoulder, then did a double take.

"Oh, geez!" The editor rolled his eyes at Lucern's nudity and turned back to the TV. "Will you go put some damned clothes on? Man! I . . . Why am I getting a sense of déjà vu here? I've never seen you naked before." He turned a suspicious glance Lucern's way. "Have I?"

Lucern ignored the question. He'd blanked Chris's memory of the other morning, but he had no intention of telling the editor that. However, he also couldn't march into Kate's room like this without revealing the nature of his relationship with her, possibly making her very upset with him. Unless he controlled her friend's mind again.

You're watching television, Chris. You don't see me.

"I don't see you." Keyes turned back to the television.

Lucern continued on to Kate's door and thrust it open. Her room was tidy and full of sunlight. The blinds were wide open. Lucern quickly pulled the door closed, then just stood there. He had seen enough to know that the room was empty. The glimpse he had gotten of the closet was enough to make his heart drop into his feet. The closet doors had been wide open, revealing an empty curtain rod and no luggage.

Lucern returned to the living room and whirled toward Chris. Releasing the man's mind, as he barked, "Where is she?"

Chris turned his head slowly. "Why are you naked?"

"Dammit, Chris, where is Kate? Her stuff is gone."

"Oh." Discomfort flickered on the editor's face. "She had an emergency. She had to leave. She asked me to keep an eye on you today and see you to your flight tonight."

It didn't take a mind reader to know Chris was lying; the way his eyes dipped to the side to avoid Lucern's gave him away. Lucern felt as if he had just been gut-punched. "Kate *left*?"

"Yeah. Like I said, she had an emergency." Chris turned back to the television, but a flush was rising on his neck. He wasn't comfortable lying.

Lucern's mind raced. "How long ago did she leave?"

"Er . . . well, about half an hour, I guess. She woke

me up. Her flight is at eight and she had to get through security and everything. She wasn't sure she'd make it on time."

Lucern wasn't listening. He had already run into his room and begun dragging on clothes from the night before. Re-donning his tuxedo pants and dress shirt, he snatched up his wallet and ran out of his room.

He ran straight out his bedroom door into the hall, rather than waste time moving through the shared living room. Fortunately, there were no resourceful fans hanging about—he would have plowed right over them. He ran to the elevator, waited impatiently for it to arrive, then waited even more impatiently for it to descend the twenty-some floors to the lobby. Everything was awash in sunlight when he hurried out of the elevator. Lucern winced and pulled his collar up to protect as much skin as he could, but otherwise he ignored it and hurried out to the row of cabs lining the front of the hotel. He leapt into the first open one and immediately took control of the driver's mind, urging him to ignore the speed limit and just go to the airport.

Even so, with traffic, it was 7:56 when he arrived. He still had to find the gate her flight was leaving from. He prayed Kate's flight would leave late. They often did, he remembered hearing. With one eye on his wristwatch, he hurried to the information counter and had the woman look up Kate's name. A little mental nudge from him made sure she didn't hesitate. Then he was running through the airport, jostling people and pushing them out of the way, and mind-nudging security guards. It was 8:02 when he reached Kate's gate—just in time to see her plane taxiing away. Luc stopped short at the door and stood, staring at the aircraft, his shoulders slumping.

"Mr. Amirault?"

Lucern turned slowly, his eyes taking in Lady Barrow's smiling face. Her eyebrows flew up at his dismayed expression.

"Why, whatever is the matter?" she asked with concern. "You look as if you've just lost your best friend in the world." Her words faded into silence as she peered from Lucern to the plane taxiing out of sight. "Oh. I saw your editor before she left."

Lucern's expression sharpened. "You did? Chris said she had an emergency back in New York."

"Hmm." Lady Barrow didn't look convinced. "Well, then, there appear to be a lot of those right now. We had one as well. I had to send the editor of my magazine home early to take care of a problem, too. She's on that flight as well."

Her gaze drifted to the plane again, and she and Luc watched it taxi around the building and out of sight. The woman sighed. "Well, you could probably use a ride. I'll give you a lift back to the hotel, so you needn't look for a taxi."

Lucern stiffened when she slid her arm through his. He really didn't want to ride back with her. He had no desire to talk to anyone at the moment, and was feeling rather raw and weary. Unfortunately, Kate wasn't the only woman with a strong mind; the thoughts he tried to put into Lady Barrow's brain obviously had no effect. Rather than drop his arm and leave him to stew in his misery as he wished, she began to tug Luc along the concourse toward the exit.

"Have you enjoyed your first Romantic Times Conference, Mr. Amirault?"

"Luc," he muttered almost sulkily. Then scowled. "No. Yes. No."

"Ah-ha." She didn't seem the least surprised at his confusion. In fact, she translated his feelings for him nicely. "I gather you were a bit overwhelmed and—added to that—under the weather at first. You began to enjoy yourself after the first day or so, but are now wishing us all to hell and back."

Luc turned a startled glance to her, and she gave him a knowing smile laced with understanding. "Watch your head."

He blinked at those words, then realized they were standing beside a limousine with blackened windows. He watched her slip into the car, then followed and closed the door after him with relief. At least he wouldn't have to worry about the sun on the way back.

"You look a little pale today," Lady Barrow commented, opening the door of a small refrigerator for him to see its contents. "Would you like a drink?"

Lucern's gaze slid over the bottled water, cans of pop and juice inside, then shifted to Lady Barrow's throat. He could use a pick-me-up, a quick nibble until he got back to the hotel and his last bag of blood. He'd been saving it for this morning and was now glad he had. He shouldn't have gone out in the sun.

"Luc?" the woman queried softly.

Lucern sighed and shook his head. He couldn't bite Lady Barrow without permission. She was far too nice a woman for that. He'd bite Chris instead. The editor deserved it for lying and not telling him at once that

Kate had left. Those few extra minutes might have gotten him to the airport in time to stop her.

"Well, I think you *could* use a drink," Lady Barrow said. He heard a clinking and the sound of liquid pouring, and he turned to see Kathryn Falk mixing two glasses of orange juice and champagne. She held one out and asked, "Did you have a spat, or is she running scared?"

Lucern just stared at her agape.

She smiled. "The sparks have been flying off of you two all week. And no one could miss how protective she was of you, or how protective you were of her."

Lucern accepted the morning cocktail. He downed it in one gulp, then handed the empty glass back. What Kathryn Falk said was true, unfortunately. But Lady Barrow couldn't know that the protectiveness on Kate's part had been purely professional in nature—she had promised to look after him and had fulfilled that promise beautifully. As for the sparks . . .

Oh, well I do try to keep my writers happy, Luc.

Lucern's mouth tightened as Kate's words rang through his head. He didn't think she had faked all of her passion, or that she had done it as part of her job, but she had left him this morning as if none of it mattered. Or as if she feared he might take it to mean more than it did and cause an awkward scene or something. And he might very well have, he realized. He might have done something as foolish as ask her to come home to Toronto with him, or . . .

His mind shied away from the "or." Lucern wasn't ready to admit his possible desire to spend an eternity with Kate. To laugh and cry and fight and make love with such passion for centuries. No, he wasn't ready for that.

A glass appeared before his face, which Lady Barrow had refilled for him. When he hesitated, she said, "She'll come to her senses, Luc. You're a handsome, gifted, successful man. Kate will come to her senses. She just needs time."

Lucern grunted and accepted the drink. "Time is something I have lots of."

The comment was to weigh heavily on Lucern's mind over the following weeks. He returned to the hotel with Lady Barrow, but didn't stay any longer than it took to pack his bags. He headed back to the airport and took the first available flight back to Toronto.

His house, his safe haven for some time, seemed cold and empty when he entered it. There was nothing there but memories. Kate sat on his couch, lecturing him about the importance of readers. She rushed anxiously to his side in the kitchen to exclaim over a head wound he didn't have. She laughed, did a little dance and gave him a high-five in his office. She moaned and writhed with passion in his guest-room bed, which he had pathetically taken to sleeping in. She haunted his mind, filling it nearly every moment of the day. But that was all she did.

Lucern got the Internet chat program she had requested he get, and he often exchanged instant messages with Lady Barrow, Jodi and some of the other writers he had met at the conference, but while he had Kate on his list of contacts, she never appeared online. Jodi seemed to think she was blocking everyone. He considered sending her an e-mail, but couldn't think what to say. Instead, he sat at his desk, listening to time tick by as he watched and waited for her to appear online. Time was something he had a lot of.

It was nearly two weeks before he grew tired of waiting and watching. In disgust one morning, he turned the chat program off and opened his word-processing program. He thought he would make his first attempt at a work of fiction. Instead, he found himself recounting the story of his first meeting with Kate, then everything that followed that meeting.

It was a cathartic experience writing the book, like being there and reliving each moment. He laughed at some of the events he hadn't found funny at the time, like his codpiece getting caught on the tablecloth, and his frantic attempt to get condoms. He didn't laugh at her leaving, so that's was where he stopped the story he had entitled simply *Kate*.

He put his last entry in the story some few weeks after he began, then pushed wearily to his feet. He felt a little lighter than he had upon leaving the conference, but not much. He was grateful he had met and spent time with Kate Leever. He would always carry her in his heart. But he was both sad and angry that she hadn't given them a chance to have more.

He switched off his computer, glancing angrily at the answering machine on his desk. Lissianna, who had insisted they all needed one since they usually slept during the day when most business was done, had bought the machines for everyone last year at Christmas. Lucern hadn't bothered to listen to his messages in the past, but he had since returning home. He'd kept hoping that Kate would call, even if just to ask when he would have another book done. But she hadn't called once. And none of the messages on the machine tonight were from her, either.

There was a message from his mother, and others from Lissianna, Bastien and Etienne. Lucern had been avoiding his family since returning from the conference, and while he knew they were worried about him, he didn't feel like talking. He didn't feel like talking to anyone, really, except for the people from the conference. He had met them all with Kate. Somehow, chatting to them over the computer made him feel closer to her. And sometimes Jodi or one of the other women had a bit of news about Kate that had made its way down the writers' grapevine. Nothing important though. She was editing so-and-so's book right now. She had rejected that model's book. She had a cold coming on. She had fought it off.

Lucern ignored the blinking light of his answering machine and headed for his bedroom. His stomach was cramping with hunger, and his body was achy with the need for blood, but it seemed like a lot of effort to go downstairs and raid the fridge. He didn't even have the energy to undress. Luc simply walked into his room and collapsed on the bed. He'd sleep for a while, he decided. A long while. He'd feed later.

The sun was just rising when Lucern fell asleep; it had long gone down when he woke up. And the aching that had nagged at him when he lay down was much worse. He had to feed. Rolling out of bed, he made his way downstairs to the kitchen. He drained two bags of blood while standing in front of the refrigerator, then took another back upstairs. The bag was nearly empty when he entered his office—which was a good thing, since the sight of someone sitting at his desk startled him enough to spill the last few drops on the floor.

"Bastien." He glared at his brother. "What are you doing here?" He glanced at the computer screen and froze as he recognized the last chapter of *Kate*.

Bastien closed the word-processing program with a click, then offered an apologetic expression. "I am sorry, Lucern. I was worried about you. I just wanted to be sure you were all right. You have neglected to return calls from any of us, and won't visit or allow us to visit you. We were all worried, so I came to see what you were up to."

"When did you get here?"

Bastien hesitated, then admitted, "I came just after dawn."

"You've been here all day? What . . . ?" The question died in his throat. He knew exactly what Bastien had been doing. His brother had read all the way through the story of Kate, he'd read every word to the last page. Luc's gaze narrowed on the younger man. "How did you know I would write it down?"

"You have always kept a journal, Luc—at least since paper became easier to come by. You always wrote things down. I often wondered if you didn't do so as a way of distancing yourself from it all. Like you do by shutting yourself away here."

Lucern opened his mouth to speak, then closed it again. Neither of them would believe his denial, so why waste the effort? Turning away, he walked over and slumped onto the couch. He was silent for a moment, then scowled and asked, "So, what do you think of my first work of fiction?"

Bastien's eyebrows rose, but he didn't call Lucern on the obvious lie. Instead he said, "I think it's a very poor attempt at a romance."

Lucern stiffened, affronted. "Why?"

"Well . . ." Bastien began to play with the computer mouse on Lucern's desk. "For one thing, the guy's an idiot."

"What?" Lucern sat up straight.

"Well, sure." Bastien's lips twitched. "I mean, here's this all powerful, handsome, successful vampire writer, and he doesn't tell the girl he loves her. Heck, he doesn't even say he likes her."

Lucern scowled. "She left before he could. Besides, she didn't tell him, either."

"Well, no. But why should she? Most of the time the guy's such a surly jerk, she's probably afraid to." When Lucern merely glared at him, Bastien gave up all pretense. "You should have followed her, Luc."

"She wasn't interested. She was just doing her job."

"I'm quite sure her job description didn't include sleeping with you. Or letting you feed off of her."

"Bastien's right," a new voice said from the doorway.

Both men glanced over in surprise. Marguerite Argeneau looked at her sons, then entered the room and moved to sit beside Lucern. She took his hands in hers, stared sadly into his eyes and said, "You should go to her, Luc. You have waited six hundred years for Kate. Fight for her."

"I can't fight for her. There is nothing to fight. She has no dragons to slay."

"I didn't mean you should fight in that way," Marguerite said impatiently. "Besides, has that ever worked in the past? Gaining a woman's attention by slaying her dragons only makes her dependent. It isn't love, Lucern. That's why you never got the girl in the past. Kate doesn't need you to slay her dragons. Though she might welcome your help once in a while, she's strong enough to slay her own."

"Then she doesn't need me, does she?" he pointed out sadly.

"No. She doesn't need you," Marguerite agreed. "Which leaves her free to truly *love* you. And she does love you, Lucern. Don't let her go."

Lucern felt his heart skip with hope, then he asked warily, "How could you know she loves me?"

"She was half in love with you before she ever met you. She came to love you fully while here."

"How would you know?" Lucern persisted.

Marguerite sighed and admitted, "I read her mind."

He shook his head. "Her mind is too strong. You couldn't have read it. I couldn't."

"You couldn't read her mind because she was hiding it from you. Kate was attracted to you and afraid of it. As I said, she was half in love before she ever met you. That scared her. She closed her mind against it and therefore against you."

Luc shook his head. "How could she have been half in love with me? She didn't even know me."

"Your books, Lucern."

He shrugged impatiently. "Lots of women think

333

they're in love with me thanks to those damn books—I saw them at that conference. They didn't know me at all."

Marguerite sighed. "Those women were attracted by your looks and success. Kate is different. She's your editor. She didn't believe in vampires, and wasn't smitten by your success. She fell for the real you. She recognized it from your writing."

When Luc looked doubtful, his mother made a tsking sound. "How could she not? You are just as surly and reclusive in real life as you were in the recounting of Etienne and Rachel's story or any of your other books. Your voice shone through. You were completely honest in those books, showing the good and the bad. In truth, you revealed more of yourself in your writing than you generally do in person, because you revealed your thoughts, which you usually keep hidden."

Lucern still didn't believe it.

Marguerite borrowed a page from his book and scowled furiously. "I am your mother, Lucern. You will trust me in this. I would never lead you astray."

"Not deliberately," he agreed. A smile tugged at the corners of his mouth.

Tears pooled in Marguerite's eyes, and Luc knew his mother wanted to banish the loss and sorrow from his past. "Trust me, son," she said. "Please. Don't give up your happiness so easily. Your father did that. He grew weary of life and gave up on it, and nothing I could say or do could bring back that spark. You were precariously close to following in his footsteps. I have been worrying about you for some time. But Kate's arrival shook you up and brought joy back to your life." She clasped his hand. "Lucern, it was as if you were reborn. You smiled and actually laughed again. Kate could give you so much you've missed—a son or daughter, a companion, joy. Don't let your pride stand in the way."

Lucern stared at his mother, her words revolving in his head along with another woman's. The psychic at the conference had said something very similar.

"You had begun to weary of life," the woman had said. *"It all seemed so hard, and the cruelties of man had begun to wear you down. But something—no, not something, but someone—someone has reinvigorated you. Made you feel it might be worth living again. That there is still joy to be had."*

"Hold on to her. You will have to fight for her, but not in the way you are used to. Weapons and physical strength will do you no good in this battle. It is your own pride and fear you will have to fight. If you fail, your heart will shrivel in your chest, and you will die a lonely, bitter old man, regretting what you didn't do."

Lucern felt the skin on his neck prickle. His gaze slid to his mother, and he asked, "How do I fight for her, then?"

Chapter Nineteen

Kate stared at Allison, her mind reeling. The head editor had caught her in the hall just outside Chris's office and stopped to tell her that she had just gotten off the phone with Lucern. He wanted to discuss the possibility of doing a book-signing tour, but he wanted Kate to fly to Toronto to explain the particulars.

Kate couldn't believe it. She didn't believe it. Why was he sending for her? Perhaps the Argeneau blood bank had run out of blood, some bit of her mind whispered snidely, and she winced in pain. It didn't matter why he wanted her to go to Toronto. She couldn't do it. She wouldn't survive another encounter with him. At least her heart wouldn't. She wasn't at all sure it had survived the conference. It was still battered and bloody.

"I'm awfully busy, Allison. Couldn't Chris fly up there in my place? Maybe he could take over Lucern altogether, in fact," she added hopefully. "It would probably be for the best. I don't think I can handle Lucern."

"The hell you can't!"

Kate whirled around as Chuck moved up the hall to join them.

"If there's a possibility we can get the bastard to do that tour, you're going. The expense of your flight there and back is minuscule compared to how much that book chain was willing to put out for this tour. And the opportunity for publicity is incredible. It means articles in newspapers of every city the tour hits, maybe even television interviews. If you want to keep your job, you'll get your tail on the next available flight and convince Amirault to do this tour."

Kate didn't bother correcting Chuck about Lucern's real name. She was too busy considering quitting. Unfortunately, she couldn't afford to quit. She had bills to pay. Taking her silence for acquiescence, Chuck harrumphed and turned to stalk back up the hall to his office.

"It'll be fine," Allison assured her with a pat on the arm. Then she too went back to her office.

"So, Lucern is finally sending for you."

Kate turned to find Chris standing in his office doorway, smiling.

"Just to discuss the book-signing tour," Kate said in dismissal. She headed for her office.

Chris snorted with disbelief and followed. "Yeah, right. Like Lucern Argeneau will do a book tour. Forget about it. He wants *you*."

Kate sat down at her desk with a sigh. "Close the door please, Chris. I don't want everyone to know about this." She waited until he had closed the door, then said, "He doesn't want me."

"Are you kidding? The guy's crazy about you."

"Yeah," Kate muttered dryly. "I could tell that by the way he's been calling and sending me flowers."

Chris sat on the corner of the desk and shrugged. "Hey, you're the one who sneaked out of our suite like a thief. You've gotta figure the guy might hesitate, maybe think you're the one not interested."

Kate stiffened. That thought hadn't occurred to her. Hope reared its pitiful head. "Do you think so?"

"I'd stake your life on it."

Kate blinked, then gave a half smile. "My life, huh?"

"Yeah." He grinned and shoved himself off her desk, walked to the door. "Well, I'm ninety-nine percent sure, but I'm not suicidal. Better you than me if I'm wrong." Then he left.

Kate watched the door close behind him, then peered at the paperwork on her desk. The conference had put her behind. She'd tried to catch up on returning, but was so distracted she seemed to just be slipping further behind. She wasn't going to get any further ahead now, either. Not till she found out where she stood with Lucern.

Grabbing her purse from under her desk, she stood up. It was time to stop moping and being miserable, and to sort this out. Especially if there was a chance . . . She didn't finish the thought. She already had too much hope building in her.

Chris stood in the hall, glanced back with raised eyebrows when she left her office. "Where are you going?"

"To catch a plane," Kate answered.

"Oh." He watched her walk past, then followed saying, "Um . . . shouldn't you call or write and let him know you're coming?"

"Like he'd answer the phone or read the letter." Kate snorted. "No. It's better this way. He wants me in Toronto. He's got me. I hope he's ready."

"Uh, lady? Did you want to get out here or not?"

Kate tore her gaze away from the front of Lucern's house and forced an apologetic smile for the taxi driver. The man was twisted in his seat, watching her with concern. He was being terribly patient. She had paid him several minutes ago, but then instead of getting out, she had sat staring fearfully up at the house.

"I'm sorry. I . . ." She shrugged helplessly, unable to admit that while determination had carried her this far, it was starting to flag and terror was taking its place.

"No, hey, that's okay, lady. I can take you somewhere else if you want."

Kate sighed and reached for the door handle. "No, thank you."

She got out and closed the door, then stood to the side of the driveway as the taxi backed out. Since she had caught a ride straight from the office to the airport—she hadn't even stopped to pack—she had come with nothing but her purse. She now gripped it with both hands and struggled to keep her breathing regular. She couldn't believe she was actually here.

"Well, you are, so you had best get it over with," she told herself.

Somewhat emboldened by her own firm voice, Kate

walked up the sidewalk and crossed the porch. She raised her hand to knock at the door, then paused as she realized that it wasn't yet noon. It was bright daylight outside. Lucern would be sleeping. Kate let her hand drop with uncertainty. She didn't want to wake him up. He might be really cranky if she woke him up. It might get this whole meeting off to a bad start.

She glanced at her watch. 11:45. There were a good six hours or more until dark. She considered sitting on the porch and waiting, but six hours was a long time. Besides, she was rather tired. She hadn't slept a full night since leaving the conference. She wouldn't mind a nap. That way, she would be refreshed and wide awake to meet him.

Kate turned and looked at the street, then sighed. She didn't have a car or any way to call a cab, so she couldn't go to a hotel. And she wasn't napping on his porch like some displaced street person. She turned back to the door again, hesitated, then reached for the doorknob. Turning it slowly, she was surprised to find that the door opened. He hadn't locked it. What kind of an idiot left his door unlocked? Anyone could walk right in and stake him. And she had already seen someone do that to him, so he couldn't claim no one would. She would just have to talk to him about that.

In the meantime, she couldn't just walk away and leave his door unlocked. She would just go inside, lock the door behind herself, and nap on his couch. It was for his own good. Kate smiled at her reasoning. It might not hold water, but it sounded reasonable enough. Almost.

Kate had closed and locked the door and made it

almost to the living room when she heard a clank from the kitchen. She turned abruptly, prepared to hurry back outside and knock, then grew still again. What if the noise from the kitchen hadn't been made by Lucern? He *should* be sleeping and he *had* left the door unlocked so that just anyone could walk in and rob him. Kate lived in New York; the crime rate was high there. Toronto was supposed to be a big city. Crime was probably rampant here, too. She had to see about the noise. She would just peek into the kitchen door. If it was Lucern, she would slip back outside and knock. If it wasn't Lucern, she would slip outside and run to a neighbor's house to call the police.

Turning back, Kate moved carefully up the hall, walking as quickly and silently as she could. Once at the kitchen door, she paused to take a bolstering breath, then eased the door open a crack . . . and nearly shrieked in alarm. It wasn't Lucern in the kitchen. It was a stranger, a woman—a cleaning woman, judging by the bandanna on her head and the mop and bucket in her hand. What had alarmed Kate was the fact that the woman was halfway across the kitchen to the door and moving fast. Kate would never get back up the hall and out of the house before the woman appeared.

Unable to think what else to do, Kate let the door slip closed and plastered herself against the wall behind it. She closed her eyes and held her breath for good measure. The door creaked open. Kate waited. She heard footsteps move past, up the hall away from her; then she opened her eyes, hardly able to believe she hadn't been caught. She stood there for another heartbeat; then, suddenly overcome by fear that the woman would turn back and spot her after all, Kate slid into the kitchen.

The door was just slipping closed when Kate saw the cleaning woman stop outside the living room and snap her fingers, then turn around. Almost hyperventilating with panic, Kate glanced frantically about the kitchen, spotted the door on the other side. Rushing to it, she pulled it open to find stairs leading down to a basement. She hesitated, but the footsteps were now audible from the hall. The woman was coming back.

Kate stepped down onto the first step. Pulling the door almost closed, she left it barely cracked so that she could see. A heartbeat later, the kitchen door opened and the cleaning woman came back in. She moved to the sink and out of sight, then came back a moment later and left the kitchen. Kate almost stepped out again, then paused and decided to wait just in case.

She stood in the near total darkness, feeling the yawning black pit at her back, aware of every single creak the house made for approximately thirty seconds before her cowardice urged her to find the light switch. She flicked it on, and the dark was immediately chased away. Kate released a relieved breath. That was better. She was just standing at the top steps to a basement.

Her thoughts stopped as she glanced nervously down the stairs. The end of a shiny mahogany box could be seen from where she stood.

"It's not a coffin," Kate told herself firmly. Moving down another step, she tried to see more of the box. "It's some kind of hope chest. Oh, I hope it's not a coffin."

She had to go almost all the way down the stairs to

see all of it, though she knew long before that it was indeed a coffin. A sense of betrayal overwhelmed her. Lucern had said he wasn't dead and didn't sleep in coffins. Or had she just assumed he didn't sleep in coffins? He *had* said he wasn't dead, though. But if he wasn't dead, what was the coffin for? Maybe he just hadn't wanted to upset her, so he had lied about the dead part.

He'd been right. She was upset.

"Oh, dear God," she breathed. "Sleeping with a man six hundred years older than me I can deal with, but a dead guy?" Her eyes widened with horror. "Does that make me a necrophiliac?"

She pondered briefly, then shook her head. "No. Lucern isn't dead. He had a heartbeat. I heard his heartbeat when I rested my head on his chest. And his skin wasn't cold. Well, cool but not cold," she pointed out. There might not be anyone to hear, but she felt better convincing herself. Until she heard her voice say, "Mind you, his heartbeat also stopped at one point."

Kate groaned at the reminder of the night Luc was staked. Then she muttered, "Surely dead guys can't get the wonderful erections Luc did. There would be no blood flow."

She'd become quite happy with that reasoning when her voice betrayed her again. "Of course, there's always rigor mortis to consider.

"Just open it," Kate muttered to herself in disgust. She had slowly eased her way to the side of the coffin, arguing with herself as a distraction. She continued to talk to distract herself as she reached out to open it. "There's probably a logical explanation for all this. Luc probably stores things in it. Things like a cello, or maybe shoes, or . . . a body." That last possibility came out as a squeak as she finally lifted the coffin lid . . . and saw the man lying inside. Then his eyes blinked open, he grabbed the sides of the coffin and started to sit up. That was when the lights went out. Kate began to shriek.

Lucern sat up, his eyes popping open. He thought he'd heard a woman scream. When the sound came again, he catapulted out of bed and rushed for the door. That shriek had been one of terror. He couldn't imagine what was happening downstairs. It sounded like someone was being attacked. He charged down the hall, then the stairs, and peered into the living room where one of the cleaning crew stood frozen. The woman was pale, her eyes wide with fear.

"What is it? Why did you scream?" he demanded.

Apparently unable to speak, the woman merely shook her head. Turning away, Lucern continued up the hall. Despite the woman's frightened appearance, there hadn't appeared to be anything wrong with her. Besides, the screaming had seemed to come from the back of the house rather than the front. Another shriek pierced the silence as he rushed for the kitchen, proving he had guessed right. But this time he could tell that it hadn't just come from the back, it had come from the basement.

Cursing, Lucern crashed through the kitchen door. He had specifically told the cleaning company that his basement and upstairs were to be left alone. No one should be in the basement.

"Jesus, how many of you people are here?" Lucern snapped when he spotted the woman frozen by the basement door. She was staring at it as if it might explode at any moment.

"Two of us, sir," the woman answered, then immediately cried, "I just turned out the light. That's all I did. The door was cracked open and the light was on—I just turned it out. I didn't know anyone was down there."

Lucern ignored her and dragged the door open, then flicked on the switch. The screaming did not stop, though it was growing hoarse. Lucern was halfway down the stairs when he heard Etienne saying, "It's okay. It's just me. Really, it's okay."

When Luc reached the bottom step, he saw his brother standing to the side of the stairs, hands held up placatingly.

"Etienne?" He barked his question and Luc's brother half turned, relief on his face. "Luc, thank God. I didn't mean to scare her this bad. I mean, I heard her muttering about rigor mortis and coffins, and knew she was going to open the lid, so I closed my eyes to give her a little spook, but I didn't think . . ."

Lucern wasn't really hearing his brother. His gaze, his entire attention, was focused on the woman he could now see standing in his basement. Kate. His Kate. Her gaze was locked with his, and while she had at first been pale and trembling, she was regaining her color—along with a spark in her eye that he hoped was passion and happiness at seeing him.

"Kate," he breathed. Smiling, he held out his arms as she rushed to him, ready to welcome her into his

345

embrace and his life. But Kate didn't exactly rush into his arms. She more or less shoved past him, snarling, "You said you didn't sleep in coffins." She started to stomp up the stairs.

Hmm. The spark was anger, not passion at seeing him. He hurried to trail her up the stairs.

"We don't. I have a bedroom," he assured her. He found himself a tad distracted as he was face level with her upside-down-heart-shaped behind, and he was unable to tear his eyes away. I really should have more stairs in my home and follow her up them at every opportunity, he thought vaguely. This was a delightful view.

"Ha! Then what was *he* doing in that coffin? Thinking?" she asked sarcastically. She burst out into the kitchen.

"Well, yes. Actually, I was," Etienne announced from behind Lucern as he followed them. "I find that the dark and silence afforded by a coffin allow me to work out some of the difficulties I run into in programming my games."

"Coffin?"

They all turned to stare at the cleaning woman still standing in the kitchen. Lucern was debating whether to blank the woman's mind when Kate made a distressed sound and rushed out into the hall.

Lucern took a step to follow her, then paused and turned on his brother. "What did you do? She's furious."

"I just . . . She . . ." He grimaced. "I heard her coming down the stairs and was at first worried it was one of your cleaning crew, but then I heard her talking and recognized her voice."

"Who was she talking to?"

"Herself," Etienne answered promptly. "She was try-ing to convince herself to open the coffin and that you wouldn't be in there."

"And what did you do—close your eyes, then pop them open and sit up to scare the life out of her when she did build up the courage to open it?" Luc asked with disgust. It was a trick Etienne had pulled on all of them at one time or another.

His brother winced, but nodded apologetically.

Lucern cursed under his breath and started to turn away, but Etienne caught his arm to stop him. "I didn't mean to scare her that badly. I mean, she half-expected to find someone in there anyway. She shouldn't have been this startled, but then the lights went out. She caught just enough of a look to know it wasn't you in the coffin, but didn't get enough of a look to recognize me before Ms. Energy Conserver over there turned out the lights."

They both paused to glare at the cleaning woman, who shrank backward, bumping into the wall under their combined irritation. The front door slammed. Lu-cern started to hurry from the room again, but Etienne stopped him. "Wait. I don't think all her anger is about the coffin, Luc."

"What do you mean? What else could it be?"

"Well, she was saying some pretty weird stuff as she tried to talk herself into opening the lid."

"What kind of stuff?"

"Er . . . well, she seemed to find it distressing enough to sleep with a six-hundred-year-old guy, but the idea of sleeping with a dead one—"

The cleaning woman gasped. Lucern scowled at her. "Leave," he said.

The cleaning woman was off in a flash. Lucern sighed and turned back to his brother. "I am not dead."

"Well, duh." Etienne rolled his eyes. "I know that. She doesn't. And she's kind of creeped out, wondering if that makes her a necrophiliac or something. She also wondered if your 'wonderful erections' are rigor mortis."

Lucern felt himself perk up. "She called my erections wonderful?"

Etienne just gaped, then raised a fist to knock on his brother's forehead as if it were a door. "Hello! Earth calling Luc! She thinks it's rigor mortis."

Lucern batted the hand away, his irritation returning. "And whose fault is that? Etienne, I don't know why you have to sleep in that damned coffin, anyway. You have a warm, loving wife at home waiting in a nice, comfortable bed. What are you doing in a coffin in my basement?"

"I'm having problems with Blood Lust Three and needed to think. Besides, Rachel isn't home. She had a staff meeting to attend at work."

"Well, next time I suggest you work out these problems somewhere else, because I am getting rid of that coffin first thing."

"Ah, come on, Luc," Etienne began, but Lucern turned and left the room.

He strode down the hall, muttering under his breath. "Rigor mortis? A necrophiliac? Where does she come up with this stuff?"

The two women from the cleaning crew had their

heads together in the living room and were whispering fiercely in panicked tones. They fell silent as he passed the doorway, and Luc could feel their fearful eyes upon him. He ignored them and walked straight to the front door. Pausing there, he tugged the blinds on the side panels aside, wincing as bright sunlight hit his eyes. It took a minute to adjust to the noonday sun. The moment he did, he spotted Kate. She was standing on his porch, staring forlornly out at the road like a puppy that had been abandoned.

Of course, she had arrived by taxi, he realized. But the cab had left while she was in the house, and now she was trying to decide what to do. Obviously, coming back into the house to call for another taxi wasn't something she wanted to do.

Sighing, he let the blinds drop back into place and pulled the door open. "Kate?"

She stiffened where she stood on the edge of his porch, but didn't turn.

Lucern sighed. "Kate. Come back inside so we can talk, please."

"I'd really rather not." Her voice was strained, and she still didn't turn to look at him.

"Okay." He pulled the door wider and stepped out onto the porch. "Then I'll join you."

Kate eyed him warily as he joined her. "Are you now going to age before my eyes and burst into flames?"

He gave her an annoyed look. "You know I don't burst into flames in the sunlight."

"I thought you didn't sleep in coffins either."

"I don't. Etienne does. He's . . . well, he's the weird one in the family."

349

"Thank you very much."

They both turned to stare at Etienne, who stood in the shadow of Luc's front entry with the door open.

"I'm going home. I'm sorry I scared you, Kate," he said solemnly. Then Luc's brother turned to him and added, "Please clear up the rigor mortis and necrophilia issue. It will bother me until you do."

Kate flushed, apparently embarrassed at her words having been overheard. Turning away from both of them, she moved to the side, apparently expecting Etienne to leave by way of the porch. When he closed the door but didn't walk past them, she glanced around, suspicion entering her gaze when she saw that he was gone. "What did he do? Turn into a bat and fly away?"

"No, of course he didn't," Lucern snapped. "He's gone through the house to the garage. He wants to avoid the sun."

"Hmmm." She didn't look as though she believed him, so Lucern just waited. A moment later, they both heard the muffled sound of a car starting; then Luc's garage door opened and Etienne's little sports car with its blackened windows pulled out. The garage door closed automatically behind it, and Etienne roared down the driveway and down the street.

Lucern waited a heartbeat, then took a deep breath and said, "Kate, I told you. It's nothing like that nonsense Bram Stoker made up. We are not related to, nor do we turn into bats. We don't sleep in coffins anymore—except for Etienne, who swears it helps him get in the mood to come up with new ideas for his games.

I am not dead. You are not a necrophiliac. Rigor mortis does not cause my erections. You do."

She flushed at his last words, though whether with embarrassment or pleasure he didn't know. He suspected a little bit of both. Her posture became a little less stiff, her shoulders easing from their military stance, but she also sighed unhappily as she turned to him.

"You want me to believe you're just like everyone else?"

"I am," he assured her. Then, to be scrupulously honest, he had to add, "Well, other than the blood hunger and living hundreds of years and never aging or getting sick and . . ." He grimaced and stopped his honest admission right there. It wasn't going to win points with her.

"Normal men do not control other people's brains, Lucern," Kate pointed out.

"No. Well . . ." He sighed. "Look, it isn't some mystical power. Our infected blood makes our bodies more efficient. We're stronger and have more endurance than the usual person. I can lift things ten times heavier than the average man my size, run longer, hit harder. I've never really questioned my ability to read and control people's thoughts, but I would assume that's just another enhanced characteristic. They say humans don't use their entire brain. Well, it would appear my kind's blood makes sure that we do. Or, at least, we use more than the average person. It's probably a survival necessity like the teeth."

He allowed her to digest that, then added, "Does any of this really matter, Kate? The fact is that I am different in some ways. But I love you, Kate. With all my heart.

Can't we get past this and find a way to be together? I'd like to marry you. Spend the next hundred years or so with you."

There! Now I've done it, Lucern thought. He'd fought his own dragons, put his pride and fear aside and told her how he felt. Now his heart and his future were in her hands. And for one moment he thought everything would be all right. Tears came to Kate's eyes and joy to her face, and she started to move toward him. Then the front door opened and the two cleaning women sidled out. They were eyeing Lucern as if he were a mad serial killer. Or a vampire.

Luc scowled at them for interrupting at such a critical moment, and they both flinched and slowed. Then one of them grabbed the other's wrist and blurted, "We quit! We've already called the company and told them how weird you are. They're canceling your contract. You'll have to find another company to clean this place."

Lucern sighed as they broke into a run, charging off his porch, down his sidewalk and to their car with the company logo, which they'd parked on the street. They left in a squeal of rubber that made him sigh again.

Forcing a crooked smile, Lucern turned back to Kate. "See, you have to marry me. I seem to scare off all the help."

Kate smiled slightly, then ducked her head to peer at her fingers. They were tangling and untangling themselves nervously. He felt the first arrow of fear hit him. "Kate?"

"I . . . How could we be together, Luc? You'll live another couple hundred years or so, never aging, and I—"

"I could turn you, like Etienne did Rachel and Lissianna did Greg," he interrupted quietly. He had thought she understood that. Apparently, she hadn't. She also hadn't said she loved him, he realized.

"Turn me?" she repeated, sounding distracted. "I'd be with you, live forever? Never age?"

Lucern was relieved to note that being with him had been the first thought, and not the living forever or not aging. For a lot of women, the last two points were temptation enough to fake love.

"What about my family? How would I explain . . . ?" She paused when he clasped her hands.

"You would have to disappear in ten years or so. The fact that you wouldn't age would be noticed, and you couldn't explain it to them without risking the lives of my entire family," he admitted. It was something he had hoped to keep to himself until after he had turned her and bound her to his side.

"Give up my family?" she whispered, obviously not happy with that point.

"Kate, come inside please?" His hands slid up her arms, caressing her. He wanted to make love to her, convince her with his passion. He knew how heady and addicting it could be. She wasn't the only one who experienced the double pleasure. He did, as well. Even as Luc shared his excitement with her, Kate had opened instinctively and shared her own with him. It was a rare experience, one borne of the trust and love they shared. At least he thought it was. He had never experienced it with any other woman. But she still hadn't said she loved him.

He didn't care, Lucern decided. He wanted her, he needed her, he loved her. His pride be damned, he would take her any way he could get her, and would use every trick he knew to do it. Tipping her chin up, he claimed her lips, kissing her with all the passion he possessed as he fitted their bodies together. It was as if she had been made for him. She was soft where he was hard, giving where he was not. Lucern embraced her tightly and groaned as he ground his body against hers. He had missed her presence, ached for her body, and longed for her smiles and soft laughter. He couldn't lose her now. And for a moment, he thought he would win.

Kate yielded against him with a sigh, her arms sliding up around his neck and holding him just as desperately as he held her. Little moans issued from her throat as his hand found and cupped one breast—but then he pushed too fast.

Breaking the kiss, he caught her wrist and pulled her toward the front door. "Let's go inside."

Kate resisted, the passion disappearing from her face and something akin to fear replacing it. She shook her head. "No, I can't. I need to think."

"You can think inside," he insisted, pulling her toward the door.

"No. You'll make love to me and bite me and my brain will turn to mush." She pulled her hand free and backed up to the edge of the porch. "I need to think, Luc. You're asking me to give up everything I know, everything I love."

"*Everything* you love?" he asked softly, pain on his face.

"No. I love . . ."

Lucern held his breath. If she said she loved him, too, nothing on earth would stop him from dragging her into the house and claiming and turning her. But she stopped short of admitting it, her expression wary. Shaking her head, she backed up to the edge of the porch. "I have to go home and think about this. I have to decide . . ."

Kate whirled away and started down the stairs, but he hurried to catch her arm. She turned frightened eyes on him, and Lucern knew she feared he would take the choice away. For a moment, he was terribly tempted. But then he recalled those words the psychic had said, and he knew he couldn't fight this dragon for Kate. He had fought his own dragons, bypassed his pride and fears and placed his heart in her hands. Now he had to trust that she was strong enough to keep it safe.

He let go of her arm and said, "I'll call a cab for you."

Kate relaxed, a grateful smile tipping her lips. "Thank you."

Chapter Twenty

Kate managed to get a flight back to New York that night. She spent the time before, during and after the flight wavering between happiness and despair. Lucern loved her. She wasn't just a meal to him. He wasn't dead, didn't sleep in a coffin, and he loved her. All of these were wonderful, marvelous things. But to be with him, she had to be "turned," had to give up her family and friends—or would have to ten years down the road. That was not marvelous.

Kate considered everything. She thought perhaps she could be with him and not turn, but the idea of aging, her body and mind deteriorating while Lucern stayed strong and sharp-minded, was unbearable. She suspected he would stay with her if that was her choice, but the idea of his hands playing over her wrinkled, sagging flesh, and leaning her gray head against his strong, muscular chest . . . No, she would never do that to them.

Of course, she could simply have an affair with Lucern, then break it off in ten or twenty years when people started mistaking her for his mother. But she could barely imagine walking away from him willingly now; doing so after loving and sharing her life with him for ten or twenty years would be impossible.

Which meant she had two options: allow him to turn her and give up everyone else she knew and loved in ten or twenty years, or walk away now, while she had the strength. Neither option seemed acceptable. Despite the distance that separated them since she left Nebraska and moved to New York, she was very close to her family. Her mother and father often came to New York to attend plays or to shop, and they stayed with her. And her sisters made several trips a year to New York, to visit, shop and just generally hang out with her. They were her family, knew and loved her better than anyone. They had encouraged her dream to write, had thought her intention to be an editor in the city was admirable. They were her support, the foundation of her life. But to have Lucern, she would have to give them up. Or to have them, she'd have to give up Lucern.

Kate hardly slept that night. In the morning, she showered, dressed and went out to catch the subway to Roundhouse. Her mind had been going in circles all night and she had yet to come up with an answer that would allow her to keep both Lucern and her family. It was making her crazy. She was desperate to get away from the concern for a bit, and hoped that some work would take her mind off of it.

Chris was in the office when she arrived. It wasn't surprising to Kate; all of the other editors worked long hours and weekends. Chris, however, was terribly surprised to see her.

"I thought you'd be in Toronto right now, playing kissy-face with Luc," he teased, but there was concern in his eyes as he saw how pale and weary she was. That concern was echoed in his solemn voice when he asked, "Was I wrong, then? Did he really just want to discuss a tour?"

Kate shook her head and walked past him along the hall to her office. "You weren't wrong. We didn't discuss the tour at all."

"What did you discuss, then?" Chris asked, following her.

Kate set her briefcase on her desk. She stared down at it silently. Then, instead of answering, she asked, "Chris, if you could live forever, would you?"

He gave a bark of laughter. "Shit, no! Live forever and have authors chasing me for eternity? Dear God, you'll give me nightmares."

Kate smiled at the exaggerated horror on his face, but said, "I'm serious, C.K. Say you didn't have to deal with writers anymore. You could live somewhere else, with someone you love very much. You would have money, love, live forever and never age."

"What's the catch?" he asked with the cynicism she expected.

"The catch would be that, because you didn't age, you would have to give up your family and friends and disappear from their lives forever. To have your one passionate, almost all consuming love, you would eventually have to give up many people you love."

Chris whistled softly. "That's a tough one." He

thought about it briefly, then said, "Well, I guess it would depend upon how much I loved her. I mean, family are special, but they have family of their own."

Kate frowned. "What do you mean?"

He shrugged. "Well, couples have kids who grow up, fall in love, move away and have kids and a family life of their own. The original family are still important to them, but their own children become a priority. When push comes to shove, their own family comes first."

"Yes, but—"

"Is this character a man or a woman?" Chris interrupted. Kate blinked.

"What?"

"The character? I presume you're fretting over the plot of a book, yes?"

Kate hesitated, then nodded. She could hardly tell him that it was real life. He'd think her nuts, she'd gone off her cracker. "A woman."

Chris nodded. "That makes it easier, then."

"It does?"

"Sure. Women have been faced with this decision down through ages. From medieval times on, they grew up, married and moved away, usually far enough that they didn't see their family ever again," he pointed out. "After all, it wasn't as if they could hop a plane."

"No," Kate agreed slowly.

"Heck, you even faced a similar choice when you came here to work. You left your family in Nebraska."

Kate frowned. "That's different. They're there if I need them. It isn't like I will never see them again."

"Well, they'll still be there for this character, too. It isn't like they will die when she disappears from their lives. She could probably see them from a distance, keep tabs on them. And if there was an emergency, and she really had to, she could probably approach them in the future. Somehow."

Kate nodded slowly. She hadn't thought of that. She might not be able to speak to them but . . ."

"Is this a modern book or an historical like his first?" Chris asked.

Kate hesitated. He obviously thought she was concerned about Lucern's latest book. "Modern," she said at last, leaving him his delusion.

"Hmm, that makes it a bit harder," he decided.

"Why?" Kate asked.

"Well . . . if it was a medieval like his first one, the heroine could move away and still correspond with her family. They would never know she wasn't aging. But nowadays, it would be hard to move somewhere that wasn't a flight away."

That might work, Kate thought to herself. She smiled at him. "You're pretty good with plot devices, my friend."

"That's why they pay me the big bucks." He gave her a wink.

Kate laughed. None of them got paid big bucks. They were underpaid, overworked and stressed most of the time. And she had moved all the way from Nebraska to do it. They were all insane, she thought with a shake of the head. But they loved books. She picked up her briefcase and headed for the door.

"Where are you going now?" Chris asked with interest. He fell into step beside her.

"Home to bed. I need more sleep before I can consider your suggestions properly."

Kate slept long and hard, mostly because she was sure there was an answer to her problem in what Chris had said. If she could just think clearly, she would find it. That belief eased the ache in her heart and gave her some hope for a possible future with Lucern.

It was mid-afternoon when Kate awoke to the sound of knocking on her door. Stumbling sleepily out of bed, she dragged her fuzzy pink robe and pink bunny slippers on over her flannel bunny nightgown and made her way into the living room.

"Who is it?" she asked through a yawn when she reached the door.

"Marguerite."

Kate stiffened, her weariness disappearing in a heartbeat. Lucern's mother? Dear God.

The smile she offered in greeting was a wary one when she opened the door. "Mrs. Argeneau. What a surprise."

"I imagine so." Marguerite's smile was confident and amused. "May I come in?"

"Of course." Kate stepped out of the way to allow the woman to enter, then closed the door and followed her down the short hall to the tiny living room. "Would you like something to drink? Coffee, tea, juice?"

"No, thank you." Marguerite settled on the couch, her gaze slipping over the manuscript on the coffee table, then to the computer set up on the small dining-room table. "I see you are a writer like Lucern."

Kate's gaze dropped self-consciously to the first ten

chapters of the story she was writing. She'd printed them to edit, then never got the chance.

"It's no wonder the two of you deal well together. You are the same in many ways, but the opposite in others."

Kate shifted uncomfortably. "Mrs. Argeneau—"

"I asked you to call me Marguerite, if I recall," she interrupted calmly.

"Marguerite," Kate corrected. "I—"

"I came to help you," Luc's mother interrupted again. "Not to badger or berate you, but to help you make what is probably the hardest decision of your life."

Kate hesitated, then asked, "Can you? Can you really help me? Lucern is your son."

"Yes, he is. But I also had to make this decision myself several hundred years ago. I know how hard it is."

Surprise flickered in Kate. "You mean, you weren't—"

"I was human like you when I met Luc's father, Claude. He was dark and sexy and seemed all-powerful to me at the time. I thought I loved him. I thought he loved me. He didn't. His heart had been given to another long before he chose me to mate."

Kate sat back, feeling as if she had been punched. She had questioned whether she could give up her family for Lucern, but had never questioned her love for him. Not since admitting it to herself in that hotel bathroom at the conference. But what if she didn't really love him, but was merely dazzled by his charm and powers and . . . Her thoughts died when Marguerite burst out laughing.

"I'm sorry, my dear," the woman apologized, covering her mouth for a moment. She explained. "It's just that your thoughts are quite the silliest I have heard in a long time. Dazzled by his charm and powers? You are half repulsed by those powers—they frighten you silly. As for his charm, Luc is my son and I love him, but even I must admit he is sadly lacking in charm. The man was as surly and grouchy as a bear with a burr up his butt until you came into his life."

Kate was shocked to hear the woman use such modern terms, but she was more concerned with: "You can read my mind?"

Marguerite nodded.

"But, Lucern said my mind was too strong for him to read. He said—"

"*He* couldn't read your mind," Marguerite assured her. "You guarded it from him because you were already half in love. You don't bother to guard it from me, however, and I have read your mind and recognized your reluctant respect and love all along. Never doubt your love for him, Kate. You recognized his true character from his books, and that his off-putting behavior hides a sensitive soul. You have learned much more since meeting him and you do love him . . . despite those special abilities you find so abhorrent."

Kate was silent for a moment. "But you didn't love your Claude."

"No. Not with the kind of love you and Lucern share. Claude wasn't as strong as our children have grown to be. He was an essentially weak man, though I loved him as such. By the end, he was like a fifth child rather than the partner and helpmate a husband should be. He didn't seem to have hope—I think that's why he turned to drinking from alcoholics and drug addicts and died the way he did." She sighed. Then, shrugging, she said, "But that does not matter. What matters is that, despite that, I have never regretted my decision to cleave to him. I have four wonderful children and two children-in-law from it. I have seen the world change and reshape in ways I never imagined. I have done almost everything I ever wanted, yet every day I come up with more things I want to do."

"But what if I'm not strong enough? What if I turn out to be like Claude?"

"You are strong enough," Marguerite assured her. "I have seen your mind. You, Lucern and all my children—you have hope. No matter how bad the situation gets, or how low you feel, there is still one little grain of hope left in your heart, and that makes you strong. It forces you eventually to wipe away the tears, slap a bandage on your wounds, and reenter the fray. You would do well as Lucern's lifemate."

Kate agreed. But that still left one concern. "My family?"

Marguerite's expression turned sad. "Yes. Your family. It must seem like we are asking you to give up everything to be with one special man."

Kate suddenly held her breath as Marguerite's words made her recall the psychic: "*He is special, your man. But to be with him you will have to make a choice. You will have to give up all. If you have the courage, everything you ever wanted will be yours. If not . . .*"

"We would be your family, Kate," Marguerite said softly. "And so long as they lived, you could always have contact with your other family."

"Lucern said that after ten years—"

"Yes." Marguerite interrupted. "After ten or twenty years, Kate C. Leever must not be seen by those who know and love her—at least not those who are not of our kind. But you could still write to them. They must simply never see that you are not aging. You will have to avoid them and travel, make excuses not to visit or not to attend funerals. It would be easier for Kate to have an accident and be thought of as dead, but there are other more intricate ways to work things out. Surely Lucern is worth that effort?"

"Thanks," Lucern muttered as Bastien closed the van door on the coffin he and Lucern had just moved out of the basement.

"No problem," Bastien assured him. "I'll store it in my basement until Etienne can bring himself to part with it. I'll just tell my housekeeper not to bother cleaning down there for a while."

Lucern shoved his hands into his pockets and nodded. He supposed he should invite his brother in for a drink or something, but he really didn't feel like talking much right now. His mother had come by that morning to see how he was doing. Apparently, Etienne had mentioned that Kate had come by. Marguerite had made him tell her what had happened between them, then had left him to his own devices. He suspected that Bastien's coming by to pick up the coffin had just been an excuse to check on him again, and he fully expected that Etienne and Lissianna would find their way to his home sooner or later to check as well. He supposed he should be grateful for the distraction they offered. He had been driving himself nuts pacing his home, waiting for Kate to make up her mind.

"Well, I should . . ." Bastien paused and glanced up the driveway as a car pulled up. "That's Mom's limo."

"Yeah." Lucern sighed, thinking he would have to put a good face on and pretend that he wasn't slowly going bonkers. On the other hand, he had never bothered putting a good face on things before. Why bother now?

"Hmm. Well, I'd better get going."

Lucern glanced at his brother with surprise. For a moment, he thought Bastien was trying to avoid their mother, but then he glanced toward the limo and saw a blonde getting out of the car.

"Kate," he breathed. He just stood there as his brother got in his van. The limo backed out of the driveway, leaving Kate behind; then Bastien's van followed. Still, he and Kate just stood there, staring at each other. It wasn't until both vehicles were long gone that Kate moved forward. Lucern found his feet carrying him closer as well.

Meeting halfway, they stood staring into each other's eyes. Then Kate said, "Can we go inside?"

"Oh." Lucern blinked. Those hadn't been the first words he'd hoped for. But they were better than a kick in the ass. Last time she was there, she hadn't been willing to go into the house. This had to be a good sign. But he was impatient to hear her decision, so he snatched her arm, turned on his heel and rushed her up his sidewalk.

Entering the house, Lucern closed the door behind them with a thud, leaned back against it and ate Kate up with his eyes. Would she make him the happiest man on God's earth or the most miserable man that ever existed? He was hoping for the happy option.

"I love you."

That was a good start, Lucern decided.

"And, yes, I will marry you and spend my life with you."

Lucern started to reach for her, then caught himself. "What about your family?"

"I can't entirely give them up, Luc," she admitted apologetically. "I love them. But I will stop seeing them and only write them when it becomes obvious I'm not aging."

Lucern pushed himself away from the door and gathered her in his arms. Her solution was wonderful. He kissed her with all the relief, love and gratitude that he was feeling, then swept her up in his arms and ascended the stairs, heading for his bedroom.

"I love you, Kate. I'll make you happy. You won't regret this," he assured her between kisses on her face.

"I know I won't," she said softly, her arms around his neck. "And *we'll* make ourselves happy." They were nearly to his room before she cleared her throat and asked, "Umm, Luc?"

"Yes, love?" he asked as he pushed through the door. She finally saw his room. Any thoughts she'd had that he might sleep in a coffin immediately slid from her mind. There was no doubt in the world that this was Luc's room. Like the man himself, it was a masterful mix of black, silver and alabaster. The windows and the bed were covered with black drapes that would block any sunlight from entering.

It wasn't until Lucern had laid her in the center of

the bed and come down on top of her that she recalled what she had wanted to ask. Putting her hand to his shoulder to keep him from kissing her, she asked, "Is it going to hurt?"

Lucern paused, his eyebrows raising. "The turning?"

Kate nodded.

"Well." He frowned. "I'm not sure. I've never turned anyone before." He hesitated, then started to sit up. "I'll call my mother and ask her. She should know."

"No." Sitting up, Kate hugged his shoulders and pressed her face to his back, then finished, "No. It doesn't matter if it hurts. I'd go through the fires of hell for you."

She felt his back vibrate with a laugh; then he said, "And rob a blood bank and offer yourself up for me to feed on."

He turned on the bed and framed her face with his hands, then added, "And even eventually give up personal contact with your family." He bent his head to press a soft, reverent kiss to her lips. "I am a very lucky man."

Kate nodded solemnly. Then her lips curved mischievously and she said, "Let's hope you're still saying that a hundred years from now, when I'm nagging you to take out the garbage and change the baby's diaper."

Lucern chuckled and forced her back on the bed. "It will be my pleasure. Everything with you is a pleasure."

Kate merely shook her head and pulled him down for a kiss. She wasn't foolish enough to believe that they would never fight, or that the garbage detail would be a pleasure for him, but she felt sure they could weather whatever storms the next few centuries brought. After all, they had hope—and so long as they had that, anything was possible.

Love Bites
Lynsay Sands

Etienne Argeneau's three hundred years of bachelorhood are at an end. He can only "turn" one human in his lifetime, and most of his kind reserved that power for creating a life mate. He has to save Rachel Garrett. He doesn't know her very well, but the beautiful coroner had saved his life. To save hers he would make her immortal.

Rachel Garrett awakes surprised. All she'd wanted was to get off the night shift at the morgue; now here she is staggering to her feet naked and in a strange place. Then she sees the man of her dreams emerging from his . . . coffin? She just hopes he tastes as good as he looks.

What She Wants
Lynsay Sands

Earl Hugh Dulonget of Hillcrest is a formidable knight who has gotten himself into a bind. His uncle's will has a codicil: He must marry. And Hugh has just insulted his would-be bride by calling her a peasant! How can he win back her hand?

Everyone has advice. Some men-at-arms think that Hugh can win the fair Willa's love by buying her baubles. His castle priest proffers *De Secretis Mulierum*, a book on the secrets of women. But Hugh has ideas of his own. He will overcome every hindrance—and all his friends' help—to show Willa that he has not only what she needs, but what she wants. And that the two of them are meant for a lifetime of happiness.

LYNSAY SANDS
The Reluctant Reformer

Everyone knows of Lady X. The masked courtesan is reputedly a noblewoman fallen on hard times. What Lord James does not know is that she is Lady Margaret Wentworth—the feisty sister of his best friend, who has forced James into an oath of protection. But when James tracks the girl to a house of ill repute, the only explanation is that Maggie is London's most enigmatic wanton.

Snatching her away will be a ticklish business, and after that James will have to ignore her violent protests that she was never the infamous X. He will have to reform the hoyden, while keeping his hands off the luscious goods that the rest of the ton has reputedly sampled. And, with Maggie, hardest of all will be keeping himself from falling in love.

___4974-0 $5.99 US/$7.99 CAN

Dorchester Publishing Co., Inc.
P.O. Box 6640
Wayne, PA 19087-8640

Please add $2.50 for shipping and handling for the first book and $0.75 for each additional book. NY and PA residents, add appropriate sales tax. No cash, stamps, or C.O.D.s. All Canadian orders require $5.00 for shipping and handling and must be paid in U.S. dollars. Prices and availability subject to change. **Payment must accompany all orders**.

Name _____

Address_____

City_____ State _____ Zip _____

E-mail _____

I have enclosed $_____ in payment for the checked book(s).

❑Please send me a free catalog.

CHECK OUT OUR WEBSITE at www.dorchesterpub.com!

Everyone loves a little meddling *help* from Mom ...

A Mother's *W* Day
Romance Anthology

♥

Lisa Cach, Susan Grant, Julie Kenner, Lynsay Sands

Is it the king who commands Lord Jonathon to wed, or is it the dia-
bolical scheme of his marriage-minded mama? After escaping her
restrictive schooling, Miss Evelina Johnson wants to sow her wild
oats. Mrs. Johnson plants different ideas. Andie never expects the
man of her dreams to fall from the sky—but when he does, her
mother will make sure the earth moves! Jennifer Martin has always
wanted to marry the man she loves, but her mom knows the only
ones worth having are superheroes. Whether you're a medieval
lord or a marketing liaison, whether you're from Bath or
Betelgeuse, it never hurts to have some help with your love life.
Come see why a little meddling can be a wonderful thing—and
why every day should be Mother's way.

___52471-6 $5.99 US/$7.99 CAN

Lynsay Sands

Bliss

If King Henry receives one more letter from either of two feuding nobles, he'll go mad. Lady Tiernay is a beauty, but whoever marries the nag will truly get a mixed blessing. And Lord Holden—can all the rumors regarding his cold heart be lies? The man certainly has sobered since the death of his first wife. If he were smart, Henry would force the two to wed, make them fatigue each other with their schemes and complaints. Yes, it is only fitting for them to share the bed they'd made—'til death do them part! Perhaps they will even find each other suitable; perhaps Lord Holden will find in his bride the sweet breath of new life. Heaven alone knows what will happen when the two foes are the last things between themselves and the passion they've never known they wanted.

___4909-0 $5.99 US/$6.99 CAN